M000078463

THE HITMAN'S MISTAKE

Love Thrives in Emma Springs, Book 1

SALLY BRANDLE

SOUL MATE PUBLISHING

New York

THE HITMAN'S MISTAKE

Copyright©2018

SALLY BRANDLE

Cover Design by Syneca Featherstone

This book is a work of fiction. The names, characters, places, and incidents are the products of the author's imagination or are used fictitiously. Any resemblance to actual events, business establishments, locales, or persons, living or dead, is entirely coincidental.

All rights reserved. No part of this publication may be reproduced, stored in a retrieval system, or transmitted in any form or by any means (electronic, mechanical, photocopying, recording, or otherwise) without the prior written permission of both the copyright owner and the publisher. The only exception is brief quotations in printed reviews.

The scanning, uploading, and distribution of this book via the Internet or via any other means without the permission of the publisher is illegal and punishable by law. Please purchase only authorized electronic editions, and do not participate in or encourage electronic piracy of copyrighted materials.

Your support of the author's rights is appreciated.

Published in the United States of America by
Soul Mate Publishing
P.O. Box 24
Macedon, New York, 14502

ISBN: 978-1-68291-750-3

ebook ISBN: 978-1-68291-714-5

www.SoulMatePublishing.com

The publisher does not have any control over and does not assume any responsibility for author or third-party websites or their content.

To Brian, Mark, Neil, and my little buddy, Iris,

who believe in my writing success.

Thank you for the faithful encouragement.

Love, Sally

Dear Wendy —
I'd love to know
what you think of
Emma Springs!
Happy trails,
Sally Brandle

Acknowledgments

Anne Mitchell, my mom, was a reader. Romance novels, magazines, newspapers, and cereal boxes came under her scrutiny and often succumbed to a pair of sharp scissors if an article pertained to her offspring. Her willingness to dive into any adventure nurtured my love of reading and the confidence to give writing a try. We all need a support team growing up, and I was fortunate to have a bevy of tenderhearted but strong-minded women, along with patient brothers and a tenacious dad.

Writing has been a journey of meeting new friends and welcoming their constructive criticism. Many thanks to my critique partners and talented authors Jodi Ashland, Susan Wachtman, Becky Oosting, C.B. Williams, Kent and Lynette Allen, Alix Adamson, Jen Hilt, Kathleen Ekstrand, and others whose comments improved the story.

Special indebtedness to By Your Side editor Dana Delamar, editor CJ Obray, editor Shannon Kennedy and Soul Mate Publishing editor Sharon Roe for her patience and dedication to bring this project to completion.

Chapter 1

Frissons of apprehension raised the fine hairs on her forearms. A shadow moved near the stairwell.

Stepping inside the elevator car, she hit the button for the lobby with her fist, refusing to allow the reminder of her heartbreaking mistake to take hold in her head. *Must be weird evening lights playing tricks in the empty building.*

The car bumped to a stop on the ground level of Seattle's Justice Building. Taking a deep breath, she stepped from the elevator onto the slate floor. The energy that normally pulsed from harried workers and pre-jailed patrons had dissipated into an eerie void.

Hesitation inched over her skin. She'd sworn she'd never ignore that warning again. Her gaze passed over the unattended metal detector and scanner tables, then flitted to the dark interior of the tiny Coffee Klatch snack shop. Stuffing her pruning shears in her apron pocket, she shook her head and chided herself. *Serene Interiors Plant Care is yours. Be thankful, and quit moping about working late.*

She pressed her palm into the embroidered purple stalk of lavender on her apron bib and looked out front.

Hazy bulletproof windows allowed a view of the dwindling stream of pedestrians in their typical Friday night exodus to their families.

No open arms would greet her tonight. Her stomach tightened while a bleak, wintry pall settled into her heart. She tugged on her ball cap. It restrained her braided auburn hair while she worked, but more importantly, it provided a lifeline.

Time to start pruning. Her hand brushed against a branch of her oldest bonsai, a Douglas fir. The bark had cracked and split for the tree to grow in diameter. If only a shattered heart did the same.

She studied her collection of potted, six foot tall green sentries jutting out in a perpendicular row from the elevator doors. They neatly concealed the ugly wall behind them and farther down, the corner stairwell holding her storage closet.

"Live shrubs produce a calming effect on visitors" was the pitch she'd given to GSA's building manager to get the contract. She'd repeated the phrase today at noon to the Regal Hotel's upper management. And they'd bought it, ensuring a few more dollars each month toward owning a wooded lot of her own, where she could build a fire pit and pitch a tent on weekends.

A hollow chant of regrets beat in her chest at the thought of watching a campfire fade to dull gray, all alone. Her hand touched her brother's Mariner's cap. The smoky scents had faded, but images of smudged faces and starry nights stayed woven into its threads.

She plodded across sunbeams of September's golden light, walking beside knee-high pots containing her ten foot indoor hedge. Her gaze swept heavenwards, up to the atrium ceiling. She blinked. Streaks across the glass distorted the brilliance of the setting sun.

Geeze. Wasn't anyone proud of their work? The creepy window washer on the scaffold last week should've been working harder instead of staring at her.

Her breaths of still air quickened. He'd watched her working.

Big deal. Maybe he had a sicko mommy-thing for women in aprons.

A trowel and her spritzer rattled in her tote while she rounded the end flower pot and moved to the backside of her overgrown fourth plant. Dim light flickered through the leaves, casting shadows onto the brick wall, barely illuminating the narrow aisle leading to the stairwell door.

She took a swig of coffee, sat with her back to the stairwell, and set her drink on a cold slate tile. Facing the front windows did little to help. The lighting in the corner sucked. After stuffing a clean cloth for polishing leaves into a side pocket of her cargo pants, she tugged on gardening gloves.

Squeaks from her mom's old pruning shears echoed in the large, vacant room. She pulled another uneven limb of the Chinese Elm closer to her face and squinted. While she clipped, a peppery fragrance released from the wood.

A twig grazed her cheek, making her flinch. She brushed the neckline of her purple T-shirt with the back of her hand.

The place threw off the vibes of an abandoned morgue. *Chill.* She released the limb, let out a long breath, and grabbed a lop-sided branch from overhead. Tonight, even a rude prosecutor's voice rupturing the tranquility would be welcome.

Not happening this late, but Ike would be descending in the elevator any minute. Hopefully in a better mood than when she'd watered the jade plant in his judge's chambers earlier. He'd been tense, without the fatherly banter he doled out when she visited him and his wife, Shirley.

Soft taps came from a few feet behind her. She tilted her head.

Footsteps? From the stairwell? Miranda released her grip, and the tree limb sprang free. She swung her head and watched the branch skim the fly of the trousers on the man now towering over her right shoulder.

Not Ike. She froze.

"What in the hell? Oh, didn't see you there—" he sidestepped, and her cup scrunched in protest under his big boot. The lid popped off and the double shot of Kona glugged into a mocha-scented pool.

He jumped to avoid the puddle. "Damn energy conservation put you in the shadows. Sorry, I nailed your coffee." His swinging backpack missed her nose by inches.

She twisted her body and scooted her butt until her shoulder jammed against a carved pot.

"I didn't mean to frighten you."

"It's okay," she mumbled, keeping her head lowered to avoid further contact with the bag-wielding klutz wearing black trousers. Must've been him she'd glimpsed a few minutes ago, while the elevator doors had closed on the floor below Ike's.

"I've never been attacked by a branch. Must say, you deployed it well," the deep voice announced. He stopped directly in front of her.

His hiking boots made her size-nine high-tops appear dainty.

Not the shoes of a snobby lawyer or a lost, post-trial pimp trying to find his way out of the building. Still, the flailing branch served him right for sneaking up on her. "I didn't hear you."

"And I shouldn't text and walk," he said in a lighter, almost sexy tone. "I'm Grant." He dropped his pack and stuck out his hand.

An FBI tag printed 'GRANT MORLEY' hung from the bag.

She peered from under her cap's brim and gulped.

Him.

Agent of Interest. Her heart took off at a gallop.

His brawny physique had inspired nasty daydreams while she'd snipped plants and snuck peeks while he pumped the coffee dispenser in the lobby café. "Nice to, ah . . . meet you." The last words squeaked out while she raised her hand. His warm grip sent an unfamiliar humming deep, deep down.

He released her hand and smiled, transforming his no-nonsense face to attentive. "You're—?"

"Aware you didn't plan the assault on my coffee," she blurted out like an idiot. She fumbled the clippers, her palms sweating worse than windows in a greenhouse.

"Size fourteen assault," he quipped. "I'll wipe the floor and get you another cup. Glad to hear I'm absolved."

Absolved? Her thoughts dipped well below religious. A snicker escaped. "I've got paper towels. The clean-up's no biggy."

Agent of Interest now stood close enough to get his precisely creased pant legs pruned. She thumbed the handle on her trimmers while he glanced at the Coffee Klatch Cafe. "Then my mission's to get your caffeine replaced." He sheepishly grinned at her, and a single dimple appeared in his cheek.

She closed her gaping mouth and inhaled his faint scent of woodsy cologne.

Hazel eyes . . . she'd guessed the color correctly. "There's an espresso shop in the next block."

Outside, a car horn honked in bumper-to-bumper traffic.

He checked his phone, and the dimple disappeared into a frown. "You'll have coffee pronto. Give me three minutes at the Coffee Klatch."

Grant Morley's smooth, measured steps echoed across the vacant rotunda. FBI, CIA, they all strode with poised determination, and this man personified the confidence of an alphabet agency's elite.

There ended the similarity in stature to the other bureau boys. Linebacker shoulders to long legs, every inch of this agent was perfectly proportioned male.

Anticipation thrummed in her veins. She'd imagined those well-muscled arms wrapped around her during a dance, or more.

She tossed a wad of towels onto the puddle, and sprang up, doing a fist pump. Her dream hunk had smiled. At her.

She bent to corral the spill and then pitched the wet mess into a trashcan.

Her poor departed mocha had been five bucks well spent. Tracing his path, she trotted through the back of the unlit body scanner.

Grant stood at the glass door of the Coffee Klatch. He tapped his key, and then raked a hand through thick hair the color of polished walnut.

Her fingers tucked strands of her own wayward hair behind her ear while she slowed and then crossed the foyer to him.

It might've been the set of his jaw, or his chiseled face— one scrape short of fierce—which signaled his determination. It wouldn't matter if he had to trek to Colombia, track down Juan and his donkey, roast the beans, and grind them himself in the back of this shop. He'd make coffee happen.

"Hey, they're closed." She blushed. An ordinary citizen could make that conclusion, much less a G-Man.

He rapped again. "The owner does bookkeeping Friday nights." He yanked a wallet from his backpack and let the pack drop to the floor. An Alaska Airlines itinerary stuck halfway out. At the top, "Seattle to Three Falls" stood out in bold print.

"I think he's gone," she said. "The espresso shop stays open late. What time does your plane leave?"

His head snapped around as if he'd deflected a punch. "How'd you know I'm flying?" His cop's stare penetrated, colder and darker than burnt tree bark.

"Observation." She smiled and pointed to the exposed paperwork. "Going on a tropical vacation?"

"Not really a vacation. Sorry. The agent in me is always questioning people's motives," he said, then pulled out the itinerary and tucked it in his pocket. "Bad timing workwise, but I'm headed to Montana to ride up a mountain." His relaxed eyes shifted to her worn green apron where bits of tree trimmings clung.

She brushed off a twig. "Oh, near Yellowstone?"

"No. Emma Springs, bet you haven't heard of it." He glanced at her worn ball cap and at the slight crook in her nose, then turned and tapped the glass again. "The owner's gotta be in the back. He'll have coffee."

"Fashionable attire isn't a prerequisite of the espresso shop." She stepped back and tugged her cap low to hide her flaming red cheeks.

"You got it wrong. You rock those tactical pants." He flashed a sexy grin. "I'm just short on time."

Before she blushed more, two honks came from an SUV navigating to the curb.

"There's my ride." He straightened his tie, lost on such an expansive chest. "Duty to help my dad calls."

"Family isn't a duty." Her hand flew to her heart. "Cherish every moment," she warned, "as if it's your last together."

"Pardon?" His eyebrows pinched together.

"Nothing. You've got a flight, and I can work without coffee."

"Okay then, I owe you." His final assessment consisted of one long pass from her tennis shoes up. Her skin tingled while he checked out every curve on her body. "I'll make it special," he promised.

"Sure." She gulped.

"Hey, if you need help trimming an unruly limb, I'm your man." His dimple reappeared. "Scout's honor."

He issued a two-fingered salute, lifted his pack, and jogged toward the exit. "Quit punishing those shrubs and go home."

"Bye," she whispered, and brushed her lips.

From deep inside came a longing for strong arms to hold her while she sat in front of her next campfire. A former explorer scout might suffice, if he owned an exquisitely molded butt like the one bounding off to Montana.

He'd crossed the lobby and reached the revolving doors leading outside. Stepping into the glass chamber, he shouldered his backpack, exposing a holstered gun.

Frostbites of reality withered her girlish fantasies. Grant Morley carried a weapon.

All agents did. However, seeing it . . . foolish of her to think her past wouldn't haunt her. Squeezing her lids shut, her chest tightened.

Nothing would bring her family back. *Damn guns! Damn them to hell!* Her fingernails dug into her clenched palm.

Damn daydreams. One late night at work, and life reverted to an emotional roller coaster. This afternoon she'd endured Ike's impatience and now the gun-wielding player.

Muffled honks drew her attention to the street where Agent Grant Morley opened the passenger door of an SUV.

Better to write his type off. Probably a size two girlfriend at the wheel. Their weekend plans included moonlight kisses and sipping champagne after hiking his stupid mountain. And target practice.

The car pulled into an empty lane and disappeared.

Shirley's right. Find a new man of your dreams, and not one wearing tasseled Italian loafers, gangster Jordan's, or new hiking boots.

"Modest and mild, modest and mild," she whispered. Her perfect dating mantra.

An old-fashioned wall clock chimed in agreement, alerting her the Number 10 bus home to Capitol Hill had pulled away from the stop.

Too late. She'd have to catch the next one. She trudged toward her plants while staring at her faded purple tennies. Dull and comfy.

She stopped by the bag scanner, and bent to tie her shoelace.

The toe of a tiny pink sock caught her eye.

She plucked it from behind the table leg and fingered the hand knit stitches.

A baby. The world needed the innocence of babies. A soft smile came to her lips while she imagined rocking an infant in her arms.

She passed through the body scanner, headed back to her Chinese Elm, and tucked the sock in her tote. Monday, she'd hand it off to the security guard in charge of the lost and found box.

Guards. Her pulse quickened. She searched the empty lobby.

The TSA officers had been on normal duty scanning every visitor when she'd arrived at four. There had to be a night watchman. A shift change?

Why hadn't she noticed their absence?

Because you've been too busy admiring Agent of Interest's butt, that's why.

She pinched off a brown leaf. Maybe the one stationed at this post got delayed.

By what? Hardly any traffic. Everyone else except Ike had clocked out to go home to their families. The brittle elm leaf crushed to bits in her grip.

A muffled pop disturbed the silence.

She tilted her head, straining to hear better.

Elevator cables groaned a nerve-wracking whine while a descending car eased to a halt.

This better be Ike. Shirley complained he often stayed too late.

If not, she'd go check. When she'd seen him earlier, she'd sworn his fingers trembled enough to cause the travel brochures to flutter.

Why'd they want to send her on a trip now, anyway? Oh well. She leaned around the ficus at the end of the row, faced the elevator, and prepared to give Ike a bright smile to lighten his spirits.

The doors opened.

A gray-haired man wearing a leather jacket and black jeans backed out a step.

Holding a gun.

She choked down a scream and slid behind the next plant over, her bushy Bamboo Palm.

Fan-shaped leaves skimmed her cheek while she squinted. *Oh no! A* body slumped against the rear wall of the elevator car. *Was it—?*

The gun's barrel stayed aimed at Ike's bloody shirt.

This can't be happening again!

Not to Ike and Shirley, people she loved.

Gripping a slender trunk of bamboo, she hunched behind the thickest section. A sickening wave of panic welled in her stomach.

The killer shoved his revolver inside his jacket, stepped over Ike's legs, and took out a knife. He pried a bullet from the back wall with gloved hands, and then pinned Ike's right arm to the hand rail. He raised the knife.

No! She plucked out her trowel.

He turned and stood motionless. Wearing a scowl, he surveyed the lobby and then looked out the front windows.

She held her breath. A few leafy branches and four feet of open space separated her from Ike's assassin.

He slid the knife into his boot and stepped out.

It felt like troops of aphids crawled up her spine.

A bright green snake tattoo wound around his neck— with its jaws open and fangs poised to strike the gunman's earlobe.

A shudder caused the leaf at her elbow to move as he

strode by her, surely close enough to hear her heart thumping in her chest. A can of spray paint stuck out of his back pocket.

He headed toward the front entrance and pressed a phone to his ear. "Tell Maneski the judge bled out, per his request . . . No time to chop off proof, the street's still busy. Painted the cameras."

She looked at Ike's hand and gagged.

Air whooshed through the revolving doors.

Snake Neck ran out, jumped into a black sedan parked at the curb, and drove off.

Leaves rustled when she expelled the breath she'd been holding. *Get down and get busy, you can worry later.* Mom's old saying flew through her mind.

She yanked off her gardening gloves, dialed 911 on her cell, and dashed to the elevator.

Ike lay sprawled on the floor, his shoe holding open the bobbing doors. Elbowing the elevator's emergency stop button, she withdrew the cloth from her pocket and pressed it into his bloody chest.

She searched Ike's neck for a pulse. Faint beating reached her trembling fingers.

"911, what's your emergency?"

"I need an ambulance."

"For yourself?"

"No." She stuck her phone between her shoulder and ear. "There's been a shooting. A bad chest wound." She squeezed Ike's cool hand. "Ike, it's Miranda."

He didn't squeeze back.

"Ike." She clasped his shoulder. His eyelids remained closed in a face the color of dull clay.

"What's your location?" the voice demanded.

"Seattle Justice Building, the main entrance." She took a breath of air tainted by paint fumes. "His pulse seems weak."

"An ambulance has been dispatched. Stay on the line until they arrive. Put pressure on his wound."

"I am."

"Where's the shooter?"

"Gone. He drove away in a black car. Ike's lost a lot of blood."

"You know the victim?"

Her heart clenched. "Yes. Judge Isaac Gilson. I need to call his wife."

His arm nudged her. "Not yet," he said.

"Hold on," she told the operator.

Pain-filled eyes met hers. "You're not safe," he uttered in a ragged whisper.

Her phone slipped from her hand. "There's another gunman?"

"No," he choked out.

"The one who shot you left."

He nodded, and his eyes closed.

"Stay with me, Ike." She slowed her voice to a calm tempo. "They're sending an ambulance." Wedging her back into the corner steadied her body.

The revolving doors swished. A bearded man entered the lobby wearing a Seahawks cap and a black jacket.

"Help's arrived." She leaned forward to attract the man's attention.

Ike clasped her wrist. "Don't." His eyes flashed hatred. Detective Karpenito. Dangerous. Get far away. Now. Call Shirley for instructions."

"I will."

"Promise me, leave the state. Tell no one." His grip loosened. "You're . . . child we always wanted." His eyelids drooped. "Don't trust cops . . . crooked. Tell Shirley I love her."

"I'll call Shirley right away. Stay awake, Ike. I hear the ambulance." All the breathable air vanished from the tight space while panic rose in her chest. She craned her head around the bank of buttons to see the street.

After agonizing moments, the blaring ambulance passed by without stopping.

The detective stood at a front window and motioned the aid car to the right.

She snatched her phone and pushed it into her cheek. "Operator?" she hissed.

"Yes?"

"Tell your ambulance to ignore the guy in the window. We're near the west entrance they passed a second ago. Under the glass atrium."

"I'll direct them back to you."

The sirens faded while uneven footsteps from leather-soled shoes approached her. "Ike, he's coming. Stay still," she whispered.

The detective's squinting eyes honed in on her bloody cloth. His fleshy face reddened.

He stretched his hand toward Ike's neck. "A call came in about a shooting. I must check for a—"

"I've searched his neck and wrists, no pulse," she assured him. Her free hand balled into a fist.

"Horrible tragedy. I'm a Seattle detective." He shoved an SPD badge toward her.

The last numbers were thirty-one, but his pudgy fingers covered the rest. "Your name, miss?"

"Miranda Whitley." She fished out her building ID and bus pass from under her apron, and gave the empty lobby a fleeting look, willing anyone else to appear.

"Ms. Whitley, I'll need your statement after I secure the murder scene." He flipped open a spiral bound notebook and scribbled a note. "You're in danger if the killer's nearby." He looked around the empty rotunda. "Did you see which way he went? Can you describe him?"

She swallowed. "No, I'd been . . . in the bathroom."

"I see." His lips pursed. "Your home address?"

Fury and anguish roiled in her gut. "I live at 1201 Pike." She'd invented a number, hopefully an apartment building. They'd figure it out pretty soon, but with any luck, she'd be gone.

He pulled out a wallet, thumbed through a wad of bills, and held out a fifty. "You did your best. The poor man's passed. Grab a taxi home. I'll come by shortly for your statement." His voice had smoothed to reassuring.

A cop would never send her away. She kept one hand on Ike and took the bill. "Okay."

"You've done what you can. The building's not safe." He checked his watch. "I'll come by for your statement within an hour. You need to wait for me at home. Do you understand?"

She looked at his ear to avoid his probing eyes. Clear streaks ran beside his beard. *Glue?* She dropped her head and focused on her shoes. "Yes. I'll go to my apartment. Give me a minute."

He shuffled his feet, and his body teetered for a brief instant while he balanced on platform soles. "Hard to see a guy die," he stated.

"Yeah." Her nails dug into her palm.

The sirens became louder again.

"A man waving a gun!" Karpenito shouted to her. He pulled out his revolver before dashing around her plants toward the emergency exit. "Get out now!" he yelled. The door to the alley banged shut behind him.

"There's no gunman, Ike. The lying cop ran from the ambulance." She stroked his wrinkled brow.

He responded by raising his eyelids a fraction, then they closed.

Lights flashed out front and an aid car stopped at the curb.

No one got out.

She grabbed her phone. "Operator?"

"Yes?"

"The medics are sitting in the ambulance. We're inside."

"Protocol for a shooting," she stated. "The police need to clear the building."

"Screw protocol." Miranda dropped the phone and put Ike's hand on the cloth. "Push it against your chest, Ike."

His hand stayed in place.

She ran to the revolving doors, gave them a shove, and dashed to the front of the ambulance.

The passenger-side window rolled down.

"He's dying," Miranda pleaded. "You can't let him die! The shooter drove off."

The driver bent forward and stared at her, and then a look passed between the two men.

She gripped the window frame and leaned in. "Please. Give me the stretcher. I'll bring him to you. I can't lose Ike, too. I can't." Tears streamed down her cheeks while she stumbled backward.

"Okay, ma'am," the passenger said.

Both men jumped out at the same time. One grabbed a supply box and the other opened the rear door, removing a gurney.

They checked Ike's vitals quickly, bandaged his wound, and wheeled him out.

She trailed behind them.

"We weren't needed at a nearby fender bender. Lucky break," the driver said.

Lucky? The crooked cop wanted Ike dead and her gone. She scrunched a corner of her apron.

"We got clearance to transport." The other medic opened the rear door. "Police are enroute."

"Which hospital are you taking him to?" she asked.

"Seattle General. Don't worry. He'll be there soon." His authoritative voice convinced her, at least for a moment.

"Thanks, guys." She leaned over and kissed Ike's cheek. "You're going to be fine. I'll phone Shirley."

Ike blinked once.

The metallic smell of blood hit her again. A wave of nausea threatened. Silver flecks danced and flickered in her vision. She leaned against the building and hugged her sides until the light-headedness subsided.

Sirens blared when the ambulance took off with Ike.

He was alive, but the detective and killer thought he'd died. Flashes of kindness from Shirley and Ike wound through her fractured mind. Then her brain skipped back to his killer. The name he'd used. Maneski.

She'd seen it in print.

In a headline.

'Maneski-The Butcher-Indicted.' Ike had presided at the trial of the notorious head of a drug cartel known for dismembering his enemies.

Mobsters. She'd better get a move on if she wanted to outrun them. She dashed inside and reached for her tote. Blood covered her hands. Grabbing her spray bottle, she misted them, then swiped them across her apron.

The trigger lever caught on her badge lanyard.

I'm screwed. The dirty cop would run her ID. She grabbed her tote, ran to the cabinet under the stairs, and shoved it inside. Now to get away.

Pushing open the stairwell's heavy door, a tiny beam of light travelled from the top of her Douglas fir to the atrium ceiling above the lobby.

"Please Ike, fight," she whispered. "You're going to be fine." A chill swept over her. She'd said the same fateful words to her dad.

No. This wasn't her fault, and she'd be damned if she'd go out without a fight, for her and for Ike.

She shoved open the exit door to the alley and stood in fading light.

Finding safety required cash.

"Crap. My purse," she muttered. She caught the closing door and stopped.

"Like I said, 1201 Pine. Whitley." Karpenito wheezed from somewhere near the elevator. "Get some hearing aids." Rubber-soled shoes squished closer.

Every nerve ending went on alert while she crept inside and ducked behind her palm tree again.

"Caucasian. Five eight. Medium build. Reddish-brown hair," he said. "Finish it now. No evidence."

An image of her body lying in the morgue flashed in her brain. Who'd come to lift the white sheet and identify her? She clutched her keyring in a death grip.

Her wall of foliage blocked her while she tip-toed to reach the stairwell closet. Using her butt, she propped the door open, extracted her shoulder bag, and stepped into the narrow aisle.

The latch clicked shut behind her. She crouched behind the fir. Crap. Had he heard?

The detective bent down at the other end of her plant hedge. His stumpy hand reached between the potted palm and the ficus to snatch her glove from the floor.

Every muscle screamed to run.

She was trapped.

Chapter 2

Karpenito's steps grew softer, fading down the hallway.

Miranda dashed into the deserted alley and headed toward the sidewalk.

The acrid stench of burning plastic filled the narrow lane between the two buildings. A plume of smoke curled skyward from the bent lid on a dumpster.

She pinched her nose and ducked her head. Ike's blood stained her apron.

Her stomach lurched. She yanked it over her head, threw it atop the smoldering heap, and jogged around the corner.

After pushing open the familiar door and inhaling the aroma of coffee, her thumping heart eased.

The rail-thin barista narrowed her eyes. "You work in the Justice Building, don't you? What caused those sirens a minute ago?"

A few customers looked up.

Miranda shrugged. "A dumpster fire, I think."

"Vagrants," the woman sputtered.

Could they see her shaking? "Uh-huh. Back in a minute. Pit stop."

The deadbolt to the restroom slipped into place on the second try. Her badges clattered together while she tugged the lanyard off. She grabbed her phone.

"Hello?" Shirley answered on the first ring.

"It's Miranda. Ike's been shot, and he's in an ambulance headed to Seattle General."

"Dear God, help us. It's happened." Her voice faded.

"A crooked cop tried to send the ambulance away."

"No," Shirley groaned.

"The cop left. Ike insisted I leave town right now. Do you have anyone to help you?"

"Thank God you rescued Ike," she said. "He wouldn't believe the threats came from a Seattle police officer. He blamed Maneski's thugs. Hold on, there's pounding at my door."

"Don't answer it! Shirley!"

A man's voice rumbled in the background.

Miranda collapsed against the sink, keeping the phone pressed to her ear.

"A policeman Ike trusted will take me to the hospital," Shirley said. "Keep us in your prayers."

"Of course. Ike said to tell you he loves you."

A door clicked shut from Shirley's end. "Sweet, sweet Ike. He'd want us to stay calm," she whispered. "Don't trust anyone until I talk to him. Follow his orders."

"Where should—" The phone disconnected, severing the connection to the one person who understood the danger.

Bulging eyes stared back at her from the mirror a foot away. She touched her nose, broken during a wrestling session with her little brother, Kenny.

Blood covered her wrist.

She cranked the water to full blast, dunked her forearm, and watched a pinkish stream swirl down the drain.

Her world had spun out of control again.

She pulled open the door and checked each chair out front. Executives and tourists chatted in clusters or studied phones while they sipped drinks.

A laptop for customer use sat on an empty table in the middle of the room.

Anything would be better than using her phone's browser on a low battery. She slid into the chair and then tugged off her ball cap and shoved it into her pocket.

A bell jangled, and the door opened. She whipped her head around.

Not Karpenito, but he'd be searching for her soon enough, backed by the Seattle Police Department and the money of Maneski's cartel.

She removed the stretchy yellow band securing her braid and laid it on the table. Running her fingers through the long strands freed them to hide her face.

Her gaze dropped to an empty drink container sitting next to the laptop.

Absently, she picked it up, turning it in her fingers. Her life seemed emptier than the cup she held. She'd lost her family, and now she might lose Ike, too?

She clenched her fingers, watching the cup crush between them.

The noise triggered an image of one very determined FBI agent. Grant Morley had headed out of state, and he wasn't a local cop. He could recommend a safe place to hide. Maybe she'd qualify for witness protection.

Her fingers rested on the keyboard and then typed in a search for flights to Three Falls.

No seats on the single flight leaving today. She pressed her fists into her eyes. Why not a bus? She depended on them every day.

The Greyhound schedule told her one heading through Montana left in an hour. The station wasn't far—she'd make it.

Her foot tapped the floor.

What was the town's name? Emma something. She typed in Montana, then Emma, and Springs appeared next to it. A side ad showed a dude ranch provided the closest lodging.

They had a room, and for an extra fee, they'd shuttle passengers. She'd book it, even though it meant she'd wipe out her savings.

Their site showed photos of trail rides and a quaint lakeside town, situated in the shadows of a craggy mountain. Grant's mountain.

She wrote the ranch's number on her forearm and typed in Morley. A Google map pinpointed two homes owned by Morleys near the Lazy K Ranch.

Ike would approve of her getaway, all paid by cash. Would sixteen hours on a freeway be enough miles to stay alive?

She rubbed her temple with chilly fingers, then pulled a windbreaker from her purse and zipped it to the collar.

A whiff of coconut hit her nose, Corrin's answer to skin care. Corrin, her best friend and the most sensible paralegal on earth. She'd loaned her the jacket, and could be trusted for anything. Even escape.

The skinny clerk leaned over the counter. "Did you need another coffee today?"

Miranda gulped. Act normal. "Oh, sure. Kona mocha special, please, the one with cacao nubs. Extra foam." She left the table, walked to the bathroom, and hit speed dial. "Where are you?"

"Happy Friday to you," chided Corrin. "I'm entering my home-sweet-apartment. Court got out early. I missed my noontime jog. If I change out of my work clothes, I can meet your bus and we can go for a quick speed walk in Volunteer Park before dark."

Miranda smoothed a flap on the pocket of her cargo pants and glanced at her shoes. A knot of tension tightened in her gut. "Hold on." She eased the bathroom door shut. "Ike got shot in front of me."

"What? Is Ike alive? Are you okay?"

"Ike's on his way to Seattle General." She squeezed her eyes shut. "I'm okay."

"Who shot him? Does Shirley know?" Corrin's voice rose.

"I called Shirley. I'll need a ride to the Greyhound station ASAP."

"Greyhound? Aren't you talking to the police??"

She turned away from the sink. "I'm headed to the mountains."

"Okay, slow down. What mountains and why?"

"Rockies," she stated. "Grab my old cowboy boots, a pair of beater jeans, and a sweatshirt from our storage unit. Whatever you see first. And don't ask questions. It'll put you in danger."

"I can do more than pack your travel bag, and I've got a key to your apartment."

"Stay away from my apartment. It's got to be this way, trust me." She drummed her fingers on the sink. "Do it fast. Get in and out. Quick."

"Why? Miranda, what's going on?"

"Just do as I ask, will you, Corrin?"

"Okay, okay. I'll use my gym bag. All right, warm clothes. Mountains." Corrin's keys rattled.

The door to their assigned storage area squeaked.

An outside entry in the vintage brick building had been converted into a walled-in storeroom separating their apartments. What had been the exterior wall to each unit still contained the twelve-inch pass-through delivery boxes used in the 1950s by milkmen.

She and Corrin had a knee-high view into each other's kitchens, if they left the little metal doors open. This morning they'd made plans for pizza tonight, their voices carrying across the open space.

"There's piles of stuff. Where exactly?" Corrin asked.

"Try left, in the boxes on the bottom of the stairs."

"Got it. Boots, jeans, and a sweatshirt. What else?"

How much time had passed? Images of Ike's bloody body slumped against the elevator wall flooded her head.

Miranda's throat tightened. "Nothing. Get out now. Ike's gunman might come."

"Gunman? You said it happened—" Corrin gasped.

"What's the matter? Corrin?" Miranda squeezed the phone to her ear.

A lock clicked.

"Corrin!"

"I'm okay. Wait, you're already done giving a statement to the police?"

"Ike ordered me to vanish." She cracked the bathroom door and peeked out.

A young kid sat at the laptop while his mom ate a scone.

The barista caught her eye. "Four ninety-five please."

"Leaving a crime scene before giving a statement isn't normal," Corrin said. "Who's talking in the background?"

"Gotta pay for my coffee." Coming out of the bathroom, Miranda fished out the fifty-dollar bill, flattened it on the wooden surface, then wiped her hands on her pants.

"Your drink's next." The woman handed her a fistful of change. "Are you feeling okay?" She nodded toward the bathroom.

"Ate a spicy lunch." Miranda stuffed the top bill into the tip jar and slipped back into the bathroom. "I won't be alone, Corrin. I met an FBI agent today. He'll help."

"A total stranger? I can do more than wave a pen over a legal pad. I'll help you."

"Ike insisted it be this way. Where are you?" Miranda sank onto the toilet.

"Leaving the—" A door slammed in the background.

"What's happening?" Miranda demanded.

"I saw a shadow in your apartment, through your open milk box."

Miranda jumped off the toilet seat. "Get out of there!"

"Done. I'm outside." Corrin's car engine revved.

"Hey, you never close your blinds. Did you close them this morning?"

Miranda's pulse hammered in her temple.

"Miranda, did you close your blinds?"

"No. I left them open for the plants."

"Bloody hell. Someone broke into your apartment. The blinds are lowered to the sill."

"Describe the shadow," Miranda demanded.

"Maybe a guy wearing dark jeans."

"He's the gunman," she whispered. "Was a black sedan parked nearby?"

"Bloody HELL. I think near the corner. Can't verify it, I'm already heading downhill."

"Please hurry."

"Where are you? Are you certain you're safe?"

"I'm at the espresso shop on Third and Vine. Nowhere's safe."

"I'll be there soon. Shouldn't drive and talk. Bye."

Miranda splashed water on her face, and dialed the ranch's number.

Her future depended on a hasty offer from Agent Morley. She had no other options.

She made a reservation, pocketed her cell, and took a breath before emerging from the bathroom. Montana might work. The trusting ranch owner hadn't even demanded a credit card.

Outside, a Seattle Metro bus rumbled past several police cruisers parked in front of the Justice Building.

No one else noticed the flashing lights. The boy continued to tap on the laptop she'd used.

Moving to a corner by the window, she hid behind a rack of tourist brochures featuring glossy photos of the Space Needle and the Ye Olde Curiosity Shop.

A silver vehicle swung into the bike lane at the curb. Corrin.

Hope fluttered in her belly. She dashed outside and hopped in the front passenger seat.

Karpenito ran out of the Justice Building.

She slunk down. "Go, go, go, Corrin!"

~ ~ ~

A plant girl had duped them. Venom blew out a frustrated breath and rubbed his gloved finger over the tattooed pit viper on his neck. So much for him striking his prey.

His phone vibrated. "Yeah."

"Where are you?" Karpenito's voice pierced like jagged glass on a jugular vein.

"I'm in the plant girl's empty apartment. The real one." He glanced at a three-foot-tall rusty pitchfork hanging on the kitchen wall and then out to an open living room. A framed portrait of a family of four hung on the wall. The boy in it had a side cowlick, like his grandson.

"The Whitley girl bolted out of a cafe next door and fled in a Firebird," Karpenito wheezed. A car horn honked in the background.

"You told me you'd sent her home in a cab. We're next on The Butcher's list if we don't silence her soon."

"No lie. Typical idiot female who doesn't follow orders. Hold on."

Venom stood close to the front door, listening. "She gave you a fake address. I didn't buy into this. She might've talked."

"Not likely . . . Hey, I think we got a break," Karpenito said.

A chair scraped across a floor. "Move it, kid," the cop ordered. "I need this computer."

Venom glanced at the boy in the portrait, and his stomach tightened. "What the hell are you doing to a kid?"

"Nothing. I spotted Whitley's hair band. Gotta call you back." Karpenito hung up.

Venom left the apartment and strode to his car. After he slid behind the wheel, his phone pulsed to life.

"Search history on the computer shows your problem's cruising to Montana," Karpenito crowed. "Time stamp matches."

"Did you say problem? She's not my problem."

"She's your problem if she fingers you," Karpenito snarled.

"You failed to empty the lobby." Venom twisted the key in the ignition and pumped the gas pedal. "Damn piece of crap," he muttered, pumping harder.

"How was I to know she'd be working late? Maneski's lawyer kept you out of the slammer. A fact you'd better not forget."

"For another hit you nearly bungled." A bitter taste hung in his mouth. "Nope. My fee was for the one final whack. I'm done."

"Maneski will double your fee, and I'll add in generous expenses."

Venom's brakes squeaked while he jockeyed out of the tight parking space. He gritted his teeth. "Okay. Give me what you do know."

"Whitley's riding a Greyhound to Three Falls and booked at the Lazy K Ranch. She searched for someone named Morley near Emma Springs. Bury the body and bring back an eyeball. Maneski wanted Gilson's hand that signed his warrant, and he'll want the eyeball that saw the hit." The phone clicked and went silent.

Venom rubbed his wedding band. "Stupid, stupid plant girl." A frown creased his face while he pulled into a parking lot and found the ranch's number. He rummaged in his pocket and then shoved a handful of antacids into his mouth. What body part would The Butcher demand for a hitman's failure?

The ranch phone rang twice. "Lazy K. May I help you?" asked a cheerful voice.

"I believe Miranda Whitley's joining you soon. I need to send my sweet lady roses to apologize for a misunderstanding I created. Do you have a local florist?"

"Oh, how romantic. Hold a moment and I'll find the number for Petal Pusher Flowers. They deliver, but maybe you'd rather bring them in person?"

It'd be a personal delivery all right. "What a wonderful idea. Our secret?"

She laughed and agreed.

Maneski didn't tolerate screw ups. The lawyer who'd delayed a purchase agreement for his mansion had landed at the bottom of Puget Sound with a boat anchor attached to his legs. Actually, two anchors—the body had been chopped in half. Nobody cared four hundred feet down.

He rubbed the sweat from his brow. If a delay moving into a house sent the mobster off the deep end, killing the plant girl ensured his own survival. His family, too. Mankeski ordered hits like his grandson ordered fries with his burger.

And the little feller devoured burgers. A double fee ensured there'd be plenty of money to raise the boy under fake identities.

An orange leaf fell onto his faded hood. He leaned back, sinking into the tattered upholstery.

Ah, the unpredictable outdoors. Perfect for a hunting accident.

Elk don't talk.

~ ~ ~

Traffic stopped mid-block.

Corrin used the pause to contemplate the fastest way to the bus station. "Miranda, what northbound route's best on a Friday night?"

"The one speeding us away from the Justice Building." Panic sharpened Miranda's voice while she scrunched into the seat and folded her long legs under the Firebird's dash. "Maybe Fourth Avenue?"

Corrin signaled a move to the center lane. "Fourth it is," she offered calmly. "Not exactly fast getaway traffic, but buckle up, kiddo."

Miranda brought the belt across and jabbed it into the buckle.

"Thanks." Corrin watched while Miranda's green eyes darted everywhere, front to back, corner to corner. Her best friend, her sister-of-the soul, ducked and bobbed like a wild creature trapped in a cage. No, a hunted creature. Goosebumps rose on her arms.

"Thank God you're okay," Miranda said.

A horn honked when Corrin inched their bumper into a space between a Smart car and a van. "I'm fine. Who shoots a federal judge?"

"Please don't grill me."

"Sorry, force of habit from questioning clients. What else can I do to help?"

Miranda twisted her head to see out the back window. "Leave your apartment for a couple nights."

"Easy enough. Should I tell the police someone broke into your place? We know he closed the blinds."

"Don't report anything." She turned around. "The killer would know you spotted him." Her color paled. She scratched at a speck of red on her tan pants.

Ike's blood.

Corrin gripped the steering wheel. "I hadn't thought of the creep seeing me."

"I pray he didn't. They think Ike's dead, and I'm next. You'll not be added to the list."

A bead of perspiration formed on Corrin's brow. "I'll go, too."

"No. Dad always said you never bring trouble to your back porch. Ike insisted I vanish, and I'll lead them out of town. If anyone hurt you, I wouldn't forgive myself. No one's followed us yet."

"None of this makes sense to me. Talk to one of my firm's attorneys if you can't trust the police."

"No time. I skip town now, or I'm dead. And your apartment's not safe. Do you understand?" Miranda's hand shook on the purse she clutched to her chest.

"Vacate. Got it. Aunt Iris loves company, and she's in a secured building," Corrin said. "Ike has contacts at city hall, but we need to determine who'll advise you if—"

"Ike's going to be okay. He has to be. No more funerals, no more headstones . . ." Miranda choked back a sob.

"Sure he is." Corrin softened her voice. "You shouldn't go through this without someone you trust." She turned a corner onto a one-way street.

Miranda rose enough to watch cars over her shoulder. "You join me, and there's a bullseye on your back. I've got an FBI agent."

Corrin checked her rearview mirror. Had the bigger car sped up? "An agent you just met." She stomped on the gas to make a yellow light. "I can get help in Seattle. Does the agent know someone broke in to your apartment?"

The black sedan ran the light and came alongside them.

"Watch out!" Miranda shouted.

Corrin swung into the next lane and jammed on the brakes to avoid a taxi. They both pitched forward.

The car sped by, occupied by a woman and two kids.

"False alarm."

"Bloody hell!" Corrin clenched the steering wheel. "I can't jump over the row of cars and onto the sidewalk."

"Sorry," Miranda said. "Traffic should delay Snake Neck."

"Snake Neck? You know the killer's name?"

"No." Miranda poked her head between the seats. After righting a blue gym bag, she straightened Corrin's stack of folders in a satchel on the floor. "It appears your pivotal case needs attention this weekend. You've got homework."

"Deflection won't work against me." Corrin said. "Snake Neck? What else do you know?"

"Don't. Ask." Miranda's steely voice didn't match her trembling hands. "You told me appeasing this client rated a make or break for your legal career. You've been the brilliant understudy long enough."

Corrin loosened her grip on the wheel. "A delay won't kill me. I mean, there's more important things in life than impressing the partners. Like assisting my BFF."

"I have a plan."

"Against a guy named Snake Neck?" She groaned. "I may be petite, but I'll face your gun-toting reptile."

"I need you here. If Ike's condition deteriorates, you'll give Shirley wiser advice."

"Typical Miranda, always thinking of others." She squeezed the shifter knob. "You and me, we're two Phoenix birds rising from the flames of our past. Please, be careful."

"I'll be okay. I promise." Miranda smiled weakly. "Can I borrow your phone charger?"

Corrin stopped the car at a red light, yanked the charger from the lighter, and handed it off. "Don't worry. I'll be there for Shirley and Ike."

A crowd passed in front of their bumper.

Miranda clutched the cord and hunkered in her seat. "I know."

Outside Corrin's window, a lone bicyclist dodged cars, trying to push through a swarm of traffic. Miranda's next path sounded risky and unprotected, too. "Where are you meeting Mr. FBI?"

"A mountain rendezvous," Miranda said.

"Shooting a judge means life in prison. You shouldn't use a credit card. They can be traced," Corrin said.

"I never got a card. Find me an ATM and keep your car running. The cops may monitor my bank account. I'll pay cash for my bus ticket, and I didn't pay for the du—hotel yet."

Du? Of course, she'd packed for a dude ranch. No protection there. "When's this stupid light going to change?" Corrin thumped the shifter knob.

LEO's accessed everything—building surveillance, all kinds of stuff. How would Miranda vanish without a trace? Her law firm's in-house PI could find a way to monitor the bus route. "Use my Firebird."

"I don't have a driver's license, and I've never driven a stick." Miranda pulled her hair over her face. "I'm ready to withdraw cash."

"You sit for now. We'll use my money." Corrin steered into a parking space fronting a bank. "How much?"

Miranda squeezed the bump on her nose, revealing a phone number written in ink on her wrist. "Two thousand should be plenty."

"Be right back." Corrin strode to the cash machine. She pulled a pen out of her pocket and jotted the first digits of the phone number onto scrap paper. How much stress could Miranda handle? She wasn't cutting all ties this time to avoid dealing with death—she was bolting to stay alive.

Corrin counted the twenties from the machine. What amount saved your life? She slid back into her seat and handed Miranda the cash. "I added three hundred." She gently squeezed Miranda's hand. "You'd better get some photos of this place. Sounds pricey."

"Thanks. I will."

"So, I didn't know the circumstances before I stuck your birthday gift from Aunt Iris and me into my gym bag. It's bling. Don't open it on the bus."

"I need a lucky talisman."

Corrin forced a fake smile. "It's got our guarantee for happy trails." She turned into the Greyhound parking lot.

At the far end, two busses sat in an angled row, their fumes puffing white clouds into evening air.

Arrivals and departures flashed on a sign above the door.

"Good driving. We made it in time," Miranda said, and pointed to the top of the reader board, where a Chicago departure pulsed. "My bus is still loading."

Corrin pulled into a parking space and shut off the engine. "Call me when you arrive."

Miranda's fingers wobbled while she arranged strands of hair over her face. "After my phone's charged. Thanks again. For everything. Gotta run."

Corrin leaned over the consul to grasp Miranda in a hug. "Hold steady. You're one of the strongest people I know." After they pulled apart, she clutched Miranda's shaking hand as she memorized the rest of the inked number. "I love you."

"It's what kept me going." Miranda tugged the gym bag from the back seat and touched Corrin's cheek. "Sister-of-my-soul, you be careful, too."

Corrin fought tears.

"Bye," they whispered to each other.

Miranda stumbled through the door. She emerged holding a ticket.

Corrin waved the 'give me a call' hand sign, like she did every day heading out for work.

Miranda blew her a kiss, flashed her ticket to a uniformed driver, and boarded the bus.

Corrin followed her dark form until she took a seat. She swiped off a tear. Ike could die, and a killer named Snake Neck had broken into the next-door apartment. Miranda's life depended on protection from a virtual stranger who'd left for a mountain.

The bus backed up, then slowly rumbled across the parking lot. At the street it turned right, toward the I-90 ramp.

She pulled her phone and a tissue from her purse and dabbed at her eyes. The call to her Aunt Iris went to voicemail.

She shifted to reverse, and did a head check before she eased the Firebird backward.

Brakes screeched.

Corrin shoved in the clutch and twisted around.

A black sedan driven by a man veered around her trunk. The car slowed opposite the entry doors, then jetted out in the same direction as the bus.

"Idiot," she muttered. "This isn't the Indie 500."

Bloody hell. Could he have been the gunman? Her mouth went dry. Seattleites owned thousands of black cars. But still . . . She hadn't told Miranda to change out of her work clothes.

Please, oh please, let Miranda's phone have the juice to receive her warning call. She pulled out her cell.

Chapter 3

Stepping out to firm Montana ground, Miranda's eyes traveled across a little crowd to a wiry cowboy holding a sign marked 'Whitley.'

She flicked a wave at him, and his weathered face brightened in a friendly smile. Deep creases in his cheeks proved he'd given out many. Heck, she'd bet he'd blown out over seventy-five candles on his last birthday cake.

Behind him, tall posts bearing fluorescent lights scattered beams onto a dark expanse of blacktop. They shone a path to the Gas N Eat's covered fuel pumps and convenience store.

No bus terminal at her destination. Just another ten-minute pit stop for some passengers, while others would depart for home from the parking lot, carrying their assorted bags and bundles.

Evening air held the crisp scent of fall.

She rolled her neck from shoulder to shoulder, loosening tight muscles.

A cattle truck turned in from the highway and rattled toward the pumps. Whiffs of animals and hay brought precious childhood memories of Dad and horses. He'd promised they'd visit a dude ranch someday. She swallowed hard.

Her cowboy approached. "Howdy." His slow drawl matched faded jeans and a sweat-stained Stetson. "You're our Miss Whitley?"

"Yes, sir." Every muscle in her body begged for rest, but habit forced her lips into a pleasant smile—the phony one she'd honed for strangers.

"My friends call me Pitch. On behalf of the Langleys, welcome to Montana." He gave her hand two quick pumps.

A gray-haired woman bustled past them. "Excuse me." She waved frantically at a uniformed Marine stepping off the bus.

The soldier caught sight of the woman and flashed a crooked grin, exactly like her brother's had been. Miranda dropped her eyes to the ground.

Brown, withered leaves blew across the pavement in front of her. She squeezed her eyes shut and took a breath, letting it out slowly.

"Nothin' like a good homecoming for a soldier," Pitch offered.

She cleared her throat. "Montana's beautiful. Hope you knew about the delay."

"Sure did. They post arrival times on the Greyhound website. Wait 'till you see our spread. You'll get an eagle's eye view during tomorrow's trail ride. I'm assumin' you had a good trip, 'cept for being a few hours late?"

"No complaints." Stars sparkled in a bluish-purple sky, unimpeded by Seattle's twenty-four-hour neon glare.

The bus driver stood over the luggage he'd removed from the open storage compartments. "Get your baggage tags ready, folks."

"Let's grab your suitcases and be off," Pitch said.

Corrin's duffel bag sat at the end of the row laid out on the pavement. Miranda pulled out the receipt for the driver. "Mine's the blue one."

"Any more?" Pitch lifted it using two fingers.

"Nope."

"You pack mighty light for a gal."

"A good friend insisted I needed a retreat. You got me on short notice, carrying the bare essentials."

He patted her bag and grinned. "Works for us. I need to

tell Kat I collected you." He pulled out a cell and tapped in a message.

Should she borrow his phone? No. The incoming call might display the ranch name. Calls to check on Ike and relay how safe she felt would be her first priority tomorrow morning, after her old phone charged. Her gaze shifted to a few dusty pickups parked out front of the convenience store.

Pitch pocketed his cell and ushered her toward a faded red truck, sitting at least a hundred feet away, under the light pole closest to the highway. "The drive isn't long, but it'll be full dark before we get home."

She rubbed the sides of her arms and walked faster through the vacant end of the parking lot. "Seems plenty dark to me now."

"No city lights out here and no traffic jams. My old Chevy and I prefer the slower pace."

Binder twine secured the dented tailgate of a pickup straight out of the 50's. "Hope you don't mind it's not a fancy limo."

"Any ride's good, even a donkey cart," she said, and headed to the passenger side.

Gravel scattered while a black sedan veered into the lot. The front plate displayed Washington's Mt. Rainier.

Miranda's pulse spiked.

"Anything in particular you want to do at our ranch?" Pitch stepped between her and a view of the driver while it passed by. He swung her bag into the bed of the truck.

"Ah, let me think." Her eyes followed the vehicle crossing the parking lot, heading toward the bus. "I'd like to sleep without hearing traffic, eat country cooking, and enjoy your scenic trail ride." She mentally ticked off the highlights from the ranch website.

The sedan's brake lights flickered bright red before it slowly passed the end of the Greyhound. A silhouette outlined a lone driver, his head turned toward the passengers milling around the bus door.

She ducked behind the outside mirror on her side, spun around, and crouched by a metal Chevy emblem mounted on the front fender.

The car cruised on to the store and backed into a spot too far away to see the driver.

Pitch came around the truck and fished a ring of keys from his pocket. "Got your bag secured." He cocked his head. "You drop something?"

"Ah, no, cool emblem." She patted the silver insignia on the fender. "It caught my eye. I love horses and pickups."

"The single thing still shining on this old girl. Wouldn't have guessed you're a cowgirl by your baseball cap and sneakers. Most of our guests arrive toting spanking new cowboy hats and boots."

"I packed my old boots, and my hat's a keepsake." She pushed the crown of Kenny's ball cap onto her forehead. It didn't provide any sense of invisibility from the car.

"Yup, there's more to being a cowboy than wearing the boots," he chuckled. "Most've our keepsakes emit a cowpony essence." Pitch rested his hand on one side of the outside mirror while she stayed crouched on the other.

Come on dude, get out of your black car. "I'm looking forward to everything I brought smelling horsey."

"That's good." He opened her door. "If you're done admiring the Chevy emblem, we can hit the road."

She scooted around him and hopped onto the seat.

He glanced over his shoulder toward the dark car, then back to her. "I'm pretty good at readin' people, and I'd say you're carryin' a lot more than a jacket on your shoulders."

"Hard to sleep on the bus is all." She pulled her door shut.

Rounding the front fender, he glanced at the car again, then slid onto his seat and started the engine. "My boss,

Trey Langley, says I possess an uncanny ability to unriddle folks."

Great. "That's nice." She turned her head to the window.

His hand wiggled the gear stick jutting from the floor. "I get a peculiar notion when somethin' deep down's botherin' a person. Yup, they say if you haven't fallen off a horse, then you haven't been riding long enough."

"Excuse me?"

He grinned at her. "Old cowpoke saying. Our horses are well-mannered."

"Happy to hear." She strained to grin back. "Was that the Lazy K's brand painted on my door?"

"Yup, a tipped K in a circle." He backed up, and steered onto the highway. "You've come to the right get-away spot."

The black car hadn't moved.

"Exactly what I needed."

"Our Lazy K's a balm to heal strained nerves, or strained relationships."

Her only relationship problems were losing Venom and finding Grant. A lot of people drove black cars from Washington through Montana. Her body sank into the worn seat. "I'm ready to relax." The yawn she produced wasn't faked.

Pitch thumped his palm on the steering wheel. "Yes, ma'am. A good dose of ranch livin' and a heap of my Loretta's cooking will have you bright-eyed and rosy-cheeked in no time."

During the eighteen-hour bus trip, she'd scrutinized every vehicle in sight and each new passenger. While Pitch drove through miles of open country, she focused on what lay ahead. At the bottom of a hill, they turned left onto a smaller paved road.

Pitch slowed at a bend. "We're following alongside Spruce Creek. In a moment, you'll see the bridge over

Plunging Rock Canyon." He glanced twice in his rear view mirror.

She looked over her shoulder. Lights blinded her from the vehicle riding their tail. "Are we being followed?"

"Nah. A car wants to beat us to the old span bridge." He slowed before another twist in the road. "I was taught, if you're ridin' ahead of the herd, look back every now and then to make sure it's still there behind ya."

"I didn't know the lodging came with a wagonload of cowboy wisdom. I like it."

"Glad to know."

Their headlights swept across a steep cliff and a dark chasm topped by a silver bridge. Its guardrails hugged the roadway.

Pitch checked his mirror again and clenched the wheel. "Hold on!"

A jolt threw Miranda against the window.

Her front bumper glanced off the railing and banged a warning. The rickety section of posts and metal tipped toward the drop off to the river. "Look out!" she screamed.

Pitch cranked the wheel, veering back to the left. She scooted her butt to the middle, the lap belt cutting into her waist. "They hit us!"

"Damn right! Clipped my bumper!" He shoved the shift knob into low gear. His white-knuckled grip held them on a straight path.

Reflected lights flashed in her side mirror. *Too close.* She twisted around. A single form darkened the front seat of the black car behind them. It surged toward their tailgate.

"They're going to ram us again!"

An air horn blasted from in front of Pitch's truck.

Miranda spun around.

Headlights beamed into their cab while a semi crossed the narrow bridge, using both lanes.

Pitch continued to straddle the pavement and the narrow, graveled shoulder leading to the bridge.

The tractor-trailer barreled by and tooted the air horn.

Miranda clutched the dashboard while they rattled onto the bridge. A dark stream wound below the span. Way, way below.

"We could've been pushed off the cliff," she stammered, and inched back toward her door.

"Not on my watch." Pitch gunned it to cross the span. "I drove jeeps in the army over bamboo bridges. Car behind us wanted to pass is all. They decided not to play chicken with an eighteen wheeler."

She looked behind them. Only the semi's fading taillights flickered. "Where'd the car go?" Her empty stomach ached. "Pitch, I'm worried—"

"Nothing to fret over." He took off his hat and laid it on the seat. "Ahh, I remember our Sheriff said there's been reports of crazy teenagers on this stretch." He shook his head. "Teenagers. Universal hormone hazards at the wheel."

"Ramming us?"

"More than likely. Don't matter. In a few minutes, we'll be at the lodge. Here's our driveway." He downshifted and turned.

They drove onto gravel and under an arched iron gate. A bend took them into a grove of tall pine trees.

Pitch braked, killed the lights, and swiveled his head to face the road.

"Why'd we stop?" She leaned forward to see between tree trunks.

A dark car sped by on the highway.

Her throat went dry.

"Well . . . you see." He rattled the floor shifter, the truck lurched to a halt, and the engine died.

Miranda's knee bumped the dash.

"Missed first gear. Sorry 'bout that." He restarted the motor. "I paused here, cause if we come in quiet, we might spot fireflies." He took out a handkerchief and wiped his brow.

Hell no. She'd caught lightning bugs on a family trip to Michigan, and one fact blazed in her memory. The insects came out for a short while in early summer, not in fall. "I don't see any blinking bugs."

"Guess they're not out tonight."

Did Pitch think the car meant to shove them into the gorge? *Oh please, not Snake Neck. No. No. No.* It must've been reckless kids. She grasped the edge of her seat, feeling each strand woven into the scratchy fabric.

Pitch turned the high beams back on and steered between canopies of drooping, dark branches.

Their truck lumbered at a faster clip than she'd expect. On a private road. At night. Transporting a paying guest.

Every bump jolted through her until she spotted an illuminated three-story lodge. Golden light beckoned from large windows recessed into logs the size of Redwoods.

Outlined against a starry sky, it resembled a giant version of a rectangular fortress Kenny had once built out of vintage Lincoln Logs.

One long side faced woods, the other side overlooked a meadow. On the short end, furthest away, a river-rock chimney rose above the roofline. A thin ribbon of smoke wound skywards.

Closest to the driveway, a porch faced two red barns, which created bookends to a fenced area between them.

Pitch parked under a light mounted on the smaller barn. "I forgot to give you this form about your riding abilities. Kat's careful choosing who sits atop her ponies." He pulled a folded paper from his pocket and then patted her arm. "You'll see, life's path is easier to walk with a horse between your legs."

"So I've heard." Miranda took the form. "I'd prefer an old gelding."

"Speak a' the devil. Trey Langley's heading into the barn." Pitch tried to jest, but his tense voice said otherwise. "The boss does a final night round on the ponies."

Miranda glimpsed a man wielding a flashlight while walking the center aisle of the larger barn.

"There's Kat, I mean Miss Kathleen, waitin' for you at the back door." He pointed over his shoulder.

A diminutive woman with curly blond hair stood on what Miranda's mom would've called a veranda.

Stairs led to the wide porch, which wrapped around to the woodsy side of the property. Rocking chairs and small tables were scattered across the raised deck.

"I gotta talk to Trey. Miss Kathleen's excited to meet you." He hopped out, and marched off toward the largest barn.

She shoved open her door. "Thanks for the lift," she called to his backside.

Her stomach issued a loud growl into country silence. Heat rose in her cheeks while she crossed the driveway.

"Welcome, Miss Whitley. I'm Kathleen Langley, or Kat." A genuine smile took years off her middle-aged face. "We hope you'll enjoy our ranch. If you haven't eaten, I can warm supper." She stuck out her hand. "We're glad you've joined us."

Miranda gave a quick shake and then put her hand on the railing and her foot on the first step. "A snack sounds great. Sorry I arrived late."

"No worries. We noticed the bus delay, and while I served the guests, Loretta fixed a plate for you from tonight's dinner."

That damned sense of aphids climbing her back returned while they lingered out in open view. Had the car doubled back? She needed protection, not dinner. With luck, Kathleen stowed a loaded shotgun under her bed. Wasn't being a crack shot a cowgirl requirement?

Miranda drew courage from deep within and smiled back. "It's nice she saved me a meal. Pitch told me you treat everyone like kinfolk."

"We try. I'll have you dining on meatloaf in a jiffy, and afterwards we'll walk you to your cabin. I bet you're beat."

"Cabin?" Miranda squeezed the railing until the wood bit into her palm. "I reserved a single room on the top floor."

"Oh, we upgraded you. You're staying in our most secluded spot, nestled in the woods."

Why hadn't she called Agent Morley to meet her? Should she divulge the real reason for her visit? She trudged up the stairs behind Kathleen. "I'm fine in your beautiful lodge."

"Our cutest cabin's all ready for you." Kathleen had reached the porch. Her gaze dropped to Miranda's worn tennis shoes. "No extra charge."

Miranda reached the top step and turned her face into the shadows, then ran her palm up and down the railing. "Very kind of you to go to so much trouble."

"My great-grandparents homesteaded here for the unspoiled beauty and passed on their wishes to share its calming effect. Their descendants live in all directions." Her hand motioned in a wide circle of pride, then pointed to the pickup and a man with ginger-colored hair streaked by silver. "There's my husband, Trey." Her face beamed with pride.

He examined the front bumper while Pitch stood next to him, scowling.

"Come here, Trey," Kathleen called to him.

Flashing a grin, Trey strode over and then jogged up the stairs. "Last guest of the season accounted for, so all the chicks are safe in our hen house."

Safe? Miranda edged her feet across wooden planks toward a screen door. A brightly lit room shone from the other side of their back door.

"My partner in the ranch operation," Kathleen smiled at him. "Trey handles creatures, I handle comforts. And he's the handsomest man west of the Mississippi. Trey, this here's our Miss Whitley."

He shook Miranda's hand. "Pleased to meet you." He leaned into Kathleen and started to speak, then closed his mouth. Instead, he stroked his wife's hand.

A sad smile crossed Miranda's lips. Her father used to touch her mother in the same affectionate manner. "Glad to meet you."

"We hope you'll get R & R," he said. "Let us know how we can assist." Trey kissed his wife's cheek. "Kat's the best horsewoman and hostess in Hanlen County. Tell her your needs, and she'll make it happen."

Regrettably, no one turned back time. The bleak, wintry feeling hung in the night air. Miranda shook off the chill. "Home-cooking and sleep sounds perfect."

A loud thump boomed from behind them.

Her pulse jumped. *Relax, it wasn't a shot.*

She turned in time to see Pitch swing a rubber mallet at a block of wood he'd placed at the edge of the bumper.

"Did Pitch hit something with his precious truck?" Kathleen asked Trey.

"Nope. Nothing," he cleared his throat. "Encountered those wild driving kids on the highway. All's well." He drew his finger across his lips and patted the chest pockets on his denim shirt.

Kathleen cocked her head. "Kids . . . Right. Oh-kay."

Had Trey given his wife a signal to button up? Miranda swallowed. "I need to—"

"Eat. You must be famished. Come on in." Kathleen held the door for Miranda to enter.

A hallway began at her left and beyond it stretched an open kitchen with stainless appliances.

"Please sit at the prep island, while I warm your meal," Kathleen said. She stepped to an industrial sized refrigerator, removed a covered dish, and slid a plate heaped with mashed potatoes, carrots, and a slab of meat into the microwave.

Scents of spices and beef lingered in the air, and carried a sense of calm. Miranda's mouth watered. She plopped onto a wooden barstool. "Wow, meatloaf beats the bus stop offerings of burritos and greasy chicken wings."

"You'll get all country cooking this week, served family style in the dining room behind you," Trey said.

Miranda swiveled her seat to face an open-beamed room holding a built-in buffet on one side. In the room's center sat a long wooden trestle table and chairs for at least twelve.

Trey set a glass of milk at her place. "You landed here pretty fast. Most of our guests book months in advance." He winked at Kathleen. "I guess absence makes a heart grow fonder."

"I won't miss Seattle."

Trey handed her a napkin wrapped around silverware. "Our ranch is good for any broken up—"

Kathleen poked her husband in his ribs. "Quit your teasin'."

Miranda studied Trey's smirk. She rubbed her chin. "Not many singles visit here?"

"We get an assortment of guests," Kathleen said. The microwave chimed, and she moved the steaming plate onto her placemat. "Be careful, now, the food's piping hot."

Miranda dug into spuds topped by melting butter.

"Our Wagyu ground beef's from my cousin's ranch, and the vegetables are grown here." Kathleen wiped a spotless counter.

"My family helped in Mom's garden," Miranda said. "Come fall, we'd take turns using an old potato fork to find root veggies and then sit at our scarred oak table enjoying the feast."

"How lovely. Here in Emma Springs we pride ourselves in treating one another like extended family," Kathleen said.

Miranda savored the last bite of homegrown carrot, trying to recall the tinkle of Mom's laughter when she threw her head back and chuckled at one of Dad's jokes. A hollow emptiness filled her chest. "Your townspeople sound very friendly."

The screen door banged shut. Pitch wiped his boots on a bristled mat inside the doorway. "Except for a few young rascals." He crossed to the end of the counter. "I declare, Miss Whitley, you polished off the meatloaf quicker than a stray dog. Loretta will be tickled."

Kathleen gathered her empty plate and glass. "We cherish our community, especially the old codgers." She pinched Pitch's cheek. "The other flashlight's out in the barn. Can you get it?"

"On my way." Pitch headed back outside.

"Anything else we can get you, Miss Whitley?" Kathleen asked. "Tomorrow's going to be full of fun surprises."

"Please call me Miranda. Right now, a good night's sleep will work wonders."

"Yup, you're gonna need your shuteye," Trey teased.

Had she missed something? By the checked cowboy shirts and the way they flattered one another, Trey and Kathleen fit country wholesome to a T, but their sharp eyes held a hint of flat-out mischief.

"Breakfast's at eight," Kathleen said. "Pa, I mean Pitch, will show you to your cabin. He's our go-to guy." Her face shone with affection. "Good night."

Pa? Loretta was her mother? Did they know how blessed they were, two generations working together? The napkin in her hand squeezed into a ball. She smoothed it out and placed it on the counter. "Night."

"Sleep well." Trey held the lodge door open for Miranda to exit. He began whispering to Kathleen and pulled it shut.

Where was Pitch? Fluorescent lights hung in front of their barns and at each end of the fenced arena, casting a bluish glimmer onto the bare ground below.

Beyond the pasture grew giant firs. Between their trunks, it was blacker than India ink. They'd be beautiful in sunshine, but appeared downright spooky now.

Goosebumps rose on her arms. She clutched the handrail and descended the stairs.

"This way, Miss Whitley," Pitch's voice called out from her left. He stood beside a pole topped by a black dinner bell at the entrance to a shadowy path.

She increased her stride to reach the glow of his flashlight. "Here's your torch, case you need to come to the lodge."

The heavy flashlight he handed her cast a strong beam, but the farther they hiked between looming trees, the closer she tailed him and her swinging duffel bag.

Stillness magnified pine needles crushing underfoot. "No streetlights or sirens," she offered.

The moon glowed while it edged out of a bank of clouds.

"You might hear coyotes. They're night hunters." Pitch stopped in front of a log cabin tucked into a grove of Ponderosa pines. "Nothing but rolling hills behind you."

He opened the door, and slid her bag inside. "Light switch's to the right." Her room and the porch became illuminated. "Your home away from home."

"No other cabins nearby?"

"Nope. You city folks appreciate privacy, and Kat mentioned you might have company."

A branch snapped. Her eyes flicked to the woods.

Thirty feet away, a dark figure stood under a pine tree. She gasped. "Who–"

"What's wrong?" He turned to where she pointed.

"A man." She backed into the doorway. "Over by the tree."

Pitch shone his light on the area. "Branches throw

shadows. Nothin' to worry about." He put two fingers to his lips and sent out a shrill whistle.

The nearby bushes rustled and a black shepherd bounded to him like a furry bullet. The dog sat next to his cowboy boot.

"Dylan, go search." He motioned to the forest. "Rest easy. He'll bark at anything strange."

Her heart pounded. "Good."

Pitch strode to the tree and lifted a low hanging branch. The image she'd noticed bounced. "Night, Miss Miranda."

"Thanks. Night." She closed her door, slid the bolt, and checked the locks on every window before drawing the curtains shut. Her fingers shook while she wedged a chair under the door knob.

Could Venom have followed her? Her brain flashed to the bumper scraping the guardrail.

Montana wasn't going to be restful or safe. She needed to find Grant before her mind went wild from fright. What had Pitch said about company? Should she call him back?

She rubbed her temples and then unzipped the gym bag.

A pair of jeans, a cotton shirt, and her old sweatshirt lay on top of her cowboy boots. A side pocket bulged with running tights she'd wear for pajama bottoms.

She took off her windbreaker, her T-shirt, and cargo pants. The nap on the inside of the sweatshirt brushed against her skin. The tights slid across the flannel sheet.

A shiver ran through her. She unfurled the blanket from the foot of the bed and pulled it to her chin.

The dog growled close by, then barked.

Hairs rose on the back of her neck. She grabbed the flashlight and found the switch. Her fingers dug into cold metal while she slid her feet to the floor.

~ ~ ~

Venom stood on a foothill between two pine trees. His pulse had steadied to a regular beat after the rush of adrenalin from nearly kissing a Mack truck doing seventy. Damned if her geezer pickup driver hadn't held his ground instead of careening off the cliff.

Next time he'd eliminate her once and for all, with a bullet. He lifted the night vision binoculars and adjusted each eyepiece to a sharp focus. The light inside the cabin went out. "Well, plant girl, no bag ladies or soldiers hovering around you now."

A clear sky and everyone except the girl slept in the lodge. Nothing beat a panoramic view from a ridge. He did a second scan of the cabin's perimeter.

"Christ," he muttered. The dog sat under the porch light outside her door.

Could he pop the mutt and her before anyone spotted him? Decisions, decisions. He stroked the pit viper on his neck.

In the morning, she should be on the trail ride. The hunters he'd passed in town earlier presented a perfect set-up for a stray bullet.

Heck, the fool he'd seen in full camo carried a street sweeper. A good hunter needed one clear shot, not a piece carrying twenty rounds of ammo.

Better to finish the job and sever his final tie to Maneski. He pulled on a ski mask and shouldered the rifle.

~ ~ ~

The second and fourth boards creaked while Grant descended the worn outside stairs of his family's century old homestead. He hadn't noticed it last night after they'd stopped here on the way home from the airport.

He took a deep breath of fresh air, tinged by pine. Hard to relax when the timing of the old mountain hermit's yearly delivery of staples cost him a week in bureau time. Now that he'd winterized his house today, how fast could he get Stan's supply trip done and return to Seattle?

The back door squeaked, and Mom stepped outside. More gray than brown colored her hair, but the sparkle in her eye hadn't diminished. "Goodnight, dear. We enjoy your FBI stories. I hope my lasagna filled you up after you worked all day at your place." She blew him her traditional air kiss.

"Your cooking's always great, Mom. Two homecooked dinners in a row. My win. Time for me to head to my house and a chance of cell reception."

"We've got spotty coverage by the barn. Love you to the moon and back."

"You too."

Dad and Poppy joined her. He smiled at the two men of influence in his life, men who dwarfed his mom's petite stature.

Poppy's six-foot, four-inch frame might be stooped, but was still damn muscular for an eighty-five-year-old grandfather.

"We're really proud of how you're positioning yourself to reach SAC." His dad held his mom's hand. "Nothing like a son climbing the ranks." He tossed the keys to their Bronco.

Grant caught them. "Thanks for the vehicle loan. The battery in my Suburban's still on the charger. Call me if you need the Bronco tonight." He maneuvered into their old SUV. Hours at the gym after he'd arrived in Seattle and a five-inch growth spurt had freed him from being a high school runt who'd flustered his folks.

Gone was the kid needing a mounting block or the teenager whose legs didn't reach the clutch pedal on the John Deere. Gone was the kid regularly beaten by the Three Falls version of a gang. He clenched his fist at the memory of those weekly pummeling sessions under the bleachers.

His dad had shown him a few defensive moves and told him he'd dealt with worse as the kid of an FBI agent.

"My State Highway Patrol career creates a better family environment than the bureau"—those words had been his father's explanation for turning down Quantico. Had his dad regretted the compromise?

Grant cranked on the engine and glanced out the passenger window to the steeply roofed house. Why hadn't they hired out their gutter cleaning? Hell, his dad's rooftop tumble might've been much worse than a few cracked ribs. A new lead had surfaced on his case Friday morning, and he'd been relieved at the flight delay to gain more work time. Damn roof.

He pulled Stan's supply list from his pocket, tossed it onto the passenger seat, and then yanked the seatbelt across his chest. He sat back while the old engine warmed.

Poppy left the porch and shuffled toward his cottage at the edge of the pasture. In the background, Mt. Hanlen stood as lone guardian, day or night.

He threw the column shifter into reverse and backed up. Gravel scattered while he wheeled the Bronco out of the driveway and then onto open highway.

The delivery list shone on the dark upholstery like a white flag. Clearly, his dad felt embarrassed he'd miss the trek to his old army buddy this year.

Dad and Stan both needed a reality check on the limits of their aging bodies.

He grimaced. Tomorrow he'd settle for equine companionship while he rode far up Mt. Hanlen on the annual father and son trip, solo this year. A wave of nostalgia rolled through him, recalling the excitement of riding out with his dad.

A dark car approached, racing toward him. The brights flashed on.

"Asshole!" Grant swerved to the shoulder and cranked the wheel full around, adrenalin pumping while his vehicle sluggishly pulled a U-turn.

The speeding car's tail lights faded away.

His shoulders sagged. No way he'd catch it in the old rig. Nor should he.

Probably damn kids seeing what the family car could do. He'd been one of them once. Shaking his head, he completed the circle and drove another mile.

The tilted sign marked his driveway.

Trees at the entrance to his property had grown from saplings to stout silhouettes. Hadn't noticed them last night, either. Time had slipped by, limb by limb and wrinkle by wrinkle. Next trip he'd have to initiate an uncomfortable conversation with his parents regarding their future without him living nearby.

Grant parked and then entered the house he'd built in stages over the last decade.

He flipped on a light.

Where had the time gone? He ran his hand on a log. Building had begun the fall he'd turned eighteen, after his parents had sold him a hundred acres. They'd finished it together in spurts throughout the last dozen years, discussing how he'd be the Morley to reach the coveted FBI rank neither Dad nor Poppy had achieved.

He'd charted a career timeline and it required a twenty-four seven mentality. Special Agents in Charge resided in big cities. To dump his place, he'd need to hire a realtor. Dad would understand.

The custom oak dining table glowed. A memory of sunny days varnishing with his dad brought a smile. He ran his hand across its smooth wood. On it sat the freshly scribbled list he'd made of what would go and what could be sold. The table had made the 'keep' list.

His woodworking skills had proved useful while he'd mentored juvies in a tough Seattle high school. The kids had convinced him to coach basketball at the Y. He smiled, recalling their insistence they needed a father figure like him.

Those mandatory volunteering hours had flown by. He'd quit three years ago, maybe four? Hopefully, those kids got into college, but more likely, jail. He should've kept in touch.

His phone vibrated in his pocket. Teens in the pre-thug stage were someone else's worry.

Three bars. At least they'd gotten better cell service in parts of Emma Springs.

The text had been marked urgent from Sam two hours ago, while he'd been scarfing lasagna. He banged his fist against the counter.

Sorry to bother you on vacation, but you're needed ASAP. Judge shot in Seattle's Justice Building-Friday 6 PM, he read aloud.

An assault of a federal judge warranted his department leading the investigation, and it appeared his boss assigned him to be in charge. He took a deep breath, expanding his chest.

The attached report opened. Whoa, they'd shot Judge Gilson. Had Maneski responded to his stiff sentence by ordering the hit?

Friday, 6 pm. "Damn," he muttered. Right after he'd left the office and stumbled over the woman.

Other Fridays during lunchtime, he'd watched her lanky frame bend and stretch to trim lobby plants. Why'd she been there late? Had she seen anything?

His finger had brushed a silky lock of her hair while he'd zig-zagged to avoid stepping on her.

Now wasn't the time to think of a russet braid and blushing pink cheeks.

Solving the case could advance him.

But the woman. She'd peppered him with questions, and made a snide comment. He rubbed a full day's growth of stubble growing on his chin.

Yeah, she'd chastised him for calling a family visit a

duty, and told him to appreciate time together. Odd remarks then, maybe worse now.

Sam Coswell, his ASAC, would be at his computer tomorrow, sending out any case updates.

He tapped, "*Need to talk*" in a text to Sam.

Recall the details, Morley. Her name?

Nope. She'd cut him off. The lookout? He thumped his hand on the counter.

Judas Priest! Had he flirted with an assassin?

Chapter 4

Miranda bolted upright, bunching the sheets in her grip. The loud clang repeated.

Oh, right, the breakfast bell. Exhaustion burned her eyes. Intermittent dog barks near her cabin throughout the night had proven worse than the nightmares.

Her cell phone rang, and she rolled onto her side to grab it.

"Hi, Shirley." Her heart gave a funny little jog. "How's Ike?"

"You saved him," she cried.

"Thank goodness. Can I speak to him?"

"He's sedated right now. Needs another surgery due to complications."

Miranda's pulse quickened. "What happened? What are the doctors saying?"

"He lost a lot of blood, and the bullet punctured a vein."

"That's bad, isn't it?"

"They can operate and fix it, but—" Shirley abruptly stopped talking.

She gripped the bedframe. "But what?"

Static buzzed.

"The FBI stopped a gunman last night. They're determined to kill Ike. Are you safe?"

She squeezed the blanket. "Yes, I'm in—"

"Don't tell me where you are. Stay put, and don't trust ANYONE until Ike gets you help. Promise?" Shirley pleaded.

"I promise." Anger roiled in Miranda's belly. "We'll beat the crooked cops and mobsters. I'm safe, get Ike better."

She threw her legs over the edge of the bed and sat up. "I wish I were with you. Call Corrin, she'll help you."

"I will." Shirley sniffed. "We love you. They might be tracing my calls." The connection ended.

Miranda dropped her phone as if it spat flames.

The room had grown cold. She'd not said goodbye, told Shirley she loved them. Her lip trembled.

She got dressed and then held back a corner of yellow-checked curtains while searching for a glimpse of the Langley's main lodge.

Nothing except woods and foothills, the kind she'd hiked as a kid. So many memories of exploring outdoors beside her mom. Her fingers glided over her worn cowboy boots, grass stained and dusty.

She tugged them on and shoved Kenny's hat into one jacket pocket and her phone into the other. Corrin deserved a few photos of Montana.

Steady Corrin, except around horses.

She rummaged in her purse for her lip balm and vial of lavender. At the bottom sat the velvet case embossed with the logo from the jewelry store Corrin's aunt had once proudly owned.

Miranda lifted out a heavy gold neck slide hanging from a bolo tie. Dark red jewels outlined the body of a rearing horse. Corrin had probably broken out in a sweat while packing it.

Nothing in Aunt Iris's shop had been faux. She'd bet Corrin's uncle had worn the garnet-laden piece before he'd died from a heart attack.

Would *she* survive to see her twenty-fifth birthday in ten days? She'd done the right thing, to vanish and protect Corrin.

She grabbed the blue windbreaker, yanked her door shut, and snugged the rearing horse to her shirt collar. Every step on brittle needles put her on edge.

She slowed her breaths. You've dreamed of living surrounded by trees and flower-filled meadows your children can run through, she reminded herself.

Dylan bounded up, his black tail wagging.

"Busy night. Wish I knew dog-speak." She scratched under his chin. "Good boy."

The cast-iron bell pealed again, boosting her into a jog. Her nerves needed people, specifically Grant Morley.

In the clearing ahead, sunshine glazed a dewy pasture dotted by spider webs, their jeweled threads sparkling. Horses pulled at tufts of grass.

A welcoming aroma of biscuits, bacon, and coffee fought to overpower the scents of pine and wood smoke.

She climbed the porch stairs and pulled open the screen door.

"Good morning, Miranda. We've got a fine fall day to ride." Kathleen stood at the end of the kitchen counter. She motioned to the built-in buffet in the dining room, which held steaming dishes and platters of pastries. "Enjoy breakfast. The other guests just got started."

Five or six Asian men and several families filled their plates.

Glass windows behind the wooden dining table afforded a view of Mt. Hanlen—a tall, jagged peak.

"I smell fried potatoes and biscuits. Yum." She handed over her completed riding form. "No rodeo mount, please." She smiled her sweetest, while searching the kitchen for a phone. "Oh, by the way, there may be a college friend living in town. Cell's dead. May I make a local call?"

"You bet." Kathleen pointed to the hallway. "Our phone's in the alcove."

Chattering voices receded while she moved away from the sunny dining room.

A dog-eared phonebook sat on the counter. Her finger

ran over a short column of *M's* and stopped at *Tom and Pat Morley*.

Their phone rang twice before a woman answered. "Good morning."

"Hi, I'm vacationing in Emma Springs. I attended college with a Grant Morley from this part of Montana. Do you know him?" She squeezed her eyes shut, praying she sounded normal, praying he wasn't already mountaineering, and praying he'd offer protection.

"Grant's our son," the woman declared. "What a funny coincidence, he's visiting from Seattle and should be here for breakfast soon. I'm happy to take your number and have him call you before he heads up Mt. Hanlen."

She bit her lip. "No worries, I'll try again in a few minutes. Thanks."

"I'll let him know."

Miranda fumbled the receiver to hang it up. She thumped her forehead. Grant might've brushed her off as a nut case. She had to find him on the trail, or go to his house to explain.

She walked into breakfast and spotted an unoccupied chair between a techie-looking boy wearing ear buds and a smiling older man. No snake tattoos in sight.

She tossed food on her plate and slid into the seat.

"Hi, I'm Andrew Chen, from New York," the man said, while he offered a hand sporting a gold Rolex. "I'm leading a group on a team building exercise."

"My name's Miranda."

His colleagues wore yoked Western shirts in different colors.

Andrew put down a ripe plum. "Are you from the East Coast, too?"

"Nope. From Seattle."

"I've been there, a beautiful city. What's your favorite place?"

She brushed her napkin across her lips. "I provide indoor plants, so buildings facing west get my vote." *Crap.* She'd said too much—not smart for a person in hiding.

The other guests continued chatting. No one turned her way.

A bearded young man sitting across from her passed a baby in pink overalls to his wife. "She's all yours, honey."

The woman pursed her lips. "Yeah, I got ambling in the corral yesterday and you get cantering in the woods."

Miranda sighed. What she wouldn't give to be a mother holding a round-cheeked baby.

"I'd guess you've done this before." Andrew pointed at her boots.

"The first time I wore them I sat behind my dad on Trixie, my grandpa's old horse." Her heart ached at the memory. "These are my best-ever present from my twelfth birthday. Mom bought them big, and they've ridden many miles."

"Hope I don't scratch my lizard skin ones today," he said.

She stabbed a potato. "They'll polish back up."

"Well, folks." Kathleen circled by diners to reach the front of the room. "I hope you enjoyed breakfast."

Miranda nodded while others murmured in agreement.

"Good. Busy day ahead of us. You'll be riding to the base of Mt. Hanlen. We measure in miles here, not blocks." She gestured to a framed watercolor painting. "We'll cross the meadow and climb the foothills at the far side of Sunrise Lake. You'll finish by parading through Emma Springs. Today's the chance to experience a drive-thru on horseback. This time of year, you may want coffee."

The painted landscape was laid out in a diamond formation, the mountain being the top point and Emma Springs the bottom. The Lazy K sat on the left, and from what she remembered of the geography on their website, the Morley's place would be to the right.

From the drawing, Grant could be ten miles away. Miranda squirmed in her chair.

"After working you in the corral yesterday, we've matched you to a horse." Kathleen smiled. "Time to mount."

"I hope your team has fun," Miranda said to Andrew Chen.

"Me, too. A few of my group decided to go hunting. They're doing firearm safety first, followed by target practice."

A vice squeezed her chest. Images of the weapons they'd used to kill her family flashed in her mind. Thirty-one bullets had wiped out those she loved. "Oh."

"They certainly own enough rifles." He pointed to a rack Kathleen uncovered, holding an assortment of shotguns.

The chair tipped while she snatched her jacket from it.

Her brain locked onto the memory of the horrible security video the police had played during the questioning session following her family's murder.

Dull gray clouded her vision. She'd seen the empty parking lot, then the killer's car and guns aimed out the windows, imagined the crack of bullets firing and her parent's screams. Thank God, they weren't recorded.

The shooters had gotten away, but every night her room became a prison, and her pillow absorbed tears of remorse for her role in their deaths.

She stumbled outside the lodge and leaned against a post for support. Guns and bullets. She'd never escape them.

~ ~ ~

Had they lost another judge? Grant rechecked the three bars showing on his cell this morning. Sam should be awake by now, and he needed answers. He parked the Bronco next to his parent's barn. Sunlight inching onto dark swaths shaded the nearby foothills.

A rooster crowed an invader alarm.

Dumb bird, sunrise was hours ago. He cracked the window, allowing whiffs of hay and horses inside the cab before placing the call.

"Coswell," Sam answered on the first ring.

"Did Judge Gilson survive?"

"So far," Sam replied. "Bo confronted an attacker approaching the judge's room last night. Sorry to cut short your time off. What flight you on?"

Sam's strained tone meant bad news.

Grant pressed his palm into the old leather seat. "How bad's Bo wounded?"

"Shoulder took a bullet."

"Damn. I should've been there. I don't have a wife and kids depending on me."

"Bo won't have permanent damage."

Grant clenched his jaw. "How'd they know what hospital?"

"Gotta' be a mole. Chatter indicates Venom pulled the trigger on Judge Gilson. Sending you the ID photo of a person of interest who left the scene. We haven't figured out her role yet."

His pulse thrummed. "Priors?"

"None, and we believe she knows the Gilsons socially. The judge's wife won't divulge their relationship. When you returning?"

Grant's eyes followed a cloud while it blocked out rays of sunlight high on the mountain. "Tuesday flight. You'd think Mrs. Gilson would want to help us find out who tried to kill her husband."

"The whole case is odd. A Detective Karpenito arrived first from SPD. He hasn't been available for questioning. Isn't he the Seattle Detective cleared a couple years ago of money laundering?"

"The name's familiar. Sorry I'm not there to run a thorough check. I haven't nailed a crooked cop yet," Grant said.

"It doesn't warm your heart. No record of the woman at the scene until we interviewed the medics who transported Judge Gilson."

It couldn't be her. He pictured her shy smile after she'd recognized him. "So the ambulance showed before an officer did?"

"The medics weren't needed at a nearby car wreck when they heard her 911 call. The woman might be an accessory by her actions. In the initial report Karpenito said he arrived right after the ambulance took off with the judge."

Grant tapped a square icon on his tiny screen and his gut tightened. The woman he'd nearly stomped on photographed well, except for her lifeless green eyes.

'Miranda Whitley' was printed on her badge. To think he'd admired her soft hair and long legs. "Well, hell," he muttered.

Sam cleared his throat. "Cares for plants, doesn't she?"

Heat rose from under his collar. "Correct. I literally bumped into her working in the lobby around eighteen hundred hours Friday night."

"You spoke to her? A couple more minutes and you'd have been in the action."

Muscles tensed in his neck. "Yes, the Whitley woman and I spoke. What happened to the night watchmen? There's always one stationed out front."

"Called to false break-ins on several floors. Ice cubes propped open the security doors until they melted and set off alarms. They'd all left their posts on the first floor. Security cameras were painted over. We need you here. Now."

Judas Priest. He hadn't noticed their absence. He'd been looking at her. "I'm locked into staying in Montana until an old mountain hermit gets his yearly supplies. Delivery's tomorrow."

"Hire someone. We'll cover expenses. Maybe you can extract information on Ms. Whitley out of the judge's wife."

"I can't fly out until after the supply drop. I made a commitment, and the guy doesn't trust most people. These are the only supplies he gets to survive a Montana winter."

"Solving a high-profile case would fast-track your promotion."

"My dad's laid up, Sam, and the guy will shoot if he sees a stranger. It's a day and a half horseback ride on a forested mountain, not UPS territory." He straightened. "I'll check for a milk route flight to get back Monday night."

"I understand the power of family commitments."

"Exactly why I avoid them. I'll find the earliest flight."

"Okay, opinion time. The Whitley woman entered the espresso shop after the ambulance left. Employees said she acted atypical before she dashed out and left in a Firebird. She doesn't fit a killer profile, but the way she took off doesn't match a witness, either. How'd your interaction with her play out?"

He closed his eyes. "She was sitting on the lobby floor trimming plants when I exited the stairwell. I'm texting my ride and smashed her coffee cup. At first, she approved of me replacing her drink and acted friendly by asking a lot of questions."

"Such as?"

"Wanted to know where I was going. She became more intolerant of my attitude than nervous."

"Clarify."

"I wanted to grab her a replacement in the Coffee Klatch, not sit and chat in some espresso shop. She believed I'd judged her on her clothes. Before I left, she warned me to cherish family time."

"Interesting. Keep watch for her at airports on that milk run to get back here. We found Mexico travel brochures in her locker. We're going over the passenger manifests to see if she left the country. No car's registered to her."

"Maybe Maneski pegged her being familiar with the building and threatened to kill her family."

"Still searching for any relatives. After the ambulance left, she ordered a coffee from the shop next door, and paid for it using a fifty. She's a noontime regular who never flashes big bills. Rushed out without her order."

"Not wise if you've iced a judge one building over. I've previously seen her at lunchtime."

"There's more. Shortly following her departure from the shop, a guy fitting Karpenito's description came in and paid for his drink using a fifty. Only two fifties in the till and the serial numbers are three off of consecutive."

A sour tang rose in Grant's throat. "What else did they do in the coffee shop?"

"Ms. Whitley spent a lot of time in the bathroom and used a café owned laptop. They're pulling prints. Friday's website history was deleted. Karpenito sat at the same computer. The barista said he whistled when he left. That's all she recalled."

And he'd recalled Miranda Whitley's full mouth, her blush, her perfect butt. He hadn't dated in months, and then a pretty thug with killer lips had misled him. "She could've left the cop a message. Twice she suggested we move to the espresso shop to replace her drink. I didn't have time."

"Her role might've been to clear the building before the hit."

He closed his eyes. "I didn't notice anxiety while we spoke."

Papers rustled on the other end of the line. "She called 911 and kept pressure on the judge's wound until the ambulance arrived. She ran out crying and begged the medics to come inside before SPD arrived. Said she couldn't lose Ike."

"First name basis with the judge. There's got to be a link."

"She doesn't appear in stake-out photos of Maneski."

Women's appearances or opinions changed with the ease of chameleons. He'd seen it, and Poppy had lost a female's key testimony on an important case. "Being the lookout and seeing the mark bleed out are two different scenarios. Her ID photo doesn't show it, but I noticed she'd had a broken nose."

"I'll add that to the notes. Karpenito said his ID got stolen on Thursday."

Grant rubbed his chin. "Karpenito's role is off. Hey, I couldn't rouse the Coffee Klatch owner. He routinely does books on Friday nights."

"At a ball game. He found two box seats in the tip jar. Here's another twist—someone torched the alley dumpster, still smoldering when SPD arrived. Contents are at the lab."

"Very professional job. After you get updated, try calling, then text me. There's a couple of spots in cell range on the mountain."

Grant pocketed his phone. He sat back and rubbed his neck while scanning the countryside.

Mom and Dad's house hadn't changed, and Mt. Hanlen hadn't changed, but things inside him had. He'd been attracted to a woman who'd caused him to miss critical elements in the moments before a crime. So much for his sixth sense predicting danger.

Each step felt leaden as he entered the kitchen where his mom stood, her pancake turner raised for action. Strong coffee scented the air. "Good morning, Grant. Sleep well?"

"Not really. All hell broke loose at work."

"Oh, dear." Her mouth tightened. "I can do the trip to Stan if you need to leave." She slid a plate of pancakes onto the table next to a jug of maple syrup. "Still prefer orange juice?"

"Yes on juice, negative on your riding to Stan. I'll make the delivery and head home."

"You've always liked to help people in need, and Stan needs you." She leaned over and kissed his cheek. "Dad's been worried sick about not going."

He pulled off a hotcake and doused it with syrup. "I can handle it." Each bite took an effort to swallow. He put his fork down. "Thanks for breakfast Mom, hits the spot."

"Kind of a small spot. You've hardly touched my flapjacks. They're chock full of wheat germ and protein powder. I hope you're not sick."

"I feel great. I stopped being the underweight teen like fifty pounds ago."

Grant's dad shuffled to the table. "We noticed. Your biceps are bigger than our Christmas ham."

"Tom, I can ride for six or seven hours," she said.

"No, Mom. Busted ribs aren't fun." Grant pushed out of his chair. "I could do this trip in my sleep. Can I borrow your Stetson, Dad?"

"You bet. If Poppy offers to go, turn him down. He needed two nitro pills after my fall. Your mother got him an appointment at the cardiologist on Wednesday."

"Is it serious heart trouble?"

"We hope not." His mom handed him the hat.

"There's still cell phone reception by the jagged rock." Dad caught his eye. "Call and I'll send a rider pronto."

A good cop never lost his shit-was-happening sensors. Too bad his own had been compromised by a lanky redhead. "You two are compulsive worry warts." Grant plucked his coat from the stand. "I'll give your regards to Stan."

Mom hugged him as if he was going off to war. "Oh, a young lady called for you earlier."

No woman knew his weekend plans, or any others. He stopped. "Did she leave a name or number?"

"Nope. She knew you from college and promised to call right back." His mother collected their plates and took them to the sink.

The phone hadn't rung. "Maybe she recognized me at the airport. Give her my cell number next time. I'd better head out, kinda getting a late start."

"Don't rush. Stan's not going anywhere," his dad joked.

He put on the coat, running through what he'd told the Whitley woman. Damn. He'd mentioned Emma Springs. "Dad, do you still keep your sidearm handy?"

"Sure do. Need it?"

"I brought my Glock."

"Next year, it'll be the two of us." His dad held out a packet, taped across each end. "Here's the envelope for Stan."

Agitation crept into Grant's gut. "Sealed and secret. Always wondered what they trade."

"Not our business. Stan will give you a crate for Roy Werner. Needs to be handled carefully, you know the drill."

"Right." He leaned over his dad's chair. "Load your gun," he whispered.

Dad nodded. "Figured as much. Safe trip, son."

"See you." Grant strode out the door. His muscles felt stake-out tense.

Two mules were tied to the pasture fence.

Poppy looked up from loading them. "Didn't know who you'd ride or I'd have gotten a horse saddled."

"I'll ride Brasso after I lunge him first to remind him of his manners."

"Good idea. Tom doesn't lunge much anymore."

He studied the grazing horses. "Hadn't noticed that Brasso's a hand taller than the other geldings. Dad must've hedged his bet that his shrimp of a kid would acquire the famed Morley height someday."

"He wanted a good horse for his son when he bought him," Poppy shot back.

"I know." Grant grinned and put a halter on Brasso. The horse danced while they entered the corral.

He let out the twenty-five-foot rope he'd attached to the gelding. He pointed for Brasso to circle to the left—first at a walk, then a trot, and finally a canter. After he'd made several smooth rounds, Grant reversed the direction and repeated the drill.

His focus wasn't on Brasso. The encounter with the woman kept surfacing. He couldn't forget her initial reaction of scrunching to hide next to the potted plant. Was she in danger? He clenched the cotton rope. Or involved?

After he praised Brasso, he led him out of the corral.

Poppy leaned against a rail. "Fall weather's unpredictable. You need to skedaddle." He pointed to a reining saddle on the fence. "Old and comfortable."

"Good." Grant tacked up Brasso while Poppy buckled panniers onto the mules' packsaddles. A crate of apples sat atop one, cushioned by pouches of dried apple slices.

"My joints ache a snow warning." Poppy rubbed his back.

"Thanks for helping gather Stan's supplies." Grant tightened Brasso's cinch, and slid a rifle into the saddle scabbard.

"I'll never forget how Stan saved your dad. Hunting this trip?"

"I share your opinion that shooting wild animals isn't sporting."

"Glad you do. I can ride alongside you, and Buttercup needs exercise." Poppy nodded to his swaybacked buckskin mare.

"Not this trip." Very few strands of hair remained on his grandpa's head. "Mom may need your help with Dad."

"Good point." Poppy adjusted one of the mule's halters. "I'll be expecting a full account Monday night at supper."

"I may need a rain check." He grabbed Brasso's mane and mounted. "There's an assault case in Seattle I'm needed on."

"Sure. Ride easy." Poppy handed him a woven lead line, then placed his weathered hand on the stirrup. "I'm mighty proud you followed my example by joining the bureau. Just don't let the quest for the title of SAC eat you from the inside out."

Grant settled into his old saddle. "I thought you loved your work from the stories you told."

Poppy stepped back. "It satisfied me until I realized my gift for helping people wasn't utilized. You have the same gift. I remember you defending the underdogs at five or six years old. A shame they started picking on you because your Pa was a cop."

"It toughened me up, made me want to clear the streets of bullies."

"Still wasn't right. Tom meant well, being hard on you. It killed him to see you coming home beat-up. Keep in mind, the people you love mean more than a rank."

He flinched. "In order to focus on my career, I needed to disengage from our family. I always thought you believed in me."

"You'll never know how much." Poppy's eyes became misty, and he pulled one of his neatly folded, faded bandanas from his chest pocket. "Bet you don't carry a handkerchief." He handed it to Grant. "Every cowboy worth his salt carries one. Smooth riding, boy."

Fabric softened by time warmed in Grant's grip. "I'm lucky to have you in my life, Poppy." He tucked the bandana in his vest. "Go put your feet up. I'll be back in record time."

Grant clicked his tongue, and Brasso began the trek up Mt. Hanlen by crossing their meadow. Solid horse muscles under his thighs relaxed him. At the edge of the grassy land, a barren patch led straight to the tree line.

He reined Brasso onto the packed earth. Two steps in, he spotted a prairie dog hole. Other mounds rose in the distance, with no clear route through them. "Whoa, back to the path." Rule number one: never put horses in danger.

In a similar way, Judge Gilson held to a strict rule in his court—evidence. Underneath his placid demeanor, he'd been fearless enough to add years to Maneski's sentence. One of the toughest judges on crime, he now lay in a hospital bed, fighting for life.

Grant clenched the reins. He'd get the evidence to convict whoever shot the judge.

If the Whitley woman had socialized with the Gilsons to gain their confidence, he'd be certain she got her replacement coffee in jail.

The sun strained to get through a cloudy sky.

Brasso lowered his head and snorted. His rear hooves slid on a steep part of the trail, sending a rock bouncing downhill.

One of the pack mules brayed.

"Easy, now." He turned to the jennies, then froze. What the hell?

A dark form moved in the woods below.

Or was it shadows from a branch?

All of his senses energized, including the sixth one that alerted him to shitstorms.

Chapter 5

No more rifles. She needed the infamous Sunday morning trail ride to begin. Miranda stepped off the lodge's front porch.

An unmistakable equine scent drifted to her on the breeze, pushing away horrors of snake tattoos and shotguns. She inhaled an aroma pleasant to true pony girls—the ones who never grew out of loving horses. A beloved memory of her dad showing her how to flatten her palm to feed a horse filled her with comfort.

Her gaze drifted to the path winding up the steep mountain. "Please ride a slow horse, Agent Morley," she whispered.

Next to the barn, saddled mounts tested the ropes, tying them to split-rail posts.

Each step deepened the soothing smells of horses and well-oiled leather.

At the far end of the mares and geldings stood a garnet-colored mule with a light golden mane and tail.

Miranda fingered her bolo tie. A mesmerizing sensation permeated the hollows in her soul.

The mule turned his head and stared at her.

Her intense longing for peace stretched out like filament strands to the towering animal.

She nodded, he blinked, and their deal was set.

This trip didn't require a spirited horse, but an armchair on four legs who knew each rock and bush well enough to allow her to concentrate on finding Grant.

Trey ambled over and reached to untie a strawberry

roan. "Miss Whitley, I've put you on Brandywine. I read everyone's riding history, and it appears you're our most experienced guest. Do you and your boyfriend ride often?"

Every muscle tensed. "No boyfriend. What gave you such an idea?"

He patted the mare's rump. "Kathleen mentioned a phone call. Um, I must be mistaken, sorry." His grin flashed before he turned toward the saddle. "So, let's get the stirrups adjusted."

She stuck her shaking hands in her pockets. "Haven't ridden a mule yet. May I try your fine specimen on the end?"

"The mule?"

Appearing jovial took every shard of remaining courage. "If it's not too much trouble?"

"Customer's always right." He shrugged his shoulders and unhitched the mule.

Up close, the red giant stood close to sixteen hands. Ears at attention, he bowed his head in front of her.

"Big Red's lazy, I only saddled him for a spare." Trey tipped his hat back. "He's a strange animal, doesn't care how far he lags behind."

"I'm not herd bound, either."

"You'll need to prod him to keep up." He checked out her boots. "Want spurs?"

She shook her head. "I've succeeded using calm words of encouragement without belly pokes."

"I'm glad you declined. We believe in kindness," he said.

The mid-morning sun reflected off the bit on a bridle hanging from his saddle horn.

"May I finish tacking Big Red?" she asked.

"Okay, have Pitch double check it, then show him you can get Red to walk and trot in the corral."

"Got your hands full of new riders?"

"Yes, ma'am." Trey crossed back to the chattering

businessmen. "Gentlemen, you did great yesterday. After I get your horses bridled, I want you to head into the arena for a warm up. Today we leave the fences behind."

"Better be soon," Miranda spoke in soft tones to her mule. She opened a vial she'd tucked in her coat. Sweet, relaxing traces of lavender drifted over her while she placed drops on her collar and hands.

Big Red's chocolate-colored eyes blinked after he snuffed her hair.

"This helps me sleep, and I enjoy the fragrance, but I've heard that bugs don't." She scratched his gleaming russet neck. "I missed the Langley's Friday night mixer, and no cool cowboys are in sight, so you're my guy."

With a few strokes, she'd dabbed oil around his eyes and ears to discourage flies. "You smell good enough to date." Putting her cheek beside his, she took a selfie. After Ike sent word, she'd text Corrin.

She held her phone to her chest. Ike had to live. He'd guided her when she needed help. Like now.

Poor Shirley. How would she survive without Ike?

Red nudged her arm.

"Got it. Time to gear up."

He stuck his nose into the bridle for her, and took the bit. "Good boy." She ran her fingers down his mane, and stopped at an inch wide gap. A rugged scar cut through where long hair should be. "Bet that hurt. Odd place for a cut." She smoothed out the mane on either side and studied the split rail fence. No barb wire in sight.

Pitch opened the gate to the big arena. "I approve of your gentle hands on our horses, Miss Whitley," he called to her. "Bring Red in any time."

"Be there in a second." She ran her hand past Red's rump to his quiet tail, rechecked the girth, and put her foot in the stirrup. Swinging onto his back, creaking saddle leather eased her last jitters.

She settled her grip on the worn reins, and concentrated on the texture of the smooth, soft leather. Her muscle memory took over after her body shifted to a relaxed seat. "Okay Red, walk on." Slight leg guidance encouraged him to amble into the roomy corral.

"Get him to move." Pitch leaned against a wooden rail.

As she collected Red using a light touch, her brain cleared. After two rounds and a click of her tongue, the mule changed to a smooth trot.

"Nice job. Red could pass for a gaited Tennessee Walker the way he lifts his feet for you." Pitch slapped his pants, a cloud of dust providing evidence of cowpoke enthusiasm.

"Please call me Miranda. Red has a rocking-horse stride, and after the bus ride, my butt appreciates the break." She made a kissing sound and leaned forward with her shoulder and hip. They circled the corral in an easy canter.

A gun blasted, she lost her rhythm, and her foot slipped in the stirrup.

Red shifted his shoulder and centered her body. He slowed to a trot and then a walk.

"I didn't expect them shooting so soon." She jumped off and hustled Red over to Pitch.

"Should've warned you. Sorry. We've got a customer with horse allergies, and they're letting him pop a few bottles. He patted her shoulder. "You all right?"

"Yeah." She rubbed the mule's neck. "He corrected my balance while I slipped. Your animals are bomb proof."

Pitch grinned from ear to ear, showing two gaps in his teeth. "Wouldn't push it, but you're close as bark on a tree. Good reaction time on your dismount. Let's lengthen those stirrups a notch."

Trey ambled over. "I'm impressed with your seat, even on a mule."

"Thanks. It's all in his hooves," Miranda grinned.

"I'd disagree." Trey turned to Pitch. "Gotta call a

neighbor to ride drag. Our new hand called in sick and Kat needs my help."

Miranda straightened her horse bolo tie. "I'll ride in rear position. If it's okay?"

"Fine by me," Pitch said. "If Trey saves you the juiciest steak tonight."

"Deal." Trey walked back to the group.

"May I graze Big Red before we leave?"

"Sure." Pitch mounted a buckskin and trotted past Miranda. "Red's been a pack mule, and his load stayed put. Glad he's found someone who appreciates him."

"Oh, it's mutual," she called.

Horses grounded her. For a few moments during the practice ride, Ike's pale face had receded. "You've found an admirer." She rubbed Red's flank.

Pitch stopped his horse while the other guests rode single file into the fenced arena. "Okay folks, hang those fancy cameras around your neck or in the saddlebags tied behind you." He gathered his reins. "Remember, you don't drive a horse with reins, you nudge it using your legs. See how loose I'm holding my straps?" His voice stayed calm, while his eyes darted between customers.

"Mine keeps moving," complained the techie boy.

"Yup, you're squeezing his belly with your knees. Consider his sides are your gas pedal, too. The stirrups will keep you in the saddle if you keep your heels down."

Miranda checked her watch. *Crap.* Another half hour delay. She glanced at the house where Kathleen sorted through a pile of lassos on the back porch.

"Time to clarify a phone call, Red." She remounted and nudged him over to the steps. "Kathleen, did a man call here for me?"

"Can't rightly say." Her eyes held a twinkle while she coiled a rope.

Miranda fumbled the reins. "Please let me know if anyone calls for me."

"I will." Kat threw her a bright smile. "You have a peaceful ride."

"Hope to." She looked at the jagged mountain and then wiped her palms on her old jeans.

Red nervously sidestepped.

"Sorry, boy." She leaned over and scratched his neck. "It's been a tough morning."

Trey approached her. "The group's ready." He tipped his hat back. "Hate to put you to work. You sure you're okay following the pack? I can call my buddy from the next ranch."

No more delays. She'd spin her own cowboy tale. "I've helped on trail rides before. Please don't give it another thought."

"Okay then." Trey led each horse into a line, and then stopped by Red's side. "Thanks again, Miss Miranda. Hope you see wildlife, now or tonight."

"I'm a tame duck kind of girl, but I'll watch for critters. Is there something you're not telling me?"

"Can't say. See you at dinner." Trey patted Red's rump and whistled while he walked toward the lodge.

An uneasy feeling settled in the pit of her stomach.

"Off we go folks. Mt. Hanlen's beautiful today," Pitch's voice drifted back to her.

She followed the plodding group in a single file line past the barns and across the meadow.

A wide, tubular stock gate opened out to the foothills. Three horses passed through. The next one, a pinto, danced a tight circle.

The rider's arms flailed wildly with a rein in each hand. "Mr. Pitch, help! I need you to lead me," one of Andrew's team screeched. The whites of his eyes showed.

"It's okay, sir. Hold on a minute folks, until I get a lead line on." Pitch dismounted and fished a ten-foot rope out of his saddlebag.

A rifle shot cracked twice.

Miranda flinched. Instincts deep in her gut urged her to break away on Big Red, gallop into the thick forest ahead, and scream for Grant.

"You okay, Miss Miranda?" Pitch asked. "Target practice is all."

"I hate gunshots." She rubbed her ears and then glanced his way. A rifle butt stuck out of a scabbard on the other side of his tooled saddle.

"You'll hear more shooting today. It's hunting season for deer, elk, and black bear." He clipped on the lead rope, hopped back on, and wound the line around his saddle horn. "My Winchester's only along in case we need to scare off a bear. Hitch that gate shut behind you, please."

The remainder of the group ambled through. Miranda hopped down and secured the chain. She pulled out her phone to get a pic of the lodge below.

A text loaded from Corrin. *Black sedan followed bus from Seattle station.* Miranda gasped.

Red's ears went straight up.

"Easy there." She patted his shoulder, then switched her phone to airplane mode.

At the tree line, the rumps of horses disappeared between trunks of tall pines. She grabbed Red's mane, stuck her foot in the stirrup, and mounted. Her legs squeezed Red's belly, and he trotted to catch the group.

Thick clouds moved across a peaceful sky. Their round formation and feathery tufts resembled the plump underbelly of a gray duck, until they split and skittered across the sky.

The woods were chillingly darker.

She pulled out Corrin's jacket. A wind gust caught the blue, shiny material and filled it like a sail.

The woman ahead of her turned. "I wish I'd brought a heavier coat and a thick sheepskin cushion."

"Stand in your stirrups to stretch your legs," Miranda offered. Her butt didn't ache, but her nerves were another story.

She stopped Red at the beginning of the woodsy trail and searched the landscape.

Grant should ride toward them from the other side of the lake. Precious time to find him in open view ticked away.

She pretended to photograph Mt. Hanlen. All she spied was dense forest ahead, and no one using the trail on the ridge across the meadow.

Movement in the trees on the other side caught her eye. A rider? "Settle, Red." She squinted. "It's gone. Walk on."

Chattering guests became static on the breeze.

Red's hooves thumped against packed earth while he trotted to catch the string of moseying horses.

By the way the others squirmed in their saddles, Kathleen should charge double for icy padded chairs at dinner.

A smile crossed Miranda's tight lips while they wound up the gradual mountain trail, ambling for hours at a slow pace.

"Time for a picnic." Pitch's words brought a cheer from the group.

She dismounted onto a thick layer of pine needles. Scents of fir trees tickled her nose.

Grant's cologne came to mind. *Crap.* Maybe she'd missed him.

"Come get your lunch sacks, folks," Pitch called. He'd chosen a crescent-shaped clearing holding a couple of rustic benches.

While the guests ate, she helped him tie off the horses. A loud rumble erupted from her stomach.

"Well, Miss Miranda, you must be hungry," Pitch teased. "Loretta packed her famous fried chicken, an apple, and homemade cookies for you." He grinned and handed her a paper bag.

"Wonderful." She smiled and sat on a stump by the horses.

"You're still troubled," Pitch said. "Anything I can help with?"

She swallowed a bite of chicken. "You moonlight as a counselor?"

"Nope, but I'm a good listener."

"When you took me to my cabin, did you say you'd heard I was expecting company? I'm not. We got distracted by the bouncing branch."

"Maybe Kat had the guests mixed up." He kicked a rock with his boot and bent to rummage through his saddlebag, wearing a big grin.

"Pitch, what's going on? I need to know."

"Some guy wantin' to send you flowers is all I heard."

She swallowed hard. Her eyes flicked between the valley stretching beyond the edge of the trail and Pitch's rifle scabbard. "How much longer to where we head downhill?"

"Another hour. You worried about bears?"

"No, a little sore in the rump."

"You've got a relaxed seat, I'd figured you owned a horse."

Maybe the mystery-guest thing amounted to a cowpoke game of telephone. One was confused and the others parroted. She pinched her nose. "I was five when I rode alone on my grandparent's old gelding. I spent all my summers at their farm."

So many wonderful memories. She held her apple out for Red.

His soft muzzle pushed against her fingers while he gently lifted it from her hand.

Sweet smelling apple juice dripped from his jaw.

"You're a lucky girl," Pitch said.

She shoved her hand into her pocket and rubbed her thumb across Kenny's hat. "In most of the family trip pictures I'm petting a horse."

"Well, your type's the backbone of our ranch, so tell your family and horse-loving friends. Thanks for watching for stragglers today. Appears these folks don't want to be more than a foot from the horsetail in front of them." Pitch bit into a cookie and motioned to a wide gap in the trees. "I hope they raise their chins once in a while to appreciate our mountain."

"Good idea." She stepped out to see the mountain better.

Where the trees thinned, dark lines crisscrossed the upper slope. She shaded her eyes. "Is this the main trail ascending Mt. Hanlen?"

"Depends on where you're headed. There's one from the other side of the lake. The rest are deer trails. Here, use my binoculars."

She stepped away from the group. A spider web of possibilities outlined narrow paths of brown earth crisscrossing the mountain. Their trail and the one opposite intersected a long way up.

"The Google Earth photo can't give you a sense of the vastness." She returned the glasses and bit off a piece of sugar cookie, then took a swig of water to get it down her dry throat.

Pitch pulled out a red bandanna and wiped his chin. "Postcard ready, isn't it?"

"In a remote way." She rubbed her arms. "I need photos of craggy peaks and critters for a girlfriend."

"You grab any shots you need. Big Red knows his way home to his evening oats. Just keep in sight of us. And bring your friend next time."

She shuffled her feet. "You bet."

His gaze shifted to the group of men. "Sure hope Mr.

Yang's doing better than he looks with that peaked face." He cleared his throat. "Mount in five minutes, folks."

Rumbles of sore butt complaints overpowered squawking jays fighting for dropped crumbs.

"There's a stump you can use for hitching those behinds back into the saddle." Pitch motioned to where she'd been sitting. "A little farther before an easy descent. Tonight we're barbecuing Wagyu steaks, the beef you'd pay a hundred bucks a pound for in the city."

The group grumbled and climbed onto their mounts.

"Let's move out," Pitch said.

An overhead canopy of tree branches shaded the trail from afternoon light. Miranda leaned out to spot Grant. Nothing moved in the ravine full of trees or on the other bank.

The horse being ponied alongside Pitch danced wherever the path widened. "Mr. Yang, your legs clamping your horse's middle gives him the signal to go. Can you relax a little?" Pitch asked. "You don't want to be exhausted when we parade through town."

Mr. Yang bobbed his head, but his legs stayed firmly planted against the brown and white sides of his horse.

The men ahead of her chattered less, and the mom's shrill voice no longer attempted to identify each plant.

Miranda swayed in her saddle, listening to the rhythmic scrunching of hooves on dry needles.

She nudged Red to the outside of the path and stopped to scan across the gorge.

Rocks clattered while the group climbed a narrow, steep section of trail winding through two boulders.

A few feet to her left stood a thicket of withered huckleberries. Behind it, babbling water coursed down a mountain stream.

"Hey Red, I bet you're thirsty, and I need a wake-up splash."

She edged him off the trail and eased out of the saddle.

Light sparkled atop the ribbon of water. She dipped her hand and brought chilly drops to her cheek. Red took a long drink, then moved his nose to a stretch of grass.

Under a nearby pine, thousands of needles formed a dense carpet. She tweezed one and leaned against the tree's trunk. Her body softened and slid to the ground.

Red methodically tore tufts and chewed to a steady beat.

She inhaled soothing pine and let her lashes flutter shut over achy eyes. Her breathing slowed.

A hawk screeched from overhead.

Miranda's head jerked. Red stood downstream, munching grass. Late afternoon shadows darkened the stream. She tilted her wrist to see her watch. "Holy crap. I slept over an hour. We've gotta catch up."

She grabbed the reins and swung into the saddle.

The trail came to a Y twice. Branches littered the route, and the cut-offs were narrow deer paths.

No sign of the sorrel's dusty rump they'd followed all morning.

"We've picked the wrong freakin' trail," she muttered.

Red stopped, his ears alert. A squirrel chattered while scampering across a fallen tree.

Drooping, dark limbs brought goosebumps to her arms.

From an uphill treetop, a flock of birds took flight, squawking a warning.

~ ~ ~

The hunter's trail-map of Mt. Hanlen fluttered against the side of the saddle. Venom refolded it on the worn creases. His eye twitched.

He raised his binoculars to pan out from the ridge where he stood, scanning across the canyon, separating him from the plant girl's path.

A rag-tag group of figures hiked downhill. The camo-outfitted posers hoping to hit an elk or deer had given up.

His focus shifted to the opposite bank.

A flash of blue stood out against dark tree trunks. His new favorite color of windbreaker was a vibrant shade of sky blue.

She'd solved one problem by lagging behind after lunch. What the hell had kept her so long inside the tree line? A nap?

His gaze travelled to where he'd watched the rest of her group move into woods below him. No sign of them.

The glasses dropped to his chest. He steadied the rifle against his shoulder while he sighted in on the female figure appearing in his powerful scope's cross hairs.

He lowered the gun and spit on the ground. Her damn mule stayed inside the timberline, where tree trunks stood too close to risk an inaccurate shot.

The trail she rode skirted the ridge in a few hundred feet. He stowed his rifle, and nudged his horse toward a better vantage point.

"Good old horsey, calm as the ones for tourists at the beach." He dismounted, patted his mare's side, and then slid his Remington from the rifle scabbard.

"Well, plant girl, there's no semi-truck or yapping dog today," he whispered.

A breeze flipped the leaves to their lighter side. He didn't hear their rustling. Too many shots had finally wrecked his hearing.

Didn't need to hear to hit a target. His tight lips curled into an unaccustomed smile while he raised the gun to his shoulder, molding his eye to the cold scope, centering her in the cross hairs . . . waiting. Never point a gun at what you don't want destroyed.

His steady trigger finger held taut, while thoughts of the kill quickened the beating of his hunter's heart.

Chapter 6

No chatter, no piles of horse manure, and no sign of Grant or Pitch. Miranda huffed on her pink-tipped fingers.

"Five more minutes and we head home to your oats, Red." She pulled Kenny's old ball cap out and eased it onto her head. "Agent Morley will be relaxing by a campfire while my teeth chatter."

Red's ears twitched, and birds scolded back an answer from treetops.

In a few more steps, they wove into open terrain. Red stopped, swished his tail, and turned his upright ears to the wide gap ahead.

The dirt trail changed to rock, forming a cliff.

"Good eye. We ought to be able to spot a rider." She nudged him to move forward.

He pinned his ears and kept his feet planted.

"Come on, Red. Take me to the overlook." Her calf pushed harder into his left side. "Don't prove you're a mule now."

He took a tentative step, and stopped.

"Five more feet, please?" She clicked her tongue and leaned forward.

Red shuffled onto the outcrop of flat rock, which jutted out a few feet from the path.

He stopped and pawed, launching stones into the canyon below. Where it ended, Sunrise Lake resembled a puddle.

"Crapola. We're up too far."

Above and to her left, taller trees dotted the top of a bluff.

No Grant, and no Pitch.

Red backed up.

"Settle, I can't see." She looked right, grabbed the saddle horn, and stood in the stirrups.

Sunshine shone against metal across from her. The crack of a gunshot echoed.

A powerful blow threw her backwards.

She clutched the horn. Ripping, searing pain tore into her side.

Red crow-hopped, and she scrambled to stay aboard, throwing herself forward over his neck. His hooves danced inches from the drop-off.

"Whoa!"

She threw her shoulders back, pulled the inside rein, and brought his nose toward the woods. "Go!"

Red spun around and bolted down the trail.

Another bullet bit into a tree near his head. Splinters hit her face.

Red veered to the right, toward the bluff and the shooter below.

"No!" She steered him uphill, through patches of snowbrush and brambles.

A thick branch smacked her forehead, throwing her backward. She grabbed the pommel, dropping the reins. "Whoa. Slow down."

He ignored her and lunged on.

She grabbed a hank of Red's mane and tightened her grip. A jolt shot into her side. She pressed into damp warmth. *Blood.*

Red slowed.

Fading light blurred her visibility. She twisted to look behind and gritted her teeth. Far away from the trail. So far. So lost.

On they crashed, until Red stepped over a log and into a tiny clearing. She sagged forward.

One of the dangling reins snagged in the crotch of a dead branch.

Red jerked to a stop.

"Good boy. Venom won't find us here." Her chest slumped over his neck, while her hands slid limply down his heaving sides.

Bone numbing tiredness overtook her fear.

The mule lowered his front legs and then his hind end.

"Thank you, Red," she whispered, and let her body roll to the ground.

Dampness seeped through her jeans. She shivered, struggling to keep her eyes open.

Have to get away.

Her palm sank into soft earth. She raised her elbow, but her arm buckled. Her cheek landed on moist leaves.

Flicks of silvery light didn't brighten the forest. Dark to black.

She'd die cowgirl style—with a mule, on a mountain, from a gunshot wound.

No one would ever find her.

~ ~ ~

Grant zipped his down vest and pulled on his Carhartt jacket.

He looked over his shoulder. The setting sun dropped the temperature from brisk to Montana chilly in a few heartbeats.

No hunters below and no more gunshots echoing over the valley.

He'd ridden the same route his whole life, but this trip seemed longer. Didn't matter. He'd do the drop and head back.

Brasso snorted, and lumbered up a slight rise in the narrow trail.

A distinct whinny-bray of a mule erupted from behind an outgrowth of choke cherry bushes.

His two pack mules brayed in response.

Hairs on the back of Grant's neck lifted. He stared into shadowed forest, while his hand shot to his hip holster. The Glock grip pressed into his fingers. "Who's there?"

Pawing permeated the brief quiet between brays.

"Whoa, Brasso."

An outline of a saddled mule bobbing his head came in and out of view. He stretched his neck, restrained by the bridle.

The rope holding the pack animals dug into his thigh. "Relax, jennies."

The other mule spotted him, bared his teeth, and issued another ear-piercing command.

"Okay, I get it. You're caught." Grant shoved the gun back and tied Brasso to a tree trunk. He picked his way in dim light toward the wide-eyed animal.

A dark blotchy streak flowed across the mule's shoulder.

"Easy, big guy." Grant ran his hands over its withers and onto its rump, which displayed his cousin's familiar brand.

The hide had a few scratches, but no gashes or scrapes. He freed the rein from the branch and turned to lead him out.

The mule grabbed the shoulder of his jacket with his teeth and pulled him backward.

"Hey there," Grant growled, and spun around.

In the shadow of a low hanging branch, a person in a blue jacket lay curled on their side.

He skirted the mule and knelt down. "Are you okay?" A long braid hung down her shoulder. He pushed it back and pressed his finger to her carotid artery. A steady beat thumped in her neck.

Red scratches crisscrossed her pale cheeks. A lump bulged above one eye.

He leaned closer and furrowed his brow, then rolled her over.

The coppery smell of fresh blood tainted the air.

Her eyes remained closed while he lifted her blood-soaked shirt.

"I need to check your injury," he said.

A ragged flap of skin covered raw flesh on her side. Dark residue indicated a bullet wound, luckily shallow.

She wasn't dressed in camo.

"Judas Priest," he muttered. His jaw clenched.

He squinted into the dense forest and put his fist down to balance on warm ground next to her.

"You're a smart mule. Laid down by her didn't you?" He patted the mule's muzzle hanging over his shoulder. "Don't worry. I've stitched up worse dings in trainings."

Grant took off his coat and wrapped it around her body. Placing one hand under her legs, he lifted her and pulled her to his chest.

The mule's head remained by his shoulder while he headed back to the trail.

"Damn idiot hunters. Elk don't wear bright blue." He dodged a low branch. "Who's the idiot? I'm talking to a mule."

He shifted her head to the crook of his arm and pulled her close to step over a log.

His eyes widened. Broken nose, auburn braid . . . he studied her lanky body.

He'd cleared the log, but his boot caught on brambles, pitching them forward. His heart drummed while he lumbered from tree to tree until he spotted a mule's ears rising above a dense thicket.

No whinnies or snorts from the animals.

He panned the area and then tied her mule to the end jenny. Brasso flipped his head, his nostrils flaring at the scent of blood.

"Easy boy," he crooned to his dancing horse. "She needs our help. If you ever pay attention, now would—"

Her mule nickered, and Brasso stood still.

"Good boy," he soothed.

He rubbed his cheek. How to mount a horse balancing another hundred plus pounds?

Shifting her to hang over his shoulder rotated her long legs to lie against his chest. Legs he'd admired more than once. *Get back in the saddle, Morley.* One giant jump squat should work. Then what?

They'd passed a flat-topped boulder on the trail, which meant another twenty minutes to the cabin and supplies. *Ride downhill?*

Too dark and Stan wouldn't wait.

No options.

With her weight centered on his left shoulder, he pinned her to his chest with his right arm.

He grabbed the reins and a section of Brasso's mane, put his left foot in the stirrup, crouched, and leapt into the saddle.

He let out the breath he'd been holding. "Good boy, Brasso." He shifted her butt to sit crosswise on his lap and gathered the lead line.

Dark red stained his leather glove. The Winchester groaned while he raised it a bit out of its scabbard. He unsnapped the cover on his hip holster.

He'd be on his own to find the cabin in the dark, toting an injured woman. Sweat beaded on his brow. Damn roof accident of Dad's.

No. Your bad, Morley. Should've been home to help. "Walk on, Brasso."

Her head swayed to each plodding step.

A hoof cracked a branch. Her eyelids never fluttered.

His muscles remained tightened to full alert. Nervous because she'd been shot on the mountain he considered his back yard?

No.

Deeper, darker.

Killers roamed near Emma Springs.

The reins compressed in his grip.

An owl hooted. Shadows lengthened into eerie fingers over the path.

The owl's second hoot boomed.

Grant's head jerked skyward, toward the night hunter staking his turf.

A glowing moon rose in an indigo sky.

"Pick it up, Brasso." He squeezed the animal's flanks.

Thirty feet ahead, a mountain juniper grew at an odd slant.

His grip relaxed.

First time he'd trekked the mountain alongside his dad, he'd heard the tale of how a giant used his foot to tip the shrub and mark the entry to their hidden cabin.

Grant nudged Brasso onto the narrow side trail. He adjusted his hold to protect her injured side.

Branches brushed his cheek while they wound through a stand of pine trees.

The path led to a small clearing. The moon popped out from behind the clouds, exposing the steep-sided rock wall guarding Mt. Hanlen's summit.

At this side of its base sat the huge cave his great-grandfather had discovered. He'd fashioned it into their cabin, the back having stone for walls, the front built in weathered wood, a perfect blend of man and mountain.

Last year he and dad had caulked the seam where the wood met the rock on the outside. Tonight, the interior should heat quicker.

And she needed heat. "Hold on, we're close." He shifted her in his arms, longing for a head nod, a mumble, anything.

None came.

A fancy jeweled neck slide dangled from her shirt. Even in near dark, it shouted bucks. Her scuffed boots and faded jeans didn't.

Had she worked late in the lobby as the hitman's lookout, or simply been an innocent bystander?

What in hell brought her here?

Every move he took felt like sliding a foot along a tightrope strung over the Grand Canyon.

~ ~ ~

Miranda struggled through a thick, hazy fog.

Another sizzling pop broke the stillness.

An ache centered in her side. Dim light came into her focus.

Scents of musky smoke and pine startled her awake. She pushed up on one elbow, wincing, and scoped an unfamiliar room.

A few feet away sat an unshaven man wearing a cowboy hat low on his brow. His chair skidded across rough planks while he pushed it to the edge of her bed. He continued staring at her.

A fire blazed behind him, shining onto the open neck of his shirt.

No tattoo.

She said a silent prayer of thanks, met the stranger's piercing hazel eyes, and recognized his square jaw and wide shoulders. Relief washed over her. "Grant," she sighed.

"Why'd you follow me, Miss Whitley?" he demanded.

She studied his tense face and narrowed, accusing eyes. "Did they shoot at you, too? We've got to leave, we're in danger." She grabbed for his wrist. Pain pierced her side.

"I'll protect us." He pushed her hand back to the edge of the bed.

"I know." She smiled weakly.

"You're a long way from the Langley's trail ride." He crossed his arms over his chest. "I stitched your flesh wound and put arnica on your temple. Your jeans are drying by the fire. What happened?" he persisted.

She blinked and looked down at her chest, covered by someone's loose T-shirt. Her shaky fingers tugged down the hem to mid-thigh. "Last I remember, I'd hit cold, wet ground. Is Red okay?"

"Who's Red?" The sinews of his neck stiffened.

A log sputtered and tumbled off the grate and onto the wooden floor.

He turned his broad back to her and jabbed it with an iron poker.

Angry? Why? Her head ached. Wait a minute, had she given him her name? How'd he know about the Langleys?

Her eyes darted from him to a sloped rock wall to her left, which trapped her in bed like a butterfly pinned to a board. A half-clothed butterfly.

The fire grew uncomfortably hot. "Red's the mule."

He turned back to face her. "I left you in Seattle and found you in the middle of the woods. Why?"

Where were they? She avoided his glare. A tiny cabin?

The recessed fireplace dominated another rock wall behind the headboard. The rest of the small room was open, and mostly wood.

"I got lost on the trail."

"Before. Tell me exactly what happened so I can evaluate the situation." The air crackled from the burning logs and his distrust.

What about the shooter? Why'd he keep interrogating her as if she'd committed a crime?

She raised her chin and met his eyes. "I'm vacationing at a dude ranch. We'd gone on a trail ride . . . I got separated and stopped on an outcrop to see better when I got shot."

His expression never changed. No shock, no sympathy, and no acknowledgment of her plight. "Did you see the shooter?" he asked.

Had she made another deadly decision Friday night? Agent Morley had told her to go home, too.

Trust no one, Shirley's warning.

~ ~ ~

The Whitley woman appeared too nervous for being rescued in the woods. Grant mentally erased reactions from his face while he sat back in his chair.

Images of creamy soft skin in firelight while he'd dressed her in his undershirt danced in his mind. Nothing inappropriate, but his body remembered all too well tugging off her wet jeans and skimming those lace trimmed panties.

He filed his fingertips across two days growth of rough stubble on his cheeks. Greenhorn guests weren't allowed to wander off by themselves on a trail ride. He'd called the Langley's earlier, and they'd been gearing up to search for her.

Impulsive or deceitful? She'd ignored him long enough. "Did you see the shooter?"

She cleared her throat. "Ahh. No."

Hesitation indicated numerous things in his line of work, none of them endearing him to the woman. Damn, the lump on her forehead had darkened in color. "If you have a bad headache, or nausea, tell me."

Her eyes darted around the room again like a cornered rat.

Not symptomatic to a concussion. "How'd you pick Emma Springs? Twenty-four hours ago, I would've guessed you didn't know the town existed."

"I Googled it." She touched her temple before she pulled the covers to her neck. She patted her throat. Dismay crossed her face.

"Your horse slide's clean and drying on the table in front of the fire," he said.

"I was worried I'd lost my lucky talisman." She threw him that shy smile again. "You cleaned it for me?"

Wow, her eyes were the shade of a clover leaf on a lazy summer day. He swallowed. "I imagine it's valuable."

"Probably. A close friend gave it to me before this trip." Her eyes glistened from tears. "I owe her . . . a lot . . . for helping me." She struggled on the last words.

She'd be dead if he hadn't found her. For a split second, he longed to comfort her in his arms.

A lock of hair fell across her face. He reached out, and she propped herself on one elbow, her eyes willing an embrace.

Instincts compelled him to pull her against his chest, whisper, 'it's going to be okay,' and crack open his tightly screwed down bureau life.

Life as an agent following a protocol. He checked himself. She'd been pegged as a possible accomplice to attempted murder, for Christ's sake.

Keep her talking and learn. He grabbed a box of Kleenex and set it beside her. "Why were you working so late when we met Friday night?"

She dabbed her eyes. "Had to." Her full lips became pressed into a grim line. "I'd interviewed a new client at noon, which disrupted my schedule."

Bureau training included noting the briefest concealed emotions. Hers vacillated between relief, anxiety, and sorrow. Now she'd switched to wary.

"You're safe here."

A red ember shot near his boot.

Miranda jumped, and then stared at the cinder's glow.

What's with her? She'd done the same ping-pong routine during the coffee incident. She'd flirted, become annoyed about a replacement coffee, and scolded him regarding visiting family.

"Tell me what happened next." He shoved the burning shard of wood into the stone fireplace with a poker and then rested it against the nightstand.

She inched into the tight corner where the roofline met the foundation. Her bright eyes scanned the front of the cabin. She put her hand to her mouth, and her face went ashen white.

He whipped around. The blind was shuttered and the solid door still closed.

His hunting rifle sat tipped in the corner.

Did she think he'd shot her? "Are you afraid of me?" He turned and asked.

She'd grabbed the fire poker.

Loud steps thumped onto the wooden porch.

Grant pulled his Glock, adrenaline thundering through his veins. "Quiet," he hissed.

The cabin door rattled from an outside force, shaking against the hinges.

A piercing mule's bray bellowed from the other side.

"Red," she called.

He stepped to the window, his gun trained on the door, and tipped the blind. "Clear." His shoulders relaxed while he slid his pistol back into the holster. "Yup, you have a four-legged guardian."

"Big Red bolted us away from the ledge after the shot." Miranda rose to upright and tipped the poker against the rock wall. "Could you please let him see me?"

Grant opened the door. The mule pushed his shoulder in a get-outta-my-way-dude shove and clomped to the end of her bed.

"Hey." Grant raised his hands. "Easy. Unless you plan to leave hide on the doorway."

"Careful, Red," she warned.

"Greet your rider, and then I'll return you to your friends."

"Come here, buddy." She held out her arms.

The mule stretched his neck over the bed. "Such a good boy," she crooned. "You saved me."

Hell. No woman had ever gazed at him with such moon-eyed devotion. He could remind her again exactly who'd brought her out of the woods and stitched her up.

Red dropped his head, inviting her to scratch the base of his copper-colored ear. His lips twisted while her long fingers combed his forelock.

Grant raked his fingers through his own hair.

"Red got me away, but I need to thank you, too." Their eyes met briefly before she pulled the mule's nose to her chin.

"You're welcome." He squared his shoulders. "If I don't end the reunion soon, the cabin will emit *Eau'de* Mule until spring, and my mom might object."

"Mine would've felt the same way. Dad liked horses."

"You grew up on a ranch?"

"I spent summers visiting my grandparents on their dairy farm." She stroked Red's cheek. "Your family lives nearby, don't they?"

He'd mentioned his dad, another fact he recalled. "Yes, at the base of the mountain."

"It's a beautiful area for children to grow up."

Most Seattle women balked at the idea. "Woods and horses makes us country tough." He caught the side of Red's halter and clicked his tongue. "Back up."

The mule's wide rump edged out through the doorway.

Grant led him to the line holding Brasso and the others. "Let's get you secured, Houdini." He scratched the mule's neck. "I want to help your mistress. What's the truth?"

Cop intuition, honed to a razor's edge from countless interviews, supported her innocence. Her abbreviated story, expensive necklace, and eyewitness accounts of her actions at the scene pointed to a different theory.

Hard facts were hell.

~ ~ ~

Grant certainly spoke gently to Red while he led him out. Miranda bunched a pillow under her good side.

She couldn't afford misplaced trust again. Her head ached with dull pain. Was she being paranoid?

No. Her dad had insisted human nature relied on strong doses of trust for survival. She'd assured her family it was okay to trust Jacob, her deadly ex-boyfriend. Lesson learned.

She should've faked amnesia and been clueless to the trail ride. Anyone might be on Maneski's payroll. But if he wanted her dead, he would've left her in the woods.

He'd asked why'd she'd been working late, minutes before Ike's shooting.

She pressed her palms into her eyes. *He needs to know who you've talked to, stupid.* Corrin has to be warned.

Cold air rushed into the room.

He stepped inside, and bolted the lock. "Your mule's tied up and happily eating."

"Thanks for everything." She struggled to shove her legs out, clenched her fingernails into her palm, and smiled. "I'm rested. If you'll saddle Red, I'll get dressed and head to the Langley's."

"Not possible. It's pitch dark out." He stretched his fingers to the glowing embers. "The Lazy K sits on the west side of Mt. Hanlen. My place is on the East side. Don't know why your mule didn't head home."

"Red started to. The second gunshot crossed over his nose. He spun around and bolted into the woods to get us away. Neither Red nor I checked a map."

A muscle in his cheek twitched. "We'll head down the mountain after you're stable."

Her wound, her problem. No one would sway her decisions, the way she'd let Jacob. She pulled her bare legs under the covers. "I'll go back tomorrow morning."

"Maybe." He sat in the chair at the edge of the bed. "I need to know how and why you came here."

A question she'd answer. Still, her throat felt dryer than parched earth.

She sipped water from a glass on the nightstand. "You flirted with me. I had vacation coming, and at a friend's insistence, I booked the trip."

True statement. Nerves were why she hadn't told him her name before. How ironic. If he knew how she'd admired his buff body for weeks. . . Heat flamed in her cheeks.

He touched his temple in a salute. "Agent Grant Morley, at your service, Miss Whitley."

The crooked detective had used the same placating tone. Had Grant followed her on the trail ride? Why'd he gone from accusatory to patronizing?

Geeze, her head hurt. "My first name's Miranda, and I'm at your mercy, Agent Morley."

"I need to check your bandage for redness or swelling. I put manuka honey on the wound to fight infection." He leaned in, his hand resting on his knee. "So, how'd you get here? My flight was full."

A G-Man could verify anything. She inched the covers from her chest. "Greyhound. Leave the driving to us."

"I see." He set a plastic box onto the bed and shuffled through assorted bandages and ointments. "My mom outfitted the cabin with basic first-aid supplies. The bullet shredded your blouse. I figured my T-Shirt would be the softest." His color deepened. "Please hold the material so I can check your wound."

She gathered his shirt against her bra. Every nerve ending quivered while he leaned over her. Warm, strong fingers probed her ribs.

A heady sensation numbed the throbbing in her side. "I'm glad you found me."

"This will hurt when I pull off the gauze."

The sticky tape jerked free of her bruised skin, and she winced.

"Sorry. Your wound's clean." No trace of sorry, his eyes had become polished stone. "Lucky the bullet grazed your side. It missed any major muscles or organs." He ripped open the wrapper on a new gauze pad and taped it in place.

"I hate the word lucky. I rose in the stirrups just as they shot. I guess it's my love handles to the rescue."

His lips curved, softening his jawline. "Shifting your position saved you."

"I couldn't spot the group."

He wadded the wrapper and threw it in the fire. "Who wants to kill you?"

The bump on her head throbbed. Could she fake a concussion? She swallowed hard. "I don't know. Can't remember much. I'm dizzy."

"Lay back and sleep. We'll talk later." In one movement, he unfurled another blanket and covered her.

She sank into the pillow and closed her eyes.

Nothing pushed away the image of his rifle.

Chapter 7

Miranda Whitley had a price on her lovely head by now, innocent or not. Did she deserve it? Grant stared at the sleeping woman.

Her eyes fluttered open, spotted him by the table, and closed tight.

"Hope you got a little sleep." He stood up. "I leave tomorrow at daylight to deliver supplies to a mountain hermit who depends on them for winter survival."

"You're going away?" Relief, or surprise in her tone?

He banked the fire. "Not until tomorrow. No one except my family knows our location. You'll have food and my gun."

"Don't want a gun." She turned her face to the wall.

"Might be a bear around, it's a safety measure."

"No. No gun." She'd turned back. Her eyes held a pain he'd seen before, in victim's families.

Compassion stirred inside him. "I'll show you the basics. You won't need to touch it unless there's an emergency."

"Whatever." She tucked her trembling fingers under the covers.

Good sign she'd rejected the firearm. "Our bathroom's behind the sink. There's a bucket of water on the floor for flushing."

He grabbed a knit hat off a peg next to the door and pulled it on. He'd watched his mom create it, one of several she'd made him.

Why hadn't Miranda asked to talk to anyone? No family who'd care?

His would.

The idea of Maneski's men on Mt. Hanlen brought a sour taste to his mouth. His family and a town full of innocent citizens could be in danger. "I need to water our horses before I turn in for the night."

"Okay."

Deep, deep in the pit of his stomach, he wanted her above suspicion. Too bad her story didn't add up.

~ ~ ~

"Corrin, watch out!" Her scream pierced the midnight quiet.

Grant yanked his gun from under his pillow, stumbled over a chair, and nearly fell head first into the fireplace.

Her legs thrashed in the blankets.

"Easy, you're having another nightmare." He sat on the edge of her bed, laying his fingers on her arm. "Relax. I'm here."

She pulled her hand across her chest, out of his reach. Her eyes remained closed.

While he stoked the fire, he watched her breathing even out.

In the flickering light, dark red hair accented her pale skin. Sleep smoothed away signs of her mistrust.

If she wasn't involved, it must've been horrific watching the judge suffer. What made her track a stranger way the hell up Mt. Hanlen?

He kneeled on the stack of blankets he'd assembled on the plank floor. Not as if he'd sleep during duty. He punched an indent into the pillow before pulling up a quilt.

She had one person she'd protect, named Corrin. Too scared to call her? He slid his bedroll next to her bed. Her chest rose and fell again in relaxed breathing.

Miranda Whitley presented a complicated puzzle. Soon

enough he'd prove she'd either been a witness and was justifiably panicked or a cold-blooded criminal.

~ ~ ~

Dawn's first light streaked through slats in the cabin's shuttered windows.

Grant tucked his Glock into his waistband.

He tiptoed in his sock feet, gathering gear and getting organized before waking her to say goodbye. Dark shadows underscored her closed eyes.

If she stayed in bed and rested while he rendezvoused with Stan, she might be strong enough to leave tomorrow. Then, he'd get Doc Kyle to his ranch to check her wound before they flew to a formal interrogation in Seattle.

He pulled the door shut and stepped off the porch. Four equine heads turned toward him. He approached her mule. "You'll be on guard duty after I leave, so put those big ears to use."

Red curled his lips back. A low nicker from him caused the two pack mules to whinny.

Grant scratched Red's neck and patted the animal's rump near a branded K. "Make it a loud bray."

Protecting a witness or delivering a suspect hadn't bothered him. Ever. Until today.

Frost rimmed the animals' water buckets and puffs of breath rose while they munched feed pellets.

He inhaled through his nose. Imminent hints of snowfall lingered in the crisp air.

Poppy was right. Winter on Mt. Hanlen would come early.

He stepped onto the porch. Fear behind Miranda's eyes pulled out emotions he'd held in check with other witnesses under his protection. She'd be safe, but telling her goodbye for the short trip twisted his insides. More than once, he'd gotten the same scared critter vibe he'd seen when he'd smashed her cup.

Painfully shy? Hell, she worked alone, kept to herself, and never engaged anyone. He'd wanted to approach her, but the timing never seemed right. So, he'd watched, sipping lousy coffee in order to glimpse her working most Fridays.

Yet two days ago, she'd flirted back. And it hadn't been fake. Not the fist pump he'd caught out of the corner of his eye. And damn if it hadn't made him feel ten feet tall. One little fist pump and he'd shot to the sky, and then a day later, torpedoed into the unknown.

This woman launched him like a catapult loaded with desires he'd held in check for way too long, and heaven help him when they hit.

~ ~ ~

Miranda opened her eyes and inhaled the aroma of fresh coffee. Sunlight gave the cabin a bigger feel.

Grant stood at the table, stuffing Corrin's bloody jacket into a plastic bag.

Time to get out of here. She closed her eyes and waited until he'd taken a step. "Morning," she said.

Grant smiled. He finished fastening the buckle on a saddlebag. "I'm running late to meet old Stan. He needs winter supplies. I split my breakfast ration with you."

Her body felt like she'd gone through a meat grinder. "Sorry I'm such an unexpected pain."

An old-fashioned coffee pot perked on a grate over the fire. "I could drop a couple of pounds. Coffee's ready. I found ibuprofen, which'll help your healing."

"I'm not very hungry, but I'll down a pill with a cup of coffee."

He picked up a pillow and the pile of blankets from the floor near her bed. "Try to eat."

She rubbed her arm, recalling a gentle stroke and soothing words during the night. "Sorry I put you on the floor."

"You needed rest, and I can sleep anywhere." Steam rose while he filled two mugs. He set hers on the nightstand.

"I feel like a spoiled princess being served by the knight who saved my life." She put her hand over her mouth. It must be the injury—brain in neutral, mouth in overdrive. Her gaze travelled to the door.

No rifle.

She curled her cold fingers around the mug, relishing the last warm drink before she'd leave.

"Technically, your mule deserves the rescue medal." He handed her a thick slice of bread topped by Swiss cheese. "A few bites would help you gain strength."

The first taste of homemade bread brought an image of her Mom, bent over a soft mound of yeasty smelling dough in a big earthenware bowl. Had a wife or a girlfriend baked for Grant? He didn't wear a ring. "Thanks for breakfast. How long will you be gone?"

He surveyed her, then continued to brush crumbs off the table. "Hard to say. Rest, and I'll return in no time."

She nodded.

"Who's Corrin?" He pulled his gun from his belt.

Swallowing the bite of bread rivaled downing a lump of sawdust. She swigged a gulp of hot coffee. "A friend, why?"

"You called for her during a nightmare."

The crooked detective might've seen Corrin's license plate. "Sorry I woke you."

Sparks flew after he threw a bulky log onto the coals. He stared into the fire. "I'm leaving my Glock. Have you fired a gun?"

"If knocking tin cans off of posts counts." She averted her eyes. "Years ago, my brother taught me to shoot his BB gun."

"Mine's heavier. Give me your good hand." He put the gun in her grip and wrapped his fingers around her shaking hand.

Horrible memories resurfaced while she stared at its black barrel.

He kept his hold steady. "Use both hands and expect a kick." He slid back the top part. "That action chambered a bullet. Aim and shoot." He took it away and placed it on the nightstand. "No safety, and the trigger's touchy. You okay?"

Corrin needed her to appear fine. She nodded. "Yup. Touchy trigger. Got it."

"Stan's probably desperate for fresh supplies, especially knowing a snowstorm's on the wind." He stood. "The quicker I get going, the sooner I'll be back. There's more ibuprofen in the medicine kit." He waved and pulled the door shut.

Sunlight flickered off the shiny black gun. She'd die before she'd use it.

Or would she?

~ ~ ~

Grant rolled his head side to side, while his eyes scoped the perimeter of the cabin's clearing. Clear so far.

If Maneski sent Venom from Seattle to finish off Miranda, she'd be dead. It had to have been one of the dumb ass hunters he'd seen carrying flashy gun cases at the airport. Half of them would shoot anything that moved.

He checked the tack on Brasso and the mules.

The animals appeared relaxed, unlike his own hyped-up nerves. He glanced at the cabin.

Her wound couldn't handle the tough ride today. Hell, he'd be sore after going straight uphill in parts, and they'd be totally exposed for a good stretch.

Fresh snow covered their hoof prints from last night.

The cabin's shield of surrounding trees rose taller than ten story buildings.

He took a breath of clean, crisp air. His family had never found where the smoke came out of the stone fissure doubling as their chimney.

He put his foot in a stirrup and swung into the saddle. He pulled his gloves from his pocket. The blood stain darkened the yellow leather.

A wave of unease matched the chill of the morning cold.

~ ~ ~

Brasso scrambled to climb a steep patch of rock. His heavily muscled shoulders bunched under his thickening winter coat.

Grant adjusted his weight forward, his thigh muscles strained from uphill travel.

He steered around boulders and over logs, heading into the thinning tree line. He stopped and tipped back his hat. A curl of smoke rose above the next big boulder.

The unmistakable click of a bolt-action rifle slide being racked shattered high-country silence.

Grant grinned. He'd heard the Winchester thirty-aught six announcing her presence every fall since he'd turned seven. Same drill, merely a different year. He raised both hands overhead.

"Name?" a gruff voice demanded. A bearded man in a furry coat stepped from behind the huge rock, pointing the gun at him.

A white streak divided a head of shaggy brown hair.

Grant smiled. Same mountain man-not as if the woods teemed with codgers toting antique guns.

Stan had no idea of the value of the Model 70 Pre-64 Varmint Predator. The last one Grant had seen at auction went for over four grand, too spendy for the rifle collection he'd begun in eighth grade.

"It's me, Grant."

The muzzle stayed put. "Grant who?"

"Crazy old coot," he uttered under his breath. He tipped the brim of the hat. "Stan, it's me, Grant Morley. Solo this year."

"Tie your ponies over there." The barrel followed his movements while he walked his three animals around the boulder to a clearing. Beside a campfire sat the old army tent, its sides still covered in bear skins.

"I brought everything on Dad's list, lots of apples."

Stan lowered the shotgun. "Didn't recognize you sporting the whiskers and sunglasses."

Grant dismounted and held out his hand. "Figured as much."

"Yup, you're even broader. I remember you being a scrawny kid a few years back." Stan's firm handshake meant business. "Your dad's all right, isn't he?"

Grant shrugged. "Can't ride with cracked ribs from a fall off the roof. The gutters won the battle. He'll be glad to know you're ready and waiting. I'm needed below, so I'll unload and head out."

"Sure, boy. You know my operation. I see you brought my favorite jennies." He patted each mule nose before moving to the fire. "Time for a cup of coffee?"

Coffee. It plagued him at every turn. He reached into Brasso's saddlebag and pulled out the manila envelope. "A quick one."

Stan poured liquid resembling motor oil into a tin cup. "I'll trade for those photos. Good java always hits the spot."

"If yours makes it to the bottom of my gut." Grant slugged a brew which must've simmered for days. "Photos of what? Maybe not a good question to ask an isolated bachelor." He grinned.

"Smart ass. Roy Werner sends pictures of the clock figurines I need to carve to replace broken ones from all over the world." Stan untied straps on the panniers. "Ran out of these last week." His eyes brightened while fingering a package of dried apple slices.

"Figurines, as in tiny?" His gaze settled on Stan's beefy paws. "That's what's fragile in the return crates?"

"Yup. Your pa orchestrated the deal. The money's allowed me to purchase more mountain and live in peace all these years. Can't thank him enough."

Grant emptied his cup, did a couple stretches, and climbed back on Brasso. "Dad's happy if you're happy. Sorry I can't stay longer. If we need to contact you, is there a signal?"

"Your pa knows how to reach me." Stan tied on two wooden crates and handed Grant the lead lines. "Make certain Roy gets them first thing. Handle them like your first girlfriend."

"Sure."

With a grubby fist, Stan grabbed Brasso's bridle. "Lame response, boy. What's wrong? Are your folks okay?"

"They're fine." Grant checked the tree line. "Keep an eye out for strangers. Mt. Hanlen may have thugs hunting two legged creatures."

Stan let go of the horse. "I'm not worried. I've got Myrtle." He patted his rifle.

"You're welcome to use the cabin or stay at either of our houses. No time limit. Dad's told me how you dragged him to safety across a battlefield."

"Long ago." Stan stepped back. "Thanks for bringing the supplies and the warning. I'm not ready for civilization yet." He shouldered his gun. "You're cut from the same cloth as your pa, one of the finest men I've ever known. Trust your instincts."

Grant nudged Brasso to the path where a breeze ruffled branches. "Got it. Door's always open to you."

"I know. Safe travels," Stan said.

The tangy scent of Rocky Mountain Junipers soon replaced campfire and coffee.

Hooves moving at a quicker pace beat out a measured clip–clop cadence in the wilderness silence.

Patches of blue dotted a heavy gray sky. Malevolent clouds banked across the horizon. Soon snow would cover this trail for four or five months, becoming a thick blanket, insulating Stan from anything urban.

He buttoned his jacket. Miranda needed medical clearance before he could escort her to Seattle, and he needed to uncover her real story.

Uncover—bad word choice. Memories of her soft skin and russet braid taunted him. *Quit. Her fake smiles potentially cover a layer of deceit. That you know from experience.*

Could he separate facts and conduct an investigation, or would unwanted emotions impair his judgment with a disastrous result?

Damned if he'd let it happen, even if his heart fired quicker than a fully loaded automatic every time he got near her.

He sat back in the saddle. A pile of very green horse manure stood out on the trail ahead.

Alfalfa green, from a stabled horse, not one of his dad's pasture ponies.

It hadn't been there on the trip up. Blood pounded in Grant's ears.

No elk hunters came this far.

Chapter 8

A jay squawked.

Miranda lurched awake. She blinked twice.

Sunshine spilled into every corner of the cabin.

Three slivers of scorched gray logs remained on the grate.

"Crap." A bedpost steadied her while she struggled into her stiff jeans. Dull pain shot through her side.

A sweater and an old backpack hung from the back of a nearby chair. Gritting her teeth, she pulled the thick sweater on, while her focus stayed locked on the door. She used the bathroom and returned to the open room.

Grant's gun sat on the nightstand. Clutching the edge of the table, she wormed into her cowboy boots, and shoved the gun into the pack. She hobbled outside.

Red raised his head and whinnied.

Cold blasted her face, while the sight of his giant ears made her grin. "I'll need your mule version of GPS tuned to the Langley's." She shut the door. "Down to the barn we go!"

Her leather sole hit the icy porch and sailed her forward. "Whoa!" She stumbled across uneven ground, fighting to remain upright.

Frozen earth and the backpack broke her fall. The woods spun for a moment. She tried to stand, but her boots slid out from under her.

Big Red brayed twice, and stretched against his tether.

"Hold on." She rolled to her knees, gathering strength.

From the trail, branches broke and hoofbeats thumped on packed snow.

Someone had heard Red. The horses drew close.

She flung open the pack and wrapped her hands around the gun's grip, her finger hovering near its trigger.

The barrel shook while she pointed it at the split in the stand of trees hiding her.

Grant cantered in on Brasso, towing the other mules.

His wild-eyed concern steeled to planes of anger. He pulled on the reins of his horse using one hand, while he yanked out his rifle with the other.

She threw the handgun on top of the backpack, and then kicked it away with her foot. "I . . . I didn't know it was you."

He shoved the rifle into the scabbard and jumped off. In two strides, he reached the pack. "Worried your partner came to silence you after you saved the judge?" Cop eyes bored into her. He grabbed his Glock.

"You knew about Ike's attack all along?" she cried. "If you're going to kill me, do it quick." She steepled her hands and met his glare. "Please, let Red go."

His shadow draped her. "Damn it, I'm a good guy that you're lying to. Straight answers, now." He shoved the Glock into his waistband. "I want to believe you, but you're making it difficult."

"So do you."

"I need to cool the horses off. Start talking." He loosened the saddle straps. A trench formed in the icy snow while he stomped around her, his body ramrod straight.

A gust of frigid air whipped her hair, the bite penetrating into her bones. She hugged her chest. "How'd you know my name? I didn't—"

"I'm asking the questions." He untacked his animals and strode to her, landing a giant boot two inches from her thigh. "Who else conspired to shoot Judge Gilson? Who? Tell me."

Betrayal burned into anger—thorny, dark red anger. She thrust her hand to the ground for balance and raised her chin. "I saw the gunman who shot Ike and a detective who came in right after. Sound familiar?"

"Not those facts. Your name and ID photo were broadcast over law enforcement channels. You're wanted as a person of interest."

She jerked. "Me, kill Ike?" She put her hand over her heart. "Shirley knows the truth."

"She won't discuss you." His tone could freeze ice. "Describe the gunman."

A killer would've asked who else she'd talked to, wouldn't they? "Green snake tattoo on his neck, near his ear. Gray hair."

He balled his fist. "Venom."

"You know the gunman?"

"There's a mob assassin inked that way."

"I call him Snake Neck. Venom's more appropriate." She struggled to tuck her foot under her. "He mentioned Maneski on the phone before he left."

Granite held more warmth than his eyes. "You're turning blue around the edges. Get inside before you freeze."

As if he cared. She pushed off the frozen ground, raising her butt an inch. Cold air hurt her lungs.

Grant leaned down, put his hand at her waist, and lifted her to wobbly legs. "You're too weak to walk."

"Am not." Her boot slipped again.

In a swift movement, he draped her in his muscled arms, with her feet dangling. "You thought you'd ride down a mountain?"

"Whatever it took to warn Corrin." She stiffened her back. "Red would've found the Langley's."

Grant held her away from his chest, the way she'd carry a bug-infested log.

She angled her neck to avoid touching his shoulder. Geeze. Even furious at him, his cradling made her giddy. Damn every inch of infuriating, dutiful, and sinfully buff Grant Morley.

"Why don't you trust me?" He stopped, one foot balanced on the porch.

Her calf bumped his revolver. A hitman wouldn't have left his target holding a gun. "I'm scared. Ike told me to escape and not to trust cops. You know my name and carry a rifle."

"I told you before, I'll protect you, and my antique shotgun didn't make the clean gash in your side. I need a detailed account, which I'll relay to my boss. The longer we delay, the more risk." He kicked open the door and set her on the bed. "Stay put by what's left of the fire." He threw her a quilt.

With two puffs of his anger-fueled breath, embers sparked to life. He laid on kindling and fresh logs.

"I've never seen you in the building after hours. Why Friday night?"

"I told you, I met a new client at lunchtime." She clutched the quilt to her chest.

While she relayed the horrid events, Grant's scowl softened slightly. Her secrets slowly lost their leaden power. She stretched her hand toward the fire. A jab pierced her side. "Ow."

"Your fall could've busted your wound open. Doc Kyle will kick me if it's worse." He gently lifted a corner of the bandage. "No broken stitches."

"I had a good seamstress," she offered.

He smoothed her shirt down. "Please don't move until I return. No joking." His voice held kindness. "Crawl under the covers if you're still cold. Gotta make a call. I'll be gone a few minutes, tops. You won't be unguarded again, I promise."

"I'll be fine."

The door slammed shut.

Her finger traced where his hand had been. While he'd ministered to her injury, she'd felt secure, a comfort as familiar as her mom's love, which she'd taken for granted until the hellish call reporting their murders.

She'd fled memories of her former life and escaped to Seattle, where Venom chased her away. Too much running, too tiring.

No, her family would expect her to fight with Grant's help. She pictured him on horseback, tall and unwavering, carrying the stony determination of a conquering warrior.

He couldn't mask everything. After she'd described Venom's snake tattoo, his eyes flashed alarm.

Over dinners, Ike had tried to describe to Shirley and her the FBI's allegiance to uphold the law. As a judge, he had great respect for their dedication and the danger. Now she knew why.

Grant's type, bonded to the bureau, would die in the line of duty, even protecting a stranger he didn't trust.

~ ~ ~

What a tangled mess. Grant unsaddled Brasso. "Now, you're done for the night, big guy." He stowed the tack.

The call to Sam hadn't offered reassurance. Maneski's confirmed involvement by Miranda's story and Karpenito's apparent disappearance escalated the danger factor of protecting her by ten.

By the looks of things, a traitor could've infiltrated their own team, and Sam shared his fury at the thought.

Grant stomped snow from his boots, swung the cabin door open, and strode in.

Miranda had hunkered by the glowing fire.

"We'll stay tonight and head out at first light. It's a long ride to my house. Doc Kyle will ascertain if you're ready to fly."

She shook her head. "No. I promised I'd check with Ike."

Should he tell her Judge Gilson remained in ICU? "He'd approve of FBI protection." He grabbed a vase from a high shelf and shoved in a couple branches of serviceberry which had hit his face on the way down. "Hallmark closed early. Here."

"Oh." She stared at the makeshift bouquet. "I haven't gotten flowers . . ."

They weren't a dozen roses, but her eyes had turned bright as a child's on Christmas morning.

A spark hissed.

She rubbed her forehead. "Oh my gosh, I have to let Kathleen know I'm all right. She said someone called to send flowers. It must've been Venom."

"I already phoned her."

"Did they think I disappeared on purpose?"

Grant placed the vase on the table. "They didn't have time to make any conclusions. Shortly after your lunch break, one of the horses being ridden by a kid got stung by a bee and took off downhill. His bolting horse launched a panic attack in another guest, and all hell broke loose. Kat's my cousin. I told her we're friends and you're going to hang out at my ranch for a few days."

"Crap. I left Pitch shorthanded. He'd asked me to be the drag rider."

"Don't worry. No injuries. Pitch got antsy you were late, but I caught them before they started a badly timed search."

"Why badly timed?"

"Venom needs proof you're—"

"Oh." Worry lines creased her brow.

He brushed his fingers over his forehead. "Kat wondered if I'm the boyfriend who'd contacted her first."

Color drained from her face. "I haven't had a boyfriend for years."

He crossed his arms over his chest. "Your friend, Corrin, called shortly after him. Who all did you give their number to?"

"No one. I booked right before I left and didn't tell Corrin any details."

"You don't have family?"

She covered her face with both hands. "None since I turned twenty." Her voice dropped. "They were murdered after I gave them bad advice."

Murdered? Bad advice? He'd never put his own folks in harm's way. Miranda seemed so innocent.

He'd need to get to the bottom of her past eventually, and maybe more. "I'm sorry for your loss. I can't begin to imagine how horrible that feels."

She turned her face to the fireplace. "No, you can't. I need to call Corrin."

"I'm certain the ranch told her you're fine."

"Corrin thought Venom followed the bus." She shuddered.

"Well, hell." He bunched his fist. "To catch him, I need to know how he found you."

"I have no idea. I used a pay phone in Idaho to alert my business clients I'd be gone."

"How'd you reserve your room at the Langley's? Your cell phone?"

"No, it needed charging. I used a public laptop at the coffee shop next door."

"Bingo." Grant grabbed a pencil and paper. "Give me the best description you can remember of the detective who appeared in the Justice Building after the gunman left."

Miranda closed her eyes. "Ike said his name's Karpenito, and he's a crooked detective. Seahawks ball cap and blue jacket. Brown slacks, my height. His badge number ended in thirty-one, and he had a beard. I think there was glue on his face next to the sideburns. He walked funny."

"Good memory. How'd he walk?"

"I sit or kneel by my plants and see a lot of shoes pass by. His gait seemed awkward, not limping. He wore platform shoes."

"That's a new one. My boss needs to know the lying bastard's involved."

"Ike's opinion, too."

"Smart judge. From now on, we stick together, whether Venom's out there or not. Maybe he's concluded you're, ah, not going to be able to testify."

"You can say dead. I know I'm the hitman's mistake."

Her words pierced him like a dagger. "I need to feed the animals. Be right back."

He closed the door and ran his hand down the weathered outside wall. Venom hadn't counted on him finding Miranda. They were one step ahead. For now.

Red nickered when he approached, then nuzzled his left pocket.

"Clever boy, already figured out where I stash the oat wafer treats." He whistled to the jennies while filling their feed buckets.

Judas Priest. Might as well shoot off a flare gun. Funny thing, he couldn't recall whistling in years.

He finished and slipped into the cabin. Hopefully she'd taken a nap.

Evening sun bronzed Miranda's profile as she sat on a chair, finger combing her hair.

Miranda projected a sweet innocence. She wouldn't survive a New York minute in his world.

Didn't matter. He'd been tasked to solve the high profile case, and she held the brass ring.

No harm in enjoying her company afterward, maybe dating her in Seattle until he got promoted.

He bent to grab a log. His gun pressed his side.

If they both survived.

~ ~ ~

By admitting one more lie to Grant, she'd have a clean conscience. Miranda sat on the edge of the chair and watched him rummage through cupboards. "You need to know—I followed you here to ask for your help, and I talked to your mom on Sunday."

He turned and faced her. "Why me?"

Her cheeks became warm, and not from the fire at her back. "I didn't know anyone else who'd protect me."

The sexy dimple in Grant's cheek appeared. "I'm glad I found you, or rather your mule found me. Hungry?"

Her mule. The prospect touched her heart. "I've never been shy around food."

He set a jar on the table and pretended to cast out a line. "There's a fishing hole not far away."

The movement pulled his Levi's tight across that perfectly rounded rump. Miranda's eyes widened. "Fishing and campfires. Boy paradise."

"Yup. In summer we'd catch a couple brookies first, then dive in for a swim. We'd climb out and jump back in. Second time, the mountain stream's a lot warmer."

Wow, Grant in a Speedo. A ripple of unexpected heat ran through her veins. "Is it canned trout in the jar?"

"Yes ma'am. Poppy and Dad put them up if we get a nice mess."

"Your dad and grandpa sound fun."

"Most of the time. Dad retired from the Montana State

Highway Patrol, my grandpa from the FBI. I finally meet their expectations."

"So, three generations of law officers. Bet you got the gun gene early."

"Poppy's bureau stories made me want to reach Special Agent in Charge, or SAC. It's been my goal since before I turned eight."

"Eight? At that age I pretended to swaddle babies and learned how to braid hair. I inherited Mom's knack for gardening, though."

"Shows in how you care for your plants." Grant rotated the glass jar. "This was a sixteen-inch brookie I caught. It'll taste like summer."

Her breath caught in her throat. His grin took twenty years from his face. The same pride Kenny had displayed after landing any fish. "How long have you lived in Montana?"

"My whole life."

"And your parents live nearby?"

"A country mile from my place."

What would it be like to have family so close? "How wonderful to have your folks nearby and live in a beautiful area." Miranda gently rubbed her nose. "You must be in the platinum air club with the commute to Seattle."

"I don't make it to Montana much. My job demands a lot of time. I'm going to sell my spread."

Her bullet wound was nothing compared to the jolt to her heart.

~ ~ ~

Venom let out a long breath.

His horse stood a few yards away, yanking out tufts of brown grass. If he approached from behind, he'd catch it. Who'd of believed a rental horse for hunters would bolt at a gun shot?

"Hey there, horsey, a little longer until you get back to the barn. He grabbed the dragging reins, and studied the final shades of twilight.

Damn if the light hadn't given out in the woods, right after he'd found the trampled area and blood.

He slid his rifle into the scabbard.

Too bad he'd missed on the second shot. Her mule had zig-zagged better than an Army Ranger in combat training.

Tracks didn't show she'd headed downhill, and no birds circled overhead to indicate a carcass. He reached into his saddle bag and grabbed the flashlight.

He'd start from the bloody patch again. She had to be in the woods somewhere. Probably bled out, like the judge. If not, the cold would finish her tonight.

Dead-lips blue would be his new favorite color. His mouth twitched into a smirk. Yup, dead-lips blue could be a popular paint chip.

He pulled a handful of feed pellets from the saddlebag and tossed them onto the ground by the horse's nose. Good thing the army taught him preparation.

Didn't miss the long marches, though. He rotated one ankle, then the other. The dogs were a barkin' tonight.

He pulled off his gloves and wiggled his phone from his pocket. Two service bars—a miracle. A text from Karpenito appeared. *Judge Gilson survived.*

Christ. And the girl would've heard him confirming the hit to Karpenito—if she'd been hiding behind her plants, like the cop believed.

He slammed his fist against a tree trunk, then dug into the pack for a water bottle and antacids. Crunching them to bits didn't extinguish the burn in his stomach.

She would've heard him mention Maneski's name, too. He grabbed a package of jerky and his goose down coat. Even zipped, the chill penetrated to his bones.

He huffed on his fingers and dialed. "Hey darlin'. How're you doing?" He grinned. "Miss you more. Did you clean out the bank account?" He pressed the phone closer to his ear.

"Say again? Good girl. Listen, if I'm not home tomorrow night, drive you and the boy to your brother's cabin. Maybe we can get our old jobs back as wildfire scouts. Give the little feller a hug for me. Bye."

He pocketed the phone. Maneski would be furious he'd taken the payoff on a judge who hadn't croaked. Tonight he'd earn the hit money offing the plant girl.

You didn't cheat a mobster. Now it was her life or his.

He ripped open the package and tore off a section of stringy jerky. The salty brine lingered on his tongue.

A coyote howled in the distance. Night hunters, same as him. He flicked on the Maglite.

"Time to earn your keep, horsey." He wedged his foot in the stirrup and swung aboard, his leg grazing the fold-up shovel strapped to the top of the saddle bag.

The tall rider he'd seen earlier leading two pack mules could be a problem.

If mule-man got in the way, there'd be a second body rotting in a shallow grave come spring.

~ ~ ~

Grant stopped talking and tilted his head. He stepped to the window and peered out.

Her body froze. "Someone out there?"

"Nope. Checking the animals. You kept pretty quiet during my Morley family history session."

"Your childhood sounded special."

He patted the table. "I've had some great times here."

The realization stung. Grant must've amazed other women using his skills at the remote hide-away, ones impressed by the size of his . . . gun.

She wasn't invited, she was a duty. The sooner she parted ways with her heartbreak-ready-to-happen, the better. "Can you arrange for me to be in witness protection?"

He narrowed his eyes. "We'll see."

"Am I considered a criminal?" Her cheeks flamed.

A big fry pan clanged while he hooked it to an iron arm and rotated it into place over the center of the fire. Oil sizzled after he slid in the trout. "I don't think of you as a criminal, and I'll protect you." He opened a can of green beans and dumped it into the pan beside the fish.

The aroma of pan-seared trout filled the room, and for once it wasn't pleasant.

Her whole body ached for Ike to be okay, for home, for a rewind of her low-profile life.

Grant dumped a can of sliced apples into a smaller pan and sprinkled on sugar, oatmeal, and cinnamon. He flipped the fish and moved the big skillet to their table.

Dessert now hung over the fire. "As a kid, Mom and I used to cook together. I think she wanted a daughter, even got me a rolling pin one Christmas." He faked a grin. "I didn't appreciate my first culinary tool."

"Sorry to break the news, Agent Morley. Life doesn't always give you what you want." She thrummed her fingers on the table.

"Nope." He transferred a chunk of fish to a plate, added beans and slid it in front of her. "Speckled trout hold their pink color. *Bon appetit.*"

"I'm certain it'll be the most delicious fish I've ever eaten as a prisoner. *Merci.*"

"Welcome." He ate in silence while she picked at the green beans and bites of fish.

Cinnamon perfumed the room.

He plopped a scoop of apple brown betty onto her plate and dug into the huge portion he'd dished himself.

She put down her fork and pushed away the untouched dessert.

"Just because I believe your story, it doesn't mean I can skip over the bureau's rules for this type of situation," he said.

"Story, as in fable? Seems you've questioned my innocence and then sugarcoated your views like the apples on my plate."

"Your words, not mine," he said quietly.

"Whatever." She jabbed a tiny piece of apple, and chewed it slowly. Irritation thrummed in her chest. "I'd bet lots of lucky women have found you at this hearth with your baking tool, Agent Morley."

His eyebrows shot up. "You owe me a home cooked feast after that comment, Ms. Whitley. Five course dinner and dessert."

"Your personal chef? I think not. Maybe I'll spring for a real cup of coffee for you at the espresso shop to pay my debt."

He cast her a side eye. "Too good for the Coffee Klatch? I observed you spying on us a couple times when you weren't bending over your pots."

She raised her eyebrows. "Bending is what you noticed?"

Crimson rose from his collar to his cheeks. "Whatever."

Logs sputtered in the fire.

"Corrin needs to know I'm safe. My phone's zipped in my coat pocket, with my tube of gloss." She rubbed her fingertips across her dry lips.

His eyes followed the movement. "Your cell got damp. We'll use mine." He fished the gloss out and placed it on the table. "Let's make the call before the temperature drops anymore."

"Good plan." She grabbed the strawberry scented lip balm, ignored the arm he offered, and took small steps out to where the animals stood huddled together.

Red's distinctive mule-nicker welcomed her. "You're happy I'm here, aren't you?" She ran her fingers through the warmth of his winter coat, and rubbed slow strokes the length of his cheek. "With a fearless mule, who needs a G-Man?"

"Oh brother," he grumbled from a few steps behind her.

She turned sideways, took out the lip-gloss and slowly glided it across her upper and then lower lip.

Grant stopped dead in his tracks.

His blazing eyes were anything but dead.

~ ~ ~

Blood pounded through Grant's veins. Her scent, her warm curves, and that smart mouth. Every cell screamed for him to pull her into his arms, and show her exactly what a G-Man could do to those shiny lips.

Worse trouble than an empty magazine in a standoff, but she might be worth the burn. He took a step back. "You forgot a coat." He held out a giant oilskin cowboy duster.

"I think it'll fit," she said.

He pointed to her borrowed sweater. "Mom's first knitting project. The raincoat belongs to my skyscraping grandpa, or Poppy, as we call him. Didn't want you getting cold."

Miranda slipped it on. Her fingers didn't poke out. "They grow 'em big in these here mountains." She tilted her chin to look him in the eyes.

As he smiled down at her, that feeling of being ten feet tall struck. Collateral damage of the worst kind. "Let me handle alterations." He cuffed four inches on each sleeve. "You need a hat. Check the pocket."

Her eyes grew wide. "Where's my Mariners cap? Blue with a white S emblem. Did you find it in the woods? It must've fallen off."

He tugged a soft knit hat from her pocket. "No, I didn't see a ball cap, but this should work."

"I need the Mariner's cap," she pleaded. "I'll call Corrin tomorrow. Let's search the lower trail."

"Your ball cap will have to wait, there's no light."

Her whole body became still. "It belonged to my little brother. He wore it constantly. It's all I have left of him."

No one could fake the sorrow in her eyes.

Needle-like twinges pricked the back of his neck. "We'll keep our eyes out. We'll spot it."

She rubbed the bump on her nose before pulling two fuzzy mittens out of the coat's pockets. "These have beautiful knit patterns. Did you make them in your spare time?"

"Mom knitted those for Poppy." He fought a catch in his throat. "She loves to knit and paint."

"My mom loved to garden, and my dad loved to read. My brother and I studied pollywogs. You're blessed to have them in your life."

Loving parents waited for his return. He'd sidelined them for too long and that needed to be rectified. Miranda didn't have that option, and worse than anything—she'd played a role in their death. How could you overcome such guilt?

"Corrin will be worried," he said. "It's not a long way to where we get a signal. We can ride bareback."

"Sure." She leaned against Red. "As in you're on Brasso, and I'm alone on Red?"

"Nope. You'd face plant."

"Can we ride double on Red?" She moved to pet Brasso.

"I guess. He's plenty big to haul us both for a short ride."

Her mule opened his mouth for the bit. "I'm already hosed," he whispered. "I don't need a four-legged conspirator."

"Excuse me?" she called.

"Need a boost up?"

She walked back and stood beside Red. "Unless there's a spare mounting block."

Grant centered his fingers on her hips, and lifted her onto Red's back. "You going to be okay?"

"After I call Corrin and find my hat."

He swung up behind her and settled his arms around her waist before gathering the reins.

The mule's hooves thumped into soft snow.

An intense battle raged deep inside while he fought to maintain a detached exterior. Her physical appeal became painful at times, the growing respect was worse.

He had to face it. A woman who'd made him laugh and enjoy life again existed between her pushbutton panic mode and her emotional pain. When the feisty woman surfaced, it scared the hell out of him.

"I've never been on a night ride in the woods." Her back nestled perfectly into his chest. "The floating snowflakes fade out to present a peaceful, moonlit wonderland."

Poetic words of what he'd been thinking. No one except the Morleys used their cabin, yet Miranda fit in as if she belonged. Especially tucked in his arms, in the quiet forest. He took an easy breath. "You hair smells nice." Damn, he'd spoken aloud. "As compared to your—"

Red snorted, and his ears went upright to alert mode.

Grant's hand shot to his gun.

An owl hooted from high in a tree.

He released his grip on the Glock. "You'd think a Montana mule would be used to nighttime noises."

"He's my guardian mule. Always on duty."

Did he want to be more than her guardian agent? He opened his mouth, then closed it. The cost would be high.

The woods offered silence until they reached the pointed rock where they had a chance of reception. The odd shape threw off a foreboding, jagged shadow. Venom could be hiding behind it.

He continued to scan the ground for prints in the snow or broken branches.

Miranda wriggled. "I smell nice as compared to what?"

"The mule."

"If you're too embarrassed to be seen with me, I think I can pull a teenage mutant warrior trick." She slunk into the coat, imitating a turtle pulling into its shell.

Grant laughed. "Wasn't expecting that." He tightened the reins. "Whoa there, big guy. First call's to the bureau." He tapped on the tiny screen. "Hey, Sam. I'll bring Ms. Whitley down the mountain tomorrow. I booked us on the next flight."

"Sorry you're alone protecting the witness," Sam said. "Not protocol, but between your location and what's going on here, you need to stay put until further notice. Street chatter implies Maneski's put a six-figure bounty on Judge Gilson's head, probably on Ms. Whitley, too."

"I understand your concerns. I'll book a Three Falls hotel for tomorrow night."

Sam let out a long breath. "Best to keep her at your place. Can't explain right now."

"Got it. Any information from Karpenito?"

"Humph." Sam grunted. "Local cops exhibiting little man syndrome are the worst."

Grant moved the phone to his outside ear. "Explain your syndrome statement."

"I remembered him. The guy's a fireplug. Maybe five-four and pudgy. The Whitley woman's description didn't match up. No one's ever seen him wearing a beard."

He clenched the reins. "Repeat, please."

"Short guy. Clean shaven, pasty jowls."

"I'll call you tomorrow from my home. We've had a bit of a fishy day."

"Maybe time to charm your way into her confidence," Sam said.

Judas Priest, another unexpected twist to her tale. "I'll consider your suggestion." Grant hung up, and scowled.

Wait, she'd described an odd walk, and glue by the beard. The cop wore a disguise.

"Your turn. Please keep it short." He handed his phone to Miranda.

She tapped in numbers. "Corrin, change of plans . . . Grant's phone. The agent. How'd you know where to call? . . . The number on my wrist, of course. Anyway, I went on a trail ride and got shot . . . No, I'm okay. He's trustworthy. The mule who saved me and the bureau boy."

Grant cleared his throat.

She leaned forward and patted Red. "We're heading back tomorrow to have a doctor check my wound . . . In his folk's mountain cabin. Don't worry, I'm fine."

His ears were trained for details, and his bullshit radar pinged. Corrin didn't trust him, either.

"Thanks for checking on Shirley. Hey, I keep a list of commercial accounts on my desk. Maybe you can find someone to water plants Tuesday?" Miranda asked. Her body relaxed. "Thanks, I don't know what I'd do without you. Miss you."

"I need to speak to her." He took the phone. "Agent Morley here. Please stay out of your apartment building until we clear access."

"I live next door and need to replenish my wardrobe and get the list, sir. Miranda will kill me if her plants wilt," she challenged.

"Agent Sam Coswell will contact you regarding an escort. We're not taking risks, ma'am," he shot back.

"Listen up, Mr. FBI agent. I'll comply on one condition."

"Which would be?"

"Miranda's family to me, so if you've got any ideas, they better have good intentions, or I'll track down your government regulated ass and pound the daylights out of you. I don't care who you work for."

"Yes, ma'am."

Corrin hung up on him.

Whoa. Her friend was a piece of work. He jammed the phone in his pocket.

"Something wrong?" Miranda asked.

He carried the badge, and he'd sure as hell done nothing to deserve Corrin's threat. Had a guy burned Miranda? His hands clenched the reins. "Nope. Friend check complete." He squeezed his left leg, and Red turned around.

"I wouldn't get by without Corrin coaxing me to push on."

Nothing beats a deranged drill sergeant. "She sounds nice."

"She's been a lifesaver more than once."

Another statement he'd investigate. "You'll see her soon. Now we head back to the cabin."

"The woods are lovely in shimmery moonlight. I wish Corrin could see it. Oh, crap. I forgot to give her my flight number."

"I'll handle it."

Red stopped, front feet splayed.

"Come on mule, we're freez—"

A sharp crack broke the stillness.

Grant drew his gun as Miranda's shoulders jolted into his chest.

A dead limb crashed onto the trail, its branches laden with snow. It dropped where they would've been in a few steps.

He released his tightened hold on her waist. "Good call, Red." He rubbed a circle near the mule's withers. "You're one smart boy."

"I knew the noise wasn't a gun." She frowned at the broken limb. "You think Venom's out there, don't you?" Her body trembled.

The less she knew the better. "Agent reaction. Can't imagine anyone staying on the mountain in the snow."

"I wonder if I'll ever sleep a full night again."

"Your normal Seattle routine will help."

Another lame response. She needed to be scared until Venom and Karpenito wore cuffs. "Walk on," he said.

Red's steps gained speed the closer they got to the cabin.

A deep-set need implored him to hold her nestled tight and keep riding into the night.

During Maneski's trial, she might land in witness protection, or be out of his jurisdiction. Still . . .

The bent tree jutted out. His focus shifted to a branch hanging at an angle a few feet down the trail.

Had it been broken when they'd left? He'd been too preoccupied getting a Miranda fix to notice.

He nudged Red's belly to turn him toward the cabin. Scrunching needles resounded in the still night.

As soon as they passed through the fir trees, light shone through the window like a beacon. He stopped where the animals were tied and searched for fresh footprints.

"Wait here a minute," he whispered before he slid off and checked the cabin. "Nothing out of place."

"Good boy," she crooned to Red.

He strode back and grabbed for the reins. While their bare fingers collided, jolts shot through him.

He shoved his hands into his deep front pockets. "I apologize. I didn't ask your permission to carry you earlier. My manners are rusty. Please don't hold it against me."

Her long sigh puffed into frosty air. "I'm cold and tired. I won't hold it against you if you'll hold me against you."

Without a reply, he scooped her up and pulled her closer than earlier. Her arm jammed his phone into his chest.

What would Sam think of his growing attraction? He tried to ignore her soft lavender-scented hair tickling his chin. Locking his arms and shifting her weight proved useless.

He'd dated a few street-smart women, who'd never ignited yearnings deep in his chest. If he let her in any closer, she'd be scorched by the flames. No matter what his heart wanted, he had to cut off the visions of a rosy future.

She couldn't hold a gun steady and talked of her little brother like she enjoyed kids. Parenting hadn't made his to-do list.

Who was he kidding? Tamping the increasing appreciation of every quality Miranda possessed had become as futile as muting a flashbang.

His damned luck he'd met her under the worst circumstances. One misstep and her credibility as a witness would be ruined, the case compromised, and the promise to his father to reach SAC shattered. A vow he'd made sporting a black eye and a split lip, a vow to clean the streets of bullies. Words said long ago and far away from the last three days of realizing Miranda brought his compassion back.

The short trek to the cabin seemed endless.

He lowered her legs until her boots reached the porch. "I'll chop a few logs." He grabbed the ax. "See if you can get the fire going."

With a few swift strokes, he had enough stacked for the next three fires. He peeled off a piece of bark and ran his hand over the smooth golden wood. No knots. The grain would be straight and even. It would've been beautiful varnished, maybe made into a headboard using silvery teak accents.

He gathered the logs and headed into the cabin, chilly but not cooled down.

Any touch from Miranda struck flint to steel, and the fire burned deep.

~ ~ ~

Just Hours, the cabin's name, had been carved on a varnished plank hanging above the door. Miranda glanced around. Candles, pillows and other hints of sensual promises filled the cozy room, the kind used for a rustic setting in a romantic play.

When he'd carried her after the phone call, he'd pulled her closer to his chest than necessary. She wasn't a total twit. He'd angled his chin to caress her neck with his breath.

Her mind continued to revisit his muscled forearms, and the embrace sparked the fantasy of a shared life, not inconspicuous, but bold.

The trip through the woods had been magical, even counting the branch scare. His dorky wisecracks added a different dimension to his character. Too bad the fun Grant rarely surfaced, or maybe just as well he didn't.

He relied on a gun as his constant companion. A lump of deadly metal he grabbed out of habit, and a huge part of his life.

Tiny threads of tenderness appeared infrequently. Anger or distrust he couldn't always hide.

She sat on a backless bench and stuck her feet close to the fire. Her fingers began yanking out tangles. It wasn't good timing to start a romance, no matter how tempting those biceps were. Not with Venom hunting her.

The door opened, sending a frigid draft against her back. "It's me."

A loud thunk indicated he'd dropped a load of wood into a bin.

Hesitant footsteps came closer. He reached over her and his hip brushed her shoulder, sending tingles through her, awakening unwanted urges.

"Want me to detangle your hair?" he asked.

The room stilled, energy crackling between them. He'd have to tug out snarls, which wasn't sexy. "Sure. Have at it."

He lifted a wooden box from the mantle and took out a carved, wide-toothed comb. The chair scraped across the floor. It groaned from his weight, and his knee brushed her hip from behind.

Grant generated heat stronger than a blast furnace, and strength from him seeped into her. "Forests are peaceful," she said.

"Poppy used to say, 'quiet as a plow laid aside at the furrow's end.'"

With competent strokes, he methodically worked from the bottom, teasing out knots.

Damn Grant Morley and his magical petal-soft touch!

Gentle pulls sent chills through her body and made her insides as soft as a pool of melted caramel. His fingers brushing her skin sent shivery sensations deep.

She'd been wrong again. His way of untangling her snarls was so, so sexy. An inner glow wrapped her in a warm cloud of pale peony pink, while every female component of hers ached for attention. His attention.

Sparks shot into the chimney.

Sensibility kicked in. If she wasn't on a mountain, held together by stitches, she'd imagine falling against his muscled torso. The one bearing the gun holstered at his hip.

Still, what harm in enjoying a little cat and mouse sparring? After she'd gotten one matter cleared up.

She rotated her head. "So, you appear to know what you're doing. Does your wife have long hair?"

"No, can't say she does."

Miranda jerked to upright.

"Don't strain my stitching. No wife, or girlfriend. My dad used to make me comb out horse tails before he'd show them at the Spring Round-Up each year. I've practiced on long tangles, but yours is the silkiest I've worked on."

His voice had deepened to a low, husky tone.

By the soft tugs, he'd begun gliding his fingers down the length of her hair. "It's like holding a perfect sunset."

Perfectly sinful. So the armor holding tough-guy Grant in place did bend. The thought brought a wicked smile while she rubbed her fingertips over her thumb, planning retaliation.

He massaged her neck and onto her scalp. She slumped, letting her head wobble like a rag doll. Coral petals brushed her heart. Yes indeed, he'd colored her world again.

"You'll sleep better tonight." His fingers slowed to a stop, but remained in place, touching her skin, warm and solid.

Time to stoke the forge. "Tonight we trade," she announced. "I'll sleep on the mat." She closed her eyes, prepared for a fight and then make up time.

Her turn to melt steel.

~ ~ ~

A twisting knot formed in Grant's stomach. No way he'd allow her unobstructed access to the door, even if he could justify demanding a bed from an injured woman. "Not happening."

Her shoulders tensed again.

"I'm not done yet, princess." He placed his fingertips on either side of her temples, searching for a pressure point. "Try deep breaths." He rolled her head one way, then the other.

He cradled her cheek in his hand and stroked the length of her graceful neck, then massaged the tops of each shoulder.

Damn. He shouldn't be doing this, shouldn't be getting close enough to interpret her guilt-driven declarations.

He pressed into her firm upper arms, kneading each muscle, needing her to believe he wanted to guard her from harm.

Finally, she unwound.

"Amazing," she whispered. "Nevertheless, I get the floor."

He brought her head back to center, letting his fingers glide for a final time through the tangle-free russet coil in his hand.

Fire danced around the cast iron swing Poppy had fashioned for cooking. He'd officially become the fourth generation to bring a woman to the Just Hours cabin. Too bad it wasn't for the right reasons.

"Poppy and Dad would ride here tonight and whup my butt if they suspected I had any intention of allowing m'lady to sleep on the floor. Nope, you'll stay put. Tomorrow night we'll both have beds."

She shook her head. "Nope, not if I had a front row seat to the butt whupping." Her cheeks had definitely become rosier. "It's a big bed, which we can share platonically. I assume you're over eighteen."

He'd have to be comatose. "I'm twenty-nine at present." He shifted his knee away from touching her hip. "Request denied."

Her spine stiffened. "Not a request. Corrin would tan my hide and fly here from Seattle if she had to, knowing I let a knight in shining armor sleep on the floor after he'd saved me, sutured me, and spent hours combing rat's nests out of my hair."

What he wouldn't give to be Miranda's knight, to win her devotion in a joust, and have her plant a strawberry-scented kiss on him. He brushed his fingers across his lips and moved to the bookshelf. "Sacrifices to comfort are part of an agent's day."

"It's nighttime," she scoffed.

Corrin would demand his hide get the scrape and acid treatment if she knew his recurring thoughts. "Are you a reader?" He waved a tattered volume at her.

"My nose remains stuck in a book if I'm not working. Dad read me volumes of stories. To this day, it's his voice I hear in my own head while I read."

At least one of them had a sweet childhood memory regarding reading. Special time spent by his dad's side involved throwing clay pigeons to shoot. "Odd, every book I'm finding is poetry." He grabbed three and moved to the table. Flipping one open, he skimmed an ancient Egyptian poem. '*My heart desires to go down to bathe myself before you.*' "Whoa, kind of private stuff." He shut the book, and pushed his thermal shirt sleeves above his biceps. "Temp's warm in here, you comfortable?"

She sat sideways to the table, propped on one elbow, studying him with the intensity of a laser trained on a target. Her eyes remained fixed on his upper arms while her tongue flicked out to moisten parted lips. "Purr-fect."

Judas Priest. All those triceps presses had backfired. He pulled the ribbed cuff to his wrist. "You need to get in bed where you can lean back. You need rest."

"As you wish, Sir Knight." Mischief shone in her eyes. "Turn your back. I'm not wearing my dirty jeans to bed."

But she'd be wearing those silky panties. "I'll find another book. After you're settled, I'll put the kerosene lantern close to you for easier reading."

The bed creaked.

"All settled. I'll stay in bed to read, if you'll join me." She patted the side closest to the fire.

Full lips parted and brows raised, she didn't need to utter the dare.

Grant sighed. One way or another, a long evening stretched ahead. "In a moment, you'll realize the slanted ceiling meets the cave wall we're built into. In the summer, it keeps the place cool, in winter, it becomes an icebox. You need warmth from the fire."

She skootched her butt back toward him. "Sure. You get the icebox."

Wouldn't help chill him tonight. "Here, hold the books.

He thrust them at her and then climbed over her legs, crawling to the side by the cave's wall. "Ow." He rubbed his head. "Didn't judge the clearance to the wooden beams." If he tipped his head toward her, he'd avoid splinters.

"You can sit closer to me, I don't bite."

Her earlobe looked good enough to nibble. "Book, please?"

She handed him one and opened hers to the index. Her finger stopped. "Hmm, let's see if I remember the first verse of *The Spider and the Fly*. 'Will you step into my parlor? Said the spider to the fly, 'tis the prettiest little parlor that ever you did spy.' I memorized this poem in the fourth grade. No wonder I wasn't too popular with boys."

Laughter rose from deep in his gut. He'd walked right into her web. Keeping from becoming rolled in her silky strings became harder by the moment. "Your classmates were idiots, unless they've watched a spider bundle its prey for a later feast."

"Mother nature at her finest." She yawned and set her book on the night stand. "Read to me, please?"

He flipped through several pages and found a wildflower poem. While he read, she sank into the bed. Her eyes no longer fought to stay open, her breathing became slow and steady.

The emerald-eyed gardener had fallen asleep, laying on her side, facing him. He whispered the last few lines, "She'd pricked his heart, at first a nettle. Now she blossomed, filling him, filling him. Her sweet love softer than a daisy petal."

Lifting the bedspread, he pulled it over her shoulders while judging the distance between the slanted roof and her body. His chest wouldn't clear the space without bumping her, no matter which way he twisted. Essentially, she'd trapped him in her parlor, unless he wanted to wake her.

Circles under her eyes meant she needed rest. She probably hadn't slept a full night since the shooting.

He slowly reached over her to shut off the lantern, not brushing a hair on her head.

Off came his shirt. His jeans stayed on.

"You won this round, princess. I'll be ready next time." He brushed his lips against her forehead.

The grit and determination of a true survivor dwelled alongside her rare beauty. She deserved her own family, married to a lucky guy. What would she say if he woke her and asked if he had a chance? He rubbed his empty ring finger, the question burning deep inside.

~ ~ ~

A distinct sensual warmth enveloped Grant's body. He opened his eyes and watched his breath create thin clouds. His face remained chilly, while the rest of his body blazed from under the covers.

Miranda still faced him, with her full length plastered against him.

One of her arms lay atop the quilt.

He snuck it under their blanket and laid it across his chest. Her lips quivered and throaty noises of contentment puffed out, reminiscent of a kitten he'd once rescued.

Picture a fluffy kitten, Morley, not the sexy bed partner. He couldn't. Damn, her contended breaths slammed into him like a sledge hammer through plywood.

He uncovered his left leg, needing the chilly jolt from the nearby rock. *Witness, think witness.* He silently recited the alphabet backwards.

Why hadn't he stopped to talk to her in the lobby? Maybe his sixth sense had kicked in, knowing her very essence would etch into the barriers around his programmed life, established for solo success.

He'd come too far to risk a compromise. But she challenged his mind, even while he fought off images of incredibly sensual possibilities.

A deadly combination.

~ ~ ~

Soft lips touching her forehead and a whispered promise hovered through Miranda's dream world. She woke from a deliciously warm slumber, her fingers rising and falling to a steady beat. Her forearm rested on a smooth beach.

She cracked open one eye, half-aware of a familiar spicy male scent. Through shuttered lashes, she recognized the sculpted torso inches from her nose.

Crapola. She was splayed across Grant with her cheek resting on his solid bicep and her arm slung over his bare chest. Her leg lay draped over his thighs.

Searing heat crept up her neck. She withdrew her fingers from dark chest hair.

Slowly, she lifted her ankle, inching off his blue jeans. After a painfully long time, she'd withdrawn her treacherous limbs.

The bed creaked, and her heart pounded. No other noise disturbed the room except his continuous deep breathing.

With a final teeth-clenching movement, a slender gap lay between them. She let out a long breath, her body still flushed from his heat. Every inch of her pulsed to return.

She laid still, eyes closed. Considering her track record, this might be the closest she'd ever get to a honeymoon.

Her fingers ached to nestle again in the finely curled hair on his chest. She lifted her hand.

~ ~ ~

The torture had ended, each disturbing moment well worth Grant's wait. The caress of her baby-soft skin sliding off his chest in slow motion maxed his restraint to seam-bursting.

He'd give her a couple minutes to presume she'd succeeded. Always better to catch your target off guard.

Paybacks were a bitch.

"You forgot to tell me to throw another log on the fire, Miss Whitley. At some point, parts of you must've gotten cold."

Her eyes burst open, and her lips parted in dismay.

"I took the liberty of moving your arm across me," he said. "It seemed the polite thing to do. Your leg followed of its own accord."

She scooted to her edge of the bed. "I guess I failed to tell you—we Whitley's don't have a knee jerk reaction. We have an elbow to knee response. You move one, and better expect the other to follow."

He grinned. A two-point return. "Good to know. Now you're awake, I'll make an extreme sacrifice and venture out into the cold."

"Sacrifice oozes from your government-sanctioned pores."

Smart ass. His chest skimmed hers as he slid out. Knowing what he'd touched, his pulse revved to action mode. "No sense starting a fire if you're well enough to ride."

"I'll be fine to ride." Judging by the set of her jaw, she'd clamp a stick between her teeth if necessary.

Threads of dawn filtered through the shade. "We'll get those stitches checked today. Old Doc's expecting us. No dawdling."

"I'll miss this cabin," her voice dropped, "and my first time sleeping with . . . " She couldn't turn fast enough to hide a deep blush.

Seriously? A virgin? Maybe she'd meant sleeping with him. "You must be beating men off with those well-aimed branches back in Seattle."

Her face turned beet red. She pulled the quilt to her chin, grabbed the book from the night stand, and held it close to her nose.

"Hey, that came out wrong. Your personal life isn't my business. It's just, you're mighty—"

"Corrin and I spend free time together. We both had horrible dating experiences, so no Tinder hookups."

Too many jerks, or had she been sexually assaulted? Bile rose in his throat.

He stuck her sweater and jeans under the covers to get warm. "I'm sorry. If something bad happened to you on a date, you may want to press charges and consider counseling." He took a step back. "I have contacts to assist with both."

"It's not like that. And I've done therapy, without great results." She lowered the book and squirmed into her clothes. "Your offer's kind. Not many people are willing to get involved."

"It's an honor."

Her gaze traveled around the tiny room. "I'll hold memories of you rescuing me and this mountain's beauty in my heart." Her voice trailed off, and she closed her eyes.

There had to be an explanation for the disparity in her description of Detective Karpenito. If it wasn't a disguise, he'd figure out why her version differed, whatever the cost. "Yes, there's unusual beauty here."

Their verbal jousting seemed hours ago. Sadness rimmed her eyes while she reached out to the vase of serviceberry on the nightstand and fingered one of the branches.

After the case closed, he'd find a counselor to work through whatever had happened to her family. Miranda wasn't a thug. He'd known it from the start. Hell, he'd trusted her with his loaded Glock.

Losing his heart posed a worse threat, and she affected him like no other woman. Her gentle touch pierced deeply and left a fiery imprint. His partner, Bo, had warned him this day would come, and damn it, he'd been right.

A loud bray ruptured the still morning air.

"It's Red." She threw off the covers, her eyes wide. "His alarmed mule—"

In one movement, Grant put his hand over her mouth and grabbed his handgun. "Get under the bed. Now!" he hissed.

While she slid into the tight space, he crossed the room and cracked the shade.

Twenty feet out, a hooded figure moved behind the shed.

He grabbed his rifle from behind the door and knelt by Miranda. "Shoot if it's not me." He placed the Glock near her arm. "Aim for the chest."

He cocked the rifle. The figure had moved to beside the woodpile.

Adrenalin pulsed double time. He flung the door open and fired.

The man jerked. A bullet pierced the door above Grant's ear.

Grant fired again, sending wood chips flying.

The second shot from the intruder ricocheted off the latch.

Miranda yelped.

"You hit?" he whispered, while crouching in the doorway.

The limping man had disappeared.

Nothing from Miranda.

"You okay?" he called over his shoulder.

No answer.

His heart raced in his chest. "Miranda, are you hit?" He stayed low, backed to the side of the bed, and peered under.

Her motionless outline remained still.

"No. No. No." He reached under, and grabbed her arm.

"Are you hurt?" she asked in a shaky voice while she inched out. "The second bullet hit a few feet away."

"You scared the crap out of me. I'm fine." He pulled her to her feet and put his palm against her cheek. "I need to track the gunman." He pushed her to sit on the bed and put the gun in her hands. "Keep it pointed at the door. If it's not me, use it."

Weary eyes met his.

"Okay."

He pulled the door shut. Snow crunched under his feet. Blood stood out against the snow at the base of the wood pile.

Uneven footprints and crimson drops led onto a deer trail.

Grant jogged, rifle poised, every sense on alert.

Crashing brush broke the morning stillness. A horse whinnied from downhill.

Would the gunman circle back? He couldn't leave Miranda alone.

If only he'd had a clear shot to nail the bastard. His jaw clenched.

Killers could be anywhere. Waiting.

~ ~ ~

Venom glanced over his shoulder, his short breaths creating white puffs into the frigid morning air.

No Mule Guy following him.

He leaned back in the saddle and twisted the stick on his thigh, pressing his belt into skin. Damn bullet hole had him bleeding like a stuck pig. And damn bad luck for taking so long to find the hidden cabin.

The reins tightened in his hand. Three mules had been tethered outside.

If Whitley had been found alive, she would've talked. If she'd fallen off the mule, he still had to confirm her dead. Screwed either way.

He wiggled his phone out of his pocket. Two service bars, the only good sign in the last two days. He punched in Karpenito's number. "Get a couple boys on the plane into Three Falls today, packing guns."

Now he'd wait for the perfect shot. If Mule Guy left the cabin this morning, it'd be his last trip.

~ ~ ~

Miranda plodded out the door and stood on the porch. Blood splotches dotted the snow. Grant's news that his gunshot wounded their attacker had brought her relief. She grimaced. Her new world sucked. How much worse would it get before she'd feel normal again?

With a thud, Grant closed the door on the tiny cabin. Noise from the lock made it final.

She'd always been safe in the woods. Until this trip. Dad's tender voice echoed in her head. When she'd been distressed as a kid, he'd told her to plan out deliberate steps.

Venom had pushed her three leaps backwards—emotionally and financially. Cleaning out her savings account would barely pay Corrin back for the cost of the trip.

"Let's go." Grant pulled a faded bandanna from his pocket and tied it around his neck.

"Expecting a dust storm?" she asked.

Grant's face softened for a moment. Next to the pale purple, his hazel eyes turned a smoky shade of green. "Not exactly."

She studied the animals. "Won't we be easy targets?"

"Not many options. Storm's coming from above and tracks showed the gunman's heading downhill at a good clip."

Gunmen and bullets. Her own personal hell. And Ike's. Her feet grew cold in her cowboy boots. "And he knows where we are."

"There's more than one route on the mountain." Grant tightened Brasso's girth strap and untied the rope holding the mules.

She lifted the bridle hanging from Red's saddle horn. "I can get him tacked, but I'll need a leg up to mount."

"You're not riding alone."

"Venom could shoot you by accident." She stomped in place to warm her toes. "I'm sore, but Red will keep me aboard."

He slid his rifle into its scabbard. "You gave me a good idea yesterday to protect us both." He unfurled his grandpa's coat and shrugged into it, holding the front out.

She rubbed her mittens together, staring at Grant's solid chest. "What's your plan?"

"You sit in front of me, and I wear the duster over both of us. Give it a try?"

She rested her cheek against Red's neck. "If nothing of me shows. Won't I be too heavy for a long ride?"

"We're willing and able." His color deepened. "Aren't you Brasso?" He turned away. "I'll put you aboard before I get your undercover costume in place."

"You'll have oats soon, Red." She patted him first and moved to Grant's bay-colored horse.

"Here, shove this on the saddle horn." Grant handed her a sheepskin glove.

How often had he ridden double and provided a padded cushion over the horn for his girlfriends' tender areas? Her mouth tightened. "How considerate."

"Might help, won't know until you try." His hands surrounded her waist, and he lifted her to sit astride in the saddle. "Boy Scout's creed, be prepared."

Nope, not a hint of boy. Her body stirred from contact with a hard-muscled man's strong, determined, and damn sexy hands.

She scooched forward, until her legs straddled Brasso's

shoulders and her belly pushed against the glove.

In an easy movement, he'd swung behind her, heating her back before he pulled the cowboy duster around them both. His knees pushed into the backs of hers, while her butt rested on . . . Not the time to picture that.

He carefully fastened each button of the big coat, closing her into a Grant pouch. Long panels of fabric topped their legs.

"If I move my eyes into position, I can see through the gaps between buttons." She stifled a nervous giggle. "Kind of mimicking the short man on a tall guy's shoulders in a circus act."

"You need to stay hidden." He lifted the bandana to cover his mouth and nose. "We whisper from here on out."

Circus clowns didn't have a hitman lying in wait. Sweat broke on her forehead.

Venom would kill Grant, too.

~ ~ ~

Grant rotated his head, examining the open area beyond the trail. Listening. Waiting.

Nothing.

He used his calf to nudge Brasso's side. The horse led the three mules out of the protective trees and onto the main path leading downhill. No longer would he consider the ponderosa pines a privacy barrier.

In the summertime, their bark smelled like vanilla. Today, fear hung in the air, both his and Miranda's.

Her body stayed pinned against him in the exact position from when he'd secured Poppy's coat. For an instant, his chest felt heavy, his arms weary. "Comfortable?"

"Yes, am I crowding you?"

Crowding, while she sat on his lap? Hardly. *Focus on anything else.* Like 'Grant Morley—SAC,' inscribed on a brass plate or lying in a freezer, naked.

Sensations of desire versus duty rolled through his body. Her curves fit his contours too damn well, from her head to her calves resting against his shins. "No crowding, ma'am. Your legs are longer than I realized."

"Can't help it. I'm from a family of crowd toppers."

Another cruel twist of nature. Most women he'd dated weren't tall enough to kiss without a neck ache.

He pulled a blanket from behind the saddle and draped it across her lap and onto her boots.

"Not a speck of you shows. Next, I need to find the deer trail I explored when I gathered kindling."

"Don't forget my blue cap."

"I won't" His eyes flicked bush to bush, searching for the path which cut on a diagonal to the lake. A slower route to cross the gulley, but thick trees would conceal them from a gunman with a scope.

"I found it," he whispered.

"My hat?"

"No. The path." Her body slumped as he reined onto a foot-wide break in the undergrowth.

Brasso dodged pine limbs to follow the trail. The farther they walked, the narrower it became.

Miranda's head swayed back and forth in time to the movements, while soft kitten snores came from under their coat. What he'd give to gather her up and tuck her into his pocket for safe keeping.

Would she move away from her friends in Seattle for his next job assignment and subsequent ones?

A branch broke nearby. Grant grabbed the Winchester.

A damn squirrel ran up a tree.

The longer they rode, the more his mind conjured Venom and his viper tattoo in increasingly gruesome scenarios. An agent had to play by the rules. The crooks didn't.

Movement caught his eye across the ravine. Light reflected off a smooth surface. His heart raced.

Chapter 9

Grant slid out his Winchester.

Shiny, giant antler paddles attached to a Shiras moose poked out of the tree line, then disappeared.

He eased the gun into the scabbard and let out a deep breath. This time it wasn't Venom.

Miranda stirred. "Home?"

"A little longer. Go back to sleep."

"Okay."

He'd gained her hard won trust. The warmth from her body penetrated into every fatigued muscle.

Wake up, Morley. A leg wound wouldn't stop Venom, and there could be other thugs by now.

Why the hell had Sam ordered them to stay at his Montana house without a team? Seattle posed a worse threat due to the mole? Maneski had unlimited manpower on his own turf. Where could they be safe in Seattle? He ducked under a canopy of branches.

John's secluded house on nearby Vashon Island required boat access. His college buddy would put them up in a heartbeat.

Brasso slipped on icy shale, jostling the three of them down a steep slope.

His grip tightened on Miranda's swaying body. He'd hold her tight, through anything.

"Easy boy." He scratched Brasso's shoulder. "Mastered a tough hill, and you did fine," he whispered.

Miranda stretched her shoulders back and winced. "Guess I conked out. My side hurts. Are we close now?"

That was an understatement. Her movements went too damn deep to ignore. Whatever he fell into with her wouldn't be a fling. Just like every commitment he made, he made it with his whole being. He was wired that way. "We'll travel another half hour. Do you feel feverish?"

"I don't think so."

"Doc Kyle will be waiting at my house tonight. Hopefully we won't need a trip to the hospital from infection."

Brasso plodded on, the extra weight and a long ride on a game trail taxing to a horse used to being a yard ornament. He swallowed hard. His horse deserved to be ridden more.

Smoke rose into a gray sky from the far side of a small hill. He let out a long breath. "Almost home, Brasso."

They topped the hill, and his home's golden logs stood out.

He shifted Miranda's slack weight. "Hey, we've arrived."

She poked a fingertip out the hole to widen it. "That's your house?" Her spine stiffened.

He swung his shoulders to give her a better view. "Yup, logs from Idaho, sealed to stay golden. Mom preferred the turquoise color for the metal roof. Dad and I picked the river rocks for the half wall in front."

Her body strained against the coat.

"What's wrong?" He scanned the meadow.

"Nothing. Years ago I cut out a photo of a similar house from a magazine."

"Wait until you see the inside, including the fretwork furniture we made. The technique combines dark and light wood into patterns. Everyone likes my home, except potential buyers."

Her form shrunk inside the coat.

What now? Did she think they produced a bunch of rickety sticks? "The furniture's upholstered with fabric from a local weaver. Real comfy."

"I bet," she whispered.

He aimed Brasso to his back porch.

Kyle had parked his Jeep as instructed, blocking a view from the woods.

"Whoa." Grant scowled at the two steps. He loosened the reins, and Brasso lowered his head to dive into tufts of overgrown dead grass.

"Miranda, we'll need to do a neck dismount. I'll kick out of the stirrup and lift my right leg over Brasso's neck, I need you to lift your right leg at the same time. We'll be sitting side-saddle for a moment before I hold you against me to slide off together."

"I jumped off that way a lot as a kid."

"On three." Grant counted, and eased them both off the saddle. "Stay put Brasso, you did good."

"Me, too," she muttered.

"Now the tougher part—climbing a couple stairs in tandem. I'm going to throw the blanket over my shoulder to cover the front of the duster. After I unbutton the top, turn around and wrap your good arm around my neck and your legs around my waist. I'll carry you inside. Okay?"

"Sure, whatever."

His heart pounded while he adjusted the blanket and clasped his hands together under her butt. "You're still covered."

"With your hands." She grabbed his neck and held tight while he took the first step.

The back door creaked open.

Miranda viced her legs tighter around his waist.

"It's Doc. We're almost inside," he assured her, and took the next step onto the landing.

Kyle stood in the doorway to the mudroom, then stepped inside.

Grant put his finger to his lips.

When they passed by, Kyle raised his eyebrows. "Clever way to cover your witness," he whispered. "I observed you riding alone and wondered."

"Needed to hide her." Grant kicked the door shut behind him. "Throw on the deadbolt." He took a few steps inside, tugged off the bandanna and tossed the blanket. "You can drop your feet, Miranda. We're safe."

She stood facing him, her breath pulsing against his throat.

Kyle locked the door. "You're grimier than when we go camping." He wore pressed Dockers and a white dress shirt.

"I've been busy." Grant rubbed his bristly chin. Damn. When he warmed up, he'd stink worse than a bum. Unlike the smiling doctor who'd always portrayed the trustable boy-next-door image.

"Hey, relax." Kyle said. "You sutured her, didn't you?" His eyes flashed alarm. "Does she have a fever, redness around her stitches?"

"Hope not. I've done my best." Grant kicked his heavy, beetle-shaped boot jack out of their path.

Once the trial finished, Kyle'd be perfect for a fragile woman like Miranda.

Not going to happen.

~ ~ ~

Miranda struggled to turn around, pinned by tough fabric and Grant's solid chest—hunted by Venom, now caged by Grant. "Can I get out now?"

"My back door has a window." Grant shuffled them forward a few steps, holding his hands at her waist. He stopped and undid the remaining buttons.

Her eyes blinked.

They stood in a narrow room. A closet took up one wall and a row of pegs holding keys dotted the other.

Directly in front of her, a McSteamy hunk's piercing cobalt eyes traveled from her head to her worn boots. He smiled and brushed back a hank of blond hair.

Grant rested his hand on her shoulder. "Miss Miranda Whitley, please allow me to introduce to you the illustrious, I mean industrious, old Doc, I mean Dr. Kyle Werner."

Nothing old in sight. Dr. Werner resembled a beachcomber transported to the middle of frozen Montana. She met his eyes. "Thank you for driving out here in this storm."

"You must be an out of towner, Miss Whitley. This dusting's a mere preview before the snow hits. Let's get you beside the fireplace in the living room." He glanced at Grant. "No blinds to drop."

Grant's hand moved to support her elbow. "Shades get dusty. I had a window coating put on last year to keep sun out that John recommended. It's mirrored from outside."

She stepped away from him.

Furniture inlaid with dark and light shades of wood harmonized with an open-beamed great room off the entry. Stones of different colors and textures surrounded a fireplace on one end.

She stopped and stared. Fireplace right, kitchen left, unobstructed living room and dining area in between with a stairway alongside a wall.

The perfect layout for a log house. She brought her fingers to her lips and whispered, "So beautiful."

Nothing blocked a spectacular view on either side. A pond lay in the foreground on one side, shadowed by forest. Mt. Hanlen took center position from the opposite window.

Sunset began to cast a shadow across the mountain.

"Not fancy, but all mine for the time being," Grant stated.

Was he nuts? She could be standing inside the glossy photo of the house she kept taped on her refrigerator. Corrin called it her dream fort.

"What's the matter?" Grant tightened his hold, ready to tote her again.

A real life rendering of her photo-how could it be? Goosebumps rose on her arm. "The layout's perfect. It's common for Montana?"

"Nope. My own design."

"You design homes?"

"Nah. Sketched the idea and handed it off to an architect friend. John nailed every feature."

Her legs wobbled. "I need to sit."

Grant grabbed her arm. "Rest on my couch. I'll get the furnace on." He got her settled and draped a knitted afghan around her shoulders.

Her chills weren't from the outside temperature. "Thanks."

"Your *For Sale* sign's a ragged blight on the landscape." Kyle approached, carrying a black satchel. "You've finally brought a woman home, have you given up selling?"

No other girlfriends came here? She sunk into the couch, waiting for more info.

"Are you channeling my mother?" Grant adjusted his Glock. "That's exactly what she'd say."

"And Pat's a very wise lady," Kyle countered.

"Actually, I've been thinking I should hire a realtor. No surprise there hasn't been a single offer in nearly a year. Everyone ambitious wants to leave Emma Springs, not move in." He slapped Kyle on the back. "No offense. I should find Brasso a rider, too. If you have any clients who might take good care of my pony, let me know. Dad's getting too old to exercise him."

Kyle's shoulders slumped. "Yeah, you haven't been here much. I put your requested grain and bales of hay in the barn."

"You're the best, bro," Grant said.

"No job would make me sell this home," she stated and tugged off a boot.

"He's never dreamed of leaping sheep," Kyle said. "Only a brass plate with SAC engraved beside his name."

"My house shouldn't sit empty. Times change." Grant picked up her ankle and removed her remaining boot. "Please, put your feet up. I'll feed the horses while Doc checks out my hatchet job." He turned to Kyle. "I used sterilized instruments. Infection concerns me, too."

Kyle shooed him out. "The doctor's on duty." He gave Miranda a kindly smile.

"Grant's got family here, friends, and this house. And he wants to sell?" She yanked her arm out of the loose sweater.

"Here, let me help." Kyle bent over her and maneuvered the bulky garment off her head. "We all have different aspirations."

Grant's scent released while she adjusted his T-shirt to expose her injury. "Yeah. How far's Emma Springs?"

"Under five miles. I work out of a home office and attached clinic located in the center of town."

"I bet it's a beautiful place to live."

"It suits me perfectly." He opened his case and tugged on gloves. "You've acquired a classic FBI field bandage, Miss Whitley."

"Not by choice. Please call me Miranda, Dr. Werner."

"Fair enough. My friends call me Kyle." He gently lifted the edges of the tape and removed the bandage. "I understand a stray bullet caught you near Crystal Ridge."

"Uh-huh."

He pressed each stitch. "I planned to become an agent until reading the FBI's use of force manual. I opted to study medicine. Once a year we play poker, and I hear his stories."

"I bet those are exciting."

"Depends on your perspective." He dabbed antiseptic on her wound before securing a fresh bandage. "You're healing properly, and the pain should continue to decrease. I need to examine the bump on your head."

"I could use a head exam." She pulled her shirt down. "How much did he tell you about me?"

"Mentioned you witnessed a botched murder attempt and fled for your life." His fingers barely touched her forehead.

"Abbreviated, but accurate. You must be good friends."

"Closer than most brothers. Let's check those pupils with my scope." He pulled a slim case from his bag. "You must've cut through a fair amount of forest on your mule. The Lazy K's on the other side of Sunrise Lake."

"Red bolted after the shot, and I held on. Those magnificent mule ears heard Grant." She bowed her head. "I shouldn't have brought my trouble to Grant and Emma Springs."

"We do what's best at the time." He lifted her chin and shone a pin-point of light into each of her eyes. "So you enjoy horses?"

"I never grew out of being a pony girl. I'd love to have the freedom to ride through meadows and mountains."

"If only Grant felt the same. I always assumed he did." He shut off the light.

If only Grant had been a school teacher or a handy man. If only her life hadn't been shattered by violence. If only her plans didn't include baby carriages and his an FBI career ladder.

If only would equal lonely in this scenario, unless she reshaped her dreams. Could she?

~ ~ ~

Grant returned from the barn, washed up, and began dusting dinner plates he'd left in the drying rack months ago. Miranda spoke his name, her tone anxious. He stepped to the edge of the kitchen and strained to hear the reason.

"I never should've come here," she repeated to Kyle. "I brought a horrible killer to your town."

Her regret struck him worse than a blow. How could she feel guilty getting help from a trained agent? Normal witnesses wanted one thing, for him to save their lives. Miranda Whitley wasn't normal in any way, shape, or form.

Had an infection made her bewildered? He clenched the dishtowel. "Is she okay, Doc? Do we need to get her to Mercy Hospital tonight?" he called from the kitchen.

"Nope. She's got little more than a flesh wound. Your stitches come out in four or five days."

"Her forehead bump a concern?"

"No signs of a concussion." Kyle continued to engage Miranda in conversation using his patient-soothing voice.

Grant walked in and tucked a pillow behind her. "Slide into the corner and lean back. I'll see what Mom stashed in my freezer for dinner."

He walked to the kitchen window. He'd missed his chance to immobilize Venom—could she be doubting his capabilities to protect her?

He turned in time to see Kyle place supplies back in his satchel and snap it shut. "I bet your family's worried sick." He remained sitting at the other end of the couch.

"They're gone."

"Out of the country?" Kyle asked.

"Murdered in a drive-by shooting five years ago," she said.

Grant's stomach lurched. How could she possibly be responsible? Sam had researched her family's murder. The brutal scene had made headlines, but there was nothing regarding the grieving, orphaned daughter.

"Oh, my sincerest sympathy." Kyle said. "Were you there?"

"No. Jacob, a guy I'd broken up with, drove my parents and little brother to surprise me at college on my birthday."

Grant stepped closer, then stopped.

"So they never made it to see you?" Kyle folded his hands in his lap, his body still.

"We had a nice visit." Her face tightened with pain. "Before they left, Dad mentioned he'd prefer to ride the train home."

"Did they?" Kyle gently probed.

She pinched her nose. "I talked him out of it."

"The shooting happened on the ride home?"

She stared into the fire. "Yes. An attack by gang members after Jacob pulled off the highway."

Grant gripped the doorframe. *Poor Miranda.*

"Random violence," Kyle said.

"No," Miranda stated. "The police considered it mistaken identity by the killers. I don't buy it. Jacob had started hanging with creeps."

"How horrible." Kyle shook his head.

She put her head in her hands. "Thirty-one bullets and they murdered everyone I loved. Because of me."

Grant's mouth fell open. Not untypical for family members to blame themselves and not the damn perps. He stared at the freezer, stocked with Mom's meals. How would you handle the guilt of thinking you'd killed your family?

By shutting down and attempting invisibility, her exact M-O in the Justice Building. He thrust his fingers between two frozen packages, tossed one in the microwave, and punched reheat with his fist.

"I can't imagine your pain." Kyle managed a comforting tone. He touched her hand. "I hope you realize they made choices, too."

Good response, bro. Grant kept still.

"No one can understand." She wiped tears from her eyes. "I'm sorry, I shouldn't burden you with my history."

"An important part of grieving is sharing your feelings.

I have a sense of your loss. My mom passed away from a curable illness, if only I'd diagnosed it earlier."

Grant grabbed the counter. Kyle shouldn't carry guilt from his mother's death.

"Oh, no," she whispered.

Kyle's chin dipped to his chest. "I'd recommended she go into Billings where they had better equipment for tests, but she put me and my dad off." He turned toward her, his eyes moist. "I insisted too late."

Not your fault, Kyle. Grant stared at his feet. Damn, he should've been there.

"I'm sorry," Miranda said. "So many should haves."

"Are you close to any other relatives?"

"No," she said flatly. "Lonely's a dictionary word until you live it. Cherish your father."

"I do treasure Dad." Kyle handed her a business card. "Call me anytime you need to talk."

The timer dinged. Grant blinked. Had he offered the same willingness to listen to her? He punched the reheat button.

Kyle never voiced shouldering the blame of his mother's death. Damn, maybe he'd missed subtle hints. So, so sorry, bro. He stared at the microwave's rotating glass tray.

His parents were a phone call away or a long car ride if he needed their company. He ate and slept alone by choice.

Miranda had no one.

He lifted a handmade potholder from his mother. Women created perfect nests for their kids, even adult ones. He rubbed his neck.

His career path would involve many moves, likely crisscrossing the country. Too tough for nest building?

"Your mom's cooking is worth a trip out here," Kyle called to Grant. "Need help?"

"You deserve a break." Grant entered the living room. "Mom's famous Wagyu stroganoff is on our menu tonight."

"I appreciate eating here," Kyle said. "I'll have delivered a baby by tomorrow, if my prediction's right. The mother wants a home birth."

"Never understood the fascination about babies. They cry and stink." Grant smiled at Miranda.

Her eyes blinked with incredulity.

Hadn't she recognized a joke? "Just kidding."

"When you hold your own little bundle, your tune will change," Kyle said.

Miranda nodded.

"You play the lullaby song first, Doc, and I'll see how it works out." *Big-mouthed idiot.* He returned to the kitchen, jammed three slices of frozen bread into the toaster, and set the table.

He set out dinner and approached the couch. Miranda's eyes held a sorrowful look when she declined the arm he offered her. His chest tightened. "Okay, make your way to the table for your first real Morley dinner."

She carefully slid into a chair and spooned a tiny bite of noodles and mushrooms. "I'm pretty full." She put down her fork. "Thanks for dinner."

"Take your time Miranda, you need to eat more. Right, Doc?"

"Correct," Kyle agreed. "Your body needs sustenance to heal that wound."

"Doc's patient care is his life, 24/7." Grant fidgeted in his chair. "He's memorized every vital statistic of the populace living within a fifty-mile radius of Emma Springs."

Kyle's eyes widened, then flicked from Grant to Miranda. He sat back. "Interesting comment coming from the guy who knows the muzzle velocity of each gun in his prized Winchester collection."

"Hey—my weapon knowledge has saved many lives." He slathered butter on a piece of wheat bread. "Dip this in gravy, and eat at least four more bites of meat."

"I prefer mushrooms, and I'm not your toddler," Miranda declared.

"Nope." He smiled. "You're my responsibility. Four bites and we'll talk full." He placed the bread on her plate and caught his mouth opening while she lifted a forkful to her pouty, oh-so-kissable, lips.

She ate half the bowl, then her hand struggled to hold her water glass.

He pushed his plate away. "Let's get you to your bedroom. Want a bath first?" He pulled out her chair and helped her to her feet, squelching mental images of Miranda surrounded by bubbles.

Clear, bursting bubbles.

~ ~ ~

No way would she risk falling asleep in the bathtub. Miranda choked on a spurt of psycho laughter at how bedraggled she must appear and smell. Maybe stinky like a toddler in Grant's mind.

A dull, empty ache gnawed at her soul. "I'll shower first thing tomorrow. Promise."

"Your choice," Grant said.

"I bet your host can find you something better than an old T-shirt to wear while I clean the kitchen." Kyle grinned.

Color rose from under Grant's collar. "I've ah, got pajamas which shrank in the wash." He bent toward her.

"I'm not an invalid." She stalked off. Half-way to the stairway landing, her toe caught the edge of a rag rug, flinging her forward.

Grant caught her wrist and rocked her into his arms in one effortless motion. "Nice try." He carried her to the stairs. "Your body's spent after the uncomfortable ride. Kyle will boot me if you hit the floor."

"I tripped. Put me down. He'll think I'm faking to get your attention." Words tumbled out.

"You've got my attention, and I don't care what Doc thinks. I do care if your pride prevents healing." He eased onto each step, as if she'd break from a sudden movement.

She rested her head against his solid torso, absorbing his heartbeats and the last fleeting moments spent intimately with her hero. After the trial, they'd part ways, and their shared time together would fade to memories, unless one of them convinced the other to compromise. "After I'm better, you'll see I'm no shrinking violet."

"Hadn't crossed my mind." He pulled her closer while fumbling for a hallway light switch. "I'm holding you to the promise of dinner and maybe dessert after the tool comment you threw at me."

Her pulse jumped. "I didn't know you'd be so sensitive about owning a rolling pin. I offered coffee."

"Coffee follows a meal." His breath quickened. "Served with dessert."

Chapter 10

Grant slowed his ragged breathing. He stopped inside his guest bedroom and gently set Miranda down. "Here you go." He turned on the light. "Bathroom's next door, I'll find those pj's and hang them on the handle. Leave your clothes outside, and I'll throw a load in the washer."

"You've done enough." She looked down, her lashes dark against pale skin. "Please don't worry about my clothes."

"No trouble. And listen, you made the right choice coming to me for help. With your testimony, we'll lock up Maneski and Venom."

A frown creased her brow. "I know." A yawn brought her lips close to his.

He backed into the hall. "I'll fix a good old Montana cowboy breakfast in the morning."

She nodded, her hair tousled and her eyes sleepy. "Guess I'll wash a layer of dust off my face." She headed to the bathroom while he gathered the pajamas.

He hung them outside and knocked. "Laundry service."

"Thanks again. Good night," she called through the bathroom door.

"Night." Miranda would soon be asleep. Alone and safe. He checked the locks before he moved to the living room.

Kyle eyed him. "I'd bet you'd welcome a Scotch, and I won't let you drink alone. Bad habit. Make mine a soda and I'll keep you company."

Grant pulled a can of cola from the shelf and the Johnnie Walker bottle from the cupboard. "Notice any strange cars in your wanderings to patch and prescribe the locals?" He threw in ice and poured the drinks.

"Nope, the town's quiet today. I did notice you locking the place up Seattle style."

"I winged a guy skulking around the cabin. Could be her assailant." Grant sank onto the couch. "Please check bullet wounds within a hundred-mile radius. Upper leg."

"I'll access records from my home computer." Kyle fingered the ridges in his cut-glass tumbler. "Miranda's special. She's the kind of woman who'd keep a man on his toes until he drew his last breath, and then she'd kiss him to revive him for another round."

Grant nodded. "Yeah. She would. And much more." He turned to face Kyle. "Hey, I'm really sorry I wasn't more supportive when your mom died."

"I knew you were there if I needed you."

"I appreciate how you got Miranda to talk about her family. I guess my witness-grilling skills scared her."

Kyle cleared his throat. "You used to be the one in school kids spilled their guts to."

Grant stared into the fire. "My consoling techniques are rusty. Miranda had only turned twenty the day her family died. She breaks out in a cold sweat if she sees my gun." He took a long swig of amber liquid.

"I read where the FBI charged Maneski with a list of white-collar crimes. Maybe you won't need her testimony."

"Maneski's been nicknamed 'The Butcher' for the way he chops his victims and takes one body part. He's trying to one-up his old man, the most brutal crime lord in Seattle's history." Liquor burned a path down Grant's throat.

"Well hell. Didn't know the grisly details."

"On the stand, she'll face Venom first." The Scotch was having no impact on his taut nerves. "We'll need her for both trials. She saw him holding the gun and heard his reference to Maneski."

"Viewing photos at the trial will be a trigger to her."

Grant took another swig. "It gets worse. Maneski's goons stormed the judge's hospital room and shot my partner, Bo. Protecting her scares the hell out of me."

"With reason." Kyle straightened. "You've become close to her."

He raised his chin. "They're sending sharp shooters to our mountain. They don't realize I have her, or we'd be dead."

"She was followed to the ranch, and hunted on the mountain. Insider help?" Kyle's voice was no longer in comfort-a-patient mode.

"Yeah, quite a coincidence." His fist clenched. "Sam's worried more crooked cops are involved."

Kyle downed his soda and stood. "You're chugging Scotch, and I heard you speak the word scared. So, my old friend, is the crack in your steel demeanor due to protecting a witness, or finding your perfect woman?"

"I'm tired, not cracking, and it's a heck of a time to question my alcohol consumption or my love life. Your point?"

"I'm considering what's best for the patient. Miranda might be safer in town, staying at my clinic."

Grant squeezed his glass until he identified the indents carved into the pineapple pattern.

The fire crackled.

He reined in the urge to shout his response and pushed up from the couch. "Won't risk moving her tonight unless it's a medical necessity. My guest bedroom's safer than yours. I've got motion lights, and my Glock. You're unarmed."

Kyle slapped his back. "I sense unnecessary irritability in those words."

"Quit the psychoanalyzing. And quit grinning."

"Bro, I've been ready for years for a woman to look at me the way she looks at you." He lifted his black satchel.

"You taught me outdoors survival. I'm returning the favor. I treat married couples in my practice. Miranda strikes me as the life partner my best friend deserves. Don't screw it up. See if she has a single girlfriend for me."

A shred of hope grew in Grant's tight chest. He sheepishly grinned. "She's got one who's a legal eagle. Ripped me a new one on the phone."

"I can handle attorneys." Kyle stepped beside him and wrinkled his nose. "Appears horses, or mules, work well for bait. Maybe I should borrow your Mustang convertible to scout for my dream woman."

"Yeah, smartass." Grant's muscles relaxed. "Anytime. Take the car now and freeze the smile off your face." He pretended to flick a speck from Kyle's coat. "Wouldn't want to dirty those doctor duds on a live horse."

"I'd bet Miranda's glad you ride."

"We'll see." Grant grinned. "Hey. I owe you for opening my house and checking out her injury."

"You'll never owe me. But you can bank on there being a snowstorm if I'm going to be delivering a baby tonight."

"I hope not." Grant stepped into the mudroom and tossed a set of keys from the pegs to Kyle. "Seriously, bro. Take the Mustang any time. I won't be back soon."

"Sorry to hear that. Miranda was, too. I should head out."

"Be careful. Killers are lurking out there somewhere." Grant eased open the door. Frosty air filled the room. "I smell a snowstorm's crisp dampness."

"You always predicted storms," Kyle said.

"Drive safe. And if you see any unfamiliar cars, text me."

"Drive safe? For five minutes?" Kyle tilted his head, studying him. "Take a breath. You'll protect Miranda. It's what you do best."

"Until I fell under her spell. Thanks again."

"Anytime." Kyle waved and left in his Jeep.

Grant threw on the dead bolt and followed the taillights out. What had him on edge? His reaction to Kyle hinting at interest in Miranda? Maybe. They'd never competed for a woman in college. And he'd never brought a girlfriend to Montana. None would've fit in.

Until now.

He dimmed the kitchen lights and walked to the sink, where the window offered a view of the woods.

At the far corner, the motion-activated floodlight flashed on.

His heart pounded. He unholstered his gun and peered out from each window in the house.

No branches stirred. Fluffy flakes meandered to the ground.

A Swift fox dashed toward the barn, its black-tipped tail dancing between snowflakes.

The light flicked off.

He made one more round, then tread lightly upstairs and twisted Miranda's doorknob.

Waning moonlight illuminated her serene face.

She'd piled her clothes outside the door. He pulled them to his chest, and inhaled a faint scent of lavender.

His mom insisted they all needed the plants by their back doors to keep bugs away.

No repellant worked on hitmen.

~ ~ ~

Three loud knocks jolted Miranda awake.

"Twenty minutes for a shower." Grant's voice boomed through the bedroom door. "New plans."

"Yes, sir," she yelled back and stretched. Her muscles ached a reminder of the events of the last few days.

Sunlight blazed through panes of glass near the ceiling.

Clean clothes sat in a pile inside the door. Bonus scout

badges went to Grant for cooking over an open fire and handling the laundry.

She wrinkled her nose and hustled into the bathroom. The warm water pounded her back to life. She toweled off, braided her damp hair, and pulled on jeans. No gravy stain remained on the fisherman knit sweater.

Wearing his T-shirt last night under the pajamas had been a comfort. She rubbed her palm across the soft cotton, then placed it on the dresser next to a framed photograph.

Three people posed in front of a Christmas tree. A man with Grant's square jaw and broad shoulders stood on one side of an older woman, a younger Grant stood on her other side. *His Dad and Mom?* Both men had their arms outstretched, wearing sweaters like the one she'd borrowed. The cuffs on Grant's came to his forearms, while his dad's fingers were covered. The woman wore a huge grin and a look of undisputed love.

And he planned to sell his home. Miranda jerked open the bedroom door.

Which way was his parent's place? From the top of the stairs, a panoramic view of the countryside stretched endlessly. The ice-rimmed lake bordered a pasture, with Mt. Hanlen in the distance. A sight more beautiful than she'd ever imagined, and she'd imagined a lot.

She looked down. Each wooden stair tread contained tiger stripes or burls created by nature's paintbrush. How could he sell such a treasure so close to his family?

Grant's voice drifted from the dining room. She padded down to the landing. He faced the mountain, his fingers gripping his cell phone.

"Look, Mom, Miranda's description of the detective at the scene doesn't jive," Grant stated. "I can't confirm her story until we get tests back."

Really? Miranda clutched the railing, her jaw clamped tight.

He swung a set of car keys. "I gotta go. I'll keep you and dad posted. Say what? Who's at your door? Mom!" he shouted.

Tires crunched on gravel from Grant's driveway.

He turned toward the other window, spotted her, and grabbed her arm. "You're going in hiding." He pulled her to the mudroom closet.

"What's going on?"

"Something happened at my folks' house."

He yanked open the door. A rusty rat trap hung on a hook at the back wall. A clump of fur stuck to the hammer bar.

"Eww," she said.

"Quiet!" he hissed. He shoved it aside and pressed his finger into a round fissure. The door swung inward.

A window shattered in the front of the house.

"Was that Venom's black sedan?"

"Don't move until I tell you." His face turned deadly pale.

"What about you?"

He pushed her in. "I'll be fine."

The door shut behind her. A low light illuminated a space the size of a small bathroom.

Three walls contained mounted, long-barreled rifles. Most gleamed, and all had labels like the paintings in a museum.

She spun around, facing the door. A monitor on the lock showed nine o'clock.

Her eyes rested on a tag marked, "Winchester" hanging by a thinner gun. She leaned closer and read, "Martially Marked First Model Henry Rifle with Civil War Provenance." She stepped to the next one labeled, "Winchester 1876 Northwest Mounted Police SRC." A shadow box hung beside it, containing handcuffs and several medals. The one closest to the door appeared brand new. "Winchester 1895 SRC chambered in 30-06." Same handwriting. Grant's?

She plopped onto the floor facing the monitor, and watched ninety minutes tick by. Sweat formed on her brow. The muzzle of a gun featuring Annie Oakley engraved on the stock caught her eye.

What would Annie do? She rubbed her temples.

Annie would venture out. Her finger trembled as she pulled the latch and cracked the door.

Voices. Nearby.

Blood thrummed in her ears. She slipped into the narrow outer closet, maneuvering her shoulders to avoid the rat trap. An empty hook caught her sweater sleeve.

The hidden door swung shut from behind.

Pitch black surrounded her.

"I can do this all night, Morley." Venom taunted.

Miranda's hand bumped a broom handle.

She grabbed it, her nails sinking into wood.

"Where is she?" he shouted.

"I told you," Grant said. "I found a mule. No rider. He's in the barn."

"I don't tolerate liars, Mr. Big Shot Agent." Venom's voice faded as he moved away.

Grant muttered something.

"You'll cooperate," Venom said from nearby.

Miranda swallowed hard, then put her ear against the door.

"Your ma and pa won't—"

She couldn't hear the rest. The space closed in on her, dark and airless.

"One of you stays on watch at the upstairs window!" Venom yelled. "Skankster, get outside and feed the animals. Give them water."

"Yeah, boss," said hoarse male voices from inches away.

She flattened herself to the back wall.

"The plant girl's one thing. Wastin' the geezers and him's another," whispered a whiny voice.

Something bumped her door. Would they search for a coat? She clenched the broom.

"Rather be chillin' in the cabin by the creek watchin' the geezers," the first one grunted.

She held her breath as steps receded.

"Swap in four hours!" Venom hollered. "Move it."

A door slammed shut, and her foot jerked into a dustpan. She froze.

Dull thumps came from farther away, each followed by a groan.

"How's it sitting, Morley? Tell me or the old folks get the same," Venom challenged.

Waves of nausea roiled in her stomach.

She cracked open the door to scan the mudroom.

No keys. No one in the kitchen.

Through the window in the back door, Grant's barn stood out against swirling white.

She slipped outside and crept alongside the wall to the back corner of the house. A cold breeze hit her cheeks.

The barn sat fifty feet away, not visible from the living room.

She took off.

"Don't want a bath, huh?" A growling male voice came from the open barn door.

Water splashed onto wood.

She swerved to the corner, crept to the door, and peered in.

"Let's see you kick at me again." A big man poked a pitchfork at Red, trapped in a stall. "You ugly bugger, I'll give you a reason to squawk."

The creep jabbed, and Red dodged sideways.

Red bugled a panicked bray.

Fury boiled inside her, igniting to rage.

Tools hung inside the door.

She grabbed a shovel and swung at the lowlife's head.

The blow thumped with the hollow sound of a fist striking a ripe watermelon.

"Uggh." He dropped to his knees and glared at her. "Bitch." His body crumpled to the ground.

"You're hitting," she whacked him in the chest using the flat side of the shovel, "a defenseless animal, asshole."

He rolled into fetal position.

"You'll wish you were dead by the time I'm done." She struck three more blows to his shoulders while his groans grew weaker.

Her arm shook.

She staggered to the door of Red's stall. "It's okay now."

Binder twine dangled from the latch.

She hog-tied the guy's legs and arms behind him and tightened the twine.

"You're lucky I'm injured." She shoved a dirty rag in his mouth and kicked his limp body to roll it away from the stall.

Red's front legs shuddered.

"Good boy." She stepped to him and skimmed her fingers over both sides of his sweaty body. "He better not have wounded you."

No blood.

She leaned against his neck. "We've got to find a cop, or Doc Kyle."

The mule nuzzled her shoulder.

She looked at the heavy Western saddles, and then lifted the sweater to expose her throbbing side.

Dark red stained the white bandage.

"Crap, Red. I must've busted a stitch." She removed the sheepskin-lined cinch from the nearby saddle and wrapped it around her torso, then fastened it with twine.

Her eyes darted from the thug to the empty stalls. A pile of dirty straw blocked the one closest to the outside door.

She bridled Red, looped a rope around his chest, and tied

the end to the creep. "Okay, Red. Drag him a little further to the end."

A few pitchforks of manure later, and she'd buried him. "How's it feel to be helpless?" She kicked the last lump of dung near his nose.

"Somehow, we'll find Emma Springs." She eased the back door open and positioned a bucket to stand on.

The tree line and freedom sat fifty yards from the rear of the barn.

She climbed on. The reins shook in her hands.

Warmth radiated from Red as she pressed her calves into his sides and leaned forward. "Go home."

Red's ears twitched back and forth.

She steered him out of the barn and gave him free rein. "Home, Red. Oats."

The big mule gathered into a lope, and moved them through the open area, skirting the edge of Grant's pond.

Snowflakes pelted her face.

Red slowed to enter the woods and she turned to look back.

Light shone from Grant's living room. Would she see him alive again?

A tear rolled down her cold cheek. "Walk on."

Red wound between trees, his hooves plodding on soft leaves. Light shone through a gap in the tree line ahead.

Hope touched her heart. She patted his shoulder. "A road. You did it."

They set off, his canter rhythmic while he carried her alongside the highway.

Snow stuck to her eyelashes. Her fingers went numb. She leaned forward. "Faster, Red," she urged.

He galloped up a hill. In the distance, cars moved through a town on the edge of a lake.

Relief shot through her. "Emma Springs. Good job."

They trotted through a four-way stop, toward a row of old wooden storefronts. "We need Kyle's Jeep or a police car."

But where? No officers in sight. She slowed Red to a walk, scanning a cul de sac.

Nobody.

In the next block, a sign swung in front of a white Craftsman style home. "Dr. Kyle Werner, M.D. Family Practice"

"Whoa." They stopped at the sidewalk. "You're my miracle mule."

Big Red's sides heaved while he puffed clouds of cold air.

She grabbed his mane and slid off, then trudged up Kyle's porch steps.

Two knocks, no answer.

She huffed on her red fingers and rapped again.

Kyle threw open the door. "Miranda, what're you doing here?" He rubbed a towel across wet hair and peered over her shoulder. "You rode the mule?"

"Grant's being held at his house by the killers. I think they kidnapped his folks. I need help—they'll kill them all." Everything went dark. She grabbed the door. "Red ran here. He needs cooling."

His hand shot around her waist. "Okay, let's get you inside, and I'll call for help."

"Give me a blanket for Red."

Kyle pulled out his cell. "I'll cover Red if you come inside. Right now. The temperature's dropped, and you've got to be frozen without a coat." He propelled her to a chair by his fireplace. "I've got the number for a colleague of Grant's who's in the bureau. Stay put."

"There's got to be a Sheriff or State Patrol nearby. If you wait, they'll all die because of me."

Kyle pushed his arm into his coat. "No, they won't. Sit." He stepped outside.

She turned to the picture window.

Kyle spoke into his cell while draping Red in a Navajo blanket. He led him off.

His gas fireplace threw off muted flames. Her fingers covered her heart, and she pressed into the knitted stitches Grant's mom must have created. A tremor shook her body.

Kyle returned and stood by the fire, flexing his fingers. "I spoke to Jesse, head of an HRT. They'll arrive in a couple hours."

"That's too long. What's an HRT?"

"Hostage rescue team. Extraction involving professional hit-men requires FBI experts. Did you hear plans or a time line?" He perched on a nearby chair.

She shoved her shaking hands under her thighs. "His parents are being held somewhere else. Venom mentioned offing the geezers if Grant didn't coop—" she choked back a sob.

He squeezed her shoulder. "Armed, trained professionals are enroute."

"Same as Venom." She pushed off the armrest and stood. "Maybe he'd trade me for releasing Grant and his folks."

Kyle pressed her into the chair. "Nope, you've all seen the bad guys."

"Oh."

He smoothed his damp hair. "First, we assess the situation, then formulate a plan and organize equipment and appropriate personnel."

"We'll need armed marksmen." A chilling dread of carnage weighted her chest.

"Whatever it takes. Grant mentored Jesse." Kyle put a blanket over her shoulders. "Let's plan how to transport them to Grant's house."

"Without being seen, and if we're not too late."

He timed the pulse in her neck. "You need to relax. Venom needs to find you. Remember?"

"He'll kill Grant when he realizes he won't talk. No more deaths. I can't—"

"Shh. Shh. Red's sure got good instincts." His voice slowed to soothing. "Luckily the call for my baby delivery came early. Otherwise, I'd be at their home sponging off a newborn."

"How can you raise a baby in a world erupting in violence?" She turned to Kyle. "Maybe it's just me. I'm the bad luck."

"Grant thinks otherwise. I need those brains he admires. Delivering a rescue team's our challenge."

"Right." Miranda's stomach let out a low growl. "Sorry. No breakfast while waiting in his gun locker."

"I'll get food going and check your side."

"I'm fine. Grant's the one whose life hangs by a frickin' thread."

"Take a seat in the sun room." He ushered her into a bump-out. "Sunrise Lake and Emma Springs—my favorite view."

Miranda sank into a chair.

"Trey and Kat Langley's ranch isn't far from the main road." He motioned to the right. "Red probably stomped the route all summer."

Her eyes shifted to where he pointed.

Shops began in the next block of the road she'd been on. "Emma Springs could be an ad for an enticing version of Americana, until I led killers to town."

"I'd bet you don't have these in Seattle." Kyle held out an open gray carton, exposing various sizes and colors of eggs. "From a client. She leaves the chicken poop intact to save me from salmonella. I'll wash them and scramble a batch."

"I know you're ignoring my negativity. Venom will torture the Morleys to find me." Her voice rose to an unfamiliar pitch.

"Grant's tough. You can't help me if you're running on fumes."

An ornate clock topped by merry-go-round horses chimed from a shelf over the stove.

She tapped her fingernail on a glass-topped wicker table. "That's me. Wound too tight. I'm sorry, and you're right. I need food to think straight."

"Exactly. While the pan heats, I'll check your stitches." He pulled a chair next to her. "The Craftsman across the street's my dad's. He's the town lawyer."

"My friend Corrin wants to be a lawyer. I think she gave Grant an earful when he insisted she stay away from her apartment."

"I would've paid to witness that. Not much bothers him."

"Except bringing hitmen to Emma Springs. Chalk up another deadly choice by Miranda Witless Whitley."

"Grant's glad you sought his help."

"Until it involved his parents." She lifted her sweater. "How many agents are coming?"

"Four to six. Whoa, you broke out a couple stitches." Kyle secured two butterfly bandages, then went to the kitchen. "Gotta admit, first time I've seen a girth used for a truss." He poured a cup of coffee and set it in front of her.

Outside Kyle's home stretched a calm expanse of water. At Grant's, Venom would be leaning over him the same way he'd stood over Ike.

She pinched her nose. "Four to six guys need to approach a house in the middle of a meadow."

"Not ordinary guys. SWAT trained experts. They'll breeze in."

"Doesn't the hero always die in the shootout after the posse shows up?"

"Jesse won't let that happen."

Heat from the ceramic mug didn't penetrate past her

fingers. "Grant must be tied up. Venom's a ruthless killer and has a gunman stationed in an upstairs window."

Metal clanged as a pickup rolled past the house pulling a stock trailer. Two stubby horned bulls swayed side to side.

She watched the rig until it turned a corner. "Wait. A horse trailer would hold them."

"If it wouldn't raise suspicion. They'll shoot if they smell a trap," Kyle said.

"We'll put Big Red in the back and hide the agents up front in the storage area. We can pretend we're bringing him to Grant. I'll unload Red while they climb out."

"You'd be in full view. Too dangerous." Kyle set down a plate of food.

"No one at the house spotted me, or I'd be dead." She stabbed a bite of steaming eggs.

"No can do. Grant won't forgive me if you're involved."

"That pony's left the corral." Her mouth methodically chewed and swallowed. "Look. My actions endangered Grant and his parents. Let me help rescue them. I'll wear a hat and glasses. Red trusts me." Tears wet the corners of her eyes.

"Miranda, Venom started this. Jesse may agree to utilize a horse trailer, so I'll borrow one."

He flipped through cards on an old style Rolodex. "We'll need to get Grant out of his house."

She massaged the crook in her nose. "Something broken. Or, tell Grant your tire's flat. Ask him to come out and help."

"They'd see the tire. Maybe mechanical trouble? My Jeep's always got an engine light on. That could bring him outside."

"If he can walk."

"Think positive." He sat opposite her, and dialed. "Morning, this is Doctor Werner. Can I borrow your horse trailer today?"

He gave a thumbs up. "That'd be great. Thanks." He replaced the receiver and attempted a smile. "Trailer delivery scheduled. He worried he hadn't swept out the manure."

She dropped her fork. "Kyle, I hog-tied a guy and buried him under a pile of manure in Grant's barn. If they've found him, they'll know I left."

"Let's hope they don't. I'd like to hear those details."

Not now. "I need to call my friend, Corrin."

Kyle nodded toward the phone. "Anything you need."

She punched familiar numbers. "Voice mail, wouldn't you know . . . Corrin, it's Miranda. I'm doing fine. Don't call me on Grant's phone or mine. I'll call you. Bye."

She left the same message for Shirley.

"A text came from Jesse," Kyle said. "Two sharpshooters and a squad are traveling by helicopter."

Every nerve in her body coiled into a tighter spring.

"We all need to be clear headed. Resting for a few minutes wouldn't hurt you," he said.

"There's no way I'll sleep. I need to thank Red."

"Here, borrow my coat. Gloves are in the pockets."

Miranda willed her body to quit vibrating long enough to work the zipper. "Thanks."

The rescue had to work. No one else died from another one of her stupid decisions.

This time, she'd die, too.

Chapter 11

Two buff agents dressed in pale gray camouflage marched into Kyle's living room. One took Kyle aside.

"I called Poppy, Grant's grandfather," Kyle said. "He'd driven into town, and when he came back, there were signs of a struggle at Pat and Tom Morley's house. They were gone. I alerted him you were enroute. He's former FBI."

Miranda's heart hit bottom while the agent responded to Kyle in an indistinguishable undertone.

Another man and a woman wearing camo entered the living room carrying long black cases.

She studied the group who could model the latest workout equipment, especially a ginger-haired one close to Grant's height.

The female agent had straight bangs accenting her round, baby-doll eyes. She could've passed for a kindergarten teacher until she removed a rifle from a case and deftly attached a scope.

Miranda flinched.

The tallest man stepped away from Kyle and flashed a movie star smile at Miranda. "Hi, I'm Jesse." He nodded toward the woman. "Bullseye's the one cradling her M-24 bolt action. She's normally in command, but seeing as I've been to Emma Springs, I'll be the lead."

Miranda stared at the rifle. "Venom stationed one gunman in an upstairs window."

Jesse unfolded a map. "Protocol in this type of hostage situation is to lob in a couple flash bangs and then secure Grant's house."

"Police protocol would've let Ike bleed to death," Miranda said. "They can see across the empty meadow to the road."

"Miranda had an idea," Kyle offered. "Let me show you." He outlined her suggestions to the group. "The trailer's hooked to my Jeep."

"Practice loading the mule." Jesse nodded to one of his men, who threw on a coat and headed outside. "Miranda's photo's been blasted over every law enforcement network. Karpenito would've sent her ID to Venom first thing, then maybe come here, too. Kyle, you sure you're okay to drive?"

"Anything for the Morley's," he said.

Miranda gripped her chair arm. Kyle and these agents hadn't caused this. An image of white sheets draped over the three bodies of her family flashed in her mind. No one would have to go to the morgue again because of her.

She smoothed back her hair. "If I wear a hat and bulky clothing, they won't know it's me. If Red balks for one of you and Venom suspects anything, they'll shoot your team, Kyle, and Grant."

Jesse never blinked. "We can handle the mule and the gunmen." He touched her forearm. "Grant's a lucky guy."

"Lucky? Beaten by a killer? His parents kidnapped?" She hugged her sides. "I'm responsible for all of you now, too."

"Not so. We're trained for these situations, and Grant's part of our team," Jesse said. "Your plan will save his ass."

"Nothing in life's certain, a lesson I learned the hard way. Repeatedly." She bit her lip. "The plan has to work."

"I can't get over you throwing one of them into a pile of horse crap." Jesse glanced out the window and frowned. "I won't get on your bad side."

"If they find manure man in the barn, they'll know Miranda escaped," Bullseye said. She moved closer to Jesse and looked outside. "Appears that her mule's the risk."

"What do you mean?" Miranda asked.

Bullseye pointed to the horse trailer. "No one's gotten the animal within five feet of the rear opening. Should we try a stick?"

Miranda stood up, fists clenched. "Absolutely not. I trusted Red, and he brought me here. He'll do what I ask."

Jesse checked his phone. "Run the drill using Miranda. Time's not our ally."

Miranda said a silent prayer, stepped outside, and approached Red. She took the lead rope from the agent and patted his shoulder. "In and out of the trailer, okay buddy?"

She stepped up ten inches into the rear of the trailer and he hopped in after. "Good boy." She patted him and backed him out.

Jesse stood in the open door, scowling.

"Satisfied?" Miranda asked him.

"For now," he stated. "Should catch them off guard without waving any red flags. Bullseye, try to load the mule."

"I tried earlier." Bullseye took the rope.

Red splayed his feet and wouldn't step forward.

"Not happening, boss," Bullseye said. "He only trailers for Miranda. If this is the plan, give us twenty minutes to coordinate diving out of the cargo area."

"It's the best idea. Make it fifteen," Jesse said.

Kyle offered his arm to Miranda. "You've had a challenging forty-eight hours, even without sporting a bullet wound." He escorted her inside. "Looks like you'll be Red's handler. Rest for a little bit. Please." He led her through the kitchen to a bedroom.

"Sure." She sank onto the bed.

"Is the wound painful?" Kyle slid off her boots.

"No, it's better today."

"Good to hear." He lifted her legs onto the comforter and pulled a blanket over her. "Don't worry. We'll get Grant back." He squeezed her shoulder.

"And his parents. I've never even met them, Kyle, and they're being held by killers."

"They'll be rescued." He pulled the door closed.

Murmurs of deep voices continued.

She'd landed in the middle of her worst nightmare, while unthinkable horrors unfolded as the clock ticked.

~ ~ ~

Kyle entered his typically tranquil kitchen, now command central for a SWAT team. "So many unknowns scare me worse than discovering the plague hit town," he said. The group had reunited by the table. A vibe of urgency hung in the air.

"I hear you," Jesse said. "So we're all clear—we have two critical parts of this operation—protecting Miranda, and getting Grant and his family out alive."

Bullseye leaned over the drawings. "Grant's parents must've been eliminated."

Kyle winced.

"He'll use them for leverage," Jesse countered. "Maneski's smart. Ordering a federal agent or former stater killed would be his death sentence."

Kyle stepped forward. "Pat and Tom Morley helped raise me. I refuse to believe they're dead. If they haven't been moved to Grant's, how do we find them?"

"Someone will talk." Jesse stared at the map.

Car chases, kidnappings, sharpshooters. Nothing terrible happened in Kyle's version of Emma Springs. This was a Seattle shitstorm, to use Grant's term. "I've got a wig in storage from Halloween. I'll grab it and see if it'll work to disguise Miranda," he offered.

"Good idea," Bullseye said. "We'll need to alter Miranda's appearance."

Jesse nodded. "The mule readily followed her in the trailer once, let's hope we get a repeat."

"Great," Kyle said to himself as he stomped to the garage. "Cooperation from a mule will determine if Grant lives or dies."

Chapter 12

"Get your ass down here after you checked all the places Whitley could hide!" Venom yelled from the bottom of the stairs. "Time to get serious!"

Ropes dug into Grant's wrists and ankles. Had Miranda stayed in the gun safe? And what about his folks? A cold sweat broke out on his brow. Were they tied up? Hurting?

Hostages became collateral damage.

He dropped his head and took a deep, pained breath. His chest pressed against another cord. Aching ribs took him back to grade school pummelings. Afterwards, his mom had smoothed arnica on his bruises.

And he'd not protected her from killers.

He worked his fingers against the zip ties binding his hands.

Venom limped in and waved a blue ball cap, then threw it onto the couch. "Found this on the trail below your cabin. Look familiar, Morley?"

"Nope." Grant shrugged. "I'm not into sports."

A heavy-set man plodded downstairs. "Yeah, whadda ya want, boss?"

"Apparently, Skankster can't read a text. Worthless ex-con." He jerked his thumb toward the back door. "In five I want you to take his place to watch the road from the barn."

"Lemme hit the john first," mumbled the pudgy guy.

"Who slept in your other bedroom?" Venom waved reddish-brown strands in front of Grant's nose, dropped them, and used a narrow-bladed knife to clean his fingernails.

"You'd better spill, or there'll be scalp attached when I'm through with her."

"My sister came in for a visit. She flew out last week."

"The Whitley woman Googled your parents' house. Make it easy on the old folks and tell us where she is." Venom rubbed his bandaged leg, and slid his hands into the leather gloves he'd worn during the earlier punching session.

"One of my guys is itching to hear squeals from a former State Patrol pig." Venom sneered. "I'm instructed to do whatever I need to get your cooperation." Regret shadowed his tense face before he stepped to the window.

Grant's mind reeled while he fought a wave of nausea. Agonizing minutes ticked by.

If they hurt Dad or Mom . . . He'd known Miranda had phoned their house, why hadn't he moved them?

Fidelity, bravery, integrity. Unquestionable loyalty sworn in an oath. You didn't negotiate with crooks.

Darkness enveloped Grant, seeping into his bones, choking his spirit to live. His chin sank to his chest.

"Is Maneski sitting in a cushy jail cell worth your parents' lives?" Venom pulled out his phone and swore. "Lousy reception." He walked into the kitchen. "Finally, a signal."

"Hi, darlin'," Venom crooned. "You and the little feller are on your own for a while. Don't flash the money and don't call me. I'll be in touch. Love you both."

Venom dialed again. "Hey, time to transport the geezers," he ordered. "Yeah, I can give you an address."

The clatter of metal bouncing on metal came from the driveway.

Grant sat up. A trailer chain?

"I'll text the address in a minute." Venom hobbled to the side of the window. "Don't move until I tell you!" he shouted into the phone before dropping it on the couch. He stumbled to the stairs. "Get outta the can and back to the bedroom window. Now!" he yelled.

Grant twisted his neck.

A horse trailer rolled by. A flicker of hope grew in his chest.

Venom sliced Grant's ties, nicking his skin. "Get rid of them quick, or you all die." He yanked him by his shirt collar, and kicked the chair out from under him. "Hide your face using the hood." He peeled off his own sweatshirt and threw it at him.

Grant fought the stiffness in his arms while pulling on the sleeves.

"Nothing funny," Venom said. He stood behind the door, opened it a foot, and then pushed Grant forward.

Kyle's Jeep towed the trailer another few feet and stopped.

Grant grimaced and shuffled outside.

A woman with black braids sat in the passenger seat.

The barrel of a gun jabbed his back. "Hurry up."

Her window rolled down. "Hi Grant, we appreciate using a stall in your barn for a few days," Miranda yelled out from the cab. "Do you care which one?"

"Answer them, fool," Venom hissed. "Tell them you're leaving and they need to hustle."

Grant's heart pounded. "Anywhere you put him is fine." Sweat beaded on his brow. "Can't chat. I've got an appointment."

Venom pulled him inside and shut the door. The gun jabbed his side.

"Don't move," Venom growled, and turned toward the window. "Skankster must've seen them coming."

Grant watched over his shoulder. The truck made a wide circle in the driveway and stopped with the horse trailer parked alongside the barn. The nose of the truck pointed toward the road.

Kyle walked to the back and swung open the trailer's rear door. Miranda backed Big Red out.

A knot constricted Grant's throat while he observed the perimeter.

A flash of gray material moved at the front of the horse van, then into the shadows of the barn. Had Venom seen it, too?

While Miranda led Big Red into the barn, Kyle jumped into the cab and popped the hood.

"What's the idiot doing?" Venom said. "Get them to leave." He opened the door and pushed Grant to the stoop.

"Something wrong?" Grant yelled.

"The service light blinked on," Kyle said. "Can I borrow a flashlight to check under the hood?"

Grant held his breath.

"Get the dimwit a flashlight. Probably doesn't know a wrench from a crow bar. I've got plenty of bullets and two shooters. Fix it," Venom sneered.

Grant reached into the coat closet and pulled out a black Maglite, and then lumbered on stiff legs across his driveway toward the hood of the Jeep.

Kyle covered his mouth and coughed out 'agents' from his seat fifteen feet away.

Miranda closed the trailer door and struggled with the latch.

Leave it and run! Grant wanted to scream. He slowed down and angled toward Miranda.

Ten feet remained. "Need a hand getting it closed?" he called to her.

She used her fist to pop the latch into the slot.

A long hank of reddish brown hair fell out of the wig.

Russet on white.

A window slid open on the second story.

Grant leapt forward and tackled her as a gunshot cracked. A bullet whizzed by his right ear.

They tumbled to the ground by the trailer wheel on the far side. He covered her with his body, his heart racing.

A second shot pierced the air. Broken glass scattered across the roof.

"Agents have breached the house. The inside's secured," Jesse yelled, while he ran past the trailer.

"Are either of you hit?" Kyle kneeled by Grant.

"No." Grant eased off her. "Miranda? You okay?"

Her eyes stayed shut, her body remained still.

"You probably knocked the wind out of her. Move over and let me check," Kyle said. He drew Miranda's knees to her chest.

Brittle nerves burst inside of Grant. "Please Miranda, you have to wake up." He cupped her cheek in his hands. "I hit her hard, Kyle. Too damn hard."

Miranda gulped air while her dark lashes fluttered against pale skin.

"My sweet Miranda." Grant kissed her temple.

"Grant, you're alive!" She struggled to sit up. Her eyes darted between them. "Where are your parents?"

Grant pulled her close. A brilliant light released from deep within his soul. "Thank God you're safe. We'll find them next." He pulled her to her feet.

Shouts came from his front door.

A man holding his hand against a bleeding shoulder stumped onto the porch. Bullseye pointed a gun at his chest and another armed agent followed behind. Venom limped out next while Jesse held a pistol to his back.

Two agents emerged from the barn, hoisting a trussed man. "Found your package, Miranda," one said.

After they dragged the thug by, manure fumes fouled the air.

"Venom calls him Skankster," Grant said. "Name fits."

Jesse and Bullseye held guns on Venom and his thugs while the other agents secured zip ties.

"Put them in the trailer," Jesse ordered.

Grant cupped her elbow and propelled her toward his house. "Check to see Miranda's okay, Kyle."

"Will do." Kyle stopped at the front door. "Galloping a mule in a snowstorm, planning your escape, and getting flattened by you doesn't fit into my instructions for her to rest for a few days."

"I'll try harder." Grant stepped aside for Kyle and Miranda to go inside. "Thanks, team." He yelled to the agents. "I'm assuming the window shot belonged to Bullseye?"

"You guessed it, boss." Jesse said. "You've got a couple of smart friends, including a four-legged one." He waved at the Montana Highway Patrol car speeding down the driveway. "Next, we find your parents."

"Good plan." Grant nodded approval and headed indoors.

"Miranda's unharmed and on the couch." Kyle patted Grant's back as he passed him. "Everyone's going to be okay. I'll check the bullet wound on the creep outside."

"Thanks again, Kyle." Grant knelt by Miranda.

"Your folks, we have to find them." She brushed her finger over Grant's bruises. A tear splashed onto her cheek.

"Don't worry," he thumbed off the dampness.

Jesse strode inside. "I've got Kyle's maps. Bullseye's managing local LEO's. Squad, reassemble in the kitchen, please."

"Be there in a second," Grant said. "Don't bring in any more local officers until I talk to you, and don't answer Venom's phone on the couch."

Grant lifted her hand, and brushed his lips across her cool skin. "We'll find my parents."

Her eyes pleaded for reassurance. "They have to be alive."

Scripted words of comfort wouldn't come. Damn his boss for not divulging why he'd ordered them to overnight in

Emma Springs. He should've questioned Sam for more intel. He brushed moisture from his own eyes. "I believe they're alive."

"Go." She squeezed his hand.

"Now, I can."

Urgency burned in his belly. He entered his kitchen and stood opposite Jesse. "Maneski's pushing hard to kill Miranda. Venom ordered the thugs holding my parents to sit tight until he texted them my address. He would've tortured them in front of me."

"Should we text a reply with the address?" asked a younger agent.

"No." Jesse said. "Patrol cars would scare them off. Where would they be holding your parents?"

Miranda came to the doorway. "They mentioned a cabin on the creek."

"A creek narrows the search." Grant grabbed the waist of her sweater and pulled her close. He leaned in to kiss her, then pulled back.

"Venom's phone's rung twice," the young agent announced.

Kyle strode to the kitchen sink, peeled off bloody gloves, and washed his hands. "Can you trace the call?"

"Not on short notice." Jesse smoothed a map onto the table. "Let's get searching."

Grant pulled several old phone books from a drawer and started to thumb through the pages. "We'll contact rental agencies that lease cabins."

"There's very few around here, Grant," Kyle said.

An image flashed of his mom's anxious face. He'd been worried about Miranda, and she'd survived. His world would turn to dust if he lost Mom and Dad. "Call the realtors in Three Falls listed under vacation rentals."

"On it," an agent said.

Grant smoothed out Kyle's tattered USGS map of the local area lying on his table. "My grandpa dragged me around to check on elderly neighbors. I remember cabins on Spruce Creek and on the river near Elk Drive." He pointed to squiggles on the map.

An agent replaced the handset and then handed a paper to Grant. "We've got addresses of three recently rented out vacation houses. One's on a private road, Spruce Creek Lane."

Grant marked the map, and eyed his watch. His gut tightened. "They won't wait forever for an address from Venom."

Jesse nodded. "Grant, you can get to Spruce Creek the fastest. Two of us will hit Elk Drive. Kyle, I'll text Bullseye that she's needed to accompany you to the other address."

"I'll load the house number onto my phone and then unhitch the trailer," Kyle said.

"We'll leave an agent and Miranda here in case any other calls come in."

"Stay here?" Miranda's eyes darted between Grant and Jesse.

If he'd been thinking straight, he'd have ignored Sam and gotten Miranda far away from Emma Springs. *Braindead times ten.* "There could be a shootout," Grant explained. "You're safer here." He turned to the others." Jesse drives my Mustang, I'll drive the Suburban."

From the doorway, Kyle threw the set of Mustang keys to Jesse.

Grant watched them fly through the air. He'd felt so cool after he'd bought it and driven straight to Mom and Dad's.

Would he ever see their smiles again?

Chapter 13

Miranda clutched the map, pressing her finger on Spruce Creek Lane. "Why'd Jesse decide to let me join the search?"

"The only thing that matters now is finding my parents," Grant stated.

"Right." She said a silent prayer, and then compared another hand-lettered street sign to the roads on the map. "Turn left at the diner ahead," she instructed.

The Suburban rounded the corner and sped past the Creekside Café and U-Fill-It gas station.

"Take a right on Parker Drive, and another right on Spruce Creek Lane. The cabin's a quarter mile off the road, near as I can tell."

"I came out here as a kid," Grant said. "We're close."

He downshifted and swung onto Parker Drive.

A creek flowed alongside the gravel road. Snow drifts made for a peaceful scene.

Grant's stiff posture and the knot in her belly didn't.

She pointed at a sign nailed to a tree. Rusted bullet holes pockmarked faint lettering. "There's Spruce Creek Lane."

A single set of tire tracks led past the sign.

"A car's driven in recently," she exclaimed.

He shifted into four-wheel drive and crept down the narrow lane.

Nervous energy shot through her body.

They crested a hill and the vehicle pitched to a stop. In a meadow below sat a weathered cabin alongside the creek. No cars nearby. No smoke from the chimney.

No sign of life.

Grant's shoulders slouched. "Those tracks led out. I'll move closer on foot. If I see anyone, I'll raise my hand. Immediately call Jesse and have him alert the State Patrol."

She checked her watch. "Maybe he's found them at another cabin."

"He'd of called." He handed Miranda his phone. His face mirrored her increasing distress. "If anything happens, you leave. Turn left on the highway and drive to the Montana State Highway Patrol office. Understand?"

"Yes." She glanced at the stick shift. "Be careful."

Grant crouched low while approaching the house. He veered behind snow-topped brush along the bank and then jogged to the porch. He shook his head before pushing open the door.

She stumbled downhill and skidded through the open door. A threadbare couch and TV holding rabbit ears sat on one end. Dirty footprints covered the floor.

Grant bent over the trash bin in the far corner. He plucked out a small box. "Dad's brand of antihistamine. His dust allergies would've skyrocketed in this pit." He turned to stare out the window, crushing the cardboard in his fist. His shoulders rose and fell.

She put her hand on his arm, but he pulled away.

Tears wet her eyes. "I'm sorry."

A scent of scrambled egg lingered in the stale air.

Miranda wandered to the sink and bent closer to the remaining yellow scraps in the dirty pan. "The egg in this fry pan's fresh. They haven't been gone long."

"Come on!" He strode to the door. "We'll try the gas station. There isn't another one for thirty miles. Someone may recall a non-local. We've got a chance, if they're not . . ." His choked voice trailed off while he left the cabin.

"The thugs could've Googled 'Morley' and be heading to your house." She ran to his side and her boot slipped, sending her onto one knee in muddy slush. "Don't you dare lose hope."

"Right." Grant took her hand and led her to the Suburban. "Call Jesse. They'll need to hide the vehicles at my house. He'll alert the staters."

She'd barely shut her door before he slammed the truck into reverse and gunned it.

"Jesse, it's Miranda. Grant's certain his parents stayed on Spruce Creek Lane. We're heading to a nearby gas station to see if they stopped there first. Warn the agent at Grant's to move the cars."

"Keep him calm," Jesse whispered.

"Sure." She pressed the phone to her ear.

"When it's family, an agent doesn't think rationally. We can't afford errors, both for Grant's folks and your safety."

He was still worried about her testimony? Now? What kind of men wanted this job? "We're at the gas station." She hit the button ending the call.

Two vehicles sat at the pumps in front of the convenience store.

Grant's narrowed cop eyes scanned the area. "Duck and stay put. Honk if you need me." He slowed the truck.

She scrunched low in the seat.

A white panel van stood unattended at the nearest gas pump. On the opposite side, a man cleaned the windshield of a station wagon.

Grant parked the Suburban alongside the front of the service garage, attached to the store.

"I'll be right back." He got out and strode toward a mechanic working on a car.

She looked through the mini mart's glass door. Goosebumps rose on her arm. The creepy window washer from Seattle stood at the register, doling out money.

Her eyes darted to Grant, talking to a man in stained coveralls.

Could he see her? She slid out the driver side and pulled Grant away by his sleeve. "I recognize a guy in the store. He started washing windows in the Justice Building right before they shot Ike. He acted strange, kept watching the elevators."

"Which guy?"

"Shaggy brown hair, wearing a Seahawks jacket."

"Stay behind me." Grant moved toward the door of the garage. "There's a kid in the car seat of the station wagon. The perps must be driving the panel van," he whispered. "My folks might be hidden in the back. If they're not, we'll have Jesse pull them over for questioning."

"I'll call Jesse."

Grant turned. "Go hide in my truck. Get it running and be ready to leave. Don't take any chances." His eyes gleamed with purpose. "I'll whistle if I find my parents." He pulled a pair of dark sunglasses out of his pocket. "Put these on," he plucked a ball cap bearing a greasy *Amsoil* logo off a work bench. "And tuck up your hair."

He circled behind the pumps and approached the van.

The window washer ambled out, his arms overflowing with pop and chips.

Crap, he'd hear Grant. She cranked the volume on the Suburban's radio, peeled off Kyle's coat, and hopped out, waving the map.

"Excuse me, mister," she began in a Southern drawl, then stuck out her boobs, and sashayed her hips while she approached him. "I'm lost, and I'm not the best at these here maps."

"Well, now." He smiled and then narrowed his eyes.

She lowered her cap's brim and broadened her smile.

The map fluttered on the sloped hood of the Suburban. "Could y'all spare me the tiniest minute and try to help me figure out how to get to Miss Oula? My Granny's expectin' me, and I don't have no idea the best route."

"Shame you're lost." He threw his packages into the cab of his van and pulled up his pants.

"I'm sorry to delay your party," she teased.

"Always glad to help a pretty little lady." In a few strides, he'd closed in.

The stench of cigarettes drifted from his clothing. His shoulder inched near her chest as he leaned over the hood. "Let's take a peek."

She stepped aside, holding the far corner of the map.

A tall guy with a blue-tipped Mohawk came from around the side of the garage, zipping his fly. "The can's freezing." He patted the top of his hair. "What ya need a map for? Straight shot to Three Falls after we visit the river."

The window washer scowled. "Not us, dimwit. This little sweetie needs help finding her granny." He sidled closer, using his hip to bump her thigh.

She dug her fingernails into her palm and smiled demurely. "Y'all are the kindest gentlemen."

~ ~ ~

As a kid, Grant drove his folks nuts with the "shave and a haircut" knock. He tapped the tune on the back door.

The "two bits" reply came in the form of two thumps.

He released a long breath and inched open the door. His eyes adapted to the dark interior.

Dim light outlined upright bodies sitting back to back on the floor, their knees bent to their chests. Ropes bound them, and gags covered their mouths.

He put his finger to his lips, requesting silence.

Their heads bobbed in unison.

While he tugged the rope at their waists, they scooted to the edge of the metal floor.

He sliced through the cords and swung their feet out. Placing an arm around each waist, he moved them to the far wall of the convenience store. Slashing cords, he set his dad's hands free and pulled out his Glock.

A woman's hillbilly voice carried to where they stood. "You boys are so smart. I think I may be able to find my way now. Where'd ya say you're off to? A river?"

Miranda. Grant wet his dry lips and managed a shrill note. "You two stay here while I get Miranda away from the thugs." He slipped behind the gas pump.

"Wanna have a drink? There's a tavern outside of town," the one with blue hair offered.

"Granny's waitin' for me," Miranda said. "Thanks, though."

The shorter creep moved his hip closer to hers, making Miranda struggle to fold the map.

His jaw clenched.

The outline of a gun bulged in blue-hair's coat.

Grant's fingers tightened on the Glock.

"Bye, Sugar." The shorter one blew Miranda a kiss, they climbed in the van, and drove onto the highway.

"My folks are alive," he called. He holstered the gun and dashed to her.

As Miranda tilted her smiling face to him, an undeniable truth beat in his heart. He wanted her to share his life.

He drew her against his chest and covered her quivering mouth with his needy lips. Tasting her awakened strong desires.

Heavy sighs rasped from her throat.

Pent up tension slid away while he pushed off the cap and ran his fingers through her hair.

She melted against him, her return kisses igniting more than physical senses. She completed him, every soft, warm, brilliant, and brave inch of her.

From the side of the building came a series of sneezes.

She pulled her head back. "Thank God they're alive!"

He kissed her brow, and swiped tears from her cheek.

"I never thought I'd be glad to see the creepy window washer," she said.

Creepy window washer. Yes, the whole thing had been planned down to each excruciating detail. Grant squeezed his eyes shut.

He should've figured out the computer connection. Of course Karpenito would've checked what sites Miranda had visited. Maneski never overlooked unturned stones and made sure his underlings didn't either.

But he had.

Because of her.

His textbook control of a situation had slipped, a mistake that nearly killed Miranda and his parents.

Distracted and deadly. The realization struck his gut harder than a close-range bullet fired into Kevlar.

~ ~ ~

Grant shivered, so Miranda nestled against him. They'd all survived, thanks to the crooks buying snacks in the convenience store behind her.

There'd been more than relief in Grant's sensual kisses, much more. She placed her fingertip on his swollen cheek. "I heard them beating you. It nearly killed me."

"Everyone survived." His tense tone shredded the tender moment.

Grant shrugged off his coat and draped it over her shoulders. "Stay here." He loped back to his parents, who'd shuffled around the corner of the building.

Warmth cocooned her now, but he'd changed. Impassioned Grant had left, and his eyes had gone stone cold. What happened?

He approached her, supporting a parent on each arm. His dad held his ribs, and his mom limped. "These are my folks, Pat and Tom Morley. Please meet Miranda Whitley. She was instrumental in your rescue."

From death. Now she understood his withdrawal. Her coming to Emma Springs had nearly killed them all.

"Very nice to meet you," Tom said and sneezed again.

"Extremely pleased to meet you," Pat agreed, and squeezed Miranda's hand.

She held the clasp, then stepped back. "I'm so thankful you're both okay."

"Stinky ride, if I do say so." Pat fluffed her dusty bangs, exposing red welts on her wrists.

Miranda covered her mouth. "Oh my God! Did they torture you?"

"No," Tom said. "Verbal threats. By your bruises, you got the worst, son."

Grant brushed a strand of dusty brown hair off his mom's forehead. "Miranda recognized one of your captors from Seattle."

"Good girl," Pat said.

"Got your ribs, too, I bet." Tom gave Grant a gentle hug. "Those guys planned to transport us to our final stop today, crime scene B." He ran work-hardened fingers through his short hair. "We knew you'd find us alive."

"I'd never quit searching. To the moon and back," Grant said to his mom. "Are either of you hurt?"

"Nope." Pat's hazel eyes, the same color as Grant's, blinked back tears. "Only bruised and delighted we'll see another moon."

Miranda dropped her chin to her chest. They knew how close they'd come to dying. From her mistake.

Grant punched numbers into his phone. "Jesse, my folks are safe. Heads up, there's a white panel-van coming your way. Montana plates, perpetrators on board. I'll call for backup . . . We'll stay until you signal." Next, he alerted the Montana State Highway Patrol.

"My staters will collar them," his dad said. "Can we wait in the diner?"

"Good idea. Jesse's sending agents here. I've got to call Sam." Grant turned his back to Miranda and faced his parents, first touching his dad's shoulder and then his mom's. "You three grab a spot in the cafe, and I'll be right in."

"Good plan. Your mom hasn't eaten enough," Tom said.

Miranda waited a moment, allowing them to step ahead of her.

His family reunited.

Oh, how she envied them.

~ ~ ~

Grant moved his Suburban to a spot in front of the café and grabbed his phone. "Sam. We found my parents alive. Another few minutes and they'd be laid out in side-by-side drawers at the coroner's office. What the hell's going on in Seattle?" he demanded.

"Maneski ordered a hit on his arresting officer and the prosecutor who filed initial charges. The Butcher's knives are all over the city. I figured you'd be safer in Emma Springs. Still do."

"With Jesse's team here, you might be right. Nailing Venom's gang took a few stilettos off the street. See you tomorrow." He slammed the truck door and stomped to the café. A bell jingled while he shoved open the door.

Mom and Dad sat on one side of a booth. Their white teeth smiled out from dirty faces. Dad imitated a nasty scowl. Miranda ought to be grinning, but her lips remained tight.

Yearning churned deep inside. No, an ache. She deserved to become part of his family.

After the trial. He couldn't afford to miss anything else because he was making puppy eyes at a beautiful woman. Not to mention compromising the witness' testimony. He strode forward. "Anyone hungry?"

"We ordered their pot roast special. I figured you'd finish

one off." Pat picked up her fork as a waiter set four steaming plates of food on the table.

Dad sliced into his roast. "The blue-haired guy spent way too much time sharpening a cleaver."

"Excuse me." Miranda scooted off the bench seat and then brushed by Grant, headed to the restroom.

"You'd better tell us some details." Tom speared a hunk of meat as he nodded at Miranda's vanishing back.

Grant slid in and faced his father. He kept his eye on the bathroom door while he told an abbreviated story of their escaping Venom. He left out Maneski's M.O. as The Butcher.

He caught himself rotating the ketchup bottle with shaky fingers.

His mom leaned across the table and laid her hand on his. "It must've been terribly difficult for Miranda to adjust to a new life after she lost her family. Then this. She appears to be handling it all."

"I hope she'll be okay. I need to adjust to being around her." He picked up a fork and twisted it in the mashed potatoes. "I acted worse than a clueless rookie. I should've moved you."

Miranda returned and slid in opposite Pat. She kept her head down as she toyed with her food.

"Food's great, Miranda." Grant said.

"Yeah." She pushed a piece of roast into her mashed potatoes with her fork.

Let her disengage, Morley. Get her safely to Seattle and afterwards sort things out. He took a long swig of cold water.

"I bet you'll be glad to have Bo's help. Partners are crucial," his dad said.

"Yup." Grant nodded and stared at the empty parking lot. Bo remained a field agent for a stupid reason dictated by his wife—she wouldn't yank their kids out of school to relocate. A husband might never be enough for Miranda.

"Apple pie anyone?" His mom's voice had a soft edge.

"I'll pass on dessert." Miranda's gaze moved from father to mother to son. She sank into the worn upholstery of the booth and shuttered her eyes.

"None for me, I'm happy to head home," Tom said.

A waitress cleared the dishes and left the check in the middle of the table.

"I'm full." Grant reached for the bill. His dad's grimy hand moved to cover his.

"Thank you, son. I knew you'd come through." His dad's voice was steady.

Miranda rested her palms on the table, preparing to rise. His mom reached over, clasped her hand, and stacked both of theirs on top of the men's hands. "Tom and I realized long ago, love always perseveres."

His dad kissed his mom's smudged cheek. "Pat sets the standard."

"You've both offered the encouragement I needed," Grant said.

Miranda withdrew her hand first. "I'm sorry. This horrible day's my fault."

"No," Grant said. "I did everything wrong. I should've taken you to Three Falls." He struggled to keep his voice calm.

"Both of you, stop." His dad thumped his fist on the table. "You've missed the bigger picture. The bad guys struck, and you each made sensible decisions. Crooks don't play by rules."

"No, I messed up." Grant admitted. "I'm experienced in these situations, and I became distracted. I should've questioned orders."

"We've all made decisions we regret," Pat said. "Move on and learn from them."

"I haven't learned," Miranda faced his mom. "Five years ago, I got my own family killed. I'm toxic to yours." She slid out of the booth, shoved open the café door, and stumbled toward his Suburban.

"She's so strong and yet so broken—needlessly blaming herself." Grant scrubbed his face with his hands, then looked outside. "The patrol car Jesse sent just pulled in. Give me a couple of minutes, and then I'll get you home."

"Take all the time you need, son. It's apparent you're stuck on Miranda." His dad put his arm around his mom.

"There's a scared little girl and a lot more under the surface, Grant. Be patient." His mom's eyes glistened.

"I want to help her. But I don't know if I can." Grant left the restaurant and stopped two feet from Miranda.

She leaned against the passenger door, her forehead pressed against the window while her shoulders heaved.

Every fiber of his being wanted to hold her tight and kiss her tears away. No. Rules defined impropriety, and he wouldn't break them again. He'd already put her testimony and his career at risk. And their lives.

He gritted his teeth and rested his hand on her shoulder. "This must bring back horrible memories."

She stepped away, breaking his hold.

He shoved his hands in his pockets, her suffering now definable in his world. "I know distress. I sat in my house not knowing if you or my parents were alive. I don't have any idea how horrible it would be to lose them. But think about this—what if you'd never had their love? Would you make a trade to remove the pain of loss and remove the memories of your life together?"

She hugged her chest.

"Would you?" He pressed his key fob to unlock the doors of his rig and waited for an answer, or a nod.

None came.

~ ~ ~

Grant's words pierced her heart, where cherished and joyful memories of her parents and Kenny brightened her sphere of existence. Not now. Miranda slid onto the seat.

Grant would carry the thrill of success from today, while she'd bear guilt. And they weren't safe yet. Her body collapsed into the worn leather.

Slow footsteps shuffled across cement. "Are you ready?" Pat quietly asked.

"Yes." Grant closed Miranda's door.

She shut her eyes. For the briefest moment in the diner, while their hands touched in unity, a soft glow had filled her, the likes of which she hadn't known in a very, very long time.

Memories were hell.

The back door of the Suburban swung open, and Grant's parents hopped in. "Home, my dear Patricia," his dad said.

Miranda took off Grant's coat and tossed it onto his seat. She pulled on Kyle's borrowed parka, but goose down couldn't fend off Grant's numbing insight. Loving with all your heart exacted a tortuous price.

When this finished, she'd try counseling again and a support group. Kyle understood her grief, and sadly enough, others would, too. Somehow she'd validate her need for love beat out the risk.

Grant climbed in and leaned between the seats. "I told Jesse we'd head to your house, Dad. Agents will be by to record statements after they book your kidnappers. Your staters spotted them on the highway and arrested them."

On the drive, Grant checked and rechecked the mirror.

Miranda narrowed her eyes. They were in the middle of Montana on a deserted highway, and his grip could've broken the wheel in half. *Karpenito?*

"We'll sleep better tonight knowing the thugs are in cells. Right, Miranda?"

They turned into a gravel driveway.

"Yeah," the words came automatically. She stared out the window and silently bade goodbye to emerging dreams of a life involving Grant. His kisses might set her on fire, but the FBI code remained embedded deep in his bones. Fidelity, bravery, integrity. She'd seen the plaque in his guest room. After her past traumas, no way would she step into this kind of turbulence yet. It'd be too painful.

"There's Poppy." Tom's voice caught in his throat. "What a sight."

A tall, balding man stepped away from a white clapboard farmhouse.

The moment Grant's grandfather recognized the occupants of the Suburban, he clapped his hands and gazed skyward.

The truck had barely stopped before he opened Tom's door and pulled him out. "I knew something bad had happened by the way your house looked when I came home." He rubbed his gnarled knuckles across his eyes, then hugged Pat, Tom, and Grant.

"I'll get the fire stoked and turn up the heat." He whipped a faded purple bandana out of his pocket and shuffled inside.

Miranda wiped dampness from her own cheek.

Grant led her toward a weathered porch flanked by two horse-head hitching posts. "I need to call Jesse from Dad's land line and get an update. Intermittent cell reception here."

Tom stood in the drive, facing the mountain. He placed his arm around Pat's waist. "We made it home." He kissed her cheek.

Pat supported his elbow while he took careful steps.

A flash of Miranda's own folks comforting each other after Grandma's funeral made her heart squeeze. She held their screen door open and followed them inside.

"It'll be toasty in two shakes of a lamb's tail," Poppy said and turned to her. "You must be Miranda. Glad to see you, too."

"Grant's spoken fondly of you." She shook his outstretched hand.

Their living room held familiar dark and light patterned furniture.

The clipped voice of Agent Grant came from the kitchen.

Tom eased onto the couch, holding his side. "Grant's voice softens while he talks about you, Miranda. We're hopeful good comes out of this."

She stared at her old boots. Modest and mild ran through her brain. The description didn't fit Grant. "Speaking of good outcomes, I need to call and see how Ike's doing after his last surgery."

"He's your friend, the judge?" Pat settled in by Tom.

What was taking Grant so long? Had they attacked Ike again? "Yes." Miranda paced behind the couch. "A very dear friend."

Grant thumped the counter. His tone had changed to a growl.

Pat rose. "I'll give you a quick tour while you wait."

Miranda forced a smile. "Sure."

"I removed a wall to allow for cooking and chatting with guests." She waved her hand across a wide expanse from the kitchen to the living room. "Two dormer bedrooms upstairs are waiting for grandchildren to stay overnight."

Miranda glanced up. "Uh-huh."

"Many things you can plan, others happen at the right time." Pat guided her into a short hall.

After all this danger, Pat couldn't possibly believe she'd raise Grant's children while he dodged bullets. Had she listened to her son's goals? "Unfortunately, not all dreams coincide."

Pat stopped and pointed at a framed photo of Tom in uniform. "He sacrificed an FBI career to have a normal family life by joining the highway patrol. Firing his revolver and wounding people forced us to discuss his feelings. Our marriage grew stronger."

Wounding, not killing. A dark memory of the coroner's office and identifying the bodies of Mom, Dad, and Kenny flashed in Miranda's mind. Each sheet pulled back one at a time, each face bearing a ghastly resemblance to one of her family. A part of her had died. She'd stumbled out of the morgue and drifted into a dull, gray existence. Until Friday.

She trudged back toward the kitchen. Grant wouldn't sacrifice career for family. And he probably shouldn't. He was good at his job, and her experiences had taught her just how much the world needed men like him.

"Yes, sir." Grant banged the phone receiver, and Miranda jumped. His eyes assessed her. "Come in the living room and sit down. Kyle threatened to keep you at his house if I didn't take good care of you."

"I need to call Shirley and Corrin."

Soft pressure from his palm steered her to a stool by the wall phone. She turned her head away from him and dialed. "Hi, Shirley. How's Ike doing?"

"He's still in ICU." The strong Shirley had returned. "Our contact mentioned a bust near you. How's your bullet wound?"

"Fine. A scratch. Give Ike a hug for me, okay?"

"Will do. If the FBI doesn't protect you, Ike will come unglued. He feels responsible."

"Don't worry, they need my testimony. Give my love to Ike." She left another message for Corrin and turned back to the others.

Grant sat in front of the fire, chatting. Like a weed in a drought, he'd adapt and survive wherever the bureau planted him.

He shot to his feet. "Sit near the fire." He motioned to an antique loveseat designed for two smaller people. "How's Ike?"

"He's still in ICU." Grant squeezed in next to her, his leg pressing into hers. The agent in him had controlled the steady voice talking to his father, but not the facial tick below the corner of his left eye.

Poppy shuffled into the room, balancing five champagne flutes and a dark green bottle on a tray. "I stole this bubbly from the back of your refrigerator. Seemed fitting for this occasion."

"Absolutely." Pat grabbed the bottle and stepped to a buffet behind them. "I forgot I bought it for our anniversary. I'm glad we'll have another one."

"Let me help, honey," Tom said, and joined her.

When the cork popped, Grant's hand shot to his revolver.

Her questions to him would have to wait. His parents deserved this little celebration of their long lives together. She faked a smile aimed at Pat. "Your cabin on Mt. Hanlen's one of the most beautiful places I've ever seen. I hope we didn't intrude on your sanctuary."

"Oh, never. You go to our cabin any time you want." Pat beamed at her, and then at Grant. "Maybe you can extend your visit, and we can all get to know each other." She cast a knowing look at Miranda. "For years we've wished for Grant to create his own special memories in our cabin. Glad he finally took a female guest."

His mom's grin implied she and Grant had made a different kind of memory there than the actual G-rated truth.

This wasn't a visit, and she wasn't his date. Seattle held deadlier challenges for them all. However, here they sat, sipping champagne, while her future included vengeful mobsters.

The fire turned uncomfortably warm, or maybe Grant's steel-corded thigh muscle pushing against hers unnerved her.

"No long extension on this trip." He glanced out the window. "Sam suggested we sit tight here for a day or so while we wrap it all up. An agent's coming by to interview you folks in a few minutes."

"But staying in Montana doesn't make sense. The sooner I get back to my boring apartment the better. Why aren't we flying to Seattle tomorrow?"

Grant shifted in the chair. "Ahh, flights in and out of here are filled by hunters. One of Jesse's team will be at my house in half an hour. They need statements from us, too."

Miranda squared her shoulders. "Drive us back to Seattle."

"Not an option," Grant said. "We'll fly Saturday. Monday, we'll be grilled by lawyers. Sam said one of the kidnappers offered Venom's plans in exchange for a plea bargain. Maneski's trial date will be expedited."

"I'd hoped to be home tomorrow." Miranda's throat went dry.

"Venom knew the address of your apartment, where we've posted agents." He draped his arm behind her. "Sam arranged hotel rooms in Seattle during the trial."

"I'll testify against a mobster's hit man, then what? Keep waiting in an empty hotel room until his trial ends, while another version of Venom knocks on the door?" Her body gave an involuntary shudder. "Will you be nearby?"

"I won't let you out of my sight." Grant's fingers brushed across her shoulder while he removed his arm to pick up a glass.

Protection or privacy? Had he meant to touch her just now? After the kiss she would've welcomed a tether to his side, before he'd realized the danger she'd brought to his family. "Your being close by would help."

Grant nodded. "I'll tell Sam to book a suite."

"My warm-hearted Grant has returned," Pat said. "The one I've longed for ever since the bureau sharpened him to a point."

No one uttered a sound.

Champagne bubbled in Miranda's long-stemmed glass. Tiny, golden orbs rose helter skelter and popped at the surface. Forced beads of energy, escaping from the bottom of a chamber and surging to an unknown fate. She could relate.

Grant cleared his throat. "Mom and Dad, here's to many, many more anniversaries and a lot less excitement, unless it involves your friends, family, and fun."

"Hear, hear!" Three voices responded.

"And Miranda's considered a very special friend," Pat said, and winked at her son.

She tasted the bite of champagne on her tongue before turning away.

"I'll be visiting Emma Springs more often," Grant said.

"We'll be waiting." Tom grinned at Pat and squeezed her hand. "We didn't redo the upstairs for nothing."

They'd better put dust covers in the dormer rooms. Miranda twisted her lips into a smile. "With your work, Grant, I'd think you'd welcome breaks."

"I will from now on."

"Maybe Miranda can join you soon?" Pat said.

"Maybe." Grant stood and held his hand out to Miranda. "Dad's beat. We should head out and give you time alone before the agents arrive."

Miranda rubbed her sleeves, fighting the chill of fear.

Pat gave her a gentle hug, then turned to Grant. "Thanks, honey, for bringing us home. We're proud of the man you've become." She pulled him into a firm embrace. "I love you."

Tom stretched one arm out, and Grant hugged him.

"I love you both." Grant stepped back and helped Miranda into her coat. "We'll call you in the morning. Rest easy."

"You can bank on it," Tom said.

Pungent wood smoke permeated the fresh air outside their home. A coyote howled in the distance, and another one called an answer.

Grant scanned the perimeter of the icy driveway, then supported Miranda's elbow crossing to the Suburban. "The initial questioning tonight should be brief." He opened the passenger door for her. "Then you can tuck in and enjoy peaceful Montana."

His body stayed rigid while he hopped in and started the engine. He pulled onto the empty highway.

Miranda balled her fists. "That's a crock. How many Venomettes are still here, and why can't I go to Seattle?"

His eyes flicked to check the road behind them at regular intervals. "We're simply taking the usual precautions."

"Maneski won't stop until I'm dead," she said.

A car jetted past them, cut in front, and braked.

Grant unholstered his gun.

Chapter 14

Miranda dug her fingernails into the suburban's leather seat. "An ambush?" she cried.

The other car turned onto the next dirt lane. The taillights disappeared over a rise.

"Damn drunk at the wheel," Grant muttered. "You okay?"

"Not in Montana." She studied his profile. In another lifetime, her fingers would reach out to the tight waves of his dark strands of hair or stroke his stubbled chin to calm him. Not happening in the near future. Grant couldn't divulge everything he knew to her. Lies by omission were still lies.

The Suburban's headlights flashed at the faded For Sale by Owner sign next to a mailbox with "MORLEY" printed in distinct letters above a painting of geese taking flight.

"How wonderful to have wings," she murmured.

"I commented once how I enjoyed watching flocks head south and received the mailbox on my next birthday from Mom."

Grant steered his truck to the barn. His eyes panned out to the perimeter of the pasture. He unzipped his coat and adjusted his gun holster. "Horses must be hungry. Want to help me feed them?"

Big Red's mulish whinny hailed from inside.

"No option," she said.

The barn door creaked open, and nickers greeted them. Grant flicked on a light. "Seems peaceful."

"The barn, yes." She scratched Red's long neck. "Want a little exercise?" She memorized his uneven white blaze and turned to Grant. "My one staunch beau would appreciate being turned out in your pasture."

He tossed a halter to her. "I'm assuming he put in his written request?"

"Tapped out in hoofography," she added.

"Right." He walked down the aisle, looking in each stall. "The middle stall opens onto the meadow, and your mule's smart enough not to wander."

He'd called Red her mule again. Could she afford her apartment and pay to board him? "I'll help you feed and muck out the stalls."

"Give them each two scoops from the covered tub."

She dug a metal scoop into a grain bin, where tiny pieces surrounded her hand. Grant and his family tried to protect her from all sides, tried to close all the gaps on all the outside forces. It provided false comfort.

How long before they'd get through the trial? Could she even locate a stable near Seattle? She bit her lip.

Red stretched his head to reach her.

"Mind reading mule." His nose felt velvety soft to her touch. "No more city slickers riding you on trails."

"He's bonded to you." Grant split a bale of hay. "Hard to believe Red took you to Emma Springs instead of cutting thru the woods to go home. Maybe he remembered the peppermints the drive thru gives to any horse coming by."

"No. He's my miracle mule." She filled his bin with grain. "I knew the garnet horse slide held special magic. It sounds woo-woo, but after Red saw me, we trusted each other."

"Smart animal."

"Too bad you can't bottle trust."

Red's ears twitched to catch each word.

Grant ignored her comment. "The animals are happily munching. Let's get you inside. Jesse and the group should arrive soon for your statement." He stepped onto the porch and stopped.

A dull ache began in her forehead. "The last time I was interrogated, it concerned Jacob and—"

His hand shot into the air. "Wait," he whispered. He slid his key in the door and pushed it open.

Warm air reached her face.

"Don't move." He yanked his gun out. "Intruder."

Miranda's feet remained anchored to the porch. Her heart thumped double time. Not again, not this soon. Her eyes adjusted to dim light.

Grant's body disappeared into near darkness after he crouched and entered, his revolver pointing the way. His form, plastered against the wall, stealthily climbed stairs.

She bunched her gloved hands into fists, taking gulps of frigid air. Her pulse drummed in her ears.

The hallway light flicked on, illuminating Grant standing a few feet from her, his face an iron mask. "They've come and gone."

"How'd you know?" She hugged her arms to her body.

"A series of short, wide footprints on top of ours in the snow. Not familiar."

Chills continued. "Karpenito?"

"Can't say. We're not sleeping here tonight. Head upstairs and pack. I need to call Dad."

Outside, the craggy outline of Mt. Hanlen appeared deceptively peaceful against a dark sky.

She grasped the handrail, pulling her body upstairs. Each step drummed into the silence.

Karpenito had been here. Hunting her.

She ran into the guest room, stuffed Grant's T-shirt into her pocket, and headed downstairs.

"Hey, Dad, we had a prowler," Grant said. "I'm moving us all to a safer spot." He wedged the phone on his shoulder and took off his coat. "I'll call Kyle. Someone will get you in ten minutes."

Miranda studied the stress lines crinkling around his eyes. Remnants of dinner churned in her stomach.

"Miranda. I forgot this." He reached into his front hall closet, and removed a blue cap emblazoned by a white *S* on the front. "Venom brought this to my house. He found it in the woods searching for your . . . for you."

"Kenny's hat. I thought I'd never see it again." She clutched it to her chest and brushed her chin with the crown. "He only removed it to sleep."

He nodded toward the door and tapped his phone. "Kyle, slight change of plans. We've had unwelcome visitors. I need to accept your dad's offer of lodging for my family. Can you meet us there in ten?" Next, he called Jesse and gave instructions.

She tugged the ball cap on. "Take us to Three Falls. I can't put Kyle's dad in danger."

Grant propelled her to the front door. "Roy Werner's attending a regional clock conference in Billings." Grant buttoned a padded black vest over his shirt.

"Is that bulletproof?"

"Yes, Kevlar."

What would protect her heart if anything happened to him? "Standard procedure's putting on body armor in Emma Springs? This must be your worst nightmare."

He shrugged into his coat. "Nope, I've had worse. Come on. I need to call Sam to let him know Maneski sent me a visitor."

"To kill me." Her whispered words escaped into dark. "No house is safe."

"Roy's place is alarmed like Fort Knox. We fly to Seattle tomorrow." Grant stepped to the door, panned the area, and pulled her to the truck.

She climbed onto the cold front seat. "Isn't Mr. Werner a lawyer?"

"Correct. He owns a rare collection of antique automaton clocks and has a state of the art security system." He slid his hand to her knee. "We'll be safer there than at a hotel. He's told me many times if I ever needed to bring guests, they'd be welcome."

Her eyes moved from the meadow to the pond as Grant steered away from his home.

The truck tires slid on iced-over tracks in the snow.

Her fingers shook while she gripped Kenny's hat. "I'm prey, not a guest."

"This'll be over soon, Miranda."

"One way or another." She stared out the window while they drove to town.

"Here's the Werner's." He turned the Suburban onto a driveway and into an open garage. "Head through the steel door to your right. I'll meet you in the breezeway," Grant ordered.

Filigreed wrought iron covered the windows on the short corridor between the garage and house. She approached the back door, and a series of locks clicked on another steel door. Grant strode to her side and pushed her behind him while the door swung open.

Kyle strained to smile. "A few of your FBI friends beat you." He studied Grant's face. "I mean, got here first."

A figure stepped out of the entry.

"You remember Bullseye?" Grant asked Miranda.

Her chest tightened. "Yes."

Bullseye wore matching Kevlar and a grimace. "For the record, I'm Special Agent Tabatha Banks. I'll try to make this session brief."

Tabatha, a sweet girl's name. How'd she become a sharpshooter? Miranda sank onto the couch. "I'll do my best to recall what happened."

Bullseye took the overstuffed chair opposite her and opened a laptop.

"I figured you'd appreciate a warm drink." Kyle set three mugs of cocoa onto the coffee table and then left.

"Miranda, please start an hour before you saw Venom in the elevator." Grant remained standing. "Tell us any details."

She pictured the grisly scene and described each element. Grant and Bullseye listened, stopping her at unclear events.

"So, the plant hid your face." Bullseye stopped taking notes.

"Otherwise, I'd be dead." Her gaze dropped to her hands. "I pinch branches to promote growth. Mom taught me how."

Bullseye nodded and tapped the keyboard.

"They'll question your leaving the crime scene," Grant said.

"Ike's warning scared me, and the cop insisted I go to my apartment." Miranda took a sip of warm chocolate. "I knew it wasn't normal procedure."

"The man Judge Gilson identified as Detective Karpenito instructed you to leave." Bullseye looked up. "Make the judge's instructions clear in court."

"Identified as Detective Karpenito?" Miranda bristled.

"The detective's ID had been stolen, and there's a few discrepancies," Bullseye said. She glanced at Grant.

"You still don't believe Ike and me?" Miranda glared at Grant and banged her mug onto the table.

"I do, but we need tests to verify," Grant said. "You were afraid of me in the cabin. Didn't you recognize me?"

"Your disguise included a hat and a partial beard. Like Karpenito," she snapped.

Grant recoiled. "Right."

She'd leave out how she'd know those broad, carry-me-to-your-castle shoulders anywhere. "I saw your shotgun and freaked. And you didn't act sympathetic."

"A day after Judge Gilson's shooting you materialized in Montana with a bullet hole," Grant countered.

"Understandable." Bullseye kept typing while Miranda continued her story.

She caught Grant staring at her. Trust, such a tenuous thing. Beginning at her temple, she slowly finger-combed her hair down to the ends, then looked away and finished the account by describing her ride to Kyle's.

"Got enough for tonight, Bullseye?" Grant's color had deepened. He shifted his feet.

"Probably." She closed her laptop and pulled out her phone. Her lips thinned. "Jesse texted. No vacancies in the nearby motels. Okay if we bunk here tonight, Grant?" She adjusted her revolver on her belt.

Grant's eyes followed the movement. "Sure."

"The agents are transporting your folks," Bullseye said. "Jesse never plans ahead. The local hotels are full. I should've checked. We'd all appreciate a bed for the night."

"No sense driving all the way to Three Falls." Grant's placating tone had returned. "Should've told me sooner. Plenty of couch space and rooms in the attic. We'll make it a party. Okay, Miranda?"

Hell, no. One thing she remembered from a college psychology class, rambling sentences backed a lie. Three Falls wasn't that far, and there weren't any local hotels, facts she knew. She turned toward the window.

Liars. They'd be guarding overnight due to a threat.

~ ~ ~

Agents who'd arrived on the premise of needing a place to crash filled Roy Werner's kitchen. Grant scowled. Bullseye must've gotten one helluva text.

Miranda's cold shoulder inferred she'd figured out the reason behind their appearance. Details could unhinge her.

He rubbed the back of his neck, then changed hands and rubbed from the other side.

Jesse caught his eye from the entry and waved his thumb toward the kitchen.

"You gave a good account of what happened." Grant spoke calmly to Miranda. "You must be exhausted."

"Yeah." She tapped her fingers on the arm of the sofa.

"My folks retired to a guest room." He forced a yawn. "Kyle suggested you stay in his old bedroom. I recall the comfy twin beds." He held out his hand.

"I'd be fine on this couch." She wormed her back into a pile of pillows at the corner. "I won't disrupt the agents. Have two of them sleep in the bedroom." Her eyes darted to where Jesse and Bullseye spoke with their heads bowed together. "Where are the other men?"

"They're in Roy's office submitting statements from my folks. I'm still amazed you found Kyle's house yesterday." He adjusted a pillow behind her.

"Thanks to Big Red." Her hand rose toward his bruised jaw.

Grant clasped it in his. "You risked your life to save mine. I won't ever forget." He kissed her cheek, letting his lips linger on her satiny skin. His body craved to hold her in his arms. He turned away while he still could. "Thank you doesn't cover it."

"I owe you much more," she said.

He had to hold back, not tell her she'd unlocked his heart. "There's no debt between us. Let me talk to the team and figure out how we'll bunk."

The killer would attempt to strike tonight, and he needed Miranda unaware.

"Okay."

He sensed her eyes following him to the kitchen. The group had assembled in front of a coffee maker sputtering the last drops of a strong-smelling brew. He stopped behind a hanging cabinet, tapped his finger on his ear, and pointed toward Miranda and the couch. Their nods indicated they'd gotten the message that she could hear them.

Bullseye held out her phone, displaying a text from Sam. *Third murder attempt on the judge.* Grant took a deep breath and read on. *Direct link between Maneski and Karpenito. Karpenito still off the grid.*

He looked out the kitchen window. "What's next, Jesse?"

"I never complimented everyone on today's coordinated and unique efforts," Jesse began. "A foolproof plan was engineered by a smart woman assisted by her mule. Nice shot, Bullseye. Grant, I must say, your training on agility helped."

"My family's alive because of your efforts." Grant looked around the cabinet to where Miranda sat with her head back, eyes closed. "Great teamwork," he said, before lowering his voice. "Maneski has no loyalty to his lackeys. He'll deny hiring Venom and order someone else to silence Miranda. Like Karpenito."

Jesse nodded in agreement and cleared his throat. "Your face got dinged pretty bad, Grant. I assume Kyle checked it?" He cocked his head. "What else did Venom do?"

"Damn, I need to log in the additional charges." He lifted his shirt. "Kyle said nothing appears broken."

"Whoa, solid purple from pecs to waist." Bullseye snapped phone photos. "Got them recorded to add aggravated assault to Venom's booking." She returned her cell to a pocket of her tactical pants. "I want to stow my gear. Where we bunking?"

Jesse pointed upstairs. "You get the scenic view, Bullseye." He flipped his hand at the office, did a V point to his eyes, and then motioned outside. Those agents would patrol the perimeter. "The rest of you can pick a couch."

"I don't see a ring on Miranda's finger," Jesse had raised his voice. He smiled and winked at Grant. "She's smart and pretty freakin' hot. I should get her phone number."

Grant's eyes widened, then he relaxed. "Her number's none of your business. She's not going to be another one of your conquests," he announced.

"Got it." Jesse rubbed his chin while he stared at Grant. "You and Miranda take the twin beds."

At the word 'beds,' Grant's pulse jumped. If Jesse read minds, he'd be on his way home to guard the mule instead of Miranda. He let out a breath and rolled his eyes. "Duty continues," he muttered under his breath.

"All's quiet. Goodnight, everyone," Jesse said.

Grant crept to the side of the couch and knelt by Miranda. The pink in her cheeks gave her eavesdropping away. "How's my damsel in shining armor? Any pain?"

Her eyes fluttered open. "Damsel in dirty dungarees." She stretched a little yawn into a deep breath. "The couch is comfy, and I'm a little stiff, but everyone's safe."

"Whatever happens, I'll protect you." He slid next to her, allowing her warmth to overshadow his secrets. "Can you trust me?"

Distress tightened her face. "I know you'll put your own life in front of mine. It's your job."

His job. How easy it'd make things if that's all she meant to him. The chasm she'd opened in his heart expanded each moment he spent with her. "Jesse prefers for you to sleep in Kyle's room. If you want, I can crash in the extra bed. I promise I won't snore. Your choice." He held his breath.

"I'd like you near me." Her wide eyes held the scared look again. "It isn't an inconvenience?"

To hell with the bruised ribs. He scooped her up from the couch and headed into the hallway. "You're not an inconvenience and won't ever be."

"Put me down, I'm not feeble."

"Habit, I guess." His grip held firm. "Hey guys? Miranda's exhausted, so we're turning in for the night."

"We've got everything covered," Jesse said from the kitchen.

Grant stopped. Jesse could've made it easy on him and bunked Bullseye with Miranda. Nope. Time to get even. "Put Roy Werner's cat in the laundry room before you button everything up."

"There's a cat?" Miranda asked.

Guarding her all night would fall between penance and paradise. He smiled at her. "No housecat, but observation training never ends. The absence of food bowls or a litter box will strike one of them by dawn."

"Bad Agent Morley," she snickered.

He grinned at her. And boy, when she grinned back, heat radiated to every cell in his body.

Her fingers tightened on his neck, sending the jolts deeper.

In Kyle's old room, he slid her to the floor.

Glass-doored armoires filled by Roy's clocks lined the walls. The two beds were pushed together in a corner.

Not two inches of space separated them.

She pointed to a framed photo inside one of the cases. "I recognize Kyle, who's the man next to you?"

"My partner, Bo Jackson. He's the one who got nailed while guarding the judge's hospital room."

Her hand flew to her mouth. "I'm so sorry. I didn't know."

Damn. "I'm sorry, too. Injuries come with the badge. While he's on the mend, the crooks will be brought to justice if it's the last thing I do."

She wrapped her arms around herself. "Your life's a constant gamble against violence."

"After I reach ASAC, it'll be primarily tactical planning." He took off his Kevlar and placed his badge on the nightstand. "My job's still mostly patience and paperwork."

"Yeah, right. Not my impression. My shoulders ache worse than if I'd been toting a backpack full of cement."

"I can help." He flexed his fingers and moved a length of silky hair away from her neck. She sat still while he massaged kinks in her tight shoulders.

"You carry too much misplaced guilt. None of this is your fault."

"You're very convincing," she whispered.

"I've spent years in the bureau learning to tie loose ends into tight knots. I used to enjoy helping others unravel their problems."

"You didn't lose your touch." Her shoulders relaxed under his circular strokes.

"I filled the last ten years with work. You made me realize I've missed love and compassion. And my family."

"Good," she whispered.

He glanced away, to his badge. "I've got to get us through the trial before I dissect my personal life." He dropped his hands. "I'm sorry."

She turned. Anguish shone in her eyes. "Yeah, I'm sorry, too. But I understand."

No, she'd never comprehend the intensity of the two forces battling inside of him. His career drive under shadowed a need to help her overcome her fears and then pursue a list of tantalizing possibilities.

New and distracting feelings. Frustration welled in his gut. He needed time to ratchet down a notch, or ten. "I'll give you privacy to get settled."

He stepped into the hallway and pulled the door shut, his fist clenched. He'd found the right woman, at the wrong damn time. Maneski would go balls out to assassinate Miranda and his folks. They'd all made the hit list. Him, too. He'd hold himself in check, get the trial over. Keep them safe.

~ ~ ~

Grant hadn't returned from the bathroom. His absence hung like a dead leaf waiting to fall. She didn't want to sleep without him by her side ever again. Maybe an impossible dream. You didn't change a person on a defined life path and the will to make it happen. Could they compromise using love?

A pair of pink pajamas lay on the pillow. She pulled them on and realized they must've belonged to Kyle's mother.

She studied an old photo of the grinning young men. They'd sworn allegiance to quell a turbulent urban world, putting relationships secondary.

A family of her own would bring her happiness. The idea had germinated in the woods while under Grant's tender care, then grown watching Grant and his folks. If his mom thought she brought out the warmhearted side of him, she'd try.

Grant knocked on the bedroom door.

"Enter at your own risk," she called.

He stepped inside and pulled the door shut. Worry lines creased his brow.

So easily he tangled her emotions into a knot. "You look tired. I'm sorry I'm such a needy wimp," she said.

"No apology necessary. Ever. Jesse stationed a patrol outside. You may see them pass by the window."

"I thought I heard something."

He pulled off the towel draped around his neck and twisted it until his knuckles turned white. "I can't compromise this case with another misstep. My first priority is your protection. But Miranda, I'd be a liar if I said I wasn't extremely attracted to you."

Desire shone in his eyes. She clutched her soft collar.

He uncurled her hand and pulled her to her feet. "I haven't been trained in this kind of restraint. When I touch you, I lose touch with my job."

"Case before involvement." Her chest grew tight. "Okay."

"No, not okay. I see hurt in your eyes." He lifted her chin. "Do you have feelings for me?"

A different Grant demanded an answer. The one she'd begun to love. She swallowed. "You're the man I dreamed about after studying you in the Justice Building. It wasn't how your team looked to you for leadership, I sensed much, much more."

"Do you still feel that way?" His eyes pleaded for the answer she longed to shout.

Standing on tiptoes, she kissed him for the first time. Soft intensity grew while she parted her lips and drew him in. Womanly instincts flared in her soul, the curling flames awakening dormant sensual desires.

His fingers gripped her waist, pulling her to his chest. He lifted the pajama top and with each stroke of his thumb to her skin, passion ignited deep within her.

All she wanted was Grant. All of him.

Her hip bumped his holstered gun. Her body tensed. She released her fingers from his neck and splayed her hand onto the wide-muscled expanse of his chest—strong, warm, and powerful.

When she pushed away, fiery red passion blazed in his eyes, the same which flared deep inside her. "Damn you, Grant Morley, for painting my gray world into intense, wonderful colors." She brushed her fingers across his lips.

He cupped her chin, his breaths ragged. "Kaleidoscope patterns, that's what goes on in my head when we touch. The trial better be quick."

"And then you'll be after the next mobster, while I worry."

"Hey, you're seeing the worst," he said.

She shook her head and shuffled to the bathroom. Grabbing the edge of the sink, she stared in the mirror at her sallow skin and bleary eyes. Her worst damage lay deeper, and he'd glimpsed the extent.

Grant wasn't a player. He wouldn't have spoken if he hadn't meant the words. Could she become strong enough to live in his world?

The shower stall beckoned with gallons of warm water to wash her doubts away. Buried deep inside lived the girl who always longed for a husband and kids, a yard, and a puppy. Grant had hinted at the possibility.

Another yawn nearly tipped her over. She washed her face, brushed her teeth and returned to the bedroom.

He stood at the bedside, holding an old-fashioned alarm clock. Lamplight outlined his shirtless back. He turned, and his gaze traveled over her.

Shields she'd built to protect her heart collapsed. A man worth any effort stood before her.

He must've read her mind.

The clock slipped onto the nightstand and tipped to the edge. He twisted to grab it, and light shone on bruises covering his chest.

"You're hurt badly. My fault, all my fault." She put her hand out, needing to stroke the pain away.

"Please let it go, Miranda." He stepped back. "I'd prefer if you took the bed against the wall. I've had worse bruises."

"Worse? And no one to soothe them." Miranda crawled over the first bed and slid under the comforter of the other one. "I led the attacker to you."

The light went out. Air stirred after he threw back the comforter on his bed. "Listen, Dad nailed it in the diner. You're an unwilling participant in Maneski's plan, and you saved Judge Gilson."

"And met you."

"Finally." Grant cleared his throat. "For months, I watched you peer through those plants. I longed to pull you through and dance you across the lobby."

Her heart fluttered. "Oh, I used to love dancing."

"Let me get us through the trial. Afterward, we'll go dancing to celebrate." He released a long sigh. "You've haunted my dreams since I first glimpsed you," his husky voice whispered.

Her body tingled from the full out assault from Agent of Interest, the sexy, 2.0 edition. "I never knew."

Only a five-inch gap hindered an exploration of the seductive features. The craving for more of his kisses sent spirals of need through her—molten, golden pools. Her fingers pushed back her comforter.

~ ~ ~

Grant calculated where Miranda's soft body parts would sink into her mattress. Her berry-scented kiss lingered on his lips.

Stop it, Morley. He threw off the sheet. Being naked in a cornfield during an arctic winter wouldn't help him chill tonight. "Need another blanket?"

"The temperature's fine," she said.

He stretched his arms alongside his body, concentrating on the crisp texture of the sheets.

These weren't the flannel sheets his mom insisted he use for winter. His mom, who'd nearly died because of his mistakes:

Miranda cleared her throat. "I wouldn't have survived all this without you. Thank you, Grant."

"You don't know how welcome you are." Yearning grew in his heart. "After the trial, I'll make an attempt to show you."

Miranda shifted in her bed. "Deal. By the way, I never said I didn't snore."

"As a matter of fact, I know better. Night." Grant forced a chuckle, he had to appear normal. He stared into the dark.

For the umpteenth time, he played out scenarios to guard them in Seattle. The mole would know their game plan.

The furnace kicked on, breaking the rhythmic tick of the clock. Miranda finally took the regular breaths of deep sleep.

All those he loved remained vulnerable to The Butcher's wrath. Angst overwhelmed him, the likes of which he'd never experienced. He could lose them all, at any moment.

Chapter 15

Grant closed his eyes and woke with Miranda pinned against his body, his arm draped over the slip of bare skin peeking above the waistband of her pj's.

Soft hair brushed his cheek and her smooth skin created a silken state of heaven.

Her eyes fluttered open. Her lips parted.

If he pulled her closer, he'd taste her sweetness again.

In one motion, she pressed her palm into his chest, rolling him onto his back. His butt straddled the narrow space between the beds.

Daylight.

She poked his ribs.

"What?"

"You're hogging my bed."

Heat rose in his face while he quelled unwelcome surges of interest. He scooched onto his bed, threw his legs over the side, and opened the door. "I'll shower first. I need to confer with Jesse." He dashed out.

Miranda had rinsed out her lace panties and hung them on the shower head. He moved them to the towel rack and shook his head, getting his focus back to business.

Staying awake all night shouldn't have been difficult, regardless of sleepless nights since he'd met her. He'd stumbled and fallen in—way, way too deep.

His brain had checked out, and his libido had clocked in. Fatigue dovetailing into an irresistible opportunity?

No. He admired her courage, and how much she cared for others. The possibility of loving her didn't scare him. He turned the shower knob to the coldest setting to rinse off, dressed, and then ran hot water for her in the tub.

He knocked on their bedroom door.

"Enter." She sat upright in bed. "What's the matter?"

"It's too early to bother the Langley's yet for your stuff. I started the water, if a bath's appealing to you. I'll see if Kyle left any clothes in here which might work."

"A bath and something besides muddy pants to wear would be heaven, but I need a bigger favor. Trey Langley doesn't appreciate Red. If you can find a temporary pasture for him, I'll buy him and pay board."

The sooner he escaped her pleading eyes the better. "I'll make it happen. Poppy can take care of him during the trial. Water's running."

"Thanks. I could build a nest in my hair." She lifted a tangled lock and crawled out of bed.

When the door closed behind her, he pulled open a dresser drawer and removed running leggings and a University of Washington sweater.

He stood on the other side of the bathroom door. "I left duds for you outside the door. See you in the kitchen."

"Great," she replied.

Get back on your game, Morley. A shooting range with Venom's face on a target and a hundred rounds would work.

The aroma of strong coffee reached him from the kitchen. He adjusted the Glock holster and glanced out a window to a picturesque, frosty morning.

Roy's mulch pile sat at the edge of the garden. Strands of frozen straw jutted out from the edges. It reminded him of the heap of manure where Miranda had hidden the crook who'd messed with Red.

Life should be gentle in Emma Springs, or boring like he remembered thinking as a kid. What he'd give for a bale of mundane, instead of what faced him in the kitchen.

Bullseye sat at the dining room table, and Jesse stood at the stove.

Damned if Jesse didn't fit Bullseye's nickname, PB&P, for "Pretty Boy and Packing." When had the squirt buffed out?

"Roy told me to make myself at home." Jesse turned the gas flame to low. "Sleep well, boss?" he chided.

Grant leaned against the doorframe and folded his arms over his chest. "I heard Roy come in."

"Alert as always," Jesse said.

"I didn't want to disturb Miranda by greeting him." He rubbed the area on his chest where Miranda's fingertips had pushed.

"Bullseye spotted a figure crossing behind the house at dawn. Might've been a neighbor."

"Or Karpenito. Great way to start the day." Grant rubbed his eyes. "Any word on his whereabouts?"

"No." Bullseye's keen brown eyes sighted in on his face, as if positioning cross hairs on a target. "Is Miranda suspicious?"

Grant stared back. "Couldn't say. You're the one with female intuition."

Jesse snorted. "About the stopping power and range of a Hornady A-MAX 308 bullet."

"Jealous 'cause I'm a better shot?" Bullseye teased.

Grant shook his finger. "Quit fighting, children. Jesse, when Miranda appears, I have to stir those eggs. I promised her a good breakfast yesterday and got interrupted."

He pulled a mug out of the cupboard and poured himself a cup of coffee. "Hate the stuff, but maybe the caffeine will clear my head."

"You must be foggy to think you get breakfast credits, Mor—" Jesse held the spatula in midair, eyes focused on the hallway.

Grant turned. His mouth dropped.

Red and gold streaks glinted in Miranda's free-flowing hair while she glided under a skylight and into the room.

Here was a Miranda he'd never seen before-not at work and not bedraggled. He fought to stay composed while his gaze traveled the length of her body. Kyle's old sweater must've shrunk. Substantially.

The V neckline accented her bosom and exposed way too much. "I'll call Langley's and get your things brought over. Trey'll think he's lucky to sell you Red with winter feeding coming soon."

"Thank you, Grant," Miranda said.

Jesse's eyes narrowed to slits and centered on him.

Grant cleared his throat. "We'll head to the airport after breakfast."

"Okay," Miranda said. "Coffee smells good."

He handed her the cup he'd poured for himself. "Freshly brewed." Their fingers brushed, her touch recharging his soul. Downtime was all they needed. They'd go slowly, get to know each other. Once she fully trusted him, desensitizing would cure her aversion to guns. Love wasn't always painful, and he'd prove it to her.

The tick of a mantle clock methodically beat through the dead silence.

"I'd appreciate having my own clothes." Miranda adjusted the sweater, hiding her cleavage by a half inch of ribbing.

Grant tore his eyes away. "I'll call the Langley's." He walked through the arched doorway and plopped onto the couch, in sight of the kitchen. And Miranda. Sweat stuck his palms to the phone. "Trey, this is Grant. I wondered if I could get Miranda's belongings in a few minutes. We're catching today's flight to Seattle."

Jesse's eyes widened while Miranda bent to pull a carton of cream from the refrigerator. The sweater didn't conceal her shapely butt.

A growl came from Grant's throat. "Sure, swing by if it's no trouble. We're having breakfast at Roy Werner's. Hey, I want to buy Red."

Miranda straightened and smiled straight at him, and her smile would melt chocolates at twenty feet.

His pulse jumped. He managed to smile back.

Trey believed the mule had caused all the trouble. "Consider it a deal. He fits in our herd, and Miranda wants him. You name the price." He'd clean out his retirement account if necessary. "I'll send a check. See you soon."

Grant cradled the phone and took a breath.

Outside, a layer of fresh snow bent the grass in the meadow. After the sun warmed it, the blades would spring back.

In much the same way, Miranda bent with stress and never broke. She met challenges head on and would make a perfect bureau wife—after she took time to regroup when the trial finished and they all returned to business as usual.

He rubbed his temple. What would his next version of normal be? His task list had never included ousting a damn inside mole.

A picture of a Porsche Carrera flashed in his brain—the black one Sam's boss owned.

His body froze.

Their own SAC could be plotting to kill Miranda.

~ ~ ~

Grant had finished the call to Trey, and then he'd moved to look out the window facing the lake. Was she imagining that his body seemed tense?

What else worried him?

He turned. "Red's yours."

"Really?" She squealed. Oh, he was so hot when his dimple showed with a genuine smile. So, so hot.

Miranda set down her coffee and gripped the counter behind her with one hand. She crooked a finger on her other hand to motion him over.

He leaned toward her, his breath warm on her throat.

She rose to tiptoe, her mouth hovering near his lips, and then pecked his cheek. "All the thanks you get for now."

"Welcome." His voice had deepened to a throaty timbre. He fidgeted with his gun holster, and his eyes flicked between the agents.

"Tarnished reputation, agent Morley?" she whispered.

Color rose in Grant's cheeks. "I promised I'd see to Red's care. Your clothes will arrive in ten minutes." He rested his hand at the small of her back, then dropped it. "The breakfast I ordered from my former student smells ready."

Jesse piled eggs on a plate and handed it to Miranda. "Like you'd know burnt from blanched, Morley. Roy's grilling the steaks."

Kyle stepped in the room and patted Miranda's arm. "How's my favorite Seattle patient?"

"Better now. Grant bought Red for me." She took a sip of coffee. "Thank you for the use of your room. I slept wonderfully until dawn."

Grant cleared his throat. "Borrowed some clothes from your dresser, bro."

Kyle glanced at her. "No worries. Hey, do I smell the infamous Wagyu beef grilling?"

"I missed the meal where Kathleen served those steaks— had a delightful fishy dinner instead." Miranda turned to Jesse. "Yum. Mushrooms and onion in the eggs. Thanks."

"Anything for our heroine." Jesse threw her another dazzling smile.

"I'll get my folks," Grant snapped. "They'll enjoy your blanched breakfast, too." He slapped Jesse on the shoulder while he passed him. "If the bureau doesn't work out, guess you'd make a good fry cook."

Miranda did a double take and then stepped aside to make room for an older version of Kyle carrying a dish heaped with barbecued steaks.

"I'm Roy Werner." He set the platter on the counter and shook her hand. "Bet you're the Miranda I've heard about."

"Yes, thank you for your hospitality."

"You're very welcome. Dig in, everyone," he said.

The aroma of seared beef filled the kitchen. Several agents speared hunks of meat onto their plates.

Pat strode in and drew Roy into the hug of an old friendship. "Sorry to be those sleep, eat, and run kind of guests."

"Friends are always welcome," Roy said. "Darned shame about the hubbub. I'm hoping Miss Miranda will return and bring a friend for Kyle." He winked at his son. "I'll show her where I hide the spare key."

"My friend, Corrin, wanted to join me. Under different circumstances, I'm certain Emma Springs is a perfect town to visit." Miranda scrutinized a series of locks on the front door. He'd have to provide a ring of keys aided by a retinal scan by the time she returned—if Karpenito didn't find her first.

~ ~ ~

"Three Falls Airport's the next exit," Kyle announced over the drone of country music on the radio. Even from the third row of seats in the back of the Suburban, Grant could see his white-knuckle grip on the steering wheel.

Everyone except his parents were on edge. They'd fallen asleep in the center row of seats. Mom's head rested on Dad's shoulder, like teenagers on a date.

He turned and looked through the rear window. A Stater tailed them at a safe distance.

Miranda slunk further into the seat next to him and

wrapped her coat tighter. "I didn't realize until this week what I've missed most."

He leaned closer to her. "Tell me."

"Loving support. I don't have my folks to steer me over life's hurdles."

"I can't imagine how horrible that would be. I still discuss big decisions with my family and made several phone calls when I doubted my choice to join the bureau."

"I understand questioning that decision."

"It annoyed the hell out of Dad. Mom encouraged me to rethink my career path."

"Why?"

"I guess she hoped I'd become a teacher like her. She maintained I'd been empathetic since first grade."

"Maybe it's time to own those softer emotions which have begun to trickle out like a leaky spigot."

"My plumbing's fine," he scoffed. "What did your parents do?"

"My dad taught school," Miranda said. "You're like him in some ways."

Good. Grant flashed the smile he knew would show his dimple. "You can call any of us. We consider you part of our family. You saved us and alerted me to a few things sadly lacking in my life." He pulled her hand from her coat pocket and squeezed her fingers. "It's killing me to be bureau ready again."

"I'm alive because you've been bureau ready since we met, and you've all been wonderful." A weak smile crossed her lips before she pulled her hand away.

They'd all been wonderful? That sounded suspiciously like the beginning of a goodbye. She was pulling inward again. But why? He'd explained he couldn't show his attraction in front of the other agents. Or was she scared?

He wasn't exactly thrilled to be going back, either. For once, there wasn't any thrill in the take down after a bust.

His folks and Miranda had narrowly missed being murder victims. Seattle posed different problems.

Kyle turned into the terminal.

Two Montana staters flanked them while he parked in the loading zone.

"Hey, backseat lovebirds masquerading as my parents, we've arrived at the airport," he said.

"I've never seen more than a security guard here before." Pat pointed at the marked cars and hopped out. "Isn't it officer overkill for Three Falls?"

Grant winced. "Consider it preparation for an urban experience."

"Thanks again for being our chauffeur, Kyle," Pat gave him a hug. "I know you hate airports."

"Hope you make the plane," Kyle stepped to the rear and unloaded luggage. "You cut it close."

"That's the idea." Grant said. "The airline knows the situation. Everyone head to TSA."

Pain etched deep grooves in his dad's wrinkled face while he climbed out. "My ribs are telling me a plane ride's welcome. Otherwise I'd be weed whacking."

Grant maneuvered out of the back row of seats and did a quick check of the parking lots.

Karpenito could be anywhere, prepared to whack *them*.

Chapter 16

Funny, the airplane seemed to be the safest place Miranda had been in days. Security had downgraded to a beefy man in dark clothes who got on and sat two rows behind them. He had to be a sky marshal.

The rest of the passengers appeared blandly benign on a normal flight.

Pat and Tom chatted in the row behind them.

She closed her eyes, absorbing the family banter. Grant studied her again—she could sense the laser focus of his attention. No pinpointing the exact moment, but within the last two days, internal radar had kicked in, sending a pulse at the exact moment his hazel eyes landed on her.

With the slightest movement of air, her nose detected his scent. Her traitorous body vibrated in the most sensual manner conceivable from his lightest touch. Like now, while his shoulder pressed into hers, solid, strong. A shiver ran through her.

"With all you've been through, I can get the FBI to provide a counselor," Grant whispered.

"I'm ready to face my past," she said.

"Great. Let me know when you want to start." Grant squeezed her hand.

"I need a moratorium on guns first."

A grimace crossed his lips. "You'll have to identify the firearm Venom carried. I'll do what I can to hustle things along."

She placed her palm over her heart. "You make things happen, Agent Morley."

"Please prepare for landing," a flight attendant announced. Fifty-two degrees and cloudy at SeaTac Airport."

Miranda stared out to where Lake Washington and Mercer Island stretched below. "I wonder if I'll have to get used to sleeping through traffic noises again?"

Grant pushed the armrest down. "If there's any wildlife calls I can make, let me know."

If only he would move away—a little bit closer. Her brain continued the battle against her Grant-addicted body. "Howling coyotes? I think not." She turned to the window. "Sequestered in a hotel room's another first on my list."

The plane dipped toward a row of lights, blinking through a light drizzle.

"I'll be wherever you want me at the hotel," Grant offered. "Sam will meet us at the airport and provide an escort."

"Protocol, I bet."

The plane bounced twice, taxied, and the sky time ended.

"Yup." Grant turned on his phone and thumbed the screen. "Tests came back from the remains in the burned dumpster."

He stood and offered his hand to her. "They listed fibers from a wig and material used in platform soles. It confirms our suspicions. Karpenito wore a disguise." His voice had shifted to authority mode.

"No lie, Sherlock," she muttered, and grabbed her purse. "Guess we both know."

Grant's mouth opened, and then closed. His body stayed rigid while they entered the concourse.

Three men in dark jackets stood off to the left. The oldest man nodded at Grant, then he continued watching passengers departing behind them.

A nearly imperceptible movement of Grant's head indicated his perusal of the crowd.

His palm pressed into her back, directing her to the men. "I want you to meet my boss, the Assistant Special Agent in Charge, or ASAC."

Of course. The important witness offered for inspection. She veered to avoid a toddler wobbling on chubby legs. Her fingertips brushed his feather soft hair. *Someday.*

"Hi, I'm Sam Coswell. You must be Miranda. Pleased to meet you." He held out his hand. His smile played out as phony as Karpenito's beard.

She shook and then stepped back to Grant's side. "I'll be pleased if everyone survives."

"Yes, ma'am." Sam nodded. "Here's Pat and Tom, now."

Pat opened her arms to the agent. "Hey, Sam. You need to plan another fishing trip. We'd welcome your gang at our ranch any time. Bringing significant others, of course." She flashed a grin at Miranda.

"The team's busy, Mom," Grant said.

"I'd appreciate a vacation." Sam shook Tom's hand. "Good to have you folks here. Sorry about the circumstances."

"We got to meet Miranda in the deal. The rewards outweigh the plight." Tom patted Miranda on the shoulder. "She's a real keeper, same as my Pat."

"Bad analogy," Pat said. "No fish on a string reference for either of us women. Miranda's a faceted jewel. She etched a mark on us all."

"Ask the Maneski thug she left in a manure pile." Grant added.

Nice recovery on an awkward moment in front of the boss. Miranda turned to watch a woman pushing a stroller while clutching a sleeping baby to her shoulder. She stared at the woman's back until she disappeared in the crowd. Longing tugged deep into her soul.

"I'd like to hear the manure story," Sam said. "Right now, it's time to collect luggage and head to the hotel."

Grant took her elbow, while three other agents surrounded her. The group shifted to avoid a wheelchair, each man keeping two feet away from her.

A TSA attendant sat at the last security point. No one familiar stood in the crowd behind him.

"Grant, you let Corrin and Iris know my flight, didn't you?"

"Negative."

"You promised." She slowed her pace.

Grant gripped her arm and propelled her forward. "Plans changed. Couldn't risk it."

They marched around a corner, her throat scratching as if she'd swallowed sand. "I need a drink." She pointed to a fountain anchored on a nearby wall.

While she bent her head, Grant, the sky marshal, and two agents formed a shoulder-to-shoulder barrier around her.

Miranda straightened up. "Damn Karpenito," she said.

Grant met her eyes. Nothing could hide his fear.

~ ~ ~

"Same Seattle, bustling with travelers." Grant struggled to casually scan the passengers grabbing luggage from the circulating carousel. He smiled at Miranda.

She ignored him and barely looked up when Sam walked over.

"Grant, you'll accompany Pat and Miranda to the hotel," he said. "Tom rides in the second car with me and the luggage."

Miranda pulled her jacket closer to her chest. "Maybe I should crawl into a suitcase to conceal the bullseye on my back."

"Simply precautionary." Grant steered her to the left when they split into two groups at the escalator leading to the arrival pickup area.

Miranda stepped on first. He placed one foot beside hers, shifting his body sideways, creating a barrier.

Every nerve ending thrummed, while his mind focused on the perimeter activities. "I enjoy travelling together in tight places."

"Yeah, right." Her head hung as she shuffled off and toward sliding glass doors leading outside.

An overcast sky hung behind a dark SUV pulling curbside.

Grant's hand slipped to his Glock while the bulletproof window rolled down. He recognized the driver. "The women will ride in the middle. I'll ride up front." He opened the back door for Miranda.

"Whatever." Rumbling motors nearly drowned out her voice.

He smoothed her coat sleeve. "We should be at the hotel in fifteen minutes. Let's make a call to Corrin a priority after we get in the room."

Eyes hooded by dark lashes turned away.

She buckled her seat belt. "Sure."

"Maybe Miranda can point out landmarks to me on the drive." His mom's voice projected calm authority, a holdover from teaching second graders. "I haven't spent much time in Seattle."

He shut their car door and continued to peruse lanes of traffic congested by departing passengers.

Seattle. Karpenito and Maneski's home turf.

Grant adjusted his Glock, scanning the airport as familiar as the back of his hand. He slid into the front seat. "Sam signaled to get moving."

Their vehicle sped onto I-5 HOV lanes. They exited, turned twice, and stopped at a three-story brick building fronted by a green, scalloped awning.

Topiary pots dotted by white lights stood on either

side of an elegant brass and glass entry. Grant surveyed the corners of the building.

No security cameras. His pulse quickened.

The driver stopped in the loading zone.

A familiar FBI agent trailed behind a uniformed bellhop approaching Grant's side. The kid brightened in recognition while he got out and opened Pat's door. "Coach! I mean, Mr. Morley."

Grant studied the boy's dark skin and eager eyes, then stuck out his hand. "Teddy! Congratulations! You landed the job. And you've shot up in height."

"Three inches. I can grab rebounds now. I appreciated your letter of reference. Thank you, Coach."

"Glad we're staying at your hotel."

"Me, too." Teddy grinned and turned to Pat. "By your eyes, you must be related to Mr. Morley. He's the best hoop coach the Y ever had." He pretended to dribble between his legs.

"And the best son. Grant's always enjoyed helping kids," Pat said, before stepping to the sidewalk.

"I stayed off the streets for the honor of playing for him." Teddy escorted Pat to the entry doors. "So far, none of our team's done time. It's been over three years."

Miranda slid onto the curbside seat and got out. She tilted her head, eying Grant and Teddy.

Grant caught her curious appraisal. "Glad I steered a couple of you kids onto the right path." He threw back his shoulders. "Mom and Miranda, please wait in the lobby."

Another agent met the women at the glass doors and led them inside.

The second SUV pulled curbside.

Grant turned to Teddy. "Thanks for the update. I'm proud of you all."

Teddy beamed. "I'll let them know. We meet once a month for a pickup game."

"Leave the place and time at the desk for me."

"Let me know if you need anything else," Teddy called, pulling luggage from the back end.

"Will do." Grant followed his dad into the lobby.

Miranda stood quietly off to one side, then stepped out as Teddy rolled the luggage cart by her. She smiled at him. "You're proof that Grant makes things happen."

"Yes, miss," Teddy agreed. "Enjoy your stay."

Grant approached Miranda. "At around fourteen, the little buggers become tolerable," he whispered under his breath.

She turned away as an agent from his office stepped up.

"Sam cleared the third floor of all occupants except your group." He handed Grant a key card. "We swept the building and ran checks on the guests occupying the other floors."

Miranda hunched her shoulders and wrapped her arms around her chest.

"I'll confer with you in a minute." Grant ran his fingers across his throat to end the details. "I assumed I'd have support from our office."

"I rescheduled dental surgery," the agent joked. "See you upstairs."

"Okay, ladies," Grant ushered Miranda and Pat into the elevator. "This will be our digs for the week."

"I spotted a pizza place next door," Tom said. "I'll buy."

Grant nodded to Sam. "Hand your money to an agent, Dad. We're in for the night. Miranda likes mushrooms."

Exiting the elevator, he quickly unlocked their suite and walked past a spacious bathroom. "This should work well."

A mirrored closet door reflected Miranda while she trudged past.

Striped furniture sat on one side of an open area and two queen-sized beds on the other. "I put Mom and Dad in the back bedroom, and we'll be out here in front." He closed the light blockers and flimsy curtains. "Okay by you, Miranda?"

"Yeah," she mumbled.

"You two get the bigger TV and wet bar." His mom grasped Miranda's hand. "You've withered worse than cornstalks in January. I bet that call to your friend would perk you up."

Miranda dropped into an overstuffed chair. "Corrin will be anxious for news." She took the phone Grant handed her and punched in the number. "Hi, Corrin. We made it to town. Maybe we can get together tomorrow." Her eyes grew wide. "You're where? With who?"

Grant's body shot to alert.

"Oh, yes, Dr. Kyle rates my approval." She tucked a lock of hair behind her ear. "Enjoy your day off. I can hardly hear your voice over the music. Okay. I'll call."

"A drill sergeant joined mild-mannered Kyle." Grant nudged his mom. He walked over and took the phone from Miranda. "Unplanned vacation?"

"Something delayed my messages to Corrin," Miranda said. "She got concerned and caught a flight to Three Falls." A hint of mischief crossed her face. "She and the good doctor are at a cowboy dance bar. Maybe she's found a pardner in Kyle."

"I never thought I'd celebrate malfunctioning technology, but I do love your smile." He pocketed his phone. "Kyle thrives on a challenge. He owes me for delivering a single woman to Emma Springs."

Three loud knocks boomed through the room.

He grabbed his Glock, and planted his body in front of Miranda.

"It's Sam and the pizzas," his boss yelled.

Aromas of garlic, pepperoni, and fresh bread drifted in with his boss. Grant stuck his head into the hallway. "Do your men want to join us?"

"Not tonight. We have a couple things to go over before tomorrow morning. You folks will need to be ready to depart at ten hundred sharp to meet with the DA." He waved and left.

Tom folded a pizza slice in half and took a huge bite. Miranda hadn't moved.

"I can order you a salad." Grant poured sparkling water into a glass and handed it to her.

"I'm not hungry." She tipped the water to her lips, her hand wobbling.

"You might want to pick out a few veggies." Pat handed Miranda a slice. "You haven't eaten much today," she coaxed.

"If you don't eat anything, Pat will put you on vitamins like she did Grant." His dad patted her knee. "He must've grown a foot one year. Come on, one piece."

Miranda picked off a mushroom.

Grant forced down a bite of greasy pepperoni. He thrummed his fingers on his knee. "Doc Kyle will thrash me if you don't absorb some sustenance. Remember?"

She nodded and took a bite. "I can handle a slice for friendship's sake."

"Honey, my ribs are hurting." Tom said. "Let's see if we can figure out the flat screen in our bedroom." He threw Grant a wobbly salute. "See you in the morning. You two are in charge of coffee."

"Got it." Grant closed the pizza boxes and set them in the hallway.

"I think I'll get a sweatshirt on. I can't get warm." Miranda rummaged through her duffel bag before she headed into the bathroom.

Grant checked the deadbolt and slid the flimsy chain in place. He loosened his Kevlar vest.

Grabbing extra pillows, he put his knee on the mattress closest to the door and formed two body-shaped lumps in the middle, then tucked the bedspread around them.

Miranda stepped out. "You snuck in lumpy friends." Color drained from her face. "Oh, those are supposed to be us."

"Another precaution." He moved toward her, then checked himself. "We can watch TV or relax, your choice."

She climbed into the other bed. "Drift me to sleep telling me a childhood story. I need to visualize the shorter, gap-toothed Grant."

Anything she wanted to hear. Anything but tonight's danger, or tomorrow. Someday he'd be pulling her close, smoothing away cares of their world. Not tonight.

He flipped off the light switch and slipped between the sheets. "Okay. One of my favorites is Dad first letting me sit on a horse."

"We share a special memory."

He continued until peaceful breathing came in wisps across his shoulder. She'd curled on her side, tight against him.

With a flick of his wrist, he threw the spread to one side and fanned the sheet. It'd be another long night.

He savored her warmth, her mere presence. How many people withstood the pressure of losing their family, started over on their own at twenty, and then handled a mobster's pursuit? Her core appeared tough-cop strong at times, but would she make it through the trial without more emotional damage, even with his support?

Sirens and traffic noise had faded to nothing by three am.

He rolled his shoulders and imagined her at different ages wearing long braids. She'd have been a tomboy, climbing trees and catching frogs. No frilly dresses for his warrior princess.

A magnetic card slid into their lock.

He sat up and swept the Glock from under his pillow.

Two muffled beeps.

Someone had unlocked their door. Unannounced.

His other hand jostled Miranda. "Shh, stay down." He pushed her onto the floor between the bed and the window.

A sliver of light came in through the cracked door.

The chain snapped.

In one movement, Grant dropped next to Miranda and aimed his gun at the door.

The intruder stepped in, closed the door behind him and fired four shots into the pillows on the other bed. Puffs of filling drifted out.

Grant fired three times into the tall figure. The gunman groaned and bent in half.

Metal clanked onto glass, followed by a thump.

"Stay put." Grant pushed Miranda into the walled corner.

The window facing the street shattered, and a bullet struck the mirrored closet door. Light from a streetlight outlined a running figure on the roof across the street.

The bedroom door cracked open.

"Don't move Dad! Sharpshooter across the street. Keep the lights off." Grant kept his gun on the man crumpled on the floor. Under his chest, a dark splotch began spreading across the carpet.

An acrid scent hung in the room.

Grant stayed below the windowsill and crawled across the floor. He grabbed the killer's Colt.

"You both all right?" His dad poked out his gun.

"Yes. Cover him," Grant said. "Stinks like knockout gas, and he's wearing a mask."

"I have the police on the phone," his mom called from the bedroom.

"Everybody stay low. No lights. Get several ambulances. There's a chance we've got agents affected by sedation gas."

His dad crept on all fours to the gunman. "He's got a wound in the neck and abdomen."

A fist pounded on their door. "Grant, it's me, Sam! Are you okay?" He pounded again.

Grant yanked it open. Another gust of foul air entered the room. "No one hit," he reported.

Sam pulled off the cloth he'd held over his nose and mouth. "Five agents incapacitated in the hallway. Alerted about a person on the building across the street. I called it in and went to check. He got off the shot before he ran." Sam scanned the room using his flashlight.

Miranda remained scrunched into a corner, huddled under the shelf holding the lamp. She'd drawn her knees to her forehead. Broken glass surrounded her.

The shadowed outline of a 9mm pointing at them would forever be seared into Grant's brain. He knelt by her. "We're safe now." His hands shook while he stroked her arms.

She tucked in further, her white knuckled fingers clamped onto her legs. "Were Pat or Tom hurt?"

Only Miranda would think of others after her life nearly ended. "They're fine. I'm going to slide you out." He unzipped his Kevlar and wrapped his arms around her to pull her out.

Cold air blew in from the broken window.

She stayed balled while he carried her to his parent's bedroom.

"Police are getting the block sealed off." Sam flicked on the lights.

"I've got you now." Grant lowered them into an overstuffed chair. "It's over. Pass your fears into me. Let them out."

Her head remained wedged under his chin, her eyes scrunched shut.

"The bureau better have good answers," his mom said. "Tell me if there's anything I can do to help poor Miranda."

Grant shook his head. "Leave the door open, Mom. I need to hear the explanation."

Miranda shuddered with the intensity of a battering ram slamming into his bruised ribs. "Let it go, Miranda. I've got you." He tipped back his head, and took in a labored breath.

In the living room, his mom raised her voice, and Sam quietly responded.

Two medics rolled a wheeled stretcher into the room.

An icy band squeezed his heart. He shifted in the chair so Miranda couldn't view the grisly scene as they stabilized the assassin.

Miranda covered her ears while the attendants relayed vitals and wheeled out the gurney.

He stroked her back. "It's over now."

"Sam Coswell," Pat shook her finger. "I don't care if fifty agents stand shoulder to shoulder in this hallway and you park tanks outside for backup. You must protect us," she demanded.

"I understand your anger." Sam clenched and unclenched his fist. "Your security's been compromised. I've got all available agents headed here." His gaze flicked to Miranda, then met Grant's eyes.

"Who knew?" Grant mouthed the words to his boss.

"Fortuna," Sam mouthed.

Grant nodded. Their damn SAC, the leader who did everything politically and departmentally correct—for his own advancement. Grant had never fully trusted the jerk from the start. By Sam's grimace, he agreed.

If it became the last thing he did, he'd collar the filthy, murderous traitor. Where to start?

Surviving tonight.

Chapter 17

Miranda fought against the onset of the slide into immobilizing despair. "Don't leave me." Grant's firm hold while he cradled her in the chair had no effect. "Please. Don't leave me alone again. I can't go back in the dark hole." Her fingers pressed into his muscled arm.

"I'll never leave you. Talk to me. It'll help us both." He pulled her so tight, she felt his heartbeats, the same as when she'd been splayed across his bare chest.

She brushed her finger over the bruised skin under his eye. "Gunmen wait around every corner. I can't watch you die."

"Shh. Sam and I know who's to blame. He won't risk exposing himself again." He pushed a curl behind her ear.

Tom stepped in. "Maybe you two need a good stiff drink, or several."

"Can I get you something, Miranda?" Grant asked tenderly.

"Self-medicating doesn't sound bad, but I don't drink. Another anomaly, I guess."

"We'll be fine, Dad. Thanks." Grant moved her palm to his heart. "I love your anomalies. Explain the darkness. Maybe together we can brighten it."

"When I lost my family, the world turned gray. It's hard to describe living in a self-imposed tunnel. You lit a torch, then Maneski threw us into a nest of vipers, and their fangs keep striking." She stretched her fingers like a claw and tapped it against his chest.

Grant let out a long breath. "I'm sorry. The snakes will all be arrested and jailed soon. Sam told me they collared

Maneski leaving his house. They confiscated a flash drive containing contacts."

"Will they stop hunting us?"

"Thugs need money for operations. We've pulled their plug. Sam and I will figure out how to eliminate the traitor in our department."

She pressed her palm against his cheek. "You'll be in danger again."

"Nope, I'll help set the stage, and Sam will carry out the plan while I remain by you."

This time. Otherwise, he'd be in the thick of it, a human shield guarding the next witness in another hotel room. Her body went very, very cold.

~ ~ ~

Grant leaned his head back. Miranda had gone quiet. Too quiet.

"You okay?"

"Do they always strike at night?" she asked.

"They think our guard's down then." Sam stood in the doorway. "But they don't know Grant Morley. Pat tells me your group can visit a family friend in a remote setting."

Grant smoothed Miranda's hair. "Precisely where we should be right now. I clarified that his house is suitable."

"I had orders," Sam disclosed. "From here on out, tell no one the details. This hotel's getting a new room ready for you tonight. Both regional SWAT teams are enroute. Once they're in place, I can go check for damage to my trousers after the butt chewing from your mother." Sam shook his head. "And it's deserved. Your bellhop friend said the person on the roof had binoculars and a cell phone. The kid spotted him from the front door. He ran in and found me a few minutes too late for the agents they gassed, but who knows how many shots the sniper would've fired otherwise."

"Teddy's a sharp kid. Always liked him."

Sam crossed his arms. "Miranda, if you need to speak to a counselor, we have one on call."

"I've got this," Grant said.

"Miranda makes the determination."

"Don't want to talk to a stranger," she whispered.

"Understood. Let me know if you do." Sam turned. "Here's the hotel manager. I bet your new room's ready."

"She'll be okay," Grant stated. "We're discussing what happened, and I already offered a counselor."

"Okay." Sam stepped into his parents' room. "We can change suites now."

Grant carried Miranda into the hall, cradling her like a frightened child.

Three agents followed them into the two bedroom suite, mere steps away from a shattered window and a mattress riddled with bullets.

"I promise, tomorrow we'll stay in a beautiful and impenetrable spot." Grant looked down at her still body. "Think Roy Werner's, except sitting in peaceful woods."

Grant shifted her weight and pulled back the covers on the new bed. "No one knows our lodging during the rest of the trial. We'll be safe."

No response.

"Please trust me."

She scrambled under the covers and rolled onto her side, facing the wall. "I have to. Can you give me a couple of minutes alone?"

A stiletto knife couldn't have carved into him more precisely. "Sure. I'd give anything to make this go away. Maneski deserves to rot like garbage." He cracked the bedroom door and caught the agent's eye who stood at the outer door. "I'm grabbing a shower."

The man nodded.

Grant lumbered into the bathroom. Blistering hot water didn't wash away his lengthy list of regrets. He shut the spigot off, toweled dry, and pulled his sweats back on.

Light from the entry illuminated a view of her back and shoulders. She'd curled in fetal position, holding Kenny's ball cap under her chin.

He shut their door and slid into bed next to her, adjusting his weight inch by inch on the mattress.

Anxiety hung in the room like a noose.

"I need to hold you," she implored. "May I?"

"Always."

Her fingers found his wrist, and she drew his hand to her waist, then nestled her back against him. The dense fabric pushed against his bruises.

"Do they make Kevlar body suits?"

"I'll check tomorrow. Let me help relax you tonight." He eased her onto her belly, slipping his hand under her sweatshirt. Bumps of tension disappeared from her tight back muscles after his thumbs kneaded the taut areas.

He finished at her waist and pulled the sweatshirt down. Next, he lifted her hair to one side at the base of her neck, revealing pale skin.

While his fingers stroked away knots, he listened to his heart. They had to figure out a life together. They had to.

She rolled her head to the side, a pink cheek exposed against a stark white pillow. "Mmm, no more kinks. Don't tell me you learned those skills massaging Brasso."

Even now, after he'd failed to keep her safe tonight, she made him smile. "Okay, I won't, though it's the truth. I watched an equine therapist at work after Poppy's old mare injured her shoulder."

"Bless the horses," she murmured.

His fingers combed through her glossy hair. Little by little, nudging tangled strands, he worked his way to her scalp.

The more he tried to put his feelings for her aside, the more he wanted her. Every strand of hair, every resilient attitude, every panicked nightmare.

Her lashes fluttered closed in time for her to catch three or four hours sleep. He left his arm draped across her back until smooth, rhythmic breathing came from her relaxed body.

His thoughts returned to Karpenito. All fingers pointed to Kevin Fortuna being point man. If he remembered correctly, Fortuna's police career began as a Seattle patrol officer. He'd joined the FBI and quickly climbed the ranks.

Every instinct told Grant it wasn't Sam. His boss drove a Chevy and took his family camping. He didn't own a black Porsche, and he didn't belong to a prestigious country club. Fortuna had to be the traitor.

An idea of how to trap Fortuna formed in his mind. He'd talk to Sam tomorrow.

His face went slack, imagining a spring Montana breeze stirring the blooming lilac bush outside his kitchen window and Miranda pulling a branch to her smiling face.

If they lived.

Chapter 18

Miranda inhaled the scent of strong and acidic Seattle coffee. She stretched the full length of a warm bed, raising her arms over her head.

"Hey, sleepyhead. You may want to get changed," Grant said from the foot of the bed. "Sam and the guys will be here in twenty minutes."

"Another wardrobe malfunction. If I don't hit my apartment, its old jeans or cargo pants."

"You're stunning in either, but Mom packed extra business type clothes she speculated might fit you." Grant set a tall drink container on the nightstand next to her. "You're welcome to chug it in the shower."

"I need a drip line." Her duffle bag sat on the end of the bed. "Thanks for the java. Very kind of your mom to bring me dressier clothing."

"She knows how fast things happen in law enforcement. I piled the gear from her in the bathroom." Grant zipped his case and wheeled it to the entry area. "Please leave the bedroom door open while you shower."

Miranda shrugged, headed to the bathroom, and stepped under the shower head. Warm droplets sprayed away memories of the horrible night, at least for a few minutes.

Pat's skirt only reached the top of her cowboy boots, but the sweater set fit perfectly. What a thoughtful gesture. Her own mom would've done the same. A tear came to her eye.

Her damp hair was the same reddish-brown as her mother's, her skin, too. She dabbed blush on, then took another swipe of Dewey Rose powder. Funeral lily would be more appropriate.

Her make-up case snapped closed. She tossed it into her suitcase, ready for their next lodging.

Hopefully one they'd leave without a bloodstained carpet.

~ ~ ~

Grant stood by the window, watching traffic.

Behind him, his dad sipped coffee and intermittently patted the bulge of his 1980's chest holster.

"Sam, can we chat for a minute?" Grant asked.

"We'll get java refills," Sam said. "Miranda should be out by the time we get back. Same order for everyone?"

"Sounds great," said Pat. "Make Tom's decaf."

Sam held the door.

"Thanks." Grant nodded to four agents in the hallway.

Grant and Sam stepped into the dark-paneled elevator.

"I have an idea to ferret out whether or not our SAC betrayed us," Grant said. "Call Fortuna and schedule a briefing about last night in your office at two o'clock. Tell him you want his opinion on your plans to move us to a new and more secure location."

"If I can restrain myself from choking the son of a bitch." Sam punched the lobby button four times with his middle finger.

"My thoughts involve firearms," Grant muttered. "Anyway, at two-fifteen sharp, I'll phone you. Drop a pen on the floor when you hear the call come in and hit speaker phone. I'll identify myself as your contact at the Belvedere Hotel and rattle off a confirmation of tonight's suite. The bastard will think he's located our hotel."

"Hmm. Might work," Sam said.

The elevator opened on the lower level.

He and Sam strode through the lobby and into the coffee shop next door.

Sam pulled out his wallet and grinned. "My treat. I like your plan. I bet he'll take the bait."

Grant nodded and scrutinized the surrounding buildings before reentering the hotel.

"I wracked my brain all night." Sam stood at the door. "I'm pleased you figured out a trap. I can't wait to cut the balls off the traitor."

A phone beeped, and Sam read a text. "Got a confirmation of what I suspected." He ushered Grant into the elevator. "When they were SPD cops twenty years ago, Karpenito and Fortuna came close to jailing Maneski's father. Records showed that after Fortuna reached ASAC, no charges stuck on either Maneski until last month." They exited at their floor.

"So they've been paid informants all this time, and no one questioned it." Grant stopped in the alcove next to the elevator, his voice low.

"They arrested minor players." Sam said. "Appeared legit upfront."

Grant let out a disgusted snort. "Black marks on two departments."

"No one tied Karpenito and Fortuna together. Their relationship may've been dormant. I'm going higher up, to our Deputy Director, Neil Markson. I trust him."

"Me, too. We're stepping into a dangerous dance, but I think we can do it with you leading, Sam." Grant checked the hallway. "Have they found Karpenito?"

"No." Sam stopped. "I've been impressed by your fortitude. I can't imagine the difficulty of your family being involved."

"Thanks. One challenge I never anticipated."

"Hold on a minute. There's another issue, and I'm going to be blunt." He locked eyes with Grant. "Is there anything personal I need to know happening between you and Miranda?"

He held eye contact while his pulse pounded. "I've guarded her 24/7, but we haven't had sexual relations."

"Your word's good. Subject closed," Sam said, and walked ahead.

Cold facts, all he'd offer. Facts side-stepping his attraction to Miranda and betraying his own moral code. He let his shoulders drop for a moment and followed Sam. The mental tightrope now stretched over a deep gorge of improper conduct.

They travelled the hall in silence.

"Java's here." Grant rapped on the hotel room door.

Miranda sat perched on the edge of a chair, her toe tapping the carpet. She dangled an untouched pastry in one hand. "I know Ike's being guarded. Are Shirley and Corrin safe?"

They weren't the ones who'd put Maneski and Venom away for life. "Yes." Grant sat in the chair across from her. "Here's a fresh mocha brew. I'll munch on a pastry if you'll do the same."

She broke off a chunk of hers. "I have a recipe for my mom's blueberry scones. I'll make them someday."

No one would harm a hair on her head. Not if he still took a breath. "Deal."

Sam pulled out a notepad. "I need each of you to stand for measurements. We're going to switch in FBI agents after you wrap up this morning's Grand Jury." He handed Pat a tape measure and began to record sizes.

"If you need to match my height, put one of the guys in platform shoes, kind of a Karpenito ruse." Grant winked at Miranda.

She rolled her eyes.

"I'll stick with lifts." Sam shoved the tape measure into

his coat pocket. "Thanks for your help, Pat. I'll head to my office to bait the rattrap."

Four agents surrounded them while they left the hotel room. The group passed through the glass doors and onto the sidewalk, with two agents from the lobby trailing behind.

Grant scanned the crowd before they all piled into a dark van and sped through Seattle traffic.

Sleepless nights took their toll. He'd never felt raw fear. Until now.

~ ~ ~

Miranda read '*Assistant U. S. Attorney*' etched in the glass door. Her heart pounded. They'd reached the beginning of the end.

The receptionist led them to a conference room where tall windows overlooked one of the busiest streets in downtown Seattle.

Half a block away, sunshine bounced off the glass atrium of the Justice Building. Inside, her plants would be happy. She owed them a good dose of fertilizer. They'd saved her— Ike, too.

A woman in her mid-forties stood at the doorway. "I'm the prosecutor in charge of this district. Thank you all for coming. A staff member will be recording your statements, a critical component in this proceeding." She turned and moved into the office across the hallway.

Grant sat next to Miranda. "I've seen her in action. Maneski and Venom don't stand a chance."

A slim man wearing tipped up half-specs rushed into the room. He held a laptop and a cumbersome stack of files. "I'll be recording brief depositions today, we don't have much time. Considering the amount of evidence, our office wants an expedited trial date."

A satisfied and genuine smile lit Grant's face. "Important cases move to the fast track."

Miranda dropped her gaze to her lap. Threads of multiple colors crisscrossed into the skirt Pat had loaned her. Maneski's actions bound them together for now. Soon enough, it'd be over and the connection would unravel. They'd go separate ways, forming new patterns with other people and events, such as Grant's precious promotion.

Bullet holes riddled her tapestry of life.

"Let's get started." The man pulled on his glasses before extracting three disposable phones from an envelope. "The cells you requested are ready, Agent Morley."

Grant handed them out. "I need your phones. Not likely, but by now Maneski could be running tracers through your service providers. Just in case, we're going to give yours to the decoys. You'll get them returned later."

A cool detachment shaded Grant's eyes.

Miranda fished her outdated cell phone from her purse. On her fateful twentieth birthday, her dad had gifted it to her, announcing he'd found a phone with a decent camera. She rubbed her thumb across the screen before sliding it toward Grant.

The man opened his laptop and began to type. "I'll record your statements one at a time. Ms. Whitley, please begin."

Grant ushered his parents out and closed the door.

"Chronologically please, from your first sight of the shooter," he said.

Her chair pressed into her backbone, intensifying the notion of being caught between an anvil and a hammer, waiting for the fatal blow to strike.

~ ~ ~

Adrenalin rippled through Grant's body. They'd all completed their statements. He pulled Miranda and his parents aside. "The suspected traitor's at a weekly meeting.

For the plan to work, he needs to see us before we change into our disguises."

"So," Miranda whispered, "if a group of bees is a swarm, and a group of geese is a gaggle, what's a group of snakes, a slither?"

If humor eased her nerves, he'd learn stand-up comedy. Grant reached for her, then pushed his hands into his pockets. "Good question. I hope their tongues aren't too forked to hiss out confessions. Let's go."

They walked single file past a larger glass-doored meeting room. On a normal week, he'd be scribbling notes, sitting next to Sam.

Their SAC faced out, seated in the position of authority at the head of the table. The psychopathic bastard glanced up.

Grant waved and passed by, but not before he'd seen Fortuna pull out a phone. "We need to move on. One more flight of stairs."

They entered a room where one of the accompanying agents pulled four coats from a bag. "You'll need to button up, the sky's dumping," he said.

"Mom gets the hooded cape." Grant zipped his leather jacket and pulled a ball cap out of the pocket. "Miranda, you'll wear the wool coat and knit hat."

The agent collected the coats they'd been wearing. "Off to outfit our decoys. Thanks, folks."

Another agent stepped forward. He'd changed to a dark windbreaker. "We'll loosely surround you while you get into a blue mini van parked out front. Keep your faces low until we're under way."

They stood in the stairwell long enough to let the group wearing their original coats shuffle through the lobby's double doors.

Cold air shot in after their replacements left. Rain and wind slapped against his face while they dashed down wide cement steps. The other foursome loaded into an SUV.

A dark car slowed at the corner, then tailed the bait car.

After the car turned, Grant leapt into action. Sliding open the side door of the van, he said, "You three in back. Miranda in the middle." He checked the perimeter, slammed their door shut, and hopped in the passenger seat.

If they were in a 007 movie, the fast-pitched music would start. But they weren't. They were smack in the center of a real shitstorm. Grant nodded to the driver. "Let the shell game begin."

Had the disguises worked? He jammed his seatbelt clasp, put one hand on the console and one on the molded door grip. "Everyone get buckled in and braced. The evasive maneuvers trainer is at the wheel."

The red-haired driver grinned and rolled into traffic. "Affirmative." He wedged their vehicle between two cars and turned a corner. In the next block, he moved over a lane and turned again.

"Whee! This could be a tilt-a-whirl ride at the county fair." His mom swayed in her seat while holding the ceiling handle.

"Glad you're enjoying it," Grant said. "Wait until you see what's next. Remember how John's invited us to visit him at his hideaway on the island?"

Pat grinned. "A room with a view. Can't wait."

Grant braced his palm against the dash while they careened to a stop at a light. "You okay, Miranda?"

The van bolted forward, then turned sharply into an alley, dodging black garbage bags.

"I guess so." Her high-pitched voice indicated fear.

The vehicle shot out between a Fed Ex truck and a taxi. Their driver tapped his ear bud and smiled. "No one tailed us. Let's hope the decoys kept their caboose. Where to?"

"Bell Harbor Marina." Grant checked his phone screen. "Our agents arrived at the hotel, followed by the dark sedan."

Two more turns, and their vehicle stopped in a loading zone in front of a gated pier.

"Okay, clan, time to relocate," he climbed out, pulled open the back door, and panned the area.

A touch pad on the eight-foot fence allowed access to a gate. At the bottom of a gangway, elegant yachts swayed upon choppy swells.

Grant stuck his head into the van. "Once we leave the slip, I need you to wait for ten minutes to ensure we're not followed," he said to the driver. "And thanks."

"I'll keep close watch," the agent said. "Good job, Morley."

Maneski's henchmen had one last chance to strike tonight and be apprehended. "Success to our team." Grant shut the door, thumped the side of the van, and stepped onto the sidewalk.

Miranda and his folks stood huddled against windy blasts of rain.

In the marina below, John Fleckard's familiar silhouette strode toward them. He hustled up the ramp and swung open the gate.

"My favorite Emma Springs family, plus one." John flashed a broad smile, one which had charmed many a co-ed in their college days.

His mom reached John first. She kissed his cheek. "How's my world-famous architect and favorite Seattle framily member?"

"Isn't framily a term reserved for phone companies?" Miranda stopped, a few feet back from them.

"Also an expression of my mom's from our college days, when we were roommates." Grant put his hand on her shoulder to move her forward. "Friends become family, Miranda. John and Kyle qualified long ago."

"Grantster, introduce me to your lovely guest." John

pushed back his dark hair, whipping in the wind. They'd wanted to date the same girl in college. John had succeeded.

"Johnny, please meet Miranda." Grant straightened to his full height. "And the answer concerning availability is 'no.'"

~ ~ ~

Proprietary comments from Grant no longer affected Miranda. His banter often consisted of whatever made his life easier. How did he turn his emotions on and off so readily? She'd never master that talent.

"Hi, Miranda. I'm honored to be your host while you're in Seattle. It's nice to reciprocate a small portion of the Morley family kindness."

John began to shake her hand, and then rubbed it briskly between his palms. "You need heat. Let's get you on board."

Grant pulled her to his side. "I'll steady you if the walkway's slippery."

A mischievous twinkle brightened John's eyes. "Follow me folks, and I'll show you my pride and joy." He took Pat's arm.

Miranda listened to the amiable chatter between Pat and John while they strolled to a row of yachts. Tom had rushed ahead.

She inhaled deeply, savoring the familiar scents of salt and seaweed.

Gulls sat on mossy posts, cawing at their winged brethren, gliding in the stiff breezes.

John stopped in front of a covered slip.

Inside sat the sleekest speed boat she'd ever seen, measuring at least thirty feet of glossy, black hull. It reminded her of an ebony pearl, too rich for her blood.

Amphitrite was painted in silver letters on the stern.

"Here we are." John jumped aboard.

Pat ran her fingers over a gleaming silver rail. "Grant told me you're doing well. We had no idea to what extent, *Mon capitan.* Traveling aboard the Goddess of the Sea is special."

Tom hooked his arm around his wife's waist. "You three boys worked hard, and we're proud of your success."

"You believed in me more than my own family," John said. "It meant the world to me." He walked toward the bow of the boat. "Get Miranda on board and cast off the aft line, Grant."

Wind wrapped the skirt around her scuffed cowboy boots. "I'll scratch the deck."

"No worries." In a swift movement, Grant reached under her legs, lifted her, and deposited her next to Pat. "I'm certain John has a special toothbrush to polish his possessions."

Pat shook her head. "Boys. Never evolving from the mine's bigger than yours mentality."

Miranda watched Grant coil a rope. She'd welcome any distraction which removed her from the equation.

"Let's get warm." Pat held the door open to the glass-enclosed back deck. "Have you boated before?"

Miranda stepped inside. Thick carpet gave way under pressure from each step. "I've fished with my brother, but comparing a row boat to this one's like comparing a plastic horse to Pegasus."

"John's into toys." Grant closed the door. "Wait until you see his waterfront house on Vashon."

Geeze. Didn't Grant value his Montana home at all? "I appreciate quiet pastures, too," she said.

"Yeah." Grant shrugged his shoulders and kept watch through the rear windows.

Churning waves smacked the stern of the boat while John backed out and turned to head for open water.

She surveyed the cityscape from left to right. The sloped bluff below Magnolia gave way to the Seattle skyline, which curved into the industrial end of Elliott Bay. Seventy-foot tall orange metal cranes loomed over freighters, silently waiting to be loaded.

Buildings of all shapes and sizes dotted the panoramic landscape. Her apartment building sat somewhere in the middle.

"I have to maintain a low speed until we've cleared a couple hundred yards offshore." John's voice came over an intercom.

As they descended from the deck to a lower hallway, lights illuminated a narrow corridor. Open doors revealed elegant staterooms on either side. They peeked inside and climbed steps to the cockpit in the bow, where John sat at a dashboard the width of the boat.

"She's a beauty, John." Tom let out a low whistle while he leaned closer to study assorted dials and gauges.

"Thanks. Everyone grab a seat. We're going to go at a good clip for the ten-mile trip to Vashon Island," John warned. "Amphi cuts through choppy water better than a cheese knife slices into warm Brie."

Miranda perched on a raised captain's chair while John pushed throttles, shooting the boat across the tops of white caps. "This beats ferry lines," she said.

"Yes, ma'am." John lifted a pair of binoculars and handed them to Grant. "Help me keep an eye out, please."

"Anything in particular I'm searching for?" Grant braced his butt against a chair, swiveled his shoulders to look behind them, and then faced forward. "Maybe I'll spot Brie-shaped logs?"

"Not likely. However, I usually don't speed across at dusk. Snags are worth a second set of eyes."

"We'll all help watch," Tom said. "The homes in the photos downstairs are incredible. We assume they belong to your lucky customers."

"Yes, but I'm the fortunate one. My customers seek me out because they care—"

"Port side!" Grant yelled.

John swerved to miss a floating log.

Miranda lurched, straight into Grant's outstretched arm.

"Everyone upright?" John asked. "I'd like to slow down, Grant. There's no predators out here except Orca whales."

"A slower speed's acceptable, Captain," Grant said.

Pat rubbed her hands together. "I commute with a former patrolman who practices on lone stretches of highway. Today we outsmarted crooks in a getaway car shell game. Tonight I've saddled the Kraken. My life keeps getting better."

Tom leaned over and kissed her on the cheek. "You're my priceless gem, Patricia."

Grant rested his hand on Miranda's shoulder. "You began describing your clients earlier, John."

"Thankfully, my customers are interested in saving our planet's resources."

Miranda caught some of the conversation while zoning out on the peaceful crossing over water she only knew from twenty stories up. From several downtown office buildings, she often snuck glimpses of Puget Sound while she tended her plants. Someone else would be watching their boat tonight. A chill went up her spine.

"Enough sales spiel, here we are." The engines purred to imperceptible while John decreased speed.

Grant slid open a window. A woodsy scent infiltrated the sharp sea air. "Welcome to our next quarters." He gently squeezed her shoulder.

Vines and bushes camouflaged a boathouse in a small cove. John pointed a remote and a huge roll up door recessed into the ceiling.

Water lapped against the hull while they eased inside.

"Which way to the house?" Miranda pulled her coat tight.

"Head right at the bow." Grant handed Miranda's bag to his dad. "You'll experience John's barrier against urban irritations."

She stepped across a narrow expanse of dark water to a grated catwalk, leading to a mesh tunnel. A mass of vines trussed the structure. Her body relaxed. "Wow. A place where elements of nature intertwine with habitation."

"I try." John forged ahead to a two-story house made of wood and silvered by decades of sun. He pushed against carved double doors. Subtle interior lights defined an entry.

Floor to ceiling windows across the front offered a panoramic view of Puget Sound.

She stopped, stunned. "Amazing. From the outside, the exterior of your home appears to be one continuous grove of trees."

"A feat accomplished by angling glass and optimizing a special coating I sourced. It pulls in reflections of the surrounding forest on either side. It also keeps houses cool in summer and restricts heat loss during the winter." He ushered her inside.

Her eyes widened. Rich hues of wood accented every space in John's living room. Following his lead, Miranda slipped her boots onto a mat next to a two-tone wood settee near the door. "Handmade furniture?"

"Tom did that piece," John offered. "I furnished my home using the fretwork creations after learning they either utilize recycled wood or plant two trees to replace each one cut. My clients clamor for anything the Morleys produce."

"Morleys, as in plural?" Miranda asked.

Grant stopped beside her. "I help Dad whenever I can."

"Family helping framily with fretwork." Miranda smiled.

"Fretwork's our specialty." Grant said. "Designs using different species of wood for patterns are popular right now."

"Craftsmanship never goes out of style." John held out a hanger carved in the shape of an Orca. "Let me get your coat. I believe the old mountain man carved this from the arm of a broken chair."

"Correct. Dad finds them at flea markets for Stan."

She moved toward the expanse of windows while Grant pulled in two more suitcases.

"Grant, help me stow luggage." John grabbed a suitcase and headed upstairs. "We'll be right back, folks. Make yourselves at home."

The well-worn oak risers creaked, their centers bowed from absorbing decades of footsteps.

"Tom, John's got our dream stove," Pat said, and towed him toward the kitchen.

Moonlight glowed over an expanse of flat water.

Miranda remembered a camping trip to a lake. That night, her mom had professed the waning moon presented an opportunity for clearing and cleansing. Surviving the trial, she'd give her theory a try.

She brushed the windowsill, finding smooth indents of pits and notches. If they talked, these boards would tell stories. Some happy, some not.

"I hope you didn't lose something important." Grant stroked her back with his warm, strong fingers.

"The recycled lumber has a gorgeous patina." She unbuttoned her sweater and fanned her face.

"Nothing shines like your hair." He slid his finger over a wayward strand and tucked it behind her ear. "I took the liberty of asking for a room together." His earnest need for her to commit had returned to his eyes. "I guess John has another guest room, if you'd prefer your own space."

No. She'd treasure these last moments before she took time to heal. "I can't sleep alone tonight."

He kissed her cheek, and they stood in silence, gazing

at the water. Her eyes dropped to the familiar palm cradling her hand, her new lifeline. She had to find a way to hold on.

~ ~ ~

Grant placed Miranda's hand in the crook of his arm, leading her to an open-beamed kitchen where John, Pat, and Tom sat on bar stools. His shoulders relaxed. He'd brought them to safety, for now. "My fair maiden studies biology. Tell her your environmental code, John."

"Okay, fair maiden." John winked at Pat and Tom. "My designs incorporate repurposed and chemical-free products. I endorse solar panels and heat pumps. And your calling?"

"Nothing yet. I did Running Start in high school and got within a semester of my Environmental Biology degree a few years back. My friend, Corrin, is studying to take the February bar. She's bugging me to finish, but I'll never match your impressive work."

"We all start small." John handed her a business card. "If you ever need assistance during any of your classes, or a boat ride, call me."

Classwork help? Nice try. Grant cleared his throat. "I'll show you our room, Miranda."

John walked beside them to the staircase. "Enjoy my home as if it's your own."

"Thanks, Johnny. We will. Night." Grant grasped her hand. He felt another new emotion—possessiveness. But it wasn't dripping out.

"Your furniture enhances John's concept," she complimented.

"I'd like to help Dad more. Woodworking relaxes me." He guided her upstairs and into a spacious suite.

From this room, the sight of the water ended at a corner window seat.

"Seattle's amazing view," Miranda said. "Stark at

times, or a fairy town offering shimmering halos of light."
She pointed to a slow moving boat. "There's the ferry
from Fauntleroy. My family rode it to Vashon's Strawberry
Festival."

He stepped behind her and pulled her to rest against his
chest. She fit perfectly in all ways. "I hope you'll consider
the Morley clan your family someday."

"Your folks are kind." She turned to face him and took a
step back. "What's the scoop on John?"

He stretched his shoulders back, broadening his chest.
"John met a woman and got married within six months. It
ended within a year. Kyle and I couldn't do much to help
him recover from shell shock."

Miranda perched on the window seat. "He seems
grounded now."

Grounded and wealthy. A knot formed in his gut. "Not a
word I'd use to describe Cindy, his ex. Her interests remained
strictly monetary."

"What a fool," offered Miranda in a wistful tone.

Unease washed over him. John wouldn't own a firearm.
"She didn't trust he'd support her."

"How awful! He's been so kind."

*Kind, a pacifist, and owner of a fabulous house near
Seattle. Damn.* "John travels frequently. That's why he has a
top of the line security system. He's gone for weeks, dealing
with snobs." He wouldn't mention the lengthy wait list of
local philanthropists wanting green homes, or plenty of his
other qualities.

"He'll find a woman," she said. "He's funny, smart, and
handsome."

Grant forced a wide smile. "Bullseye's single, maybe
she'd be a good match."

Anyone but Miranda.

~ ~ ~

Loving Grant would be so, so easy. Morning light danced across his back while he slept face down, in an ideal position for a reciprocal massage. She inhaled a trace of his spicy cologne, while her eyes followed the rhythmic rise and fall of his shoulders.

She stretched her hand out, reaching toward him. How would his smooth skin feel?

With splayed fingers, she kneaded the base of his neck, and inched her way down, gently pressing into toned muscles. So much stronger than she'd imagined—solid and enticing.

She slid the tip of her pinky underneath the waistband of his sweats and ran it across his lower back.

"Please stop." Grant's husky voice broke the silence. He caught her wrist, rolled over, and pressed it to his heart. "Imagine the stack of dry kindling in the cabin as me. You'd be a blowtorch, igniting the flames."

"Oh." Heat rose above the collar of her T-shirt. "I shouldn't—"

He put his finger to her lips. "You should, after you give me a little more time. I made a kind of chastity vow to Sam I can't break. One final report, and my part of the case is closed. Then we're going to revisit your exploratory advances." He lifted her hand and threaded his fingers into hers, squeezing gently. "I'm falling in love with you, Miranda."

"And I'm falling in love with you." She squeezed back. "I don't know the rules of engagement, so to speak." Her blush deepened.

"With these magic fingers, you can pull me out of a hat anytime. I hope by the end of next week." His smile made her heart hitch.

"I'd better shower before I cause more trouble." She slid her legs over the bed.

"Soon, you can offer me your trouble, twenty-four seven."

The sensation of gliding while she stepped made her smile. She closed the bathroom door, imagining mornings where she'd have unlimited access to all of Grant.

For now, she viewed where he emptied his pockets at night.

He'd left his key chain and wallet on the vanity. A business card, which must've fallen out, lay on the floor near the wastebasket.

She flipped the card over. From a doctor?

A doctor proud of his bold-printed motto. "Vasectomies without the downtime."

She sagged against the counter. Precious babies of her own had been a dream which sustained her. She closed her eyes.

Grant's comments had all been negative regarding children. Loud, stinky, and annoying, he'd said.

Her dad had offered unconditional love and devotion, and after she found the right husband, her own kids would be cherished.

The disparity of their life's wishes seeped into her heart.

The card fluttered back to the floor.

This might be the end of their story. She stepped under the shower and let the flow pound against her shoulders.

What a story. Grant's muscular arms around her while they'd ridden through the snowflakes had been spellbinding. His kisses—she'd live on his kisses alone.

No, she couldn't. She turned the water to cold. He'd joked about the young man who'd been their doorman at the hotel. "Kids became tolerable after they were teenagers," he'd said. She wrenched off the spigot and got dressed.

Modest and mild, modest and mild. Could she return to inconspicuous Miranda, yearning for a man who wanted a placid family life?

Could she live without children? Her hand gripped the door handle. She plastered on a smile and pushed it open.

"Wow, my shoulders and back appreciated your massage." Grant's dimple seemed deeper in his rested face. "I hope you slept like the proverbial rock."

Until a boulder dropped on her in the shape of a business card. "I did, thanks." She towel dried her wet hair. "The bath's all steamy for you."

His focus remained fixed on her face. He threw his muscled calves over the side of the bed. "You okay? I chose John's home because I thought the natural setting would appeal to you."

Parts of her he totally understood. She flipped her head down, rubbing the last drops from her hair. "Accommodations are wonderful. Courtroom nerves is all. I've never been grilled by a lawyer."

"You'll do fine. I bet the coffee's on," he said. "Seattle coffee."

The towel's fibers pushed into her tensed fingers. "Java's just what I need. See you downstairs."

So many dreams of raising a child. She blinked back tears.

~ ~ ~

Pat and Tom sat elbow to elbow in John's kitchen, grinning like newlyweds.

Or nearly-deads because of her. Miranda grimaced. They hadn't even appeared in court yet. Her eyes flicked from the water to the woods behind the house. No barred windows or crew of agents protected them. She poured herself coffee.

John handed her a plate of scrambled eggs. "Henny Penny special."

"These are the deepest yellow color I've ever seen," she remarked.

John smiled. "I keep a few hens out back. They eat scraps and produce fertilizer. How does a boat ride today and a picnic lunch off Blake Island sound?"

Grant stepped into the kitchen. "Water's fine if we stay away from other boats."

"Talked to Sam yet, son?" Tom cut in. "We're dying to know what happened last night."

"The SAC rat got flushed out, as we expected." Grant's voice lacked enthusiasm.

"Good police work needs good instincts." Tom thumped his son on the back. "A corrupt SAC, though. What a shame for the department."

"During Maneski senior's trial, critical pieces of evidence went missing, and they blamed it on our property room managers. One officer died of a heart attack during proceedings."

"That's suspicious." Tom reached for Pat's hand. "I never dealt with anyone so ruthless on my watch."

And Grant dealt with them on an hourly basis. Miranda bit her lip.

"We've opened further investigations. Fortuna came to do the job himself last night. No one received injuries in his arrest." Grant offered them a weak smile.

"How could someone turn on the partners they'd sworn to protect?" Pat shook her head.

"Fortuna admitted he's got a gambling problem. Agents are still questioning the people named on Maneski's flash drive. The day after Judge Gilson's shooting, Karpenito put in for a thirty day leave and hasn't surfaced since."

"Karpenito won't quit hunting." Miranda clenched her fork.

"Enough shop talk." Grant's eyes flicked from Miranda to the shoreline. "Let's cruise."

Grant had kept tight lipped in Montana because he'd

believed Karpenito had followed her. She fought a wave of nausea.

Karpenito would be more confident in Seattle. What if they didn't catch him soon? Or ever?

~ ~ ~

Miranda studied John's house from where she stood in the middle of his courtyard vegetable garden. She'd needed time alone after the boat ride. Grant had suggested a welcome chore of outdoor gardening, so long as she stayed in a monitored area. So much for a restful retreat.

"The heat from the house helps things grow here." John approached and handed her a mug of tea.

"Thanks." She brushed a streak of dirt from her jeans and admired her handiwork. Two planting beds sat mulched by dark compost. "I'm going to give my friend, Corrin, a call. May I use your phone again?"

"*Mi casa es su casa.*" He led her into the kitchen and gave her a hand towel from a drawer. "Grant's taken with you, and it appears mutual. But you're holding back. If I can help, say so."

Grant's deep laugh and jovial chatter came from the atrium breakfast room.

Fibers gave way while she twisted the soft fabric. "I have to confront my past before I can concentrate on a future."

He rubbed his empty ring finger. "I understand, and I'm here if you want to talk. The Morley's are gold." He handed her a portable phone.

"Indeed." She trudged upstairs and dialed Corrin. "Are you in your apartment?"

"Yes, a patrol car's stationed on the corner. I'm currently dousing hand sanitizer on all my exposed skin. This afternoon I met an unforgettable male client."

"I'm sorry to hear you're still fighting those battles. Got a minute to talk? "

"Always. A friend of Iris's watered your precious flora," Corrin said.

"Thank you. One less worry."

"You're upset. Is it Mr. FBI?"

Miranda slumped on the bed, running her fingers over the quilted material. "His family's sweet, and they spoil me. His ranch is beautiful. Grant's a hero with a heart."

"I'm not getting any problem."

"Grant carries his gun everywhere, even playing checkers."

Corrin tapped her nail on the receiver. "Bloody hell, Miranda, he's protecting your life. You may have mutual attraction, but first and foremost, he's a clocked-in agent."

"Sort of the problem. I've got to go. I'll call again soon."

"Oh no you don't," Corrin broke in. "Listen for a second. You've drooled over hunky Agent of Interest from afar. You meet him and sparks sizzled. Right?"

"A lot happened in a short time." Miranda fell onto the bed.

"Time's irrelevant. Flash forward. You see a horrific event which triggers memories. Who stood by you when you needed him?"

"Grant."

"I remember the first Montana conversation. You'd travelled into dreamy snow land on horseback. Your voice gave your warm-for-his-form thoughts away."

"I didn't know it was so obvious."

"And who wanted you to meet his family?" Corrin pushed.

"Grant."

"Who can't face that it's hard to love, not knowing what the future holds?"

"I'm a coward, and I need more counseling." Miranda closed her eyes.

"No, Miranda. Many of us are scared to love, for good reasons. Sure, get counseling. Meanwhile, grab hold of what might be the best chance you get at happiness. Kyle told me how you and Grant fit. I envy you."

Miranda rubbed her forehead, determined to enjoy the last hours in paradise. "I envy you. You've finished your degree. Now you simply need to pass the bar exam. How is Kyle?"

"Quit shifting the conversation. Give yourself a chance at a real life—maybe in picturesque Emma Springs?"

"Not likely. Blood ties interlock the residents. If I'd been a heifer from the local herd, it'd be fine, but small towns don't embrace a stranger who's brought killers to their town."

"His family would pave the way," Corrin said.

"Doesn't matter, Grant wants to sell his ranch."

"It's not about location when it comes to love."

"You're right. It's about life with the right man." Miranda glanced into the bathroom where she'd seen the doctor's card. "Thanks again. See you soon."

She could choose a life shaded by pale baby pink or blood red.

The decision ripped her apart.

~ ~ ~

Monday morning had arrived too soon for Grant. The days of free time at John's had gone fast. They'd swapped a cushy window seat looking out on water for the hard benches in the Justice Building hallway.

He fought an irrational urge to call Sam and remove Miranda from testifying in front of the Grand Jury.

She's the key witness, dipshit. He raked his fingers through his hair. Would it always be this way, his brain going sideways if it involved Miranda?

With Judge Gilson hospitalized and still unable to give

a statement, the attempted murder charge against Maneski hinged on Miranda's testimony.

He shoved his phone back into his pocket and sat by her. "We'll testify one at a time."

"The prosecution calls Federal Agent Grant Morley to the stand," announced a female voice from the doorway of a hearing room.

Grant strode past the woman.

Two lawyers and Venom sat at one end of a table, on the far side of the windowless room.

A prosecutor placed a sixteen by twenty-inch photo of his bruised torso on an easel. His battered face came next. He'd tried to keep his stomach injuries hidden from Miranda, but she'd seen them. Another failure. He gritted his teeth.

No surprises were delivered in cross-examination by the defense attorney.

The FBI would win. Why didn't the anticipation of an impending promotion excite him? Grant held his head high while he returned to the holding area and took a seat.

Pat followed Tom in giving testimony, both returning pale and shaken.

He watched Miranda walk in. She'd gone through hell too many times.

Facing Venom could put her over the edge.

~ ~ ~

Never let them see you sweat. Miranda stood tall and strode to the witness stand. Ike deserved her best effort. Grant, too.

This, she'd provide to him. She folded her hands in her lap and raised her eyes to the prosecuting attorney.

"Ms. Whitley, can you identify the gunman who shot Isaac Gilson?"

Identify him, recognize his guttural voice, and feature him in nightmares for the next twenty years. "Yes." She pointed to Venom. "The man with the snake tattoo. He stood over Ike, pointing a gun at his bloody wound, while the elevator doors opened."

Anger welled in her chest. "He shot Ike, and then came after the Morleys and me."

"Keep to testimony regarding Judge Gilson's attack. Can you point out the gun you saw the night of the shooting?" He motioned to a nearby table.

She pictured Venom shoving it into his belt. "The third handgun from the left. The one with the long piece protruding from the barrel."

Silencer. She'd silence Venom, all right.

She answered other questions before a defense attorney hammered her.

Screw them all. She furnished every detail. A grimace from Venom implied she'd nailed him in the attempted murder of Ike.

You got what you deserve, dirt bag. She glared at him.

His snake tattoo looked a lot less frightening sitting next to the collar of an orange jumpsuit. Orange—a suitable color for a hollow pumpkin of a man. He'd nearly killed Ike, and her, and hurt Grant.

Someone should carve his ass using a dull knife. Her fingernail gouged her palm, as if she gripped a hilt.

Miranda blinked. Venom had forced one positive change. From now on, she'd fight for what she wanted. No more cowering behind anything or anyone.

"I'm finished with this witness, your honor," the defense attorney stated.

The judge excused her. Accusations against Carlisle Bartholomew Buddston, or Venom, were apparently complete.

This time they'd arrested the would-be killers, unlike the ones who'd murdered her own family. And she'd helped. She threw her shoulders back and marched out of the courtroom and straight to Grant.

He grabbed her hand and gave it a firm squeeze. "I don't know what happened in there, but I'm proud of you."

Warmth came to her cheeks. "The inconspicuous plant girl pruned Carlisle Bartholomew Buddston."

Grant laughed. "With his name, no wonder he turned to crime."

"The venomous fangs of his snake tattoo bit us, but we've pulled them out, tooth by tooth," she jested.

Pat rose and hugged her. "We're very proud of you."

"You're a real gem, little lady." Tom patted her back.

The lawyers exited the hearing room, chatting like old friends.

"Can we leave?" Pat asked.

"We should wait to see if there are further questions." Grant smiled. "Good job, everyone. Let's see what transpires."

Grant checked his phone and squeezed her hand. "Got the word you were amazing under pressure. Your testimony should put Venom away for good. You may be kitten-soft on the outside, but your core's tungsten steel."

How she wished the steel wasn't paper-thin. Miranda let out a long breath. "Thanks."

Within a few minutes, Sam approached and motioned them into an empty corridor.

"I have the best news I can give you," Sam said. "Venom's going to plea bargain for a shorter sentence. You all did an excellent job today."

"Especially Miranda," Grant said.

"Agreed," Sam said. "Neil Markson flew in. He wants to talk to you tomorrow morning, Grant. Might have an interesting proposition for you." Sam smiled while he delivered the news. "Do you need a place to stay tonight?"

"We're fine where we are, and my friend's meeting us at the Sands Restaurant. We'd appreciate a ride to the pier, if you're willing."

"Sure. Due to the success of this case, we may both be adding different initials to our titles."

"Give me a hint about what Neil's thinking." Grant matched steps with his boss.

"Can't say for certain. Heard you might be sporting a tan instead of webbed feet." Sam thumped his shoulder, a boyish grin on his face.

No return grin from Grant. He barely nodded.

Miranda stared at him. The news should have brought him total elation.

Maybe it was the known fact that crime lords, as powerful as Maneski, could operate from jail.

~ ~ ~

Grant hadn't said two words on the trip to the restaurant. He hopped out of the car and guided her toward the pier.

"How'd it go?" John stood at a corner of the popular waterfront restaurant, his boat moored behind him.

"We're done testifying." Grant smiled and placed a light hand at the base of her back. "In celebration, I'm buying dinner."

Every touch from him elicited traitorous shivers of delight. No escape to her apartment yet, Grant's orders. She stepped aside to allow John to approach.

"You don't have to ask me twice," John said. "The seafood here's fabulous and locally sourced. Plus, they've got live music tonight." He slapped Grant on the back. "And the agent of the day's paying. Life doesn't get any better."

Miranda fell in behind Grant and John, watching them like an audience member in a theater, waiting for the final scene.

Their group settled into a booth by a window. Edible flowers and fresh herbs garnished the food.

She nodded at appropriate moments, and managed to laugh during Pat's impression of Venom glaring.

"A guy could get mighty healthy living in this neck of the woods," piped Tom, while balancing a bite of halibut on his fork. "Whoa, now there's a dessert tray."

"Let's do pieces of chocolate decadence, tiramisu, cheesecake, and bring a bunch of forks," Pat put the request to their waiter.

Tom leaned back in his chair. "Tonight, we'll sleep peacefully, having full stomachs and no more concerns about hit men, disguises, or courtrooms."

At least he would. Miranda placed her knife and fork across her barely touched meal.

A little boy giggled from the next table. Pat and Miranda swiveled their heads in unison, both smiling at his cherubic face. He wore a bow tie and sat in a high chair.

"I bet Miranda's ready for the next chapter in her life." Pat raised her coffee cup. "Here's to it being a bedtime story and not a page-turner."

Pat had never seen her collection of children's picture books. Miranda lifted her water glass, and pulled her cheeks into the biggest smile she could muster, while her heart squeezed into a tight ball.

Grant's eyes flicked from her to the boy and back. "Or a college text book. Miranda wants to finish her degree and be a biologist. Kids demand a lot of time, if you're concentrating on school or a career."

"A degree's always good." Tom clinked his glass, leaning toward his son. "This case should propel you to ASAC, and then it's a short step to SAC. Good job, son."

The bites of dinner she'd eaten sat heavily in her stomach. Her priorities necessitated a choice. The right choice for both of them.

"Sam hinted there might be changes in my job title." Grant sat back in his chair, the most relaxed she'd seen him, except in bed this morning.

The waiter centered three dessert plates on the table, and John took the lead by spearing a piece of cheesecake. "So, off to the college life, Miranda? If you need a water break, Amphi's available." John offered.

"Uggh. What is it with my friends?" Grant moaned. "They all figure they can bird dog me when I find my perfect woman."

Miranda smoothed the tablecloth. Perfect woman she was not. A perfect woman would accept Grant and not break into a sweat every time his gun appeared. A perfect woman wouldn't risk asking her man to choose between his career advancement or spending a dull life with her and their children. Because she loved him, she would be perfectly miserable alone while conquering her past.

Pat tipped her head toward Miranda. "If you need a little tranquility, come to Emma Springs." She spooned tiramisu onto her plate. "You don't eat dessert?"

Miranda folded her napkin and laid it by the side of her plate. "Not tonight. I think I'll let my stomach settle after a perfect dinner."

Grant, John, and Tom fought over the last two bites of chocolate cake, sparring with their tined spears.

How appropriate, fight scenes played out before the curtain dropped. An emptiness burrowed deep into Miranda's soul, knowing the decision she had to make. She'd reached a plateau, free to move on.

Freedom brought an avalanche of new vulnerability.

~ ~ ~

Grant shifted in his chair and rotated his untouched after-dinner scotch. His sense of an impending crisis heightened to maximum alert.

He'd seen the team of agents pull up after Sam dropped them off. The restaurant building was secure.

It was Miranda's behavior that was off. She'd kept to curt responses, while his folks and John chatted happily over the background music.

A woman fronting a trio of musicians sang out a slow Patsy Cline song. On the dance floor, several couples swayed to the tune.

Dancing would soothe both their nerves. He leaned close to her ear, breathing in her scent. "I promised you a celebration dance. Join me?"

"Yes, please," she whispered.

He grasped her hand, aware of the current drawing them together. The pulse deepened after her palm rested on the top of his arm.

When he settled his hands at her waist, she draped her arms over his shoulders, resting her cheek under his chin. He'd swear his heart beat stronger, pressed against hers.

They moved together in sensual unison, their bodies attuned. The music surrounded them for precious minutes, shutting out the world.

As the last chord struck, she lifted her face, love shining in her eyes.

He pulled her close and brushed his lips onto hers. Her breathy response sent waves deep into his heart—an awakening he welcomed.

Releasing her tortured him.

Not a word was spoken between them, not at the end of the song, not after they'd left the restaurant, and not on the boat ride. A magical spell had been cast which neither of them dared to break.

She had to want a future together.

Or what the hell would he do?

Chapter 19

A step toward Morley honor could be presented to him this morning. Anticipation should be bouncing through his body, but it wasn't.

He exited the elevator on the floor housing the high-level FBI personnel and knocked on the first open door. Neil Markson, their assistant director, had stepped in until the bureau filled Fortuna's position of SAC.

"Come in, Grant." Neil minimized the page on his computer. "This offer ought to put a big smile on your face." He tipped his chin. "I hope your family had a relaxing evening."

Nothing regarding Miranda's restrained demeanor had been relaxing. She'd retired immediately after they'd arrived at John's house and had been shoveling dirt when he'd left today.

"Yes, sir." Grant took the chair opposite Neil's desk. "Thank you for inviting me."

"In reviewing your file, you'll be sitting at my desk soon. How'd you like the title Assistant Special Agent in Charge, at our resident agency in Reno?"

Grant leaned forward, holding onto both armrests. "I'm honored to be considered."

"An unrecognized criminal element's dominating the meth trade in Reno. After what you accomplished diving into this case, the department anticipates you can make a real difference in that leadership role."

Pride welled in his chest. He'd done it. "I'll accept, sir."

Neil slid a stack of papers across his desk. "Sign these transfer documents, and we'll have you in your new job by next week. They need you immediately."

Grant skimmed the top page, and turned to the second. "Nice pay increase."

"Ah, well, I need to tell you, the previous ASAC and a partner got ambushed in a parking garage. They're on permanent disability."

Considering the nearly double jump in pay, it was a justifiable risk. He suspended the pen above the page. A prick of misgiving nicked his gut, and then he scribbled his name. "I'll handle Reno."

"Deal."

Neil's firm handshake boosted Grant's optimism. "The bureau has high hopes for you. Now, and in the future. Good luck." He ushered him to the door. "Please thank your family again for their cooperation in the Maneski case."

"Sure thing." The door clicked shut behind him. He spotted a men's room and ducked inside.

Reno. Could Miranda flourish under blocks of neon lights? He leaned against the sink. In a few years he'd be able to transfer, and meantime, the casinos must use tons of plants. Hell, she'd thrive in the sunshine. She wouldn't have to work with his raise in pay.

He pulled his phone out and dialed John. "Hey, boat drivin' buddy. I hope I can trouble you to bring Miranda in for dinner."

"Matter of fact, I'm meeting clients tonight in Seattle. I can get you in at Blaine's if it's a special evening."

Grant tapped his fingers on the counter. "Yes. I'll need the most romantic table in the place."

"I'll dock at six and bring Miranda. Good luck."

A sense of accomplishment filled him, shadowed by a long finger of doubt. He punched in a memorized number.

A familiar gruff voice answered on the third ring. "Tom?"

"Nope, it's Grant." He squared his shoulders. "Poppy, I did it. I've been promoted to oversee our team in Reno's satellite office. A second Morley reached ASAC today. I wanted you to be the first in the family to know."

"Wonderful, son. Pat mentioned you and Miranda are getting along swell. She excited about Reno?"

"I'm going to tell her over dinner," he said, "and ask her to marry me." He leaned against the sink and crossed one leg over the other.

"Can't picture Miranda amongst a bunch of gamblers," he grumbled. "A good woman's worth more than a nameplate. You've sidelined everything for your career."

"I did what it took." Grant bristled.

"At a personal cost. I never regretted leaving the bureau. It gave me fifteen wonderful more years to love your grandmother. The summers the three of us spent together when you were a boy were some of the best parts of my life."

"Wait—your job meant everything."

"Yup, until I had a hothead moment after a key witness wouldn't testify. Turned out to be the best gift I didn't receive," he joked.

"Losing a big case was a gift?" Grant stammered.

"Best one except for meeting your grandmother. You were in college when she passed away. I miss her every day, not the job. You don't know the meaning of love until you've lost it."

"I'm beginning to understand."

"Can't wait to see your Miranda again. Bring her back soon."

His Miranda. He loosened his tie. "I'm hoping after tonight she'll be wearing grandma's diamond. Leave it to Mom to have packed it."

"Your dad picked a special lady," Poppy said. "Runs in the family. Good luck."

"Thanks Poppy, for everything."

He might need more than luck to get Miranda to leave Seattle and her friends. They'd work out the geography. Next on the agenda, he'd hit his closet and find his best suit.

Driving to the apartment, he spotted a pocket park, green and lush from the last rain. He slowed his car. Miranda would know the name of every sprout.

Reno however, conjured images of arid desert, strong wind, and glitzy casinos. Would Miranda relocate for him? He stepped into the bright lights of his building, and his foot stumbled.

~ ~ ~

"There's your man, standing on Blaine's dock awaiting the arrival of the woman who captured his heart." John slowed the boat.

Miranda fingered the strand of pearls around her neck. A Morley family heirloom, loaned to her for tonight in the expectation of an event which wouldn't happen. Not yet anyway.

John surveyed the duffel bag she'd brought aboard. "Remember, I'm not giving up on you two."

Her stomach twisted into a tighter knot. "And I'm not ready."

"Don't rush into big decisions." John parked the boat and threw a line to Grant.

"Hi, gorgeous." Grant took her hand, helping her from the boat to the dock. "Can you get us at ten, John? Thanks again. You've accrued unlimited vacation days in Emma Springs."

"I'm going to make time to collect." John tied off the last rope and set Miranda's bag onto the dock. He handed Grant a tiny box. "From your mom. Enjoy dinner."

Miranda shouldered the duffel and eyed the black case Grant slid into his pocket. She'd overheard Pat whisper 'ring' to John. Could she accept his life if he popped the question?

"You look radiant." He drew her into his arms and gave her a lingering kiss, holding her tight.

She committed every movement of his muscled body to memory while her heart slipped a little further. "Your mom gave me a dress she's never worn."

"Even more to celebrate." He put his hand on her back, hitting the strap of Corrin's gym bag. A frown marred his glow while he ushered her through the etched glass doors. "I'll have the maître de stow your duffel. I'd hoped you'd stay another night at John's."

With him lying beside her? *No, no, no.* Miranda stepped inside the elegant entry. "The apartment's safe, and Corrin and I have a lot to discuss."

A waiter settled them into a private alcove. An ice bucket held a bottle of champagne. "Compliments of John Fleckard," he stated, and popped the cork.

Golden liquid flowed into two tall flutes.

Trails of bubbles released from the bottom, shot to the top, and exploded. If her brain was the narrow-stemmed glass, her innermost desires to stay with Grant were the uncontrolled bubbles.

"I accepted a promotion today." Grant tipped his flute to clink against hers. "I'll be ASAC in Reno. They figure I'm ready for the challenge, which puts me one away from SAC."

His broad smile softened all the angled planes on his face.

She took a sip of champagne, and set the glass down before she spilled any of it onto the white linen.

Her golden bubbles had burst. He'd agreed to Reno without considering her feelings. Worse yet, a new crime-ridden city fulfilled his goal.

She forced her mouth into a smile, and watched

excitement animate his face while he laid out his future.

"Reno's a quick flight from Seattle," he continued. "And I bet the casinos need your green thumb." Sliding one hand across the table, he moved his other hand toward his pocket. "Miranda, you know I—"

She couldn't hear it again. "Hold on. You took a job out of state without asking my opinion. Is this how it'll always be? You make all the plans for both of us?"

"Well, no. I thought maybe you'd be excited for me."

"Is it dangerous?"

He shifted in his seat. "All cities have criminals to contend with. The counseling will help your anxiety about guns."

"I want a stable family life with children, and I saw the snip doctor's card you dropped. Kids and puppies would hold back your career."

His face fell. "Right now, they would. Maybe not in the future, say in three or four years. That card came from Bo as a joke, he'd just found out they're having their third."

Her trembling fingers undid the clasp on the borrowed pearls. Their smooth warmth weighed heavy in her hand before she dropped them into his open palm.

His color paled. "Are we okay?"

He wouldn't force her into his plans. She slid out of the chair. "I need a little time alone."

A boisterous group of diners rose to leave. She wove through them, intent on one thing. Escape.

She passed the restrooms and veered to the entry.

The *maître d'* and another man stood at the reception desk.

"Please get me a cab and my blue gym bag. Fast." The words spilled out, her voice shrill.

One of them opened a door, waving his arms. The other handed off her bag. "How else can we assist, mademoiselle?"

Her chest tightened. "You can't."

Right now, she'd convert back to a cowering mess at the first mention of gunshots. Guided by a therapist, her future self might be able to stand beside him in support.

For a moment there, she'd almost caved. His pull became magnified by how gorgeous he looked in the dark suit. His lips had quivered as he'd prepared to tell her he loved her again and propose.

One more thought of those lips, and she'd be running to their table. But only a total coward of the lowest degree wouldn't offer Grant an explanation.

Miranda pulled a business card out of the rack on the wooden kiosk. Her purse held the temporary phone, a pen, and her lip gloss.

It took every ounce of courage to write on the back of the card.

She handed the *maître d'* the bureau-issued cell phone and the card carrying her note. "Please give these to the tall gentleman in the black suit I came in with."

"Yes, of course." He helped her into her coat.

Grant began pushing his way through the crowded entry. Shock marred his handsome face.

She spun around and ran to the open door of a taxi. "Capitol Hill. Hurry."

The driver sped her away from another woman's dream life.

Music in the cab blared while tears splashed onto her lap, her heart releasing a pool of regrets.

Two written words on the back of someone else's business card changed the course of her immediate future.

NOT READY.

~ ~ ~

Grant spotted John on the dock and ran to him. "She bolted. Can you believe it?" He pulled out his phone and fumbled while punching numbers. "Agent Morley here," he announced to the bureau call center. "Miranda Whitley left the waterfront unescorted in a taxi. Please alert the agents watching her apartment. I assume she'll be arriving shortly. Keep me appraised."

John stepped to his side. "Take a breath, Grant. Your face is bright red."

"I'm fine. I need a car to go after her." He scanned the street.

Another taxi pulled into the restaurant's drop off area.

"There. A cab."

"Slow down." John grabbed his sleeve. "I've seen you in ticked-off mode. Don't confront her right now. You may say things you'll regret."

"She left without giving me a chance to talk things out." He thumped his fist on a light post.

"She must've had good reasons." John untied the bowline, and leapt aboard. "If Miranda's safe, come back to my house and make a plan."

His chest hurt as if he'd been run over by an armored BearCat. "Damn plans."

"Trust me on this one."

John should know, he'd been through worse hell. Grant nodded and stepped aboard, unable to speak. His phone vibrated with a text. *Miranda Whitley arrived home without incident.*

But what about him?

They crossed the Sound, cutting through thick fog. John moored the boat, steered him onto the walkway, and pushed him through the door.

His parents were seated in the living room.

"We're home. Not good news," John announced.

"Grant, what's happened?" Tom rose from the couch and searched the doorway. "Where's Miranda? Did Maneski's thugs kidnap her?"

Distress penetrated Grant's flattened world. "No. I got

word she's in her apartment."

His mom took his arm and led him to the couch. "You're pale. Sit down and talk through it, honey. "

"I didn't get a chance to propose and ask her to join me in Reno." He tried to clear his dry throat. "I described my promotion to ASAC. She got upset I'd accepted the job without consulting her and questioned the danger. She wants kids. I said maybe in a couple of years. She excused herself and left."

John put a glass of water in Grant's hand. "Drink this, buddy. I'll get you whiskey after your color comes back."

"I believed she loved me as much as I love her." He gulped a swallow of water.

"I think she does," John offered quietly.

The strand of pearls rippled while it left his pocket.

He handed the necklace to his mom. "No. She took these off and left me." He pulled the velvet case from his other pocket and gave it to his dad. "Won't need Grandma's solitaire."

"Grant, listen to me," his mom said. "Miranda might think this last week's typical and be scared about handling life and death worries on a daily basis. How'd you describe the new job?"

"I didn't have the chance to say much, but you're right. No one can assure her there won't be danger. I signed on for the position." He sank back on the couch. "Neil wants me in Reno because of drug activity in the last six months. I can't go back on my word to the bureau."

Tom patted his shoulder. "Tough luck. She'll come around, son."

"She knew I was an agent when she spied on me in the Justice Building's coffee shop." Grant cradled his head in his hands.

Mom laid her hand on his arm. "When she watched you

honey, I bet you didn't stir your coffee using the barrel of your Glock."

He'd misjudged multiple times in the last week, but did she really not trust him? He pushed out of the chair. "You're right. She must've hoped for a desk jockey or an IT geek. I'll give her a day, and we'll meet for coffee. Her fears can be overcome."

"Keep this." Tom handed back the ring case.

Grant shoved it in his pocket. "I'm calling it a night." Echoes of Miranda's voice questioning his move to Reno repeated in his mind.

"Their apartment building's being watched," Grant said. "She's safe. Protecting her is what matters."

But he wasn't there to watch for Karpenito.

Chapter 20

Desolation reached into Miranda's soul, cold tendrils wrapping her in a bleak sense of finality. She couldn't recall the drive from the restaurant. Had she paid the driver?

Who cared? She sank into a kitchen chair and put her head in her hands. "I needed you to be home, Corrin."

"You know me, every night out trolling for a good catch at our corner tavern. Not." She slid her a cup of tea, releasing scents of cinnamon and orange. "Give me more details."

"I wrecked Grant's idea of our future together."

"This was your big night out." Her voice had softened.

"It was, from his point of view. We sat in Blaine's drinking champagne. His promotion came through, and he's relocating to Reno." She took a sip of tea. "He had 'marry me' written all over his face, and I think an engagement ring in his pocket."

"Exactly what you've longed for. A chance to start a family of your own. Your voice projected happiness during more than one conversation."

She rubbed her arms, imagining his touch. "We did my version of blissful harmony during a slow dance. You'll never guess the irony."

Corrin pursed her lips. "Two left feet?"

"Hardly. The song was *Crazy*. Check out the lyrics. He didn't leave me for someone new, it's the same old bureau, new dangerous city."

"I know the song. You weren't crazy for loving him. He's what you need, and I'm a little jealous you found him."

Miranda rotated the steaming mug. "Jealous of my misery? Don't be. Day after day, night after night, I'd have waited for the phone call telling me he didn't survive a shootout or a car chase. I love him too much." Tears made warm paths on her cheeks. "I'm not ready for his life. I need help."

Corrin pulled a box of tissue from the counter and slid it across her Formica table. "Loving again will be hard for you after what happened to your family." She took her hand and gave it a squeeze. "If you want a life including Grant, get moving on the therapy."

"You're right." She dabbed at her eyes. "Counseling takes time. Maybe things will work for Grant and me, maybe not. I want children someday. Why wasn't he an agent packing a computer instead of a gun?"

"Because he wouldn't be your hero. Did you tell him your concerns and let him respond?"

"No. I got upset he chose Reno and a higher wrung on the agency ladder without my input."

"You didn't give him much of an opportunity to work things out. Not fair."

Miranda shook her head. "You don't know Grant. He's in charge, he's the fixer, and he'll try to fix us. I turn into a pool of melted caramel if I'm two feet from him. He thrives on an adrenalin-injected post he's honor bound to his family to ascend."

"I think you cut him short."

"You do the math on how long we'd make it in Reno before we'd hate each other because I'd want him to choose between me or the bureau. I'd rather attempt to conquer my anxieties and learn how other spouses in the same situation handle danger. I'm in love with him, and I need to be open to all the challenges of loving and having the love returned."

"Your explanation wouldn't hold in court, but I won't judge. You get a vote in your future, too." Corrin leaned back in her chair, her finger tapping her lip. "I suspect there's more."

"He has the card of a vasectomy doctor. Called it a joke."

"Oh, bloody hell. Now I understand. I've never seen a collection of kids' books like yours."

"You haven't seen the antique baby spoons."

"Okay, new subject." Corrin pulled a stack of paperwork from the counter. "I grabbed you a University of Washington course catalog."

"I don't think college will work now."

"We discussed this. I pass the next bar exam, and you finish your degree. We study together while you get therapy."

Miranda took another sip. "I probably can't afford both."

"My spare bedroom's empty, so move out of yours. They have a waiting list for these apartments, and we'd share expenses." She narrowed her eyes. "Your family would want you to graduate."

Miranda's eyes misted over. "Kenny would've been eighteen this year and be heading off to university."

"Get your degree in his honor."

It was the least she could do. Determination grew from deep within. "We dreamed of being biologists. I might be able to get a student rate on counseling through the university."

"There's the Miranda spirit. We'll be cost-conscious coeds. You can hang your mom's pitchfork on the wall," Corrin said.

"Antique potato fork. It's why the tines are flat and not curved."

"Your garden art's welcome. But I draw the line at potato planting in the sink."

"I appreciate you, Corrin." She flicked through the pages of the university catalog.

This was for the best. Grant would be confused and terribly hurt. What man wouldn't who'd been ditched at a restaurant carrying a ring in his pocket? Would he recall their dance as magical, their bodies intertwined? She wrapped her arms around herself. They'd been synchronized, and he'd been the prism directing colors into her gray life. During his kisses, she'd felt sensual excitement for the very first time.

No more maybes. Diligent effort would reconcile her past.

If Grant would wait.

~ ~ ~

How to reach Miranda? Grant rubbed the back of his neck. He'd ordered Corrin and their apartment building monitored and the agents had watched Miranda schlep in packing boxes and walk out with an older woman and a big suitcase two days ago.

He pounded his desk. They should've followed Miranda, not worried about Corrin. Why wouldn't her damn friend or Shirley Gilson answer his calls? Miranda had jetted away before he'd returned her phone.

His fault for not changing the surveillance order. His fault for waiting for Miranda to cool off and finding her apartment emptied out. He grimaced, recalling the bare space he'd faced yesterday, and the landlord informing him he needed a warrant for a forwarding address.

Nothing he could verify had been updated with a new address for her. Karpenito must've deleted her Justice Building ID info from the system to protect himself.

So Miranda, so impulsive. She'd lost her family and moved. Anticipated his marriage proposal, fled the restaurant, and moved.

Why couldn't she have faced off with her inner demons and fought for the two of them? Hell, she'd clobbered the creep poking Red. She was ready enough to do that with an injury.

Stop it, Morley. Part of her appeal came from her ability to shift into gear after disaster struck.

Yeah, he rated disaster all right, only thinking about his career move.

Grant stared out the window at the Smith Tower. Dread pooled in his gut. Once he found her, what if he couldn't convince her to make a new life together? Or if she'd changed her mind?

There had to be a paper trail for a techie to trace. Everyone ordered utilities. She wasn't a criminal on the run, and it was his duty to return her cell in person. Yeah, the word she'd hated, duty.

He slipped her phone in his pocket, typed the IT request, and began packing the files of case protocols useful for Reno. Four boxes were crammed full before a ding indicated an email.

IT had addressed every request.

He studied the screen, and frowned. Miranda paid in person for her phone bill, and her cell remained registered to the old apartment.

A life off the grid. He dialed the bank number where she'd opened her Serene Interiors business account.

After a brief conversation, his head throbbed. He couldn't lie regarding his need for the information. Stupid privacy laws.

He took a breath and dialed Corrin's cell phone for the tenth time. Business voicemail. Again.

Her friends were too loyal. Didn't they realize he wanted to make her happy?

A seminar agenda on his desk caught his eye. He'd return to Seattle to attend it in a couple weeks. He picked it up and checked the dates. Meeting her in person—always a better tactic.

The paper wavered in his hand.

He might never see her again.

~ ~ ~

Reno sun blazed onto his desk. Grant stuffed the conference agenda for "Criminal Organizations vs. Drug Cartels" into his briefcase. One thing he realized—he'd attend the Seattle seminar having better insight into the motivation of junkies a day out from a fix.

He needed a Miranda fix badly. At least one more time, to deliver news that the gang members who'd murdered her family had died or been jailed. He'd read every report and discovered her suspicions were correct concerning the ex-boyfriend's involvement. Why hadn't the detective phoned her with updates?

He stared at a stack of files loaded onto his laptop. Current crimes took precedence, a fact he knew too well. He selected one of the icons and two photos appeared of the apartment they'd raided last week. A wall held disturbing photos of the last ASAC from every possible angle.

It wasn't paranoia if your predecessor had been stalked.

He clicked his pen, in and out, in and out, and then crossed the final day off the calendar. The trip he'd planned to visit his folks and then see Miranda hadn't come soon enough.

His phone rang, and Kyle's number flashed. "Hey, bro," he said.

"Cheer up. I remembered Corrin's law firm. Meyers, Fitch, and Brine. I Googled it."

"Thanks. I traced her cell phone back to them, and she won't respond. If I don't find Miranda first thing next week, I'll visit Corrin's job site. Want me to put in a good word for you?"

"Corrin and I had a great time for twenty-one hours and thirty minutes. There's chemistry and a lot more. At the end, she kind of pulled a vanishing Miranda on me." His voice lacked all remnants of doctor-style confidence.

"No woman in their right mind would ditch you, Kyle. Must be some mistake."

"I think the same thing about you and Miranda. Don't give up."

He slipped his phone into his chest pocket, next to Miranda's old cell.

Neon lights blinked from the building across the street, a constant reminder of the underbelly he needed to gut.

An ex-Marine whom he'd come to respect approached his desk. "While you're gone, we'll keep things in check," the agent said.

"Keep an eye out for the mob leader's kid." Grant showed him a photo. "He's a real piece of work for being under eighteen."

"Yeah. Daddy buys him out of any trouble. Forget him, and have a good weekend without bullets."

That'd be tough. Since he'd left Seattle, his heart felt like it'd been used for target practice. "You, too."

Grant stomped to his car, gripping his keys. Reno didn't lack solar heat. Miranda'd be shivering in Seattle on her upcoming birthday. He'd offer her a plane ticket to soak up sunshine on a visit. Hopefully she'd agree—if he found her.

A woman approached on the sidewalk, holding her toddler's hand. The kid's T-shirt pictured the face of a beagle puppy.

The boy jerked free and jetted between two parked cars, running straight toward a busy street.

"Stop kiddo!" The mother screamed.

Grant bolted out and grabbed the boy by the waist, swinging him away from an oncoming van.

He carried the kid back to the sidewalk. "Close call, little guy. What were you doing?"

"Doggy, there's a doggy over there." The child pointed to a hooker parading a poodle.

"Yup. But no matter how exciting, you never run across a street."

"Sorry." He smiled at Grant, his eyes dancing from excitement. Round and green, same as Miranda's.

Grant imagined he held his own child. Something deep inside wished it so. "You have to hold your mom's hand and wait until it's safe. The truck could've hurt you."

"Is he okay?" The mother rushed to them. "Kiddo, are you hurt?"

The boy released his arms from around Grant's neck and reached for his mom. Grant's pulse kept pounding. So close . . .

"Thank you." She ruffled her son's hair. "Children are the most precious challenges in the world. He adores dogs. Maybe I should get a leash for him."

"Maybe you should get him a puppy." Grant smiled to the boy who'd begun pulling his mom toward an ice cream shop.

Puppies and toddlers, Miranda's dream. He hopped in his car. His gas gauge sat on *E,* and in a few minutes, he'd need a six-pack of colas for the drive. He pulled into the closest station, flipped open the tank cover, and pried his credit card from his wallet. It slid through his fingers. Another hot-as-hell day. He bent to pick it up.

A bullet whizzed by his head.

In one movement, he released the Glock and carved a half circle in the air with the barrel.

Car tires squealed from the parking lot across the street. A light-colored Audi carrying Washington plates left a trail of dust and spinning gravel.

Too many risks for a shot.

All he'd gotten was a glimpse of a short guy with a scruffy beard. Had he seen that driver before?

He rubbed the sweat off his forehead. If he hadn't dropped the credit card, he'd be wiping blood. Or worse. The police would grab the bullet sample with no DNA of his attached.

He pulled out his cell phone and called in a description of the car and driver.

The string of gaudy neon lights advertising a sordid variety of services continued to blink their message.

One way or another, this town would kill him.

~ ~ ~

"Insisting I go away with you to the San Juan Islands helped clear my head," Miranda said to Shirley and Ike. "I'm dying to try your version of the lemon-glazed salmon we enjoyed aboard the yacht."

"We wanted to treat you to a special birthday cruise. You needed a rest before starting classes, especially after vacating your apartment in a day." Shirley passed the platter of fish to her husband.

"My move entailed rolling books and plants twenty feet to Corrin's." She raised her water glass in a toast.

"We're glad you're enjoying the University of Washington. How's the counseling going? The psychologist and his weekend retreat came highly recommended."

"I've made progress understanding my guilt, and I've accepted the grieving process. Thank you for the encouragement and monetary support."

"We'd do anything for you," Shirley said, and gave Ike a meaningful glance.

"We want you to be happy," Ike chimed in. "We're proud of you for facing your challenges. The time and energy will be worth it." He pulled a card out of his pocket. "A gentleman stopped in to see me today. He pushed the card toward Miranda. "He appeared older, or maybe thinner, than he appeared in court the last time."

Her fork stopped midair, a plump bite of salmon balanced on sterling-silver tines.

Shirley moved the card to the edge of Miranda's plate.

"He stopped by here, too. A handsome young man, in a serious sort of way. Late twenties?"

A desperate need rose from deep inside. The need to see Grant. She put her fork down. "He's turning thirty at the end of this month."

Ike sat back. "He said he needed to talk to you one more time, Miranda."

Using her thumb and forefinger, she tweezed the card into her pocket. "I'll contact Grant on his birthday. My counselor agreed on the timing."

"Good, dear. Describing Grant gave your voice a hopeful tone." Shirley patted her hand. "Call him. He saved your life, after all."

Countless times every night she'd rehearsed the conversation. "I will." She cut the bite of salmon in half. "Is this the fish your friend caught?"

Conversation continued, but no matter how wonderful all her friends were, they'd never fill her longing for a husband and children. If Grant didn't want babies, they'd adopt. Plenty of kids needed homes. That might appeal to him.

"You seem tired, Miranda. I'll give you a ride home tonight," Ike offered.

She thanked Shirley, gave the necessary replies to Ike on the trip home, and trudged into the building.

Another lock had been put on their apartment door.

Miranda stuck her key in the door knob and threw it open.

Corrin rose from the kitchen table, her face pale.

"What's the matter?" She rushed inside.

"The apartment manager spent the last hour helping a locksmith install the new deadbolt. A man came to his office this morning flashing a detective's badge and asking your new address."

Miranda shuddered. "Did he tell them I moved here?"

"Thank goodness, he didn't. Our blessed manager said, and I quote, 'No warrant, and the pipsqueak gave me the willies, badge or not.'" Corrin pulled her into a hug, and met her eyes. "It's Karpenito, isn't it?"

Hairs rose on Miranda's forearm. "Yes."

~ ~ ~

Miranda shouldered her backpack full of textbooks and stomped into their apartment. She spun around and grimaced—flipping two locks had become second nature.

The light blinked on the answering machine Shirley and Ike had insisted she needed. They'd tried to call too many times after her cheap burner phone had died. She pressed the button.

"Miranda." Grant's deep, melodious voice filled the room, swirling around her weak knees.

She gripped the counter.

"I miss you, and I have to know you're okay. Are you okay? Need a dose of sun? I hope you'll call me soon, so we can talk about getting you a flight. Use the new cell number on the card I gave to Judge Gilson . . . anytime, day or night." His voice cracked. "Please call, Miranda. I need to know you're safe. I love you."

"I love you, too," she whispered to the empty room. She stood in silence for a moment, tilling under the remaining layers of angst on the top strata of her world again. Did he know about Karpenito?

Corrin opened the door, met her eyes, and ran to her. "Something happened!" She yanked out her phone. "Do I need to call the police?"

"I got a message from Grant." She hit the play button.

Corrin put her arm around Miranda's waist while they listened. "Quit torturing yourself. Call him back. He's determined to work things out and sounds miserable, too. You should tell him the creepy detective came by."

"You heard the police. We can't discuss it with anyone."

"Call for the hell of it. Get a plane ticket, and get out of here. You don't own the plant business anymore, and you're ahead in schoolwork."

"Two more sessions until I've earned a clean slate from my counselor." She rested her head on Corrin's shoulder. "I want to surprise Grant on his birthday and tell him I've wiped away the bad parts of my past and am able to write our new future."

"People aren't chalkboards. We all have history. For heaven sakes, Miranda, you're flipping tortured hearing his voice. You love him, he loves you. Make the call, or I will."

"My best friend wouldn't deliver a threat. My best friend would understand I can't contact Grant yet. This is one time I don't want to ruin everything by jumping too fast."

Corrin banged the teakettle onto a burner. "I'm here if you need me, your best friend biting her tongue."

Miranda stumbled to the bedroom. She pulled on pajamas and slid between cold sheets, then reached under the pillow for Grant's T-shirt.

His scent had grown faint. She should make the call. He'd said he loved her.

No. She wasn't quite ready. Last night a man followed her off the bus and scared her half to death. He'd recognized her from the trial and wanted to thank her for getting Maneski and his thugs arrested.

Grant made a difference by arresting criminals.

Soon she'd be equipped to support him.

~ ~ ~

Out the window of Miranda's Number 14 bus from the university, leaves blew into piles near the curb. A sliver of moon peeked through clouds. How much closer would it appear in Montana, or Reno?

Today Grant turned thirty. One phone call and her life would change for the best.

Quit stalling. Do it right now. She pulled out his card and ran her finger over his imprinted name.

She'd prepared herself to step into his world. Her phone glowed while she pressed the numbers on her key pad.

"Hold please," said a female voice, "Yes?"

Had she misdialed? "Is Grant Morley there?"

"Ahh, no. Is this his realtor from Montana? If the property got an offer, he told me to relay he wants—"

A double blow. Miranda hit the end-call button, and dropped her cell to her lap.

Maybe it was a friend answering his phone. She'd try during the day, during business hours.

She fingered her rearing horse slide, worn for luck tonight. A memory filled her heart of falling off the mule, hitting the ground, and suffering—alone and freezing to death, until Grant saved her. Her palm grazed over the site of her bullet wound, bearing the faint scars from his stitches.

"Your stop, Miranda," her bus driver called out.

"Thanks." She exited and zipped her coat, then lowered her head and braced her chin against the wind. She stuck her chilly hand in her pocket. A familiar bag met her fingers, filled with an emergency supply of bone meal for her plants. Wow, how things had changed since she'd worn it last year.

Her feet trampled brittle, dead leaves. Dried up, like she felt inside, thinking about who'd bought a cake for Grant and lit the thirty candles.

Gusts whipped into her. North of her building was always worst, blowing her around the block leading to her apartment. Maybe it'd blow her off the planet, mimicking the displaced nannies in Mary Poppins. Anything would beat facing the picture of his house on the fridge.

Time to pitch the tattered photo.

Stop it already. There had to be a good reason for a woman answering his phone.

At night.

On his birthday.

She tromped toward the corner. Why did she keep imagining his smile, his muscular chest, his very essence of loyalty?

A mule brayed.

Miranda jerked to attention.

Big Red's distinct call drowned out the metallic sounds of car doors and brakes.

She ran, her heart pumping.

Red stood in the middle of her tiny front yard, tied to a tree outside her building. He opened his jaws and let loose another round of acknowledgment to the next block.

Oh no! Grant had met someone, and she'd insisted he clean house, including Red, their miracle mule. Her fingers shook while she reached out to him. "Hey, buddy."

Her internal radar sent the pulses that Grant's gaze was on her, a wonderful sensation.

Damn her traitorous body.

The mule nuzzled her ear and issued a low whinny, then bobbed his nose at the entry.

In the shadow of the porch, a familiar figure leaned against the wall, his face hidden.

She couldn't confront him yet, hear him reject her. She clutched Red's neck, smoothing his mane over his deep scar. Her fingers caught on a leather strap.

A carved sign hung from it. 'LOVE ALWAYS PERSEVERES.'

Miranda stared at the carved lettering. Hundreds of pink buds burst open in her chest, while soul-deep warmth spread throughout her body. He loved her, he truly loved her, and she could love him in return.

She gave Red a hug before she walked to the steps. "Grant."

Gone was his stance of assurance. His intense eyes stood out in his thinner, tanned face.

Keeping his hands in his pockets, he took a step forward. "I moved to Reno, and found shallow gamblers and ruthless gangs, and you weren't there." His voice held the urgency she'd felt moments ago, before the phone call.

Tears wet her eyes. She understood the emptiness of every hour they'd spent apart.

"I've been managing a young, aggressive squad who thrive by living on the dangerous edge, and thank God, you weren't there. I came home every night and didn't sleep because you weren't there."

She took a step on unsteady legs, a foot of concrete separating them.

He offered his hand and pulled her to the landing. "I love you. Would you ever want to live in Emma Springs someday? When you're ready?"

Her heart fluttered. "Emma Springs? On your ranch?"

"Yes." He touched her lips. "Oh, how I've missed your smile. Miranda, I'll move anywhere. You, me, and Red. Is it too late to beg your forgiveness for making the stupidest decision of my life without talking to you first?" His voice trembled.

She grabbed his belt loops and pulled him close. "You're what I need in my life. Reno, Emma Springs, Three Falls, wherever. I'm so, so ready to love you, Grant."

His lips found hers, and began caressing her trembling mouth in light, sweet kisses. A moment later, he said, "I made desperate attempts to find you. Hell, I almost accosted a woman bending over your plants in the Justice Building. Stopped myself just short of embarrassment."

"Serenity Interior's new owner would've snipped you down to size," Miranda giggled.

"It wouldn't have taken much, the way I felt without you."

She leaned back and stroked his hair. "I've gotten over big hurdles through intensive therapy. You won't need to prune my clinging vine before leaving for work every day, Agent Morley."

His face softened. "Wouldn't change a thing about your foliage. The bureau part of my life's over."

She shook her head. "No. I'll handle being an agent's wife. The FBI's in your blood, and I won't have you resenting me."

He pulled her closer. "Wouldn't happen. I left Reno in the capable hands of Bullseye and Jesse."

"You resigned?" She took a deep breath. "But why?"

"Teddy gave me the first inkling I'd helped kids. Then, I had a punk kid nearly run me over. The incident prompted the idea to catch juvies before they choose the wrong path."

Non-agent Grant. Miranda searched his eyes. "What will you do?"

"I spoke to Dad, and we're thinking of creating furniture in a trade-school setting, teaching at-risk teens. Mom's excited, but if you're not, we'll work out a better plan. Back in college I got a CPA degree to meet one of the bureau's criteria."

"I used to dream about a quiet life, modest and mild. The CPA route might be too reserved. Teaching kids is a wonderful idea." She pressed her lips to his and inhaled woodsy cologne and another scent—enticingly male and purely Grant.

"I prayed you hadn't moved on." He kissed her deeply and pulled her closer.

Red issued a demanding bray.

She stuck her key in the outer door. "Let's get inside before animal control comes." A grin spread across her face. "Getting Red here must've been a challenge."

"I couldn't wait any longer for you to return my call." He followed her in. "Operation Miranda required unparalleled strategy and an irresistible decoy."

She angled a sideways glance at him before she said, "I called your cell tonight and a woman answered."

"Bullseye's turn to handle informants. She must not have changed my number yet."

Total faith in their love illuminated her insides, brighter than the first rays of spring sunshine. "I feel like dancing again."

Grant's shoe thumped onto the outer hallway floor.

A gray plastic boot encased his left foot. "Give me a week."

"What happened to your foot?"

"I stood on the wrong side of my car when the punk drove too close." He held two fingers up and placed his other hand over his heart. "Scout's honor. That life's over. Oh, I need to return your phone." He pulled a cell from his chest pocket.

"My old phone. You held it hostage, didn't you?" She rubbed her fingers across the scratched back of the copper-colored case.

"I needed to make certain it got safely into your hands." He looked out at Red. "We both would've had long faces if you'd turned me down."

"Speaking of Red," Miranda guided him to her apartment door, "I'll talk to our landlord regarding mule housing for tonight." Her hand shook while she searched for the apartment keys in her bag.

"No worries. Red's checked into a stall for a few days at Seattle's Mounted Police barn. And Dad arranged a transport horse van both ways." Grant cocked his head. "Boy, your mule's making a racket. I think us being out of sight irritates him."

She pushed open the door.

Red's loud braying carried inside.

"I wish I could tell him we'll all be together in Montana soon."

Grant glanced out the window to Red. "He'll know soon enough."

"Have a seat at the table, and I'll fix you a special cup of birthday cocoa."

"My birthday. I'd forgotten." He turned her to face him. "I'd love anything you'll give me, maybe a baby or two?" His voice had become hopeful.

"I didn't think you wanted kids."

"I gave it a lot of thought. Problem was, I wondered if I'd be a good father. Parenting beside a partner you love and trust is different. Our folks are proof. I'm excited to hold a tiny version of you, God willing."

Another dormant tendril unfurled inside her belly. "Or a cooing baby Grant."

"All in good time." He closed the door behind them and set the locks. "I'll be glad to get back to Montana."

"Me, too. I know they never caught Karpenito." She lifted a pink Taser from her bag. "I took a gun safety class and bought this for protection."

Grant's eyes widened. "Wow. I'm proud of you, for many, many things."

She smiled. "I've heard them call it riding the lightning. Fifty-thousand volts of love."

"Bullseye would approve." Grant laughed.

She stowed the Taser in her bag and tossed it to the couch. "I don't plan to use it."

"I hope not. Emma Springs wouldn't know what hit them."

One more thing had to be settled before Miranda could be sure they'd covered everything. She rested her hands on his shoulders. "SAC's the title you've dreamed of since childhood."

"The dream of a kid. Finding you clarified my adult goals. By the way, you're impossible to track. You should teach a class on vanishing."

"Corrin assisted. My determination to overcome anxiety about your job barely won out over wanting to hop on the next airplane to Reno."

"I never should've left you. Neil understood the reasons for my resignation."

He held her at arm's length. "You need my cooking. Peaceful Montana's where you belong."

She stroked a fine growth of stubble on his cheek and sighed. "Montana, Red, and you." She pointed to the photo of the log house stuck on the side of the refrigerator.

Grant sucked in his breath. "This could be our home."

Another tendril of joy unfurled inside her. "Wow. Our home, that you didn't sell."

He touched it and a smile came to his lips. "Neither of us lost hope."

She moved to his side. "Nope. Three counseling sessions a week kept me from berating myself over losing you."

"Misplaced, not lost."

She straightened a pile of books on the counter. "Corrin's getting prepped for the bar exam. I'm completing the final classes for my degree."

He kissed her forehead. "You're brilliant and stubborn, thank heaven."

She gave him a friendly jab in the ribs. "I'd call it perseverance."

His eyes shone. "I'll volunteer for whatever I can do to help. Grow moss on my toes?" He pointed to her antique potato fork, hanging on the wall by the refrigerator. "Or maybe harvest spuds?"

"Probably not necessary, but I'll make a note of your knowledge of garden implements."

"I can't wait to tell my folks. They were devastated to hear I hadn't gotten in touch with you. First though, I need a little more assurance we're good." He pulled her into a deep, breath-stealing kiss.

Red let out a piercing bray from outside.

"That's his mule warning." Miranda released her hold on Grant. "I wonder who's—"

Two knocks rapped against the door.

"The manager must've heard Red." She slid the deadbolt, and twisted the door knob open, then gasped.

Karpenito pushed a gun with a silencer into her chest, stepped inside, and shoved her against the wall. He kicked the door closed.

"What do you want?" Grant took a step toward them, his hands up.

The gun hovered a few inches from her heart. "Stay back, Morley, or she dies."

"Is it money?" Grant quietly asked. "I'll match what you're being paid."

"Hmm." Karpenito shrugged. "I figured I'd stage a routine burglary gone bad in Seattle, and then have to travel to Montana. You arrived, and I decided on a murder-suicide. Saves me a trip." He kept the gun aimed at her chest. "Interesting offer, Morley, but we both know the boss doesn't tolerate loose ends."

Grant stepped back, toward the wall where the small pitchfork hung. His hand went behind him.

Karpenito saw the action and rotated his gun.

Miranda shoved her fingers into her pocket, grabbed a handful of the powdered fertilizer, and threw it into Karpenito's eyes.

"Bitch!" Karpenito shook his head.

Grant swung the potato fork, sending the revolver flying under the kitchen table. In the next instant, he punched Karpenito in the jaw, knocking him to the ground.

Karpenito shoved his shoulder into Grant's leg cast, throwing him off balance, then grabbed the pitchfork and backed Grant to the door.

Miranda dove under the table and retrieved the gun. "Drop it. Don't think I won't shoot a spineless coward." She crossed the room and pushed the muzzle into the base of Karpenito's skull.

"You're too chicken," Karpenito turned.

"Not anymore." She racked the slide to load a bullet into the chamber. "You're threatening my wounded hero, asshole."

The cop dropped the fork.

Grant grabbed Karpenito's wrist and twisted it behind his back. He pulled cuffs off the cop's belt and secured them.

Miranda dialed her phone using steady fingers. "The police can haul this snake out of my apartment."

By the time the Seattle Police and Bo arrived to question them, Miranda's pulse had returned to normal. They gave statements and shut the door on Karpenito for a final time.

"You're amazing, Ms. Whitley," Grant smiled.

"Half of the best cowgirl and former-agent team."

"I think the Annie Oakley Commemorative rifle in my collection needs to accompany you in Montana to scare vermin. If you'd like?" Grant asked.

"I'll do my best to make Annie proud," Miranda grinned. "The gun range practice came in handy, but hopefully I'll never fire a shot."

"Our life will never be boring," Grant teased.

"I certainly hope—"

The apartment door burst open and slammed against the wall.

Corrin flew in. "There's a mule . . . you must be Grant." She dropped her shoulder bag on the floor. "High time you showed."

"Nice to meet you, too," Grant said.

"My pleasure, Agent Morley. I dodged police cars on my way in."

"Karpenito's handcuffed in one of those squad cars, thanks to Miranda's gun-toting skills."

Corrin fist bumped Miranda. "Good going, roomie."

"The last snake's been snared." Miranda grabbed Corrin's hand and gave it a squeeze. "We're all safe now, sister-of-my-soul."

"And that's a genuine smile for a change." Corrin patted Miranda's shoulder and then glanced at Grant. "I'll leave you lovebirds alone. I'm truly happy for both of you." She stepped into her bedroom and pulled the door shut behind her.

Grant took Miranda's hand. "I made another reservation at Blaine's, but I can't wait any longer." He lowered himself to the floor, balancing on one knee.

Eagerness thrummed in her heart. She'd dreamed of this moment.

"Miranda, I love you with all my heart." His eyes confirmed the words. "Will you do me the honor of marrying me?"

She put her hand to his cheek, smiling. "Yes. Come here for an uninterrupted seal of approval." She grasped his upper arm and pulled him up. While she kissed him, elation flowed in her veins. "Together from now on, for the rest of our lives."

His lips brushed hers. "Forever." He pulled out a tiny box and slid the solitaire onto her ring finger. "My grandmother's."

She held her hand to the light. "The diamond reflects the sparkling I feel inside."

"Matching my kaleidoscope." Grant took both of her hands in his. "I have a suggestion, or confession, maybe two."

Her body stilled. "You can tell me anything, Grant."

"You're old-fashioned. One of the many qualities I adore. This morning I contacted Judge Gilson, I mean Ike, to ask his permission to marry you. I hope it's okay?"

Flutters of joy filled her chest. She covered his hand with hers. "It's sweetly romantic. Tell me Ike's response."

"He approved, and said he'd be honored to escort you down the aisle, if you ask."

"I can't think of anyone more fitting," she said.

He centered the diamond on her finger. "There's one more, ah, shall we say, matter of consideration."

"You have my full attention."

"I want to marry you and start our life together. I'd bet my parents, and Ike and Shirley would want to make it a celebration. If it's what you want."

"Mom and I envisioned my church wedding and reception." She pressed her palm to his heart. "I have the handsome hero part locked in, and Corrin could help make plans."

"I'll do my best to earn the hero status." He cleared his throat. "In the meantime, Dad and Mom redecorated my guest bedroom if you want to start your life in Emma Springs before we get married. We'd have time to get to know one another outside of a pressure cooker." He loosened his tie. "Or you can stay at their house."

No more separation. Miranda turned over his hand and stroked his palm. "I like the guest room idea. At my hero's home. My classes can be completed online, so nothing's holding me in Seattle."

"Nothing's better than traveling back to Montana beside you and Red under temporary guest room conditions in our home." Grant's color deepened.

Petals of pink, magenta, and fuscia colored her world.

Chapter 21

She'd traveled home with Grant and spent her first night of undisturbed sleep in the guest room of her dream house in Emma Springs.

On the car trip to Montana, she'd learned from Grant that her family's killers were incarcerated. She could quit wondering who else they'd harm.

If a rose bush represented her life, a flowering stem would be grafted alongside a rugged, sturdy branch.

The old globe on the stand in the corner had resided by Dad's desks in each of his classrooms. Now it sat by her desk in the guest bedroom. She slipped out of bed and laid her fingertip on Montana—her perfect place. Mom's pruning shears sat on the dresser, and Kenny's ball cap hung from the hand-carved finial on the antique vanity mirror.

Her clean clothes had been piled inside the bedroom door. Grant must've done laundry last night after they'd arrived from Seattle.

A flat package tied by a pink ribbon lay on top of her blouse. She untied it and pulled off the paper to find a book, *Irish Love Sonnets*.

Inside the cover was an inscription: *To the sweetest daughter I could ever have. I hope you'll call me 'Moms,' what I called my dear mother-in-law.*

Miranda touched her heart. Pat would be her 'Moms' and a wonderful grandma someday.

Miranda placed the book next to the Scales of Justice statue Ike had given her from his office. Purple African violets bloomed from tiny pots balancing on each side.

Whiffs of coffee and fried potatoes enticed her to the stairs.

Grant stood at the bottom. "Good morning. I hope you slept well." He pointed to a steaming mug. "The coffee I owe you from Seattle will be paid back every day."

"No paybacks match the adoration I see in your eyes. Dad called Mom a precious treasure, exactly how I feel." She pulled him close and kissed him, letting her body fill with a strong sense of belonging. Belonging together and belonging to a loving family again.

"You put my thoughts into perfect words." Grant stroked her cheek. "Brasso and Red are fed and saddled. Your mule told me he's ridden enough transports for the rest of his life. After breakfast we can trot over to tell my folks in person."

Her children would follow that path to their grandparents' home someday. She sipped the coffee, pure joy welling in her chest. "I'm in."

"As a kid, I dreamed of galloping home on a horse to deliver good news. In fact, I made Mom a pair of hitching posts in high school shop class which have been waiting for the right announcement."

"I noticed those horse heads and wondered. I can't wait to tell them." She grabbed a bite of crispy potato and sipped her coffee. "I'm impressed you researched my blend of Kona and ground cocoa nibs."

"I had to get your special brew right. Did you find the book?"

"Yes, it's lovely, same as your mom," she said. "Let's go announce a wedding to my new family."

He beamed at her and brought her fingers to his lips, kissing each one. "Do you mind the four of us celebrating our engagement? Dad bought champagne before I left. He may be gruff sometimes, but he adores you. He suggested I shuttle Red to Seattle."

"Smart man," she teased. "Champagne bubbles can't match the bursts of joy releasing in my heart."

"I want to marry you yesterday." He held out her puffy parka and handed her a pair of fleece-lined gloves. "No more cold or alone."

"I know." She squeezed his hand while they strolled away from their home.

Familiar calming scents wafted out from the barn.

Big Red mule-nickered. He nuzzled her cheek while she straightened his bridle. She ran her fingers over the gap in his mane and deep scar. Another past injury. Another survivor moving forward. "Shirley offered her antique wedding dress. I'd love to ride on Red side-saddle to the church."

"Totally Montana. Whatever you wear, you'll be a beautiful bride with her groom waiting at the alter for his forever love," Grant whispered in her ear.

"My hero."

Snow-capped Mt. Hanlen rose from a landscape dotted by pines. Her new family waited across the pasture.

She had her man and her mule, and the mountain of troubles freezing her heart had melted into a pool of hope.

Grant turned and smiled. His light reflected out to her, as deep and welcoming as a fall sun, illuminating cherished memories and brightening the path to their future.

Love thrived in Emma Springs.

If you'd like to receive the epilogue to *The Hitman's Mistake* introducing Grant and Miranda's baby, Annie Rose, visit Sallybrandle.com and sign up for my email list. If you enjoyed my book, I'd love it if you'd visit Amazon and write an honest review.

Warm regards,
Sally

Torn by Vengeance

Corrin Patten is solidly on the path to partner in a prestigious Seattle law firm when an ominous threat from her past turns deadly.

Dr. Kyle Werner revels in the trust of his town's patients. But the small Montana community lacks one thing—a woman to share his life.

Can they defeat the wealthy stalker bent on mistaken revenge against Corrin?

If you like tenacious heroines, sizzling attraction, and a shadowy villain seeking revenge, you'll love Sally Brandle's *Torn by Vengeance*.

About the Author

Multiple award-winning author Sally Brandle writes clean, contemporary, romantic suspense stories. She left a career as an industrial baking instructor so that she could bring to life her stories of courageous women supporting one another while they discover men who deserve their love. A member of Romance Writers of America, Greater Seattle RWA, Eastside RWA, and She Writes, Sally's current series, **Love Thrives in Emma Springs**, is set in rural Montana.

Connect with Sally at www.sallybrandle.com